T0380392

THE NEW GENERATION

THE NEW GENERATION

Fiction for Our Time
from America's
Writing Programs

EDITED BY

Alan Kaufman

WITH AN INTRODUCTION BY JOHN KNOWLES

ANCHOR PRESS
Doubleday
NEW YORK
1987

"Veterans," Copyright © 1982 by Laurie Alberts. First appeared in *Fiction International*. Reprinted by permission of *Fiction International* and the author.

"The Vanity of Small Differences." Reprinted from *The Prairie Schooner* by permission of the University of Nebraska Press. Copyright © 1987 University of Nebraska Press.

"The Big Sway," Copyright © 1986 by Dennis Johnson.

"Things to Draw," Copyright © 1984 by Katharine Andres. First appeared in *The New Yorker* magazine, January 9, 1984. Reprinted by permission of Russell & Volkening, Inc., as agents for the author.

"I Ate Her Heart," Copyright © 1986 by Bob Shacochis. Originally appeared in *New Virginia Review*. Used with permission.

"In the American Society," Copyright © 1987 by Gish Jen. First published in *The Southern Review*. Used with permission.

"Claire's Lover's Church," Copyright © 1984 by Teri Ruch. First appeared in *Grand Street*.

"Where We Are Now," Copyright © 1986 by Ethan Canin. First published in *The Atlantic Monthly*, July 1986. To appear in a forthcoming collection of Ethan Canin's short stories to be published by Houghton Mifflin Company.

"The Incorrect Hour" by Debra Spark was published first in *The North American Review*. Reprinted by permission of the author and Melanie Jackson Agency. Copyright © 1986 by Debra Spark.

"Conviction," Copyright © 1986 by Tama Janowitz. First appeared in *Boulevard*. Reprinted by permission of the author.

"Sparks," Copyright © 1987 by Susan Minot.

"Last Night," Copyright © 1984 by Dennis McFarland. Originally appeared in *Sequoia*. Used with permission.

"In Christ There Is No East or West," Copyright © 1986 by Kent Nussey. First appeared in *The Black Warrior Review*, a publication of the University of Alabama.

"The Things That Would Never Be Mine," Copyright © 1987 by Michelle Carter. Used with permission.

"Snake Head," Copyright © 1979 by Lynda Leidiger. First appeared in *Playboy*.

"Jillie," Copyright © 1985 by Ehud Havazelet. Originally published in *Sequoia*. Reprinted by permission of Harold Matson Company, Inc.

"Hands," Copyright © 1983 by Kenyon College. Reprinted by permission of the author and *The Kenyon Review*.

"Cuisinart," Copyright © 1986 by Fred G. Leebron.

"View From Kwaj," Copyright © 1985 by Patricia MacInnes. First appeared in *Chicago*, May 1985. Reprinted by permission of the author.

"Ten Cents a Dance," Copyright © 1987 by Joseph Ferrandino. This story was originally published in *The Southern Review*, Winter 1987, Volume 23, No. 1.

"Three Maids' Children," Copyright © 1987 by Mona Simpson.

"Massé," Copyright © 1986 by Leigh Allison Wilson. Originally published in *Harper's Magazine*. Reprinted by permission of Harold Matson Company, Inc.

"Flight," Copyright © 1985 by Linda Svendsen. First appeared in *Western Humanities Review*. Reprinted by permission of the author.

Library of Congress Cataloging-in-Publication Data

The New generation.

1. Short stories, American. 2. American fiction—
20th century. I. Kaufman, Alan. I. Title.
PS648.S5N39 1987   813'.01'08   87-10034
ISBN 0-385-23951-3
ISBN 9780385239523(pbk.)

Copyright © 1987 edited by Alan Kaufman
ALL RIGHTS RESERVED

FOR *Frank MacShane* AND *Ted Solotaroff*

ACKNOWLEDGMENTS

To Marie, my mother, and George, my father, my love and gratitude for their devotion. Many thanks to Robin Straus for her warmth, diligence, and professional guidance. Many thanks to Connie Brothers (The Writers Workshop, University of Iowa), Ehud Havazelet (The Creative Writing Center, Stanford University), Doug Swift (The Creative Writing Program, Johns Hopkins University), and Jeff Goodell (The Writing Division, Columbia University) for their invaluable editorial effort and recommendations. My special appreciation to Ceci Scott and Karen Suben of Doubleday.

Contents

Preface

We now know more about America, but also understand her less than ever before. New voices are needed to explain her. We have the consequences of our predecessors' activities and decisions to cope with, but the consciousness, symbols, ideas, and alibis of their chroniclers can no longer serve to illustrate our relentless trek toward nuclear war. In the streets of our nation squats a second, homeless nation. Youth suicide, drug abuse, and financial and government scandals make the time ripe for the expression of something more than futility.

The writers in this first edition of *The New Generation* are among the most exciting new voices we have today. Bob Shacochis, Tama Janowitz, Eileen Pollack, Debra Spark, Laurie Alberts, Mona Simpson, Kent Nussey, Susan Minot, Teri Ruch, Michelle Carter, and Joseph Ferrandino, to name but a few included here, are creating a sensibility of their own. They are willful writers. They take risks. They give an unexpected twist to our condition. All are spellbinding stylists, but none are strictly obsessed with *craft:* they have something too fresh and important to say.

They inhabit an age which freezes the heart: metaphorically speaking, a Medusa. To trap her diabolical visage in their fiction, they track her to her lair, hold their imaginations up to her, catch her reflection in polished prose; dangerous work. In her image, we see our own. The effect can be jarring, as in "Claire's Lover's Church," by Teri Ruch, a hypnotically beautiful, dreamlike account of a woman's struggle against possession by the polygamous minister of a mysterious religious cult. In "I Ate Her Heart," by Bob Shacochis, a dulcet-toned black comedy of rock and roll, cocaine and smuggling on the Gulf of Mexico, an endearing man commits an act of atrocious horror. In "The Vanity of Small Differences," a gorgeously written story by Eileen Pollack, the fierce alienation between an aged breeder of laboratory mice and his punk-rocker grandson leads them to a nightmarish embrace. Laurie Alberts's "Veterans" drops like a roller coaster through a world of forgotten and scarred Vietnam veterans. In "View from Kwaj," by Patricia MacInnes, a young girl wrestles with love's indecision at the foot of an exploding H-bomb.

Not all the stories in *The New Generation* tightrope walk along the brink. Stories like "The Big Sway," by Dennis Johnson; "Cuisinart," by Fred Leebron; and "Conviction," by Tama Janowitz, stare Medusa in the eye but shield us with laughter, while stories like "Sparks," by Susan Minot; "The Incorrect Hour," by Debra Spark; "Flight," by Linda Svendsen; "Where We Are Now," by Ethan Canin; "The Things That Would Never Be Mine," by Michelle Carter, and "Three Maids' Children," by Mona Simpson, pinpoint Medusa in the least sinister of places, in our very own living rooms and backyards, the faces of the ones we love, the values and aspirations we prize and that make us the people we are.

The stories in *The New Generation* are the work of the alumni or currently enrolled students of four of the most distinguished graduate writing programs in the United States: The Writers Workshop at the University of Iowa, The Writing Division of Columbia University, The Creative Writing Program at Stanford University, and The Creative Writing Program at Johns Hopkins University. I have chosen these programs for being well known, both in their field and to the public, but by no means are they exclusive examples. In recent years, the programs at the University of Houston, Sarah Lawrence College, the University of Arizona and the University of California at Irvine, to name but a few, have attained at least equal stature. Graduate writing programs have opened their doors to thousands of aspirants, young and old, on well over one hundred and fifty campuses in this country, and today virtually every principal name in American letters is affiliated with them. They are also some of the main suppliers of the many exciting new talents currently enjoying the public's esteem.

From among a select number of these programs, and with their faculties to guide me, I will track down their most recently accomplished writers and gather them together in each future edition of *The New Generation.* Tactically speaking, taking a few programs at a time makes sense. Working alone, I am unequipped to handle the flood of material that would otherwise pour in. It is also a good way of plumbing the depth of each program.

Though intended to constitute a kind of annal of the creative writing programs, *The New Generation* is by no means their official showcase. It is an independent anthology. Nor is my purpose to attack writing programs or attempt to answer the burning question posed by many who serve on writing-program faculties: whether writing can or should be taught. Whether or not it can or should, there are excellent writers coming out of the schools and going on to major careers. In these pages, I will provide an annual sampling of their output and of what it means to be young, alive, and writing in America.

Such a collective view can, for one thing, be extremely entertaining to an audience: a way to experience, from the rich abundance of material, what is best out there. It can also yield perspectives about the impact of the programs on our national letters, particularly at a time when they are the subject of broad controversy. Most important, in *The New Generation* new American writers can assemble with a sense that they now constitute a genuine movement of their own making.

J. B. Priestley wrote in *Literature and Western Man:* "Literature, which is further removed from the centre than ever before, does what it can." And yet, today, that's not enough.

Works of art can't save us from ourselves. But if the writer cannot salvage his age, he can show its face. He can use his talent to reveal the truth, which is larger than himself, and he can best do so in conditions which are favorable to his artistic growth.

Therefore, writers should receive, in as many professional forums as we can provide them, a sense, all too rare in our literary culture, that they can address a national or even an international audience. To be heard strengthens one's voice; we need strong voices. As they grow braver, so will we, somehow. I can't imagine that Dickens or Twain, both by nature gregarious and outspoken, could have achieved the thematic scope, command of language, and bracing concern with the life of the times that characterize their writing had they not believed that their landsmen were listening. In America, particularly in the recent past, it has been one of our mistakes, I think, that we have failed to grasp, as it is still understood in Europe, the seminal importance to a writer of being heard.

Today's young writers have that opportunity, perhaps even on a scale unimaginable to Twain or Dickens at the start of their careers. Because of a significant reassessment by the publishing trade of the marketability of first novels and short-story collections, they enjoy a high degree of visibility in the literary marketplace; their works receive enthusiastic praise in the national magazines and book supplements. Among critics and editors, their peers are behind them. Theirs is becoming a singularly privileged situation. What is their responsibility to it?

I address this directly to young writers everywhere: *Out here lies a public, many of us young and literate, who are willing to purchase your books. Perhaps we think that we already know what you will say and expect to receive from you no more than confirmation of what we hold to be the last word on our condition. You can surprise us. Your appeal can effect a revolution in our expectations. You can brush aside the intellectual scarcity of current postmodernist writing fads, the substitution of tortuous craft for substance, and with the ease of your natural voice deliver imaginative perspectives which both move and delight us.*

ALAN KAUFMAN

New York City
Spring 1987

Introduction

It seems that there are more young—and sometimes not so young —men and women seriously interested in writing than ever before. They want to delve into "creative writing," they want to produce good fiction, they want to create literature. Academic courses have proliferated across the country to meet their desires; writers' conferences have sprung up on all sides; and thousands and thousands of short stories have been produced as a result.

It is unfortunate that the short story is the vehicle for the apprenticeship of these neophyte writers because good short stories are so very hard to write. You cannot afford to make any mistakes in the composition of a successful short story. The compass you are working in is necessarily small; the room to maneuver is minimal. Once you have embarked upon the story you must move forward with sureness, with economy, toward your goal, toward the final effect of your story, the totality.

In a novel you can ruminate, digress, wander off the point occasionally, introduce a character who really doesn't contribute much of anything to its final effect. But in the short story such flaws are fatal; wander off your line of development, stray into irrelevance, and the story is ruined, another failure, another nice try.

Successful short stories are like fugues in music, sonnets in poetry, small creations which, when done right, prove mastery of the medium.

And yet this difficult form, the short story, must be used in writing courses because in a relatively short period of time the students need to produce something which can be discussed, analyzed, dissected, and then have time to go on to another attempt, profiting from the lessons learned from the first try, and another attempt, and another.

That is one reason why thousands of short stories are written today, why so many students struggle to master such a difficult literary form. If few complete successes result, there are nevertheless many worthy and admirable achievements, valuable examples of the short story today, written by gifted literary artists in the process of growth.

This anthology contains a rich collection of these. I am going to leave to time, and to readers, to decide whether one or more of these stories, and these story writers, have already here entered the sacred grove of mastery. It is a site where, for example, Ernest Hemingway rests in peace, secure in his achievement as he can never be in the novel, where full mastery eluded him. It is, I think, preeminently an American domain, one of those not-so-numerous arenas in art where Americans have excelled. I don't really know why this is so, but when I visualize American literature I see a few great monolithic novelists and an entire regiment of short story writers, masters of the story, writers who establish the international standard for this form.

Publishers don't much like short story writers; short stories "don't sell." When I turned in such a collection to Random House, Bennett Cerf rasped, "Yeah, okay, but now *back to the novel.*" Not being very comfortable in the short story form myself, I willingly followed his advice.

But if publishers dislike the form for economic reasons, many readers quietly love it. They may not rush to bookstores to buy out editions when they are first published, but they nevertheless read them, get them out of libraries, treasure them, love them. Many readers crave a literary experience which is encompassible at one sitting, an experience which possesses a beginning, a middle, and an end. They are grateful for a full aesthetic experience, complete in itself, which takes them twenty minutes, half-an-hour to read.

In this anthology they will have varied opportunities for that unique literary pleasure, and they will of course be hearing the contemporary American voice, the sound of the eighties, direct, unbuttoned, sensitive, self-regarding, often eloquent.

Some of the stories have already appeared in magazines as varied as *The New Yorker* and *The Southern Review, Playboy,* and *The Kenyon Review.* We are not dealing with tentative beginners here.

The authors' backgrounds, national origins, scars of war, private images, directness, inform these stories, and so do the accomplished literary techniques of trained writers. All of these stories were written by students or graduates of the master's programs in creative writing at Stanford, Johns Hopkins, Columbia, and the University of Iowa.

Of course the ability to write cannot be taught, and of course there are technical insights which can be taught—write about what you know; use the five senses; individualize through speech and gestures; show, don't tell—and these writers have learned them.

Here we have a formidable array of contemporary literary talent working toward mastery of that great American literary form, the short story. Here are the tales they spin out of their lives and observations and imaginations; here is what they wish to show you about our times.

THE NEW GENERATION

Veterans
LAURIE ALBERTS

I'm not dressed properly. The damp creeps up through the soles of my sandals to my toes. Hugging my cotton blouse, I watch shivering while Stefan rigs the boat. He arranges lines without looking up. Quick. Efficient. Rude? After calling me to come, the least he could do is talk. Katie, whose house I'm staying at until I find my own, said she didn't know him though her boyfriend did. She heard that Stefan fished part-time and that he repaired other people's boats. This boat, low-slung, wide and wooden, looks too small to carry us out where whitecaps scar the bay. I wish I hadn't come.

Stefan offers a hand, names things: mainsheet, tiller, centerboard, boom. We push off. Groundless, the boat wobbles. Buoyancy makes me catch my breath. Stefan draws in line and the sail fills, sending us skimming along trailing a small wake. Crouched in sloshing bilge I wonder, how do I know he knows what he's doing? How do I know it's safe?

"Ready about," Stefan says.

"What?"

"Duck!"

I do and the boom swings by, missing my head. With an unexpected smile, insistent as a touch, Stefan forces my eyes away to where the channel marker lurches in the waves. He asks if I want to try. Reluctantly I accept the tiller and move it too far. The boom swings back, the sail flaps empty. Stefan draws in line. We're moving again but now we're going too fast, tilting.

"Here," I urge, "you take it. Please."

Stefan, at the tiller again, says softly, "Fear keeps you from learning." Screw him, what right has he to assume he knows me? I decide he isn't good-looking enough. Too short, with a bald spot in back and filthy nails. His eyes, I have to admit, are striking: pale, opaque, a blue unblinking stare—persistent, yet remote. I can't help wondering, when he looks at me, what shows?

Maybe it wasn't Stefan, but something in that photograph, his classic pose: shirtless, skin glistening tropic sweat, knees bent and ready, holding the M-16 in front of his belly like a gift. The weapon's weight shapes teen-aged biceps. He smiles into the camera— eager? hopeful? bewildered? He was beardless then, not like when I met him. Of course he looked young. I thought that photograph was the only thing that made him like the rest. Every veteran I'd ever known had a picture like that shot in front of barracks with a Nikon bought dirt cheap. That picture made me jealous; his history, a lover, lingered in his mind. That place I'd never been.

The next time, Stefan takes me clamming. I wear jeans rolled to the knee, sneakers, and Stefan's brown wool sweater. He wears his old army coat, name printed over his heart, and when he points out holes, I dig. After clams we hunt for mussels, tearing blue-black shells from the rocks. Stefan says, swinging his arms wide across the beach, "When the tide is out the table is set. We have everything we need." We eat mussels, steamed in seaweed, wine and garlic, and drink beer. Late that night we toss shells back into the ocean where the tide sucks them away.

When he was beginning his basic training, I was in eighth grade. In those days I starved myself and envied the survivors of Hitler's camps. I wanted a number tattooed on my arm. It wasn't

their wounds, it was their knowledge I craved. I thought I knew
wounds already. As a child I had sat on the papered table while
the night-shift intern, eyeing my father, whispered questions in
my ear. I'd been given a gauzy eye-patch and come home to swept
glass. At ten I had seen the depthless world out of one eye and
knew that in the end things went back in place. Once again the
belt would dangle between silky ties and laundered shirts with our
truncated family name printed in the collars. After every battle
the footsteps would be vacuumed out of the avocado wall-to-wall
rugs.

When the veterans came I forgot about tattooed numbers. I was
sixteen then, a long-legged long-haired girl in short skirts. When I
took the bus to Cambridge, strange men followed me for blocks.
Harvard boys with deferments offered films with foreign names
and at my school senior boys from lower tracks crowded close in
the library and lunchroom to tell me they would someday own a
bar or join the Marines. Even my history teacher with a new
pregnant wife drove me home from school one day and leaned
across the seat to breathe kisses in my hair. They all said, "You're
so pretty, so pretty, so pretty," but it sounded like "save me, save
me, save me," as if I were a lifeboat and they could slide their
bodies in.

The veterans were different. They rolled into town one day in
tattered uniforms, wheelchairs and set up camp on our common.
Lounging against historic monuments, they flaunted empty
sleeves, rage. We crowded close to hear their speeches and songs
but it was their eyes I wanted, not their words. I wanted what
they had seen. Denied their eyes I would have settled for their
stares but when I smiled seductively blank sneers came back.
They had secrets and despised my ignorance. To them I was dis-
posable, like any piece of flesh.

The dead calf hangs from the rafter by its forelegs, neck limp.
Brown Bambi eyes disturb me, so Stefan cuts the head off and
stuffs it away in a burlap sack. He insists he didn't kill the calf.
Three days old, it died from congenital heart failure on a farm up

the road. He laughs at the farmer's squeamishness; the man won't eat it but Stefan (and I) will. I watch him slicing connective membrane, tugging the hide off the carcass like a snowsuit off a child. Stefan places his knife point between dangling hind legs, at the place of unformed genitals, draws it up the belly to the chest. Peeling layers he says, "See the pericardium enclosing the heart?" An anatomy lesson. He was, before enlisting, pre-med.

Fishhooks dumped out of a pail, the pail empty under the swinging, headless calf. Stefan yanks and blue-green innards, liver, heart, kidneys, guts slither and spill, fall splat. Standing close I study the pail, intrigued by my lack of disgust. The sun, refracting off early snow, cuts through the window, polishing the glistening calf's body like a wet red stone. Stefan is wrapping pieces in foil. Meat.

Did I ever tell him of our dinners? My brother and I ate hamburgers while the Sony blared the nightly body count on the kitchen table. My father, disliking his children's voices, ate in the dining room. My mother ran back and forth between two suppers. The dog, enclosed in the kitchen because her pedigreed hair marred the rugs, scrambled to get out of the way. Every night the war was on but sounded fake. I thought it should've been loud, like the TV show "Combat," not blurry black and white and a muted rat-tat-tat mingled with fork clatter and my father's shouts that his chops were burned.

"Did you kill anyone?"

"I always shot over their heads."

He says there's nothing to tell. He means I wouldn't understand. Instead of words he offers files: discharge papers, notebooks, a letter from a Vietnamese girl who worked as a telephone operator at his fire support base. She drew little stars all over the pages.

"Did you sleep with whores in Saigon?"

"I never added to that destruction."

Later Stefan tells me he was a virgin all through Nam and only made love for the first time with his leg in a cast from a motorcycle accident when he first came home. Drunk in cast with a girl who screwed bikers.

"But you enlisted."
"Yeah."
"But how could you have *enlisted?*"
"I didn't know."

"I'm falling."
"Shh," I say, "shh," pressing my fingers on his lips.
"You have the loveliest smile I've ever seen."
How can he see it with his face half an inch away? I smile wider for him. Whatever he wants— I'll spread my thighs until he is so much inside me his fingers poke out through my fingers, his toes curl around mine. I don't care if Stefan fumbles making love. I say, "No one has touched me but you."

In high school I started hitching, Massachusetts Avenue, Route 128, just to see what would happen. A man gave me a ride and halfway there invited me into a park. He left me covered with leaves. It was interesting to learn he couldn't hurt me. Rides and rides, always men. They said, "You need a place to stay?" On a decaying ranch in Colorado a veteran played Hendrix loud, "All Along the Watchtower." When we got stoned he put his fist in my face and shouted, "You know nothing, Nothing, NOTHING!" We had a slide show and looked at his pictures from Nam. "These are Yards," he said, "Montagnards, best fucking killers around." His friend came to visit and the two of them ran around in the sagebrush shooting rabbits.

I met a veteran who liked literature. He said, "John Updike would have been the best American writer if he'd only gone to war instead of sitting around writing about banging his neighbor's wife." Another was a vegetarian. "Stop eating meat," he told me. "You're creating violence in the world," while he squashed flies against the window with a swatter. And one was an Indian boy in a Pacific Northwest town who took me to his granny's house for a shower. The old lady with a face like a clenched fist rocked under a framed photograph on the mantel. That Indian boy in that photo, brandishing his M-16, was the same picture as Stefan, the same.

These are things they told me:

"You're so young, what are you doing here?"
"Your legs are too white, you need more sun."
"If I catch you looking I'll kill you."
"I can see you been around."

Four men walked into the house, black men with leather coats and floppy hats. They locked the door and pulled a gun. I sat in the armchair saying, "Anyone got a match? got a match? got a match?" an unlit cigarette wavering in my hand.

I could survive anything. (Stefan said he had nine lives.) But when I went to the beach I was afraid of the water. In bed, I was afraid to turn out the light.

When Stefan works, his concentration is complete. Only the immediate exists. I know it's wrong to interrupt him, so I watch silently, huddling under a quilt on the greasy couch, toes near the converted oildrum stove. His head—that bald spot now familiar, endowed with power and appeal—bends over a dismantled outboard engine. I admire the surgical precision of his hands. Stefan said he'd fix this engine months ago but has only begun to work on it today. It belongs to a middle-aged guy who knocked one night while we were eating steamers in the shop. He wore a captain's hat, white plastic shoes, and seemed embarrassed. Stefan offered beer and reassurance, said he'd get to it in a few days. When the man left I asked, "Why'd you say that when you've got Herk's to do and Johnson's diesel and you said you'd fix Eddie's truck?"

"Look at the guy," Stefan answered. "He's low priority. He doesn't need that boat to eat."

"So why didn't you just say no?"

"In the long run," Stefan said, dangling a buttery naked clam before my eyes, "it won't matter at all."

Now he leaves the engine to get a beer from the shop fridge. It's only 11:00 A.M. and he's on his third, but it doesn't seem to affect his work. His beer breaks are my chances:

"Stefan, do you ever feel like the days don't go together?"

"What do you mean?" He has his back to me, his head in the fridge.

"You know, nothing seems connected. First I was little and now I'm here." (Here, this oil-smelling room, dirt under my nails, the hard new swell of my upper arms, woodsmoke in my hair.) "All this stuff happened in between but it doesn't fit."

Stefan throws his head back, noisily gulps. There is something brutal about his throat—the way the Adam's apple juts and when he swallows, a convulsive muscular roll.

"Ahhh." The beer bottle rings empty against cement. Stefan burps, shakes his head. "I don't have answers for you."

He does, I know he does, if he'd only share. Leaning over the engine, he whispers.

"What, you said what?"

It's as if he doesn't want me to hear.

We go to a party on a barge turned houseboat down on the town docks. When we step aboard, seagulls flap up squawking from a garbage scow tied nearby. The barge belongs to a man named Julio who works at a power plant five miles inland. Fake walnut paneling, rock posters, shag rug, beads and Indian bedspreads. I wonder where Julio was ten years ago, when all that was new. There are a lot of people, few whom I know, though Stefan seems surprisingly at home. "Got to keep your mind open," he urges. I sit in a corner, knees pressed shut, while Stefan makes the rounds. A man with chin-length sideburns leans over my lap, pushing a joint in my face.

"It's pretty hot in here," he says. "Want to get some air?"

"I'm here with Stefan."

The man looks over his shoulder, smiles. "He seems pretty busy to me."

Across the room I watch Stefan still talking to a blonde who wants him to fix her Harley. "I'm tired," I say. "I'm going home."

Instead I go to Stefan's cabin and fall asleep in his bed. He wakes me with crashes and mumbled cursing.

"Stefan? What happened?"

"Dishes, damn dishes. Cosmos don't care."

"Stefan, are you all right?"

"Listen!" He lurches against the bed and grabs my wrist, his beer breath sour in my face. "When the toads cross the road to mate in the spring they are squashed by the thousands. Nobody even sees them. Nobody even cares!"

"What are you talking about? Please, let go. You're hurting me."

"Don't you see it's the same? It's the same?"

"Stefan please let go. I want to go home."

"Home? Go home. Go home. You leave now I'll never speak to you again. Go ahead, go home." But he's pushing me back, pinning my wrists. When he does let go I can't move. Then he's gone, retching and gagging over the sink. I squeeze the pillow over my eyes and ears.

"You don't know how much I love you," Stefan says, standing by the bed again, wet now, stinking. "You just don't know."

So I hold him.

While I dress I watch the tiny figure of Stefan through the cabin window, down on the beach scrubbing away at his boat. The sink was clean, the cabin spotless before I woke.

I never even knew I hit it until Stefan pulls the dead bird out of the grille of my car. "Weapons," he says. I start to cry. Stefan waves the bird like a club, accusing, then carries it away, tenderly cradled in his hands.

When a fish surges out of the water, fighting Stefan's line, I'm shocked to see that life exists under that murky surface. Stefan says, "There's more life under there than walks the earth." He says he could live off the beach and the ocean; he needs nothing more. "When the tide is out the table is set." He says someday he will just head out to sea and not come back. All he needs is a knife and hook. What about me? Would he leave me here? Don't leave me here! Stefan says we have to learn new ways. There won't be second chances. There will come a time to take up the rifle. He has a pistol and a rifle; the rifle hangs in the cabin on a long strap. He says supertankers are ruining the seas. Everywhere tar and oil spills. Murder. Petrochemicals raping the earth. He speaks of nuclear disaster, says he will take up the rifle or sail away. How could he sail away from a deadly cloud? Could he sail away from me?

My mother used to take me down to our basement air-raid shelter every week to change the water in the bottles. Cans of Campbell's soup with dusty and faded labels lined the walls. I was afraid The Bomb might drop while I was in school. We practiced for that, crouching under our wooden desks, hands over our heads. What if The Bomb dropped while I was at school and my mother was at home? We'd be stuck in different shelters. Or what if she was at the supermarket, or in the car? I decided I'd run out of the shelter—it would be worse to be alone.

When I get to Stefan's cabin his boat is gone. Rounding the marshgrass, coming over the rocks, I suddenly know that it won't be there. I stare across the bay searching for his sail. He didn't even tell me. The cabin looks the same. He only needed a hook, he said, a knife. Still I ransack his files, read his notebooks and letters looking for clues or explanations. Then I see his sail and finally Stefan walking up the beach.

"I was worried. You didn't say you'd go so far. Where have you been?"

Stefan shades his eyes, stares past me toward the cabin. "On the water. Does it matter?"

"Stefan, Stefan." I wrap my arms around his neck, hug hard. He stiffens though he doesn't stop me. I feel him endure my touch.

I learned to sail his boat alone, although I didn't really want to. Take chances, he said. I learned to set nets, chop wood, tune an engine, shuck clams, pull fish on a line. I learned his face, his thoughts. I spoke his thoughts. I studied his picture. Running my fingers over that younger face, that glossy black and white, I thought: I want to be in that picture. Stefan, it should have been me.

Stefan comes out of the cabin carrying a bottle of beer.

"Where have you been?" I ask. "It's been days. We've got to talk. Won't you at least talk?"

Carefully he sets the bottle down and packs sand halfway up its sides.

"But you said you'd call, Stefan. You said."

He goes back into the cabin and I wait. He comes out carrying the pistol. "Watch," he says. He raises the pistol. My hands go up. The beer bottle flies apart—green glass shards for a second fracture the sun. The noise is nothing like on TV.

"See?" he says. "Watch. Dammit, are you watching? Watch." He raises the gun, swings around, points. Down the beach the bullet shatters the side of his overturned sailboat. Stefan goes back inside.

I turned around and walked back the way I had come, over the rocks and the marshgrass. Later I moved away.

At a party at Katie's house (she married her boyfriend years ago; they have a baby now) Stefan comes over to sit by me. His eyes look the same, and his smile, like that first time he took me sailing, but now for different reasons, forces my eyes away. He says, yes, he's still fishing; no, he hasn't made it on that long sail yet but someday he's going to just set out and keep going. He says we have to find new ways. I smile at him; I nod.

When he shows up at my door two hundred miles away I think, don't you know what time means, but of course he doesn't. He wanders my apartment in his old army coat, touching my things, fingers black with machine oil. I feel no triumph when he says that I'm the only one doing what I want to be doing, or when he asks to stay.

I have no time for Stefan. For him there is no time.

Look at me now—I'm not the same. I'm almost matronly these days. I've got a broad behind and a flat-footed nurse's walk. But I don't care; I like my nurse's walk. I enjoy my transformation every morning: I begin with cigarettes, coffee and a ratty old robe. Then I shower. I pull on underwear, my slip. I draw white pantyhose up and smooth the waistband. I like the crisp feel of my uniform and my starchy nurse's cap. I like my name clipped over my heart.

Then why does that photograph still scare me? Even now I can see his puzzled face, open arms, the weapon: a nineteen-year-old Stefan waiting for something that never came. There's something in his picture I still might want, or still might want to be, so I have to be very careful. For a long time now there's only been room in my body for one. I don't blame this on Stefan; in wanting him, I enlisted too. I accept these limitations because, unlike Stefan, I have faith: I know that a series of days, precisely ordered and stretching back, will sweep me into a future of certain change.

The Vanity of Small Differences

EILEEN POLLACK

Massey killed the mouse mother, pinched her by the tail and dipped her into the beaker of disinfectant, as he might dip a teabag. He laid the pink body just so on a towel and pierced the puffed belly. Though he heard his grandson squirming behind him, rustling the paper clothes he was wearing, Massey paid no mind. A nick here, a cut there, the uterus popped free. He tweezed it out, careful not to nip the fetuses inside, then floated the sac in a warm solution. He sealed the flask tightly and locked it inside a large tank that had two holes in one wall, with rubber sleeves and gloves reaching in from the holes.

"That thing looks like a fat farmer scratching his innards," the boy said.

"Well, it isn't a farmer," Massey told his grandson. "It's an isolator, and you can't go calling an isolator a 'fat farmer' or no one will know what in hell you're intending."

"So? Why should I care?"

Massey had felt his patience eroding with each passing hour. With restraint, he told Joseph: "Suppose you were a scientist here. How could you tell us technicians what you wanted us to do with your mice if you called things by different names from what we call them?"

"If I was a scientist here, the only thing I'd tell you to do with my mice was to stop cutting their bellies open or I'd slit yours, and you'd know what that meant, I'll bet you."

Massey raised his hand, but his fingers were bloody, and this caused Joseph to shrink inside his too-big coveralls until he appeared mean and sassy no longer, just a skinny thirteen.

"I don't know what's wrong with me," he moaned. "I say bad things like that, then I wish I were dead. I'd never slit your belly, Granddad—I'd rather slit my own."

Joseph looked so frail that Massey would have tousled his hair —if not for the mouse guts defiling his fingers. "See that you call things by their right names from now on, that's all," he said, and went on to the next part of his chore, slipping his arms into the sleeves of the isolator and unsealing the flask that he had just put there.

Despite the rubber gloves, Massey moved his fingers in delicate motions, slicing the womb and plucking the mouse pups, delivering them from the germfree uterus into the germfree tank. Four naked pink lumps no bigger than pencil erasers, eyes covered with membrane, each pup a perfect copy of its siblings, not only at skin level, but as deep as its genes, the identical products of hundreds of generations of planned incest among brothers and sisters, sin sanctioned—no, prodded—by science. Every Albino Mouse just like every other Albino, but markedly different from the nude mice called Streakers, or from the Dwarf Mice, the Obese, the Moth-Eaten.

Then there were mice deviant not in appearance, but behavior. The Waltzer, dancing in endless circles like a belle in Satan's torment. The Bouncy, the Fidget, the Hot Foot, the Waddler, the Twitcher, the Twirler, the Trembler, the Jerker, the Lurcher, the Shaker: Massey had shown them all to his grandson. These pups were Rhinos, he told the boy now. For two weeks they'd sprout fur, then they'd go bald. Their skin would outstrip them; wrinkled and baggy, their pink hides would thicken. Their ears would grow pointed, their snouts would elongate, their black eyes would sink into furrows of horned skin.

"Rhino Mice are the ugliest, most ridiculous creatures the good

Lord created," he told Joseph. Ridiculousness, he went on, was
the wages of vanity. Think how conceited these mice were! They
knew how much trouble had been expended to make their births
immaculate, to guarantee their pedigrees, to purify their eccentric
appearances. But they weren't special. Just ugly.

"I'm not ugly!" Joseph shouted, and the highstrung mice skittered in their sterile shavings. "I'm just different, and nobody has
ever paid me wages to be it. And if anybody looks ridiculous, it's
you, because your head isn't much different from a Rhino's, and
on you it looks lots worse." Then the boy withered and ran out.

Massey didn't follow. He decided it would be good to let the
boy wander through a big unfriendly building where he wasn't
important enough to get inside a single magnetically locked room.
Joseph had left his street clothes in his grandfather's locker; he
couldn't leave wearing paper. Massey decided to stop in the men's
room.

Right away, his reflection over the sink made Massey soften.
He didn't often scrutinize his appearance—not because it was
hateful to him, as it once had been, but because he had learned
long ago that no one's appearance deserved much attention. Now
he saw his hairless pink head, the scalp convoluted with age and
fat. His face was as wrinkled as a brain, his small eyes like black
nails driven in pouches, his ears made prominent by the lack of
hair around them. His nose had a red tip. All I need's a tail,
Massey thought, and forgave the boy easily.

Besides, he loved Joseph. If he hadn't loved him, would he have
been so desperate to save him? He couldn't let someone he loved
waste himself on spray-painting his hair green, getting his ear
pierced at a women's jewelry store and sticking a feather through
the hole, and turning his allowance into an ungodly large collection of record albums by bands whose names reminded Massey of
the strains of neurologically disordered inmates at the Mouse
House. He shuddered when he thought of the recent school con-
cert during which Joseph had stood up to play a trumpet solo and
launched instead into his own demented version of "The Brave
Bugler" until the rest of the band had dropped away in confusion.

Then Joseph raced off the stage; he quit the band during intermission, even before the conductor could expel him.

The boy's parents, helpless before his excesses, had sent him to his grandfather in Tennessee for a two-week corrective visit. When the boy arrived, Massey immediately went through his valise and forbade him to wear the most outlandish garments, giving him instead the shorts, trousers and perma-press shirts that the boy's grandmother had picked out at Penney's.

"You can either put on these new clothes, or you can go around naked and attract all the attention you seem to desire," Massey told him. "Now get ready and we'll take you out for a welcome-back-to-Tennessee dinner."

Ten minutes later, Joseph walked steel-eyed and naked from the front door to the driveway, with his grandmother watching. Then he lost his boldness and tore back to the house. The next morning, he came down to breakfast dressed half in his outcast's clothes and half in the new clothes from Penney's. Massey thought this made him appear even more foolish and threatened to burn the old clothes. But Joseph's grandmother took his side. She whispered her reasons to Massey: half a normal boy was better than none, and any extreme measure might cause a relapse to total foolishness, or worse, total nudity.

So Massey just went on to the second lesson. That evening, he took the boy to a field beyond the last ring of houses in Plainview Estates and showed him the overwhelming number of stars in the night sky. "I'll bet a hundred boys like you, green hair and feathers and such all, live on those planets. Isn't anything you could do to earn God's notice."

But Joseph only became obsessed with the notion that hundreds of other Josephs existed in the universe. He tried to contact them by trumpeting his theme song of sharp notes to the heavens, until his grandfather commanded him to stop, at which the boy played the keys without blowing.

"He won't need the music to hear me," the boy said, "just air waves. Or thought waves," and kept clicking at the stars.

After that, he never played a note in his grandfather's hearing, just clicked and sibilated, though he carried the trumpet wherever he went. Massey had been glad when the guard at the Mouse House ordered Joseph to leave his trumpet in Decon, to keep him from blowing germs on the rare mice.

When Massey found the boy in the locker room at last, Joseph apologized stiffly. In silence he tore off the paper coveralls and slippers, girded his cotton-covered child's bottom in heavy layers of camouflage khaki, an armor of pockets and countless brass buckles of no use, then stamped his feet into black boots intended for paratroopers, weaving and tugging the laces for minutes. Finally, he buttoned his blue shirt up his delicate white chest, along the soft crease between the rows of his small ribs.

Massey had barely led the boy out of the scrub room, glad that none of his co-workers had seen how strange his grandson looked in his street clothes, when the boy muttered fiercely: "When I get older and have lots of money from my trumpet, I'll buy this place and set all the mice free, because they're the neatest animals in the world and they deserve better than slicing."

"They wouldn't last a minute," his grandfather told him. "They've never touched a germ and wouldn't know how to get food if it wasn't mashed in a pellet and dropped by their noses. Something would eat *them.* This place is a freak house, and all freaks are weaklings."

He drove the car to the gate and jabbed his magnetic card into a sensor that looked like a cobra's head. A turnpike arm swung up. Massey looked at the boy to see if he was struck with his own insignificance in not having a magnetic card with which to tame the cobra, but the boy's eyes were burning a hole in the windshield.

"They're just mice that have airs," Massey said, and was pleased to see the building recede to an inconsequential size in the rearview mirror.

The Mouse House—really the Chatamaguchie National Breeding Laboratory—was, in Massey's opinion, a monument to the freak: six hundred thousand glorified house pests, cared for with as much religious devotion as if they had been temple monkeys in India. When a particular strain was instrumental in a discovery of genetic importance, employees of the Mouse House would boast of "their mice." All except Massey, who knew that this job didn't make him special. Getting it had just been blind fortune. He had been born in this nowhere corner of Tennessee twenty years before the mouse labs had existed. He had gone to war, and he had come back to Chatamaguchie because he hadn't known where else to go; as he remembered the place, no one much lived there, and the people who did just tried to get by and mind their own farmyards.

Driving the boy home, Massey tried to re-create that long-vanished landscape for Joseph, tried to erase the fast-food restaurants and motels of the Pike and restore the unassuming town whose peacefulness had been his sustaining memory throughout the long war.

"Must have been even more boring than it is now," the boy said. "Must have been just like any other one-horse town."

Massey couldn't help but marvel that even though Joseph had grown up in Chatamaguchie, he seemed to know nothing of the history of it: how the government had needed a swamp hole where scientists could work on the bomb in concealment, how the Army had purchased the whole place and ruined it. Massey had come home from the war and been shocked to discover a raw and sprawling village fifteen miles east of the city proper—guard towers, Quonset huts, plank walks above muddy streets, pile reactors, uranium purifiers, physicists and engineers and their families, all hidden and fenced in among the greeny vines of the backwoods.

The physicists had bred mice in a shack, to have them handy for experimental doses of radiation. After the war, biologists elsewhere began needing pedigreed mice for their research, and the Mouse House was moved to a much bigger building. Over the years, the bomb labs and the Mouse House had crawled out of the woods and gobbled up the town, so that half of Chatamaguchie was now Ph.D.s and their families, and all the rest natives who were proud if they had finished high school. The two halves lived separate, but everyone in Chatamaguchie, genius and unlettered alike, worked at the labs or the Mouse House.

Massey had been a medic's assistant in the war, so he was assigned to a job in the Mouse House. His nimble fingers had earned him such duties as chopping up tumors and teasing uteruses from pregnant mouse bellies, but most often he was just a caretaker. The mice might be fancy and favorites to others, but to him they were just tiny machines that turned big vats of pellets into big vats of mouse shit. Three dumpsters daily. Machines that made mouse pups. Three million yearly.

If the other caretakers wanted to pump up their egos because they served freak mice—Massey said this to Joseph as they turned into Plainview Estates—that was from the desperate need they shared with most people to distinguish themselves in some small way from other people. Take the man who lived across the street —Massey pointed. Just because he had gone from drinking six cups of coffee a day to none at all, he thought he'd been redeemed and was determined to save the caffeinated soul of every person who was kind enough to invite him to dinner. Or the old biddy next door, who informed everybody over and over that she just couldn't keep regular unless she started every day with a glass of cold water and ten minutes reading a book on the toilet.

"Since they're not family, I don't bother to warn them." Massey led Joseph from the garage to the house. "But I've seen what befalls such people. They try to be different at all costs, and that's what it costs them—all they have."

"It doesn't cost *me* much," Joseph retorted, "and when I get older, I'll be rich from my trumpet and it won't matter. I'll buy a neat mansion for you and Grandma so you won't need to live in a crummy house in the middle of all these other crummy houses."

Moved by the boy's generosity, Massey did not clarify his point. He just said: "Why, thank you, but your grandmother and I are very happy in this house. We have each other and such a nice family, that's enough for us." Then he gave in to his urge to tousle the boy's hair.

* * *

Late the next afternoon Massey was swabbing an operating table when he heard a command over the P.A. that he should report to the caretakers' lounge. He finished his swabbing, slid fifteen dead mothers down a chute to the furnace and obeyed the summons.

His supervisor was waiting with a dented shoebox in his small, outstretched hands. "Some hillbilly grandma left this at the front desk," he piped. "Her granddaughter passed on, and she heard we grow mice to cure cancer, so she went out and caught these. I shouldn't have even let them into the building—first thing you know and they've got loose, spread mange to the nudies, had some fun with the lady mice and mixed their bad genes in with the pure ones.

"I'd tell you to just let them go, but you know the order. Gets to be a habit, and pretty soon the environs are overrun and the neighbors start screaming. Every mouse they see, it's some dangerous mutant that's going to eat them. Get rid of these, okay? Thanks, Massey, old man. You're a good soldier." He set the box on a coffee table and pid-a-padded out of the lounge.

Massey lifted the box lid. The mice made him feel funny. Shocked, almost. Yet they were just barn mice, with gray coats and small ears. Not big mice. Not little. Just normal.

That was it. Normal. He touched a soft head. The mouse shook. Massey ran one thumb over the gray silk. His boss had been right. They couldn't just be let go. He lifted the smallest mouse. It peed in terror. Gently, he placed his thumb and forefinger just behind the gray head, applied a quick pressure and yanked the tail down. The mouse died with no struggle.

The other mice whispered. Of course, they had been whispering all the time, Massey knew. He just hadn't heard them because a man never heard anything while he was killing. Still, he felt funny. He looked at the mouse that hung from his fingers. Why should a creature die because it was normal? Maybe he couldn't set the other mice free, but nothing in the rules said he couldn't take them home with him.

He took a napkin from the pile near the coffeepot, wrapped up the dead mouse, then popped the shrouded corpse through a slot to the incinerator. He carried the shoebox to Decon, where the guard made him open the lid and explain. Being singled out gave Massey discomfort, but he told himself again that no rules forbade him. "They're a lesson for someone," he said in a high voice, and when the guard nodded, he scurried out.

* * *

When Massey drove up and saw his yard, he became chilled by
the possibility that his grandson was beyond saving: he would live
and die ridiculous. The fence had been woven with four colors of
crepe streamers. The trees and bushes had also been tied up; the
old oak was as pathetic as an invalid who'd been drawn on with
lipstick by delinquents. Strands of orange, pink, purple and lilac
rained from its branches, poured down the front path and bled
through the wet grass near the rotating sprinkler.

The boy was standing beside a clothes-drying umbrella that
looked like a maypole. His trumpet was hung with long braids of
color. His small fingers pumped the keys with fury, but the instrument made no sounds except clicks and hisses. Colored paper
encircled his thin neck and wound down a T-shirt with flamingos
on it. Below his white shorts, each skinny leg was a candy cane
with stripes.

When the boy saw his grandfather, he took the horn from his
lips. "I haven't been able to tell your house from the others since I
got here." He seemed proud and ashamed, both. "I thought of
this today."

Massey was close to strangling the boy, but Joseph looked
deeply into his horn and murmured, "I can't help it," and Massey
just pitied him. Massey knew that he himself had never fallen
victim to the vanity of small differences only because his parents
had been lessons to him, as had the Army. Blessed with this wisdom, he had come home and married a woman who believed in
the humility of plainness, a woman whom he loved and admired
deeply. She had borne him two daughters, who had always attempted to be like their girlfriends. Both girls had married nice
normal boys and raised nice, normal children—except for this
grandson. But it wasn't the boy's fault, Massey now realized.
Raised by humble people, Joseph had never been able to learn the
dangers of pride, and when his father had been transferred to
Miami the year before, Joseph had been exposed to the strange-
ness of that place with no defense against it.

"Just take down this nonsense," Massey told the boy. "If it's gone before dinner, I'll show you a surprise." On his way to the garage with the shoebox, Massey looked over his shoulder and was relieved to see the boy reaching hand over hand to pull down a streamer from the oak, though Joseph seemed for a second to be climbing the ribbon up to the treetop.

Massey was even more relieved when the boy seemed to understand the lesson of the barn mice, understand that his grandfather was not a killer and that ordinary creatures were healthier and more lovable than freaks. The boy listened intently as his grandfather told him that mice suffered if they were handled too much. At supper, Joseph refrained from his usual antics, such as jamming corn cobs in his ears to win his grandmother's laughter— Massey had told her just to ignore him, but she said she preferred Joseph's clowning to his writhing in embarrassment every time she came near him, as he had when he arrived. "Besides," she said, giggling, "he *makes* me laugh at him."

But the boy must have realized that getting laughed at was a punishment for outlandish behavior, not a reward. Encouraged, Massey took down the family album, and while his wife cleared the table, he sat next to Joseph and reviewed the photos.

He turned first to a picture of an absurdly fat man, a mountain in white clothes wearing a helmet flowing with veils. Massey Senior's beekeeping had been eccentric, but he had never made much of a living from it. No, his vanity had been his prognostication. "Come a day when the Colored Man will eat at the same counter with us." "Come a day when pictures will enter our houses with the music." And, from the humming in his hives, the weather.

But he hadn't predicted the heart attack that killed him at forty, and so hadn't purchased enough life insurance. That diminished the legend that he had been a seer and sent his wife Ruth to serve doughnuts for a living. ("That's her," Massey told Joseph, with shame and reverence. The boy gave a low whistle.)

"I must be the only person in the county who doesn't like chocolate," Ruth Massey used to inform her customers, "or coconut, either," holding her chin up. "It's a shame, because I can eat whatever I want and get no fatter than that coffee stirrer. Some women-I-won't-name say they've got thyroid. My little pinky! They come in and eat half a dozen Bavarian Cremes, then they cook up a thyroid!" She would revolve slowly in front of the mirror and admire the ease with which she fit into the smallest size of the doughnut company's stretchy peach uniform. People in the shop would nudge each other and say, "No one keeps herself from aging like Ruth Massey."

Now she sat all day tied to a wheelchair in a lineup of old men and women who were so formless that Massey couldn't tell right off which was his mother. He decided he would take Joseph to the old-age home the next afternoon.

But Joseph complained that he had already invited a couple of the other children in the development to help him celebrate the last day of his visit. Previously, he had said they were boring; Massey was so pleased at Joseph's attempt to engage in normal pastimes that he granted approval.

For the rest of the evening, the boy practiced his trumpet silently on the living room floor. After Joseph had gone to bed, Massey told his wife he hoped the boy's calmness would last long enough for their daughter to see it. "He just needed a firm hand. Not that *you* used one. How could you watch while he papered our yard and not stop him?"

"I can't scold him," she said. "He hurts worse from scolding than any child I've seen."

"He'll hurt himself worse if he goes on."

She picked up the album, replaced it on the shelf, then stated slowly: "God doesn't love people just because they're different, but He doesn't hate them either. Oh, maybe He has a few chuckles at their expense, but He loves them also, because they're His children."

He smiled at his wife. He knew she couldn't be right, but was moved by the plainness of her thoughts, the simplicity of her print dress and apron, the house she kept for him, not showy or cluttered. Since Joseph had told him he looked like a Rhino, Massey had felt vulnerable, as if he stood out. Now he felt safer. This house, this woman, made him feel hidden. He bent down and brushed his lips against her puff of gray hair.

Flustered, she drew back. "I saw some yarn on sale, a pastel peach color, and I thought I might knit a shawl for Mother Ruth with it."

He straightened. "I guess it couldn't hurt," he told her, and led the way upstairs.

*   *   *

The following day, Massey brought home a cracked plastic cage from the Mouse House. Entering the garage to replace the shoebox, he stopped dead. A crowd of boys and girls encircled the workbench. This made him angry. "A couple of" meant two to Massey, not fourteen. The last thing he had wanted by saving the mice was to make himself into the town's Pied Piper.

Joseph stood at the center of the ring. It pained Massey to think that his grandson was setting himself up for the derision of his peers. None of the fourteen, all blue jeans and sweatshirts, stood out from the others. Joseph was a blaze of absurdity in their midst, rhinestones dangling from one earlobe, steel studs on his black vest, pants that glowed orange.

"I grew up around here," the boy was saying, and they listened as rapt as if he had been a demagogue poor-boy campaigning for Congress. "I grew up around here, so I know how boring it can get. You want to feel like someone, shake everyone up, but if you do different, people say you're queer. Down in Miami—that's where I live now—everyone does it, so no one gets called queer, and life's lots less boring, I'll tell you.

"I mean, look at these mice. The reason that most mice get their necks broke in traps is because they're just plain mice, they all look like nothing. But just you imagine if one of *these* mice ran out of its hole and into your kitchen. Your dad wouldn't stomp it. He'd try to catch it and put it on TV. If all of the world's mice looked like these here, none of them would get killed and none would get laughed at."

The boy moved to one side to open the workbench more clearly to their view. Massey stepped forward. The children turned their heads.

He couldn't believe it. One mouse was wearing a little blue suit with white stripes; tied to its head was a hat like a sailor's. A second mouse was as red and shiny as a toy fire engine. A third was wrapped in a space suit of aluminum foil. Others had antlers of tree twigs, tails plumed with feathers, fur pasted with gold stars and glitter. One mouse, in a tutu, was shoelaced to a cardboard cutout of Fred Astaire.

That did it. If their skins were painted, living things couldn't breathe. And the Lord hadn't meant for His four-legged creatures to be tied in the embrace of cardboard movie stars and forced to stand upright. Massey pushed through the circle, pulled the boy roughly to him and sat heavily with the boy across his lap. Joseph was too stunned to struggle. He didn't even try to twist around, just hung limply over his grandfather's thick knees. The boy's pants were stretchy at the waist, as were his Jockeys, and before Massey knew it, his hand was slapping naked buttocks.

The first sting of flesh to flesh made the boy stiffen. After the second slap, he jumped to his feet, grabbed his pants up to his hips, tucked the shoebox under his arm and pushed his way through the other children. "Isn't any human being deserves that!" he shrilled out, and ran down the driveway.

Massey found himself sitting awkwardly on the bench with fourteen blank-faced adolescents around him, until one by one they dropped their eyes to their sneakers and drifted away. For a moment, he regretted not having punished the boy in private. Then he thought: it was high time that someone had tried to beat it out of him.

* * *

When Joseph didn't return for dinner, Massey didn't worry. He guessed that Joseph would brood on his spanking, and when the evening got too dark and chilly, he would come home and sneak upstairs. The boy knew that his bus would leave for Miami at eight the next morning; he wouldn't risk getting left in Tennessee a minute longer than need be.

Massey put on his bathrobe and started up the stairs. His wife was still at the church, cooking hot dogs for bingo—he was glad she was gone, because she would have told him to call the police.

He snapped the light off and lay on the blanket. He closed his eyes, dozed, and saw himself shoveling live mice from a squirming heap into an incinerator. When he opened his eyes, he was as wet as if he had actually been stoking a furnace. He heard only his breathing, rough and heavy, until the slow notes of a lonely horn mingled with his rasping.

At first he thought someone was playing a phonograph. The song was familiar, but he couldn't name it because the musician was turning it upside down and inside out, ruining the simple tune with a tortuous squealing and wailing. Then his ears trained on the source of the music. He went to the window over his front yard.

Joseph was holding his trumpet to the moon. No braids of crepe ornamented the horn now, only the cold, molten light, burnishing the brass. The boy stood in a circle of dead branches and colored paper. A red watering can sat by his feet, and the shoebox.

As Massey listened, the improvisation untangled itself into an unadorned Taps. This made him think of the boys in the Army, each considering himself invincible because of who his daddy was or the great job or girlfriend he had waiting for him, and the next thing you knew, he was a dead boy with no face.

Massey had not realized that his grandson could play the trumpet so it would give a person the shivers. For a second he was proud. He realized the trumpet must have been something deeper in Joseph than green hair or earrings, something he couldn't help. Maybe if Joseph were given permission for this one difference, he would give up the others.

But the boy couldn't be permitted to show off at such a late hour in such an exposed place. The phone would start ringing at any moment. Massey tied up his bathrobe, but even before he could step from the window, the boy had stopped playing. Massey watched as Joseph doused the dry wood and paper with water from the can. Then, just as Massey was seeing that the spout on the can had nothing to do with water, the flames rose in a low circle around the boy.

"Put that out this instant!" he yelled to Joseph. "Go turn the hose on it!"

The boy needed only to step over the fire to get clear, but he just looked up blankly and resumed his playing, a more frenzied song now, notes as erratic as the spastic dancing of the flames around him.

Massey thumped quickly downstairs, marking his steps by "Jesus" and "damn him" until he reached bottom and raced out the door. He was halfway to the boy when the gas can exploded.

He saw the flames whoosh up and close around Joseph, as high as the boy's head. "Run through! Run, quick!" But Joseph was an immobile dark core in the fire; from the waist down he appeared to belong to it already.

Massey tore off his bathrobe and charged with his head down. "I'm a big tough-skinned rhino," he told himself. "I'll turn pink but won't feel it," and crashed through the flames. He hooked the boy's armpits and dragged him to safety, but he wouldn't let Joseph go for fear the boy would try to run from the fire on his back and so fan the flames there. Massey pulled the vest, with its melting leather and its steel studs like hot brands, off the boy's shoulders, threw him to the ground and yanked his pants off, then fell on top of Joseph and smothered his burning hair and underwear against the damp grass.

The boy's whimpering and rambling seemed to be coming from deep inside Massey's own body. After a minute, he became conscious that he was lying naked on his naked grandson, and rolled off.

The boy lay as if dead for a moment, then shot up. "I left it! My trumpet! I left *them!* The shoebox!" He screamed from the pain that he probably didn't know yet was in his skin and not in his head, in what he thought he had lost. Then he collapsed.

Massey knelt by the boy's side and stared at the black skin, already blistered, and knew that his grandson would never again strive for notice, yet never escape it. As the neighbors came running across the yards of the development, Massey leaned forward and tried to shelter the boy from the humiliation that no living thing deserved, not even if it had been burned down to nothing.

The Big Sway
DENNIS JOHNSON

We were walking through the Public Gardens when she decided to let me know. It was the beginning of summer and Joanne had on her new jeans with the stitching on the pockets and she looked good. I didn't want to hear what she was telling me.

Aren't you listening? she said to me. Yes, yes, I told her, although I was really trying not to. I'm like a kid sometimes it's true, but I feel like if you just don't hear some things, well, you know.

So she went on. You better listen, she said. You're a nice guy and all and I don't want to hurt you but so on and so forth.

Well, I guess I'd known it was coming practically from the first. I mean, I suppose we didn't really have a whole lot in common. And though she claimed to prefer older guys, our slight age difference had been a problem. But who knows why these things happen? I liked her. She was so good-looking, and had such a calm coolness about her, that I'd become hopeful about it working out. And nobody likes getting the old heave-ho.

So, before I could really think, I started getting jumpy and asking her why and everything, and that's when she said it. Because you can't dance, she said. Which was true, but I mean, hello? Just like that, Bang! she pops out with it.

What kind of reason is that? I asked, but she only went *Tsk* like she always did when you were just supposed to know. That's one thing about her I never did like, that *Tsk*.

Anyway, she went *Tsk* and started to walk away and I got a little miffed. I had to run to catch up. I said, Hey c'mon you can't mean this you got to have reasons. And she did it again—*Tsk*—and said I *told* you. She went, Don't worry you're still kind of young. I just want to be by myself for a while, she said. And she walked away again.

Well, I knew she was just trying to get away, but she hurt me with that *kind of young* bit. I'd just turned thirty. She was twenty-two. Also, I knew it wouldn't be easy for me to get another girlfriend like she was going to go out and get another boyfriend, which was what she really meant by that be-by-myself line.

So it was starting to hit home, and I guess I was grasping at straws or something but I ran to catch up again. I started asking her, What about that dance line?—we'll just forget about my age for now, I told her. So again, of course, she said *Tsk*, but she stopped to say it. She looked at me and I could see by the curl of her lip that she was annoyed that I wouldn't give up so easily, that I wasn't hearing her. But I'm like that.

Look, she said, hissing a sigh through her teeth as she tossed her long brown hair back over her shoulder. When we go to a club you won't dance with me, she said. I always have to get somebody else to dance with me so I'm gonna try to be by myself for a little while and maybe dance around, okay?

That 'okay' really meant *so-shut-up-and-beat-off-huh?* but by that time I'd had it and I just stood there like a dummy. She turned and clicked off in her spike heels.

I was stumped. I felt like I had to say something quick, but at the same time I was trying to take in what she'd just said. I couldn't get a hold of it. Her reason, it was like some meaningless sound. All I could think was that she'd be out dancing with some tall job that very night, as soon as she got off from work at the hoity-toity record store she worked at. In fact, if she could get them to play that kind of record where she worked, she'd probably dance right there with some spiffy customer.

But like I said, I'd had it at that point, so I just stood there and watched her go off down the sidewalk and over the little bridge by the swan boats.

Hey, Okay Fine! I shouted after her finally. Out on the pond I saw this whole swan boat of tourists turn their heads. I didn't have to be within hearing distance to hear her go *Tsk* but I didn't care.

However, I did have to admit that she sure looked good in those tight jeans and the high heels and all, and she was doing her little fanny sway as she left me there in the middle of all those flowers.

On the #57 bus back to my place in Watertown I tried to think. When I had calmed down a bit, I realized it was all for the best. Of course, every time I'd broken up with a girl I tried to calm down by deciding it was for the best. You should figure it out for once, I said to myself. It seemed to be happening with increasing regularity, especially since I'd begun dating women somewhat younger than me. I'd thought Joanne was different, though. I'm not sure why. I was suddenly embarrassed at having told her, on our first passionate evening, that I loved her. Never again—another thing I always say at the end of a relationship. But I never mean it when I say never.

It was hard to figure, though, her ending a relationship that was barely a month old because of dancing. It seemed to me that she could have said something like, you know, about my age and my being just a mail clerk and all. I mean, I could have handled that. I could have said something then about her working in a crummy record store. I thought you were gonna go to Elaine Gibbs and become some lawyer's secretary, I could have said. You know, and the argument could have gone on from there.

But that dance comment—Look, at thirty years old, you think I'd never danced before? When I was a little kid I remember trying to do all the stuff the teenagers were doing—the twist, the frug, the jerk—but I was a little kid and I didn't know what I was doing and I felt stupid. It wasn't easy. You had to do the right steps to the right songs and all. But as I grew up, things got different for a while and you could do whatever you wanted. Getting stoned and waving your arms over your head and shaking was very popular. Also spinning like a top. You could just stand, just feel it, just plant your feet and sway. Or—my particular favorite—you could flail all over the place. Nobody cared, it was great. It didn't last, of course, things got back to special steps, to disco, slam-dancing and so on. I quit, because when everybody in the room is doing the exact same moves, it's just, well, weird. It's like they regulated it, for Christ's sake—*dancing,* of all things. That's not right, so I said the hell with it.

In my head, on the bus, that's what I was saying to Joanne. The hell with you, Joanne. If you just want to go out and do the same moves over and over, wearing the same clothes as everyone else, fine. Fine. Maybe we belong to different classes or something. But don't give me my not dancing as the reason to end our relationship.

You're not worth it, Joanne, I said to myself, loudly. Even if you do look good in those jeans.

But it was no good. I had to put it out of my mind, stop thinking about it. Life goes on, I told myself. I sighed. I had to go back to work in the morning. Another day, another dollar. All for ice cream, stand up and holler.

Forget it. Never mind.

It was about an hour later that I started really missing her.

I was standing at the stove fixing up an omelet, and I started feeling lonely, and there's just one plate on the table and all. And I started thinking, What kind of hardhead am I, that I won't dance? It's cost me a relationship with a beautiful woman, a well-built woman. I couldn't keep from thinking about it. I mean, I like bars and all, why couldn't I just do what everyone else does in a bar? Besides drink, of course.

The problem with that was me and Joanne liked different kinds of bars. *Clubs,* she called them. Those big, splashy, crowded places where it takes a half an hour to get a drink, which is probably just as well because all the people in those places are as thin as Joanne—they have to be, to fit into the fashions—and one or two drinks on their empty stomachs and that could become an ugly rabble. You know, the kind of place where all you can do is dance in the big crowd, or you stand on the side and watch the big crowd dance. The music from the speakers is so loud that pretty soon your whole metabolism is pumping at the same rate as the bass. There's wild lighting, flashing, or red or blue or something. See, I'm always so distracted by stuff that I could never really give the dancing part a fair shake.

On the other hand, Joanne hated the kinds of bars I liked. I like to go to bars and drink. *Bars,* I call them. Joanne, she'd drink those sweet drinks that come in pastel colors. Occasionally, she'd get a gin and tonic, but that's no beer with a shot, if you know what I mean. I like simple wooden places with a good jukebox and a bartender you can shoot the breeze with. But the only dancing you can do in those places is real late when you get a little schnookered, and you put the same song on the box two or three times in a row, and you slow-dance while they're waiting to close the place. You know, when all you want to do is lean and press up against each other. Nobody looks. But I guess that's not really dancing. And try as I might, I could never get Joanne to drink enough to do that stuff.

So I was standing there at the stove shredding some cold cuts up into my omelet because that was the only thing I could find in the fridge that smelled safe, and I was thinking about dancing, and I understood that it had been years since I'd even tried. What if Joanne had been right?

The way she said it was like she didn't think I could do it.

That's what decided me. I turned off the stove and got my jacket, and left the omelet sitting there, uncooked, those little pink shreds of baloney floating in the thick yellow mess.

The bus left me off in this corner of Cambridge where there was a funky blues bar I'd heard about. The place sounded like a good compromise between the kind of joint I liked and the kind Joanne liked. It was supposed to be a bar where you could just sit and relax and toss back a couple of boilermakers if you wanted, but they also had live blues bands and a small dance floor.

Sammy's After Hours looked just right. I stood outside in the drizzling rain for a few minutes giving it the eye. It was a small, dark place, with twisting neon beer signs in the window. A Xeroxed photo of the band was taped to the wooden door, a bunch of black guys who looked like they really knew what to do with their instruments. They were led by some harmonica guy named Cryin' JoJo. Things looked good so I went inside. I was surprised to find the place full of white people. In fact, just about everyone in there was white, college kids and hairy Cambridge eggheads and all, and I began to wonder how good the music would be. To my mind, the blues weren't exactly born in the white suburbs, if you know what I mean. But I didn't want to go home so I figured *eh.*

Anyway, what better place for me to end up in, after losing a girl, than a blues bar? Things were starting off okay—it was an hour or so before showtime and I got a stool right at the center of the bar, about fifteen feet in front of Cryin' JoJo's microphone. As soon as I sat down, I got a drink, because I knew things weren't going to be easy, especially walking in stag and all. But by the time the band had finished their first song I was finishing my third beer, and my fears about the music and dancing were someplace way in the back of my head. The band was good, I was a little buzzed, and I was just kind of checking out everyone and the situation.

I didn't budge during the whole first set, just kept drinking and observing, in that order. At first, not too many people danced, just some rowdies who were friends of JoJo's. But gradually, as the band got cooking, the floor began to fill up. The place got a little warmer. The cold beer tasted good. My fifth, I think. Maybe my sixth. The lights were low and I was beginning to feel quite swell. I had a couple more beers and tried to figure out some moves.

About halfway through the second set, I had some moves in mind and the next thing was to find someone to dance with. The thought gave me a little flutter and I decided to have another beer first. No need to hurry, I thought. Be cool, fool. When I got the foamy, dripping mug, I emptied it toot sweet and licked the froth out of my mustache. It was at this point that I suddenly realized my bladder was aching. I guess I'd been a tad preoccupied. The place was pretty crowded by then. I didn't want to lose my seat, but I really had to go, so I ordered a whiskey and a beer, slugged down the whiskey, and left the beer to mark my seat. As soon as I stood up I learned that I was shellacked. We're talking three sheets to the wind. Right off, I was having trouble just making my way through the crowd to the rest rooms. In fact, I wasn't sure where the rest rooms were.

Suddenly, just as I was able to focus on a sign that said "Gents" only a few feet away, someone touched my arm. I thought I'd stepped on somebody's toes, I was too blotto to know. So I turned a little too quickly and mumbled Sorry. There was this blond woman there and she was smiling. Wanna dance? I thought I heard her say.

It was a real dilemma. I couldn't say No I Have To Go To The Toilet. Then I thought maybe I'd imagined it, but she repeated *Do you?* No one had ever asked me to dance before. I was surprised, I was touched, and I didn't know how much longer I'd be able to stand up, so I said Sssure. I gave a final, wistful look toward the men's room, hoping I could get through just one song; then I would politely excuse myself.

The dance floor was packed by that time. The band was really wailing some slow, aggressive song. JoJo was shouting and growling into his microphone *Every Day, woman, Every Day I have the Blues,* Goddammit! and the crowd was getting worked up and shouting *Oh* Yeah! back to him. People weren't dancing so much as bobbing and weaving, clenching their fists—a floor full of boxers. I thought, All right, I can do this, forget the beers.

The woman led me to a spot just in front of the guitar player, then she turned and set her jaw and closed her eyes. She started doing this churning wiggle, really getting into it, her brow furrowed in concentration. She looked like I felt—agonized. My head. No, my bladder. I froze and forgot all the moves I'd thought up earlier. I tried to think up some more, something that wouldn't look too stupid yet—more importantly—would allow me to keep my legs together. People were bumping into me as I just stood there. It was hot, my head was reeling, and somebody had turned up the band. The blond woman danced on, eyes squeezed shut. I couldn't imagine Joanne dancing like that. Slowly, I realized that I wasn't able to do it. I couldn't seem to move. I just wanted to go to the bathroom, I wanted to go back to the bar and finish myself off. Joanne had been right. I felt stuck, heavy, stupid. I took a step and felt the beer sloshing in my stomach. My sparring partner had stopped and was looking at me quizzically. I felt bad. She looked concerned. I wanted to explain it to her, to tell her what Joanne had said.

I leaned forward, was about to tell her when I felt myself finally beginning to sway, and I think I got out a weak grin before I passed out into her arms.

When I opened my eyes the next morning I was thinking about Joanne. It didn't help when I remembered the shoving hands and laughing faces that had stuffed me into a cab just a few hours before. I sat up with a surge of anger—at Joanne, at myself—but fell right back. Crawling out of bed I only felt foolish and hung over, and all I could think of was getting into a hot, steaming shower, which is where I was when I remembered to take off my shorts. That got me annoyed at everything again.

But as the room filled with steam my thoughts more or less evaporated. It's like not waking up. Goofy, Joanne used to call me in the mornings. She found it amusing, my distracted stumbling around, my trances in the shower. *Goofy*. Actually, she only called me that once, but it sort of stuck with me.

Leaning my shoulder against the tiled wall, I reached up and adjusted the shower nozzle so the water hit me square upon the chest. It was the same staring pose I struck nearly every morning, warm and comfortable with the steam rising up all around me, a pose I went into without even thinking about it. I don't want to go to work, was what I was thinking. Thirty years old and I got to cut this crap out, was what I was thinking. Thirty years old and I'm just a mail clerk and it's degrading but I don't know what to do about it. Once, I'd tried to get out by learning a skill. I'd enrolled in E.A.R., the Electrical Appliance Repair Institute, but I felt silly in there with all those tough-mouthed eighteen-year-olds from the suburbs, plus I slipped up once and blew up a toaster.

The water misted off all over the place. It was spattering off the curtain and the tiles and off my chest up into my face and running in braided rivulets down my legs. The legs that wouldn't dance when I'd told them to last night. I ducked my head under the pulsing water.

When I got out of the shower and the fog there wasn't enough time for a cup of coffee. I was running even later than usual. It took five minutes of deep contemplation to decide to put on the same clothes I'd worn the day before. I fumbled with my keys, got my tricky front door lock to click, and thought Boy, Joanne, that was a crummy reason to leave me, even if it was true.

That thought stayed with me all the way to the bus station. A rotten thing to tell me, I'd think, *She's a jerk—then, No, no,* she was right, I hadn't tried hard enough. All the way to the bus station like that, back and forth.

There were two buses idling at the depot. My bus, the Burlington Express, had a long line of black cleaning women and Hispanic factory workers filing onto it. It would wind through the neighborhood to the expressway, to the long string of warehouses along the service road. The other bus shut its doors and revved its engine. Pale faces stared blindly out the windows. This was the downtown bus. Its last stop was at the Public Gardens, directly across from Joanne's record shop. I looked back and forth, from one bus to the other.

The downtown bus started to roll and I was in motion. I ran to it and pounded on the door. It stopped short, opened its doors, and I was on my way into town.

I went to the back. This bus wasn't near as crowded as my normal one. There were a few nurses, some students, some old ladies going in for a day of shopping. None of these people even remotely resembled a mail clerk.

What in the world am I doing? I wondered.

When I got off the bus I knew what I was doing.

Staring through the bright summer flowers and the dense, dark greenery of the gardens, I could see the storefront: clean, plate glass and even rows of white-painted bricks. I was going in there to admit that I couldn't dance, and what's that got to do with anything? I wanted to hear an answer, get some reasonable reasons. I mean, just something about my *content,* for Christ's sake, you know? Some kind of statement of thought. I was gripped by this sensation that someone, Joanne, somebody, owed me that. One *Tsk* and I'd jump her.

I was kind of wired.

As I stepped in the door, a little bell went off over my head. I Can't Dance, I announced loudly. Then I looked around, and didn't see Joanne. She wasn't there. A lone desk clerk in some very stylish clothes looked up from his work. He'd been watering one of the many hanging ferns. *Pardon?* he said.

Oh, I mumbled, nothing. Just looking.

I never had bought a record at that store, even though Joanne could have gotten them for me at a good discount. They sold only classical records, and some jazz. No rock or anything. Joanne said that teenieboppers and old hippies often came in asking for rock and roll. But, she said, we don't cater to people who *won't* grow up. So I asked her to teach me about classical music. We were at her place. She put on this thing called Bolero, which was as boring as all get out, and I told her so. She took it off immediately, even though I apologized and asked to hear it again. Or anything, I said, anything that's classical. She got a little vague and said she'd loaned out all her other classical records. I noticed quite a few pop records lying around. Those aren't for *listening,* she snapped, just for *dancing.* That was the last time I was at her apartment.

Peeking through the ferns, the clerk was watching me. I could see him out of the corner of my eye as I tried to act like I knew what I was looking for. There was a forced quietness. Faint music —strings and voices—in the background. Hisses from the water bottle. Pause. Resumed hissing. Finally, I went up to the guy and asked for Joanne. He pretended he hadn't been looking at me. *Oh,* he said. She's just gone out for some coffee and croissants. Be back shortly. He went back to his plant life.

I nosed around some more. There were no other customers. I seemed to be the first one of the day. Be cool, I told myself. Minutes passed.

Suddenly, the little door bell tinkled behind me and I braced myself. Taking a breath, I whirled around and was about to proclaim *You're Right—I Can't Dance!* when I saw that it wasn't Joanne. It was a young black woman in a white dress. Her blouse had puffy sleeves and the skirt was just a bit too long and looked old-fashioned. The clerk spoke to her—Good morning may I help you?—but she didn't even look at him.

There was something about this woman. She had a very open expression on her face: her eyebrows were high on her smooth forehead. Her wide eyes scanned the room and found the clerk, and then her hands came up in a fluid series of beautiful gestures.

It came to me. On the loading dock down at the warehouse, there was a guy who had that same look, who moved his hands the same way. He was deaf. But what would a deaf person want in a record store? I wondered. I realized I was staring—with my mouth open, no less. I do that sometimes. I hate when I do that. She's just getting a gift or something for someone, I figured, making myself look down, and I saw I was in the small but tasteful jazz section. I started flipping through some Charlie Parker records. Boy, I thought, if they knew the kind of life this guy led they'd ditch these records. It'd wilt their ferns.

I couldn't keep from shooting glances over at the deaf woman, though. She was trying to explain something to the clerk. I saw her make some more half-hearted signs, which he didn't understand. She watched him closely, like she was reading his lips. But she didn't see there what she wanted. She made a swaying movement with her hands and shoulders. He said Ballet? She shook her head, no.

I started paying even closer attention when I heard an annoyed tone enter the clerk's voice. He kept saying I'm *sorry* madam, and You should have written it *down.* I'm afraid I don't have any paper *handy,* he said, trying to get back to his atomizer. He was being a real twit, I felt like going over and knocking him down, but she was being patient with him. I started going through my pockets, looking for scrap paper, anything, when I saw the woman was counting with her fingers—first one finger, then two, then three, then one, two, three, one two three—and it hit me.

Waltz! I said, then louder, *She wants a waltz.*

The clerk looked at me with heavy-lidded eyes, and she turned to follow his gaze.

Do you want a waltz or something? I said to her, trying to move my lips around the words so she could read them. I think I spoke a bit too loudly. She nodded vigourously *Yes, yes,* smiling. She was pretty. Well which one? said the clerk, like he was in a hurry to get somewhere. Which one? I repeated, because she was looking at me now.

She came over to me and touched my blue work shirt gently. Then she made a beautiful little rippling motion with her hands. The clerk got it immediately and yelled it out like it was a competition. The Blue Danube! he called out. But he was behind us now. So I said You don't by any chance mean *The Blue Danube?* and she nodded again, but not so enthusiastically, like she wasn't so sure.

Put it on, I told the clerk. Oh *really,* he said, She can't *hear* it, and I said No but *I* can. I hadn't heard the thing in a long time, I couldn't really remember how it went. Back in junior high school, in gym class, they made us do ballroom dancing once a year, and I'd gotten waltzing down pretty good. And I recalled that the instructor had always used The Blue Danube.

Anyway, the clerk got the recording and put it on the store's super hi-tech player. It looked like it pained him to take off the opera he'd been listening to.

The woman was looking hopefully from me to the clerk and I was trying to figure out a way to describe the sound to her. As soon as it came on, with a slow flutter of strings, it was like I'd know it all my life. Starting to whistle along, I looked straight at her so she could see my lips. Then I realized how idiotic that was and I stopped but she kept looking at me with this expectant look, smiling. I started to sway a little and go da da da de dum along with it and her smile widened and her eyes widened, too. She even swayed with me a little. But I could see she still didn't get it, and before I knew what I was doing I'd put my arm around her waist and started waltzing with her. It just came back to me in a rush, all the way from junior high school, so I started waltzing with the deaf girl to The Blue Danube.

She laughed and I pulled her closer and swirled her around, one two three, one two three; we twirled and over her shoulder I caught a glimpse of the clerk with a dumfounded look on his face but it didn't matter. Somewhere a little bell chimed but I didn't even bother to look over by the door, I didn't care, I held the deaf girl and closed my eyes and she was laughing and we just kept swirling and twirling one two three one two three.

Things to Draw
KATHARINE ANDRES

On the first Saturday in May, my father and I went to a store that specialized in English riding clothes and looked at swatches of corduroy—navy blue, brown, olive drab. Then the tailor put one hand between my father's shoulders and guided him to the fitting room to measure him for a suit. The store was high-ceilinged and brightly lit. There were saddles, half mannequins wearing tan jodhpurs, drinking glasses with pictures of riders jumping brooks and hedges.

I was entirely uninterested in horses. I was fifteen and thin, and when I walked by the full-length mirrors my own walk looked odd to me, as if the whole upper part of my body were tilted back. I walked from mirror to mirror, self-consciously upright, until my father came back. "Which color do you like best?" he asked.

"The dark blue, with the narrow wale."

"So do I," he said. He would have said this no matter which I'd chosen. I picked the colors of clothes, new cars, rugs. We both laughed, and my father ordered a suit. "When can you have it ready?" he asked.

The tailor looked at the calendar above the cash register. "I think we'll need four weeks, sir," he said.

"I'd like it sooner."

They agreed that my father would pay for the suit in advance and the tailor would have it ready in three weeks. My father caught my eye to be sure I saw the lesson in this: one need only be firm. He reminded the tailor of the exact narrowness of the lapels, and we left.

I had been spending Saturdays with my father for eleven years, from the time my parents were divorced. He lived in a dark apartment on West End Avenue, too big for one person. I spent my Saturdays there drawing with Magic Markers at the kitchen table, playing Scrabble by myself, reading the books my father chose for me: "Captains Courageous," "The Call of the Wild." These books without women and children moved very slowly, but I always said I liked them. Late in the afternoon, we watched the General Electric "College Bowl" on TV. I never understood that sense of the word "bowl" and didn't ask. My father nearly always called out the answer before the crewcut college student pressed the buzzer. "And I didn't go to college," he'd remind me.

I was always frightened of doing something stupid: of forgetting to put a sheet of scratch paper under my drawing and staining the white table with traces of blue and green, of closing a door too loudly and disturbing my father's afternoon nap. He read while I was there, worked at his desk, watched football games, slept. "A nice quiet afternoon," he'd say on the telephone if anyone called. But when I did spill apple juice on the rug or rip a plate in a book of Chagall paintings, his face became deep red and he said I was a stupid girl, his voice filling the midafternoon darkness of the apartment.

"I'm sorry, Daddy," I'd say.

"Don't say you're sorry, Margaret," he'd say in a warning tone, but he didn't suggest an alternative.

The day we chose the corduroy suit, we had lunch at a Japanese restaurant, a small, pretty place with blond wooden tables. All morning, I'd had my cardboard portfolio under my arm. "What have you been drawing?" my father asked when we had been seated. He loved the idea of my becoming some kind of artist and gave me art supplies for encouragement—fat tubes of gouache, heavy white paper. I pushed aside my teacup and took out my drawings. He leaned toward them. The first had four panels on one page: views from windows. I had also drawn my mother's reading glasses and three bowls from our kitchen. These last were in watercolor, pale shades, two blue and a green. He spread the drawings out, careful to avoid the little puddle the waiter had made when he filled our water glasses. Usually, I'd show my father something every other week, and there was always this long silence. I couldn't see his eyes, because he was looking down from one page to the others, his lips pressed together. "Why did you draw these things?" he asked.

"Well, because of the seagull, partly, and I liked drawing them," I said.

The seagull had been two weeks before. It was in pastels—a seagull on a bollard, a dock in the background; bleak enough, I'd thought. In the late afternoon, we'd been sitting on my father's dark-red couch. He was drinking beer. "It's a cliché," he said. "Unless you can do something like this in some brilliant or novel way, best to leave it alone."

I had worked on the seagull for quite a while—so long, in fact, that I'd lost sight of corniness, which I really was attuned to generally. I waited for him to notice that it was at least technically O.K. The bird had the right look between placid and arrogant; the light was nice. I often came near to tears during my father's critiques. I was near tears then, and it kept me from speaking. He held the drawing, sitting forward on the couch. I looked at his thin hair, his dark eyes, his strong rounded nose, and I despaired of ever pleasing him. Of course, I had pleased him—especially when I was a child and had drawn fearlessly. He often said how sorry he was that I had acquired self-consciousness. Picasso, he said, hadn't.

I said, "What can I draw?"

"Things that aren't encumbered by meaning, by ideas," he said, finally putting the seagull down on the coffee table. I put it back in my portfolio right away, and I went home and started my views from windows in blue ink, stark on the page. I'd drawn sulking, thinking it wasn't fair for him to want me to be so good so fast.

Waiting now, holding my chopsticks as if the food were already there, I watched my father. His brow was clear; he was taking himself seriously.

"They're better," he said, as if it were an effort. "But I'm not sure I can tell by looking at them the reason for their existence. They're just *there.*"

I had recently learned the cliché about the rock and the hard place, and I thought of it now. You didn't want a drawing sloppy with meaning. On the other hand, bowls and eyeglasses were incidental. That left people, but I didn't always have people who were willing to stay still. The waiter was coming with our lunch.

"The work is very good, though," my father said, seeing the waiter too. I put the drawings away and tucked the portfolio under my chair. I wondered if I might forget it there.

The food was a signal that we were talking about something else, but I was still thinking about what to draw. We had sashimi and rice. The sashimi came on gray-and-blue ceramic palettes. It was bright orangey-pink and stood upright next to a web of grated radish, three slices of cucumber, and a green plastic leaf. We had this meal often, and it pleased us both.

"It's good," I said, about lunch.

"How is your mother?" my father asked.

"Fine," I said. "Working." My mother was an editor. She and my father had met when she returned the manuscript of his novel with an encouraging rejection. He had visited her and tried to get her to change her mind. "Bullied me," she said. She had refused. They had fallen in love with each other's hardheadedness. But slowly this must have become less appealing. They always asked after each other in this cursory way—I think to make me feel comfortable, but maybe because they were still vaguely curious.

"How are things at school?"

"Fine," I said again. "Two people in my class got suspended for selling marijuana."

"Did you know them?"

"Sort of." My stories often fell flat.

I looked at the chopsticks in my father's square hand. "What have you been doing?" I said. He'd scolded me before for not asking this question, for being self-centered, so now it weighed on me each Saturday until I had said it. It never sounded very genuine.

"Working on a television pilot. Meeting with the other writers."

"Is it going well?"

"There are very few excellent detective stories, and this isn't one of them."

I laughed. I drank my green tea and searched out the last grains of rice with the ends of my chopsticks.

My father offered me his plastic leaf.

I said, "Thanks, but no thanks." This was ritual.

We walked on Madison Avenue after that, looking in store windows. I had to keep my head down because of the sun, and my dark-blue shoes looked long and narrow to me, the way I imagined nuns' shoes.

My father was in love, and maybe because of this he seemed very young to me. And because I imagined that I'd never be in love, I seemed very old to myself. Today, his step was especially light. But Judith, the woman he was in love with, was married—a marriage that looked as if it would go on. And the next week my father had to go to the hospital for tests; the doctor wanted a look at his gallbladder, he said. He didn't ever have steady jobs and was always worried about money, so I thought that we should probably eat salami sandwiches at his apartment and that he should buy ready-made suits. But nonetheless he did seem on top of the world. I suspected that he worked at it, in order to seem young. Being young myself, I knew that blitheness wasn't an attribute of youth.

He walked me back uptown to my mother's apartment and gave me one of his solid, lasting hugs. These days, when he hugged me I just saw the top of his head. Neither of us had mentioned this; I felt enormous, afraid of becoming so tall that, unwillingly, I'd bend forward toward things I wasn't even sure I wanted. I never wanted to draw those thin, graceful animals—giraffes and gazelles. I liked the steady, bearish ones, whose strength you never doubted.

"See you soon," he called, then turned the corner, back toward the West Side.

A week later, my psychology class was taking a trip to a hospital in the Bronx. We'd been warned by Dr. Gittleman, the school psychologist and our teacher, that it would be strong stuff for high-school students, and I was looking forward to it. I sat next to Moira Jacobson on the bus.

"Have you ever been to a mental hospital before?" Moira asked.

I made my eyes wide and moony and said, "I can't remember," in a high-pitched little voice.

Moira just said, "Oh." She was the kind of person who is never sure when to laugh. I wanted to look out the window at the dark uptown buildings. For me, everything was already connected to the hospital. I was tightened for a blow, so that I wouldn't show it if I was scared.

The hospital was a tall, dark-brown building with wide steps leading to the entrance; around it were other hospital buildings and an excavation site with a construction trailer. It was a cloudy Friday afternoon.

Inside, we were met by a young woman in a white coat. She said not to touch things, not to talk to patients, and to stay in our group.

The twenty of us stood clustered together in a darkened room filled with white rats in cages. At a long table lit by a fluorescent bulb, technicians transferred a liquid the color of mint jelly from test tube to test tube with eyedroppers. Most of the rats were sleeping, some with their paws tensed in the air. There was a sour, medicinal smell in the room, and the woman was explaining about lithium and manic-depressive behavior in rats. I could tell that Scott Fischer, standing by one of the cages with a pencil in his hand, was thinking about poking one of the rats. We were all eager to get on to the real thing.

We came out into a lighted corridor. The class was quiet, as if we didn't know one another. I liked everyone for being serious. The boys were tall, ill-shaven, and looked intent on walking. Dr. Gittleman, with her light-orange hair in its loose bun and her darting glance (at school, it was said that she was trying to spot the crazies, to catch them unawares), led us down the hall. She

was fond of me, and wrote things like "Sensitive thinking" or
"Very original observation" in the margins of my papers. We
passed a cafeteria, full of doctors and nurses, then an empty room
with a cot and gym mats on the walls—"For cases where isolation
is indicated," the guide said. We went in all together and pressed
our fingers into the soft walls. Then, through double doors, we
went into the corridor of the men's ward. Even in the hall, the
light was unnaturally bright: for scrutiny, I imagined. Each door
had a window and the day's menu with boxes checked off hanging
from a clip. We went by quickly. I saw a check by "hot turkey
sandwich" and one by "ice-cream novelty." The guide said we'd
be in the recreation room next, where the patients spent their free
time.

It was a very large square room, with tables and chairs that,
though they weren't actually small, reminded me of kindergarten
furniture. There was a television set, with local news on, and two
men were facing it, though not really watching. There was a shelf
of games—familiar ones, like Monopoly and Clue. Some men
played checkers, some looked at magazines, but most just sat—
not at tables, not near the edges of the room, just randomly. They
all wore pajamas and slippers. The pajamas weren't hospital issue.
The pajamas of the man closest to me had a pattern of tiny alter-
nating keys and teacups. Some were plaid or striped. No one
looked at us. We stood in our group, and Fritz Hammer, who
stood beside me, took my hand for a second, then let it go. I was
startled. I was concentrating so hard on the keys-and-teacups
man, his short, light hair and maroon terry-cloth slippers. What
had he done? How long would he be here? It was as if he had
touched me. I thought I might have made a sound, but no one was
looking at me. Everyone in the group was blank-faced, waiting to
be led away.

Fritz and I had gone to the same school since we were five. If
I'd been asked before that moment whether I liked him, I couldn't
have said. I had that tolerance for him you have for people you've
always known. We went to the same dentist. He was sometimes a
character at the edge of my dreams. He was slightly smaller than I
and wore round, gold-rimmed glasses, and was the sort of boy

who not only knew facts in English or history but was famous for having theories. At that moment, I couldn't look at him, but I knew his face, its bony, vulnerable shape, and though I knew I shouldn't be, I was entirely happy for a moment, knowing that he was as bothered as I was, that there was something wrong about standing and watching these men. I moved closer, without actually touching him, and then, finally, we moved on to a conference room, where we were allowed to ask questions.

I was afraid that Fritz would say what we both thought, and that spoken aloud it would be brash, typical, self-righteous. He said nothing. Someone asked about the success rate of drug therapy. Moira asked something about high- and low-security facilities in such a way that I could tell that she wanted to be reassured that the men we'd seen were nice, calm crazies, not going anywhere. The prissiness of her voice made it possible to look at Fritz for the first time. Neither of our faces changed.

On the bus going back to school, we sat together. I couldn't stop shaking. I had imagined haggard women, distant screaming, the sad things being instantly apparent. The side of Fritz's head was against the window, his hands awkwardly on his knees. He said, "Are you depressed?" and then he looked at me. "You're trembling."

"I know," I said. The bus went by a stone wall at the edge of a park. Other people were talking normally again. "But in a way I feel as if I'm not quite as sad as I ought to be."

"We're too far away from it, or maybe we don't know enough."

"Sort of." I could remember Fritz a long time before, wearing corduroy overalls, sitting with his hands pressed together between his thighs, listening to stories. Even then he had had that intent forward tilt of his head. My favorite book then had been "The Five Chinese Brothers." I'd liked its black-and-yellow drawings and the way each brother escaped death through his extraordinary strength. It was calming, somehow, to think of it now, and so I asked Fritz if he could remember the talents of the five Chinese brothers.

"Having legs that could stretch to any length," he said. "And one had an iron neck, one could hold his breath forever, one could swallow the entire ocean—or were those the same one? I'm stuck. I used to wonder what would happen if I had to do any of those things and I couldn't."

I liked him for not asking why I'd said what I'd said. I could feel happiness mounting the way you feel the pressure the longer you hold your breath.

"Have you seen 'Yellow Submarine'?" he asked.

"Yes. I sort of liked it."

"I just wondered if you still liked stories about people who can do amazing things."

"*They* don't do amazing things. You never really believe in cartoons that the characters are doing things. It's too whimsical. Did you like it?"

"Against my will," he said. "I love things like that." He had a wonderful bright smile as he said this, and that intensity which made people laugh in class when he talked about Angel Clare's injustice to Tess or the Second World War. I liked watching him. My own thinness seemed brittle and inelegant to me—I'd judge it in the mornings as I got dressed. But in Fritz thinness seemed clever and flexible, like one of the talents of the five Chinese brothers. Then we were back at school.

We pulled up near the old gray stone building with red wooden doors and a cast-iron spiked fence in front that looked like a cross between a church and a fire station. It was three in the afternoon, and the street was empty, except for my mother, walking toward the entrance in her beige raincoat, and then turning toward the bus. I couldn't remember when I'd last seen her at school. "It's my mother," I said to Fritz.

When Fritz and I got off the bus, my mother rushed toward me and crouched down near the pavement, so that her arms were around my hips. I felt off balance, as if everyone who had got off the bus was looking at us. Fritz stood a few feet away, and I could feel him coming slowly unattached from me.

"Darling, your father is dead," my mother said.

He had died in the hospital while they were operating on his gallbladder; his heart had stopped.

I felt very tall with my mother crouched at my feet. I looked around me, at faces, parked cars, the blue bus we'd just been on. I felt the cool gray air of the day on my neck. Nearly everyone had gone into the school by then, but Dr. Gittleman was still outside, talking to a few stragglers, and my mother went to tell her what had happened. I didn't move, and neither did Fritz. I knew I should tell him, but it seemed too hard. Instead, I thought about the place on the sidewalk where I was standing, to the left of the red doors, by a locust tree at the curb. Every time I walked by, it would be the spot where I'd found out that my father was dead, and, odder than that, from now on he would always be dead.

Fritz waved and went inside. Dr. Gittleman came over and hugged me. I stood rigid, waiting for her to let go. "Come and talk to me when you get back to school," she said, and I said, "O.K.," so that I could escape. And then my mother and I walked home.

At home, I didn't know what to do. Everything in my mother's apartment was calm, the way it ordinarily was. I couldn't read or do homework or draw or eat. I lay on my bed, not thinking of anything, feeling sick, but not like crying.

For dinner that night my mother heated up cream-of-celery soup from the can, and we had those octagonal crackers that go with seafood. It was a long time since she had been married to my father, and I couldn't gauge what she felt. I looked across the kitchen table at my mother holding a spoonful of soup at chin level. She had already offered to call my friends, so that I wouldn't have to, and she had said that I could go back to school whenever I was ready. These were the easy things to talk about. Ordinary things—the events of the day until we had found out—seemed irrelevant, like telling jokes during the intermission of a very serious play. My mother kept looking at me, and I could feel her waiting for me to talk, so that she'd know I was all right.

"What did you have for lunch?" I said.

She went on looking at me; it wasn't the sort of thing we discussed. "I was eating at my desk when they called from the hospital."

I stopped myself from asking "What?" though for some reason I wanted to know. I wasn't doing well on my soup, but I kept eating the little crackers, one by one, while I thought of what to say next. I imagined, but quickly, since I wasn't really sure that this was what I wanted, a mother who treated me like a small child, holding me in her arms, urging me to cry. But we were separate, upright, and I treasured the idea of seeming strong. I went to my room again right after dinner.

"Do you have something to read?" my mother called from the living room, then came to my door with four books to choose from. I took "The Heart of the Matter," for no reason. When I was ready for bed, I knocked on my mother's door. She was at her desk, her room dark except for the reading light, working on a manuscript, with a yellow pad full of notes. The folder for the manuscript was on the floor by her shoes. She worked sitting cross-legged, leaning forward into the light, so that her profile was sharply, beautifully lit.

"Good night, Mummy."

She kissed me, and I crossed the dark living room and shut the door of my room. I sat on the edge of my bed and began to cry with the tension of trying to be silent. Tears made wet spots on my knees, so that they were pink through my nightgown. I got up, pulled down the shade, and went on crying. I had a fear of missing my chance. This was the only night I could cry and be comforted; any kind of behavior would be all right. My mother could rescue me, and I knew that she would do it wonderfully; it would work. I thought she might come now, as she often did, to say one more thing to me before bed. I went on crying, faintly self-conscious now, and then I turned off the light and lay still for a long time, not crying, not falling asleep.

On Monday, I went back to school. My friends knew what had happened, and there was no reason to tell anyone else. But I felt conspicuous, as if everyone knew. My homeroom teacher said he was sorry. A few friends asked how I was, and I couldn't think of the right answer. I needed time to practice saying "My father is dead" without that internal wriggle of embarrassment. I wanted it to be as easy as "My father is in Egypt," which, after all, sets you apart from other people, too.

I saw Fritz in the hall before psychology class. "I heard about your father," he said.

"Yeah."

"I'm really sorry."

We'd never actually been friends; he didn't have to say anything. In class we sat next to each other, and I was aware of the glare of his eyeglasses and the tilt of his head as he listened. All through class I felt like a living illustration of Psychology—that people were watching me, and later on would say, "I know this girl, and when her father died she hardly seemed to notice. I mean, she seemed completely normal."

After class Fritz asked if I'd like to go to the Bronx Zoo with him on Saturday. It was because my father had died. Now even Fritz's taking my hand in the ward of the hospital seemed to be because of that. I knew that I was scrambling the sense of things, but I didn't talk about it with anyone, and that made it less dangerous. "I'd like to," I said.

The day at the Bronx Zoo was the first day that didn't seem completely empty. Fritz and I walked along the paths, stopping for a long time by whatever we came to: yaks, zebras, elephants. "What do you like best?" I asked.

"I don't know," he said.

I couldn't imagine not knowing, and this seemed like a gift from my father. We stood in the sun, by a fence, drinking root beer, and I laughed. We were shy of each other, and it seemed self-conscious to talk about the animals—too easy. We sat on a bench and ate pizza that had been heated in a microwave oven. I had no idea what Fritz was thinking when he didn't speak, but I felt that he knew exactly what was in my mind. "Can you tell what I'm thinking about?" I asked.

"Your father?" This was the first time either of us had mentioned him.

"No. I don't know," I said, and looked out at the ostriches.

"What was he like?"

"That's an impossible question."

"I know."

This talk made me angry and full of energy. "Come on," I said. "Let's walk around some more."

"I didn't mean to annoy you," Fritz said in a timid way that was even more annoying. I didn't say anything, and he put a heavy arm around my shoulders, not quite high enough, because I was too tall. We walked yoked together like this for a while. I looked down at his running shoes, at my brown leather sandals. There was one of those green wooden signs that said "TO BEARS," and to break the silence I said, "My father liked polar bears best."

I tried not to mind Fritz's arm as we stood looking at the polar bears: their sleek, heavy lunges in and out of their pool, their spiky, yellowed fur. It felt exactly like one of those "moments of silent prayer" in a school assembly. I wished I hadn't told about my father's liking polar bears. It was my own fault.

We headed back to the subway station, not even stopping when animals were right up near their fences or antic in their cages. The subway was too noisy for talking unless you desperately wanted to. I read the ads for employment agencies and aspirin and thought how I had spoiled the day. In my head I composed the note I'd write to Fritz to apologize. He was looking straight ahead at the reflections of our faces in the window opposite. I leaned toward him and kissed his cheek. He turned, startled, and we jerked away from each other. I got off the train first and waved to him from the platform.

For the next week, I dashed away after psychology class to avoid my talk with Dr. Gittleman. But then on Friday I felt safe, and stood outside the classroom talking to Fritz. Dr. Gittleman put her disarranged orange head out the door and said, "Margaret, may I talk to you for a moment?"

I hadn't been in Dr. Gittleman's office before. Everywhere there were manila folders with odd-sized pieces of paper hanging out. There were primitive paintings on the walls—men, canoes, and fish, on some dry-looking animal skin. Behind her desk there was one window facing the building next door. You could see it from the psychology classroom, too, and generally someone's maid was there, ironing and folding. Sometimes I'd see the lady of the house, dressed to go out, leaving instructions. All this was riveting, and there was a lot of discussion of it after class. Now there was no one in the apartment, but I looked beyond Dr. Gittleman out the window anyway.

She smiled her I-know-exactly-how-you-feel smile at me. "How are things going?"

"Fine," I said for the thousandth time.

"Are you sleeping at night?"

"Mostly."

"Good. Is there anything you'd like to talk about?"

I thought how easy it would be to be someone else, to say: I feel bewildered all the time; everything is perfectly ordinary.

The maid came into view and began ironing.

Dr. Gittleman said, "This is quite a normal reaction to a very disturbing event. You succeed in assimilating it only to have it hit you all the harder later on."

"When?"

"It depends on the circumstances."

We both stood up then, and she came around the desk and hugged me for the second time. I thought a psychologist should know when someone didn't want to be hugged. Then she took a small box from one of the filing-cabinet drawers. "I want you to have this."

"Thank you," I said. It was an ordinary rock, white and shaped like a small potato, with a green-and-brown grasshopper painted on it next to an orange flower. I thanked her again. "It's a very comforting rock," I said.

Dr. Gittleman gave me a quick, quizzical look, but I got away with it. I put the rock in its box in my book bag.

Afterward, I had drawing class. It was in a big, white-painted studio, and mostly you were just left alone to draw. Today, there was a slender, fair-skinned model, lying on her side with her back to the class. There was the clean, sharp smell of paint in the room, and it was quiet. It was a ten-minute pose, and I was aware of other people's charcoal scratching against the paper. But I didn't have the perspective right; the shoulders were huge, the feet tiny, and I had no patience. I was exhausted. Though you weren't allowed to, I untacked my drawing, put away my board, and left the class. I went and sat at the foot of Fritz's locker, waiting for him to get back from gym.

"How was it?" I asked when he got there.

He leaned over, untied his blue-and-gold running shoes, and stood in his gray socks. "Softball," he said. He didn't have to say terrible; hardly anyone who was smart liked gym.

I was hoping he'd ask me to do something on Saturday. Though so far there had only been the trip to the zoo, I'd let myself imagine walks, movies, tea in my living room. After we'd talked awhile, he said, "My mother is taking me shopping for pants tomorrow morning. Can we do something in the afternoon?"

We agreed to meet outside the Metropolitan Museum at two, and then I said, "I couldn't draw today."

"What do you mean?"

"I was drawing and I couldn't get it right, and I just quit."

"It doesn't matter. You'll be fine next time."

"Maybe," I said. I couldn't explain about feeling nearly dizzy with the effort to get the curves of the model's body in the right places on the paper. I didn't want to risk crying.

Fritz had put on his desert boots, and now he knelt, putting books into his knapsack, spines facing up. He sat down next to me, and our thin legs stretched out into the hallway. He patted my shoulder and said, "It's really O.K." We were both so thin and awkward that any touch seemed to come too close to the bone. So when his hand touched my shoulder I did begin to cry, looking across at the green lockers on the other side of the hall. Then, with a funny, abrupt strength I wouldn't have imagined he had, he pulled me around so that my face was against his yellow shirt. The last class was about to let out. People would be coming to their lockers. But I felt heavy and inert and kept thinking, Another minute and I'll sit up.

"I'm sorry," I said. "I didn't plan this." I saw that I'd made a dark spot on his shirt. His face was worried: it had a bony, unguarded look. I was beginning to get better and said, "Do you know what your favorite animal is yet?"

"I've given it some thought," he said, "but I need to weigh and consider a little longer."

People were in the hallway. We stood up and were unnoticeable again. I wanted to throw my arms around Fritz, but the irrational happiness scared me, because I knew it wouldn't last.

We went downstairs. Fritz smiled and said, "See you tomorrow," and I watched him walk off, adjusting his knapsack on his narrow shoulders.

The next day, Saturday, my mother went to her office, and I had the whole morning. I got up, dressed, and left the house before I realized that I didn't really have a purpose. I began walking. I didn't want to go to a museum or a movie, so I walked up Fifth Avenue on the Park side, past children and their mothers, Good Humor men, people sitting on those benches along the wall. When I was hot and beginning to be tired, I turned east, then down Lexington. At a quarter of one, I was outside the Japanese restaurant where I'd been with my father three weeks before. It took me by surprise. I stopped as if it were a person I recognized. I looked in the window, past the plastic pieces of sushi and the wood-and-paper screens, and then, without thinking, I went in and sat down. I'd never eaten in a restaurant alone and I half expected someone to come to the table and very politely, for an unexplained reason, ask me to leave.

I was across the room from the table where I'd sat with my father, and I saw now for the first time the Hiroshige print on the wall above that table: people holding umbrellas, crossing a curved bridge in heavy rain. I wished with an ache that I had seen it before. If I had, I'd have specific cause to love it or, perhaps, to want never to see it again. But there would be no danger of its fading into the flatness that dulled the edges of everything now.

A waiter, the same one, came with the menu and a bronze-colored teapot. I tried to decide if it was a smaller size or exactly the same. I looked at the menu and checked to see if I had enough money. I wasn't especially hungry, but I had gotten used to my small square table, to being there and listening to the tinkling, repetitive music. I was sure the waiter would ask, "Where is your father?" He must have known we were father and daughter, and I must look wrong to him there by myself. I was deciding whether to say, "He's in Egypt, looking at the pyramids," or "He died." To the one, the waiter would say, "How nice"; to the other, "How sad"; or maybe, "Lunch is on the house." He only asked what I'd like to eat, and I said, "Sashimi and rice, please."

I kept looking over at the print: the deep blue of the water, the rain in slanting black lines. I thought about drawing things that were connected to each other instead of just things: The people carried umbrellas because it was raining. They were crossing the bridge to get to the other side. My saying this would have made my father smile. But then I thought: I wouldn't have been able to explain my way to it. I might not have thought it, even if I had craned my neck and seen the picture.

The food came, and I ate very slowly, looking back and forth from the picture to my plate and sometimes out the window.

After lunch, I went over to the museum. Fritz was there already, sitting on the steps, polishing his eye-glasses with a handkerchief. "Did you get pants?" I asked.

"Khakis," he said. Then, in what must have been an imitation of his mother, " 'Such nice quality, and perfect with your gray jacket.' What do you want to do?"

"Whatever you'd like." But I'd realized that today, three weeks after the fitting, was the day my father had arranged to pick up the blue corduroy suit.

It seemed wrong to let the day slide by, after the tailor had hurried. "I have an errand," I said, since Fritz hadn't suggested anything right away. I imagined Fritz in the suit, drowned in blue corduroy.

I didn't explain until we were right outside the store.

"What are you going to do with it?" Fritz asked.

"I'd sort of imagined having it at the back of my closet for the rest of my life."

It was odd to be in the shop again. I said I was picking up the suit for my father, and the man said it was all paid for and if there were any problems with the fit, just to bring it back. I said, "I'm sure there won't be."

Outside, with the suit in its black plastic carrying case, neither of us could stop laughing, but I saw from Fritz's face that he wasn't sure if it was the right thing. "But what are you going to do?" he said.

"Search me," I said.

"Come on," he said, and we walked toward Third Avenue. We stopped at the corner, and I stood, holding the suit against my legs. There were mostly small stores on this block—a shoe-repair, a delicatessen, and not too many people. Fritz stood very straight, a little away from the curb. Then suddenly he took the suit from me and held it out to a man turning the corner toward us. "Excuse me, sir," he said. "We're delighted to inform you that you are the winner of this handsome suit."

The man was sandy-haired, and he was close to my father's size and carried a bag of groceries under one arm. He looked annoyed. He held the suit back toward Fritz. I said, "This isn't a practical joke, really," and Fritz said, "We're with a very reputable firm. You'll find us in the telephone directory." He had his hands in his pockets, so that the man couldn't give him the suit. I said, "Wear it in good health." Then Fritz grabbed my hand, and we ran down the block. I looked back once, and the man was still standing there, but he had folded the suit bag over his arm.

I felt as if I needed both hands to catch my breath properly, but Fritz still held one. Of course, now was the time to laugh, but neither of us did.

As we walked toward the river, I imagined the man arriving home with the suit and telling his wife what had happened. He'd say he'd been perfectly innocent, practically assaulted by these two skinny, fast-talking kids. "What could I do?" he'd ask. He'd put the suit on, and they'd decide that it wasn't exactly his style but really quite nice. The wife would suggest lengthening the trousers, taking the jacket in at the waist.

"You're not mad?" Fritz said, because I wasn't talking.

"No." But I was still wondering if there was any reason in the world why it might have been better to keep the suit. We were walking slowly now, down a quiet street of dark apartment buildings. I could see the green of the lawn of the United Nations.

It was nearly summer, and the man would put the suit away. In the fall, now and then, he'd tell people how he'd got it. They'd nod and smile, but it wouldn't be much of an anecdote; there was too much missing from it. But for me it was whole, without the weight of a solid thing. "It was brilliant," I said to Fritz, and he swung my arm.

I Ate Her Heart
BOB SHACOCHIS

It was a wretched act of love and greed. I was in Galveston, playing the mouth harp with the Stank Brothers Band and crewing on the shrimp boats when they wanted me. She was another woman from Dallas who figured she'd look real sweet and sexy with the Gulf of Mexico as a backdrop. My Starlene, she was right. I fell for her hard. There was a miserable turn of circumstances. I made an irresponsible decision and took a bite from her heart. It was a sour thing.

Lord, how I suffer the loss of her. My Starlene was an inspiration to me. She smelled like a lime tree and had legs like a movie star. I never had it so good.

We met at the Wildcatters Picnic where the Stank Brothers were providing the noise. Me and the brothers noticed her right off down in front of the stage. It looked like she was reading our message loud and clear. Playing in a band you get used to a lot of girls being friendly. When the music picks up speed they start behaving like they got lightning in their pants. She was parading herself in green terrycloth short-shorts tugged right up into her crack, and a tube top of similar color wrapped tight around her bosom. Her legs were so long it looked like it would take you all day to run your tongue down them from hipbone to heel. After a few songs this old boy came up to dance with Starlene. He was swinging and dipping her. They were moving fast to the rag. I thought, My God, those tits are going to pop and sure enough one did. Without breaking step she tucked it back in like I might do my shirttail. I remember nodding to Roy Stank and saying That's a fine woman there. I remember him nodding back and smiling like a weasel.

She settled in my mind right then. I thought of her as I played. My music started coming through in a purer form than it ever did before. I blew the Texas dust through those reeds. I sucked in the frontier and the longhorn steers and the Alamo. I spoke a version of Spanish and Apache and rattlesnake. I courted my mother's mother, charmed from her her toughness and suspicion. I took all the bums of the range up the tracks to Kansas City and back. My lips were burnt by the time I finished.

She found me over by the van liquoring up between sets. I like my liquor, God knows I do, and that's a part of this story. I've always handled it well, but when you start chasing grief with booze you're in for trouble.

Well, she comes up to me. The Brothers were inside the van, and they began to caw and squeal when they saw her. The Stanks knew no restraint. They're in the back of the van hitting up methiolade and sniffing canisters of freon they tore off old refrigerators. I saw in her eyes that this woman had some tenderness to her so I said Let's you and me take a walk, thinking I'd never have a chance with her if she got in that van. She did poke her head through the door and say Boys, you make it all worthwhile. They grabbed for her but she declined their invitation with a wise little laugh. I put my bottle-free arm around her high waist and we promenaded through the parking lot.

She said, "Mouth man, you've got a talent that makes me wonder what you're truly like. You've got a style."

I appreciate words like that, and I told her so.

"You're a good-looking man too, a good-looking ugly man."

"I know how you mean," I said. It took a long time for my ugliness to smooth out into something beneficial.

"They're the best," she said. "They don't suffer without good cause."

I knew what she meant. She was talking to the history of my heart.

She stopped by a willow tree, told her name and pressed against me. I put my face into the curve of her neck. Her skin smelled like lime, a sweet, fresh, citrus sting. My nose is a weak part of me. More than once it has led me into love. I could feel it happening again.

"Mouth man," she whispered in my ear, "I'll bet you know how to treat a woman fine."

I let my hand crawl up her back and explore her curly hair. She lifted one of her long legs and hooked it behind me. We kissed and rubbed together. "I do," I said. "I do."

Starlene expected a lot out of those words, and I'll be damned if I didn't give it. Knowing what fame was for, I took her home with me that night and bedded her. In the morning fame went right out the window, and love swept in like new air filling a dead space. We spent the day licking on each other. By the time the sun went down, and I fixed her coffee, I wasn't the Mouth Man anymore, I was just me, Taylor.

You know the course of such passion. She moved into my place, came with a suitcase full of pretty clothes, a big box of shoes, a transistor radio, and a bag full of stuff that filled every spare inch in the bathroom. She cleaned things up, though in a disregardful way, and put a picture of her daddy on the shelf next to the bed. None of that bothered me. My life had taken a step up. I was grandly in love. I had been in love with women before, but I couldn't recall when or where or who or how. Starlene seemed like the one and only. Women have always been important to me. I need to treat them like queens, but I never had one before who knew what she needed from me. Starlene needed the queen treatment, and I gave it to her.

At dinner I'd cut her steak up into little pieces to save her the trouble. When she took a bath I'd scrape her skin soft and pink with one of those Japanese sponges. She'd get her monthlies, and I'd go into labor pains out of sympathy. She'd sneeze like a little kitten, and I'd get on the phone to the doctor.

The way I felt, I couldn't do enough for Starlene. I'd smell her smell, or ponder those legs, and get in a helpless state of giving. Her fondness for cocaine was not to be denied. I did my best to accommodate her with what little money I had. She'd dope up a lot, but I never said anything. It seemed to bring her so much pleasure. She didn't usually get far off like some dopers do. As I said, I go for the booze, so I'd just sit beside her and drink until she fell into my arms. We'd drag into bed, undressing as we went. She'd turn on my unit and stick in a tape, always the Bonecrushers or Nellie Slit. She'd take the headphones and put them on. I'd nuzzle down between her thighs and have my ears clamped by her hot flesh. Locked in like that, I'd play her night lips in a harmonic fashion. She'd shove into me as if she wanted to be swallowed up. Occasionally I'd look and see the ecstasy of her face on the horizon. Sometimes she'd pass right out, and I'd curl up beside her and belt myself.

Do you get what I'm saying here? I was in love. I was way down in love and never wanted to come out. It was the best thing that ever happened to me, and the worst.

After a couple of months she said to me, "Trailers ain't a decent place for life to advance."

I hadn't thought about it before. "Right," I said. "What did you have in mind, honey? One of those condo things? A cabin in the woods?"

"I like the water," she says. "I like the smell of it and the way the sun moves around like mercury on the surface."

I searched about and found an old houseboat docked at a marina in Trinity Bay. The guy wouldn't rent it but said he'd sell cheap. I was cash poor so I called up my shrimper friends Jim and Joe (not their real names). They were organizing a run to Mexico and took me along as a favor. Everything but shrimp ended up on that trawler. My cut was large enough to buy the houseboat and something special for Starlene.

When I came back eight days later she wouldn't go with me to the band jobs anymore. "Why'd you have to be away so long?" she said. "The Brothers sound like birdshit without you, Taylor."

I held her in my arms and told her how much I missed her.

"I hate being alone," she said, looking at me straight. "You were always in my heart, Taylor." She let go of me and placed my hand over her left breast. "Right in here, kicking like a baby. I never forgot about you for a second."

I said I wouldn't leave her again. I gave her the ghetto blaster I had bought her for a thousand bucks—a high technology unit that sent out enough sound to kill everything in a forest or sustain life in the barrios. My hands trembled when I gave it to her. She said Oh my, oh my, and cried.

"No one, Taylor," she said, "not ever, has been this nice to me. I've always felt like property in a war zone, seized and abandoned over and over."

"Aw hell, Starlene," I said, petting her hair.

"I suppose it's my fault. I need a lot of love and attention. Love me, Taylor. Pack my heart full."

I told her I would.

"Forgive me my sins," she added.

I told her she was without sin in my eyes, that the devil wouldn't dare come near a soul like hers.

I leased this rundown dock in a secluded part of the bay for our houseboat. We seemed alone together in the world. I could piss off the side in the daylight if I wanted. She could sunbathe bare-assed, expose her real estate to the wild blue yonder. With a fishing pole or crabnet, she'd snare creatures from the deep and transform them into spicy gumbo. The best thing for Starlene was when our house rocked cradle-like in the wake of a passing motorboat. It got to the point where she craved that rocking more than anything.

One night she said to me desperately, "Oh damnit, Taylor. I don't think I can sleep with everything so still. Even these Quaaludes won't take me out."

We made love, but still she kept her edge.

"Maybe it's the coke making me so restless," she moaned.

I'll see what I can do, I told her. There wasn't much I could do. I tried holding onto the dock and jumping up and down, but the hull had too much concrete in it to move that easily. The next day I drove over to the wharves where an old buddy of mine worked on the supply end of a drilling team. He sold me a crate of dynamite at a pirate's price. After that I'd blow a stick in the water whenever Starlene had trouble sleeping. We'd get about a fifteen minute roll out of it, and if she wasn't out by then, I'd blow another. I never heard a complaint from anybody on the bay except once from a rich lady about the dead fish in the water. I said it was my intention to eat those fish, and it was no business of hers.

Sometimes we'd sit out on the deck at night slapping mosquitoes and star gazing. We'd count UFOs. The sky always seemed full of them. If the mood was right I'd spit some blues through my harmonica. She'd hum a lazy counterpoint that would amuse me. I forget how long we had been on the boat by then, but it was during a peaceful night like this that I asked her a question that she'd been avoiding.

"Starlene," I said. "Nobody has a thirst for music more than you. When you going to come with me to another job? We're booked at Gilmore's Friday night."

The way she said *Never* made me wonder what was on her mind. Then she recovered. Her face came out of a shadow into the light of a candle that burned between us. I could tell by the set of her eyebrows that she was ready for finding fault in the world. "You ask that awful Roy Stank for a raise. Do that, Taylor," she said.

I was low on cash again, had been thinking out loud that very day on what chance I had to get on a shrimper. I knew Starlene had a good point. But I wasn't deaf to the basic revelation of her words. "What's wrong with Roy?" I asked. "You've not said bad about him before."

"Never you mind."

"What in the dickens does that mean?" I said. It was the only time I raised my voice to the woman. "Roy do something to you while I was away? He make a move?"

"No such thing," she insisted, clipping her voice. "It's *you* he's doing something to, Taylor. Roy ain't giving you what's due."

I said, "Now honey, that's Roy's band. I don't play on every song. I don't have loans out on fancy equipment. I may be the best harp man in the South, but what's fair is fair."

"We need more money," she tells me.

"Cocaine ain't salt," I said. "You have to slow down."

She changed tack on me. "Taylor," she said tenderly, "I can't have you going off on those boats. I was never meant to be alone."

"Neither was I."

"Then stay," she said, moving toward me for an embrace. "Roy will give you more money. That band pulls in a lot. Where would they be without the weight you add to their sound?"

"The question is, where would I be?" I told her. We didn't talk about it again that night.

About a week later, when we drove home from dinner at the Evil Enchilada, I noticed that the old boat had suffered damage—she was down a foot in the water. I got a bilge pump going but the best I could do was stabilize the situation. Starlene was crying, and I hated to see that. Whenever she slipped into tears it made me feel like a dog.

"Must've been the dynamite," I said sadly. "The shock waves must've cracked the cement of the hull."

"Aw Taylor," she bawled. "I loved our home. I love the creak and the sway."

"Don't you worry, baby," I said. "We'll have her hauled out and patched. You'll see."

"Homeless again," she sighed.

"Now don't worry," I told her. "We'll stay in the van until the work's done."

We rolled up our pants to keep dry and went below to collect our clothes. She spent some time in the bathroom doing something to improve her mood. When she came out she was smiling what I'd call indiscreetly. Thinking back, I'd say she was calculating how to survive the narcotic hunger she lived with.

"We can stay with Roy," she said. "He'll put us up."

I didn't think that was a good idea. Roy wasn't much of a man without a guitar in front of him, and she herself had applied the word *awful* to the fellow. The van would have been fine with me, but I went along with the scheme because I wanted her to have what she wanted, no questions asked.

We got over to Roy's place around midnight. The Brothers were just waking up. The house, a stuccoed old-style thing with red tiles on the roof, stubby palm trees and motorcycles in the yard, used to be nice but the boys had turned it into a pigpen. Between the needles and the dogs, the wall to wall shag was unkind to bare feet. One of the band's fans had taken a blow torch and written *Fuck You* and *Rock Off* in fire all over the walls. Two stereos were going at the same time, playing different numbers at top volume. Living with Starlene I had become accustomed to a certain level of cleanliness. The Stank place was reprehensible. I thought maybe I could take it for a day or two. I suppose you have to live hard to sing right.

The Brothers were gathered in the kitchen for what they called their breakfast. There was no table, but they stood around eating vitamin pills. They had no other form of nourishment that I ever saw besides Buckhorn beer and orders of ribs from Smiling Goofus McTeez, that barbecue place run by a black guy gone crazy on his Scottish ancestry.

Anyway, Roy was combing the knots out of his hair with his fingers. He looked unrested for just getting out of bed.

"Roy," I said. "Bad luck's come upon Starlene and me."

He became very concerned. He wanted to help us, he said, in any way he could. I was a Brother, he said. Starlene asked for a vitamin. Donnie threw some capsules in her mouth. I took a beer from the fridge but had to wipe brown sludge from the top of the can before I drank it. One of Roy's hounds ran through the room so fast he skittered all over the linoleum, then crashed out a small hole in the back screen door. We made powerful music together, but I sure didn't like socializing with the Stanks. Their habits were lethal. They had minds like a trash dump on fire.

I opened a second beer. There was some disjointed small talk that came from outer space. Everybody's eyes seemed connected to a rheostat—they just kept getting brighter and brighter. Starlene's too. She said Oh dear, this is *good,* and giggled. The Brothers grinned like jackasses. Buzz found a ukulele in one of the cupboards and started strumming out this calypso shit. I was bored, tired and uncomfortable.

I said, "Starlene, let's go lie down and nap."

She looked at me like I was spoiling her party. Her pupils had dilated fully, her flashing green eyes eclipsed by dark moons. Her face explored a series of expressions until it found something right, something serious and deliberate.

"Ask Roy now," she said.

"Ask him what?"

"Ask me what?" Roy joined in.

"You know," she said to me. She was by my side now, holding my arm with both hands. "Ask him."

"Ask me what?"

"Starlene," I said gently. "This isn't the right time. We're here enjoying this man's hospitality." What the hell was she doing? Maybe she wanted to be sure I wouldn't leave her alone again, but the way she kept going, I had to think it was deeper than that.

"Ask me what?" Roy persisted.

"A matter of business, Roy. Nothing much at all. We'll talk about it another time."

"Go ahead. Ask me."

"Naw, Roy. Some other time."

"Go ahead, brother."

Starlene took over, or we might have gone on like that all day. Her voice was squeaky and vicious. "Roy," she said. "You're gonna have to pay Taylor more money, or he'll have to leave the band."

"Well honey, come on now," I said, calm as I could. "That's not true."

Roy was rather delighted by Starlene's proclamation. "Is that right?" he said, looking at her, not me.

I tried to intervene. The two were making a kind of connection I couldn't break. "Roy, forget what she said. Donnie, what'd you give her?"

"Is that right?" Roy repeated.

"Yeah," she said. "You know it."

Roy howled and clapped his hands, a gesture that made me think he was a maniac. "Well how bout that," he said. He was just tickled pink. "Donnie," he yelled without ever turning away from Starlene, "how bout that?"

"Shame on you, Taylor," Donnie said.

"Buzz, how bout that? What do you think?"

Buzz pouted his lips. "This ol boy is pussywhipped."

"How bout that? Lester, you have some thoughts on this?" Lester didn't.

He had laid down on the floor with his eyes closed. He was in poor condition for talking.

Starlene was smoldering, and she broke out in flame. "Roy Stank, you are a worm," she hissed.

"But you like that, don't you gal?" he said. He smiled wickedly and finally dropped his stare. He turned to me instead. "This little bitch has got you fooled, Taylor."

"Roy, don't say such a thing," I told him.

"This girl likes to gallop up the side of heaven and shout at the angels. Starlene's in love with the snowman, Taylor. Ask her what she was up to when you was out on the Gulf."

I don't like fighting, but I was ready to strike the man. Starlene commenced to tug me out of the room. "We can't stay here," she said. She said it over and over again until we were at the door. I heard the Stanks back in the kitchen laughing ungallantly. "My honorary Brother," I heard Roy shout after me. "Just say the word, and I'll take her off your hands."

"Come back any time, Star Queen," one of the other Stanks called out. "You know how generous the Brothers can be."

Starlene ran across the driveway ahead of me, shaking her head and screaming, *damn, damn, damn.* When I caught up with her she spun around. "Hit me, Taylor," she said. "Go ahead."

I'd never do that.

"I fucked up," she said. "I did you harm. You must hate me."

I held her, cuddled her head to my chest, smelling that scent of fresh lime behind her ears and along the tense curve of her neck. "You did no harm," I told her. "You own my heart. That devil tried to twist his way in, but it didn't work."

"Jesus God, don't ever leave me, Taylor."

"I'd never do that," I said.

We had the houseboat hauled out of the bay and put in dry dock. I parked the van next to it, and we quartered there. I said no more to Starlene about what happened because I knew no good

would come from talking of it. For me the glory of the Stank
Brothers Band was no more—I had to seek other employment. I
went to see Ed Chiles of the Kamikaze Kowboys. He said the
Kowboys were going into the studio in another month or two to
cut their next album, and they could use me then. I did some
roustabout work in the oil fields for about a week. The boatyard
finished repairing the houseboat and handed me a hell of a bill.
The yard wouldn't release the boat though until I paid in full.
Starlene had no patience for anything. One day she took a job as a
waitress at a nice seafood restaurant nearby but quit before her
shift was over. She stayed in the van more and more, nodding to
the tape deck, then at night when I was there she'd whine and
complain. The tan on her legs began to pale. It didn't prejudice
my love for her. I only became more determined to set our world
back in balance.

To be precise, it wasn't more than eight or nine days like that
until Jim and Joe (not their real names) showed up in the yard the
same time I was arriving from work. They talked a lot of vague-
ness and indirection, as all of these fellows do, but from what I
gathered they were doing something big and needed me along to
replace a member of the crew who had misbehaved publicly and
gotten thrown in jail. On an operation like this sums of money are
not clearly discussed beforehand, but I was made to know that I
would earn enough money to buy a new dick if I wanted one after
the run was over. I discussed it with Starlene. She said No, she
wouldn't be alone again. I said to her Honey, this is the windfall
we need to live a life free and unmolested. She sulked all night but
finally gave in. I left before noon that same day.

Being with Jim and Joe can get dangerous because they don't
give a shit what they do. Smuggling wetbacks, guns, heroin, pot—
it's all the same to them.

This particular run was a junket for six Mexican thugs who
couldn't afford the formality of airports and borders. We picked
them up in Cancún, off the Yucatán. They gave Jim a garbage bag
full of money for their passage.

I watched them come aboard at night. I know a little Spanish, so I asked them who they were.

"Nosotros somos Los Huevos Grandes," they said audaciously, as if I was breathing air only because they allowed it.

I thought that *huevo* meant egg, but I didn't laugh. People from other countries just don't think the way we Americans do.

These greaseballs were well-heeled. They all wore silk shirts of the most terrible colors. Their underarms smelled like overcooked chili. Two of them had briefcases handcuffed to their hairy wrists, and each of them wore more jewelry than I've ever seen on any woman, except a back-alley whore. They were going to Galveston to deposit money in special bank accounts, get checked out at the gringo VD clinics, visit the cathouses they owned in the barrios, break the arms of the upstarts that were trying to move in on their action.

These Huevos liked to touch their knives and shout at each other. I tried to keep away from them as much as I could, but they were bad headlines from the word go.

Halfway through our cruise the passengers were having trouble relating to each other. A boat's not a place for people with no tolerance. Toward the end of the voyage I was fool enough to try to break up a fight between two assholes in the galley. The one they called Aguila took more than his share of rice and beans at lunchtime. One of his buddies stabbed him in the hand. I stepped in, and immediately there was a switchblade pressed across my throat. Another guy came up and wanted to slice off one of my ears to teach me the big lesson—don't interfere in the business of Los Huevos Grandes. He was laughing and thought it would be a great joke. Jim walked on the scene just in time. He told the Huevos that if any of them fucked with the crew they could tear up their round-trip tickets. That message twice saved my life.

Bad weather drove us in near Port Lavaca, which is by car not more than three hours south of Galveston. The Gulf is big, the Coast Guard small—you're always banking on luck in a deal like this. We snuck into the intercoastal waters and anchored in a tiny hideaway cove in Tres Palacios. On shore you could see the sandy tracks of a fisherman's road winding through the dunes down to the water.

After we set the anchor Joe tuned in the shortwave and contacted one of his local men for some transportation. The plan was for me to escort the passengers to a roadside motel, check them in and pay for the rooms. Then they were on their own to get to Galveston any way they could to rendezvous with the ship in about ten days. I could do whatever I wanted until it was time to head south again. In the meantime, Jim and Joe would enter the harbor to wait for better weather and then move the shrimper up to home port.

Joe gave me fifteen one-hundred-dollar bills. I was to pass a thousand of that to the wheels man, pay for the motel and keep the rest for pocket money. I ferried the Mexicans ashore and told them to lay low in the dunes until the transportation arrived. Rain kept falling the whole time. I longed for Starlene. I wanted that lime smell to open my nostrils. I wanted those sleek legs wrapped somewhere around me.

Jim came along the last trip and returned the Zodiac to the boat. From shore I watched the props churn up mud as they reversed out of the cove. I was alone with the six goons and didn't much care for it. I was also dying for a drink, a little taste to relax with. Nobody had much to say to me. I tried to be as polite as I could because I knew damn well there wasn't five seconds worth of trust among us. Paranoia isn't something that bothers me much, but this group wasn't exactly the Jaycees. I knew I had to be careful.

Los Huevos passed reefer back and forth and talked in shrill, bitch-like voices. Then one of them, Aguila again, the fellow with the appetite, found a sea turtle. It was a female. She had recently crawled up on the beach, probably thinking this was a quiet enough spot to scoop a hole for her young. They chopped her open and ate the eggs. When they were through, they stood around telling one another how virile they would all now be. I thought to myself, these savages make the Stank Brothers look like Young Republicans.

What there was of the sun was fading into general bleakness by the time the transportation arrived. A big International Harvester all-purpose vehicle, its side and back windows blacked out, came roaring across the sand flats to where we were in the dunes. We packed in and got the hell out of there.

"Jim says there's a motel you know of that guarantees privacy," I said to the driver. He nodded once, kept his eyes straight ahead. We bumped and banged our way out to a surfaced road that led to Point Comfort.

"When you see a liquor store, stop," I said. "I got to buy a bottle or I'll go crazy. These egg fellows are bad on my nerves." He offered me some reefer but I passed it up. That stuff makes me sleepy and loosens my overall confidence. I had a night ahead of me and needed to be in control.

We stopped at a small bait and lure shop with a package store attached. I bought a fifth of whiskey. The Mexicans bought a couple of cases of good scotch, a case of Winstons, and a box of beef jerky. I was impressed by the quality and quantity of their thirst.

At the motel we came to everybody waited in the vehicle while the driver went inside. I considered going with him but then thought better of it. I looked like a tramp, unshaven, clothes dirty and wet, smelling like diesel fuel. I cracked my bottle and drank from it like it only held water.

The driver reappeared. "Gimme two hundred bucks," he said. I did. He left and came back within a minute, handing me a single room key.

"What's this?" I asked.

"Waz thees?" one of the Huevos echoed, his voice full of hostility. I had the sense this guy wanted to start a war.

"That's all the man had. Be thankful for it, buddy."

"This is bad," I said. "These boys are already claustrophobic from the boat."

"Keep a low profile now," the wheels man said as he returned to his seat. "Don't bother other guests. Everybody's got to be out of there in three days."

I paid him off and escorted the passengers across a dark patio to the room. They griped a lot among themselves about being forced into one room, but they didn't pester me with it. As soon as we got in there they began to fight over who was going to use the bathroom first, who was first on the phone, who would get to sleep on the twin beds. I told them not to be so loud. They told me something which I think meant fuck off. I began to worry that being with them was becoming bad for my health.

Bring us food, one of them told me.

"Alright," I said. "What do you want?"

They wanted Kentucky fried chicken. A lot of it.

"Right. Try to hold it down while I'm gone," I warned them quietly. Like I said, I was just trying to be a nice guy, do my job, and get back to Starlene, as quick as I could and in one piece.

The motel was on the edge of a commercial strip. Once I was outside, I placed a long-distance call to Starlene from a booth across the street. I phoned the boatyard and had somebody go get her on the line. Her voice sounded very weary when she asked me where I was.

"Starlene," I said. "I'm with a bunch of people I don't like. Come rescue me."

I gave her directions and hung up. It was about eight o'clock. I walked down the road a ways and bought three buckets of chicken and a tub of cole slaw. By the time I got back to the room the Mexicans had dug into the booze and were celebrating their safe arrival in Los Estados Unidos. They wolfed down the chicken and slaw and were soon noisy again. I tried my best to pacify them, but it was useless. Each of them had his own bottle of scotch. A few of the guys were tying off their veins and shooting up. Somebody came toward me with a hypo, but I waved him away. He threw the thing at me as if it were a dart. I dodged it, and the needle stuck in the lampshade behind me. He laughed, and I joined in nervously to let him know I could take a joke. If I had any sense I would have gotten out of there, but I figured I was safe, that business is business, and Jim had warned them not to harm me.

I lay on one of the beds drinking heavily from my bottle, my nerves all jangled, wondering if I should stay in the room until Starlene showed. By ten o'clock I had finished my fifth but didn't feel the way I wanted. I started in on some of the Mex's scotch. The head honcho, who still had a briefcase locked to his wrist, kept dialing the phone, making contact with his people in Galveston.

This gang liked a fast track. They didn't impress me as being a tightly run organization though. You can never trust low-life to stick together, even if they are goddamned eggs, or Big Balls, or whatever the hell Huevos Grandes is supposed to mean. I had not before been with men of such petty and brutal character. One of the junked-out boys accidentally burned Aguila with his cigarette. A knife was drawn and brandished. He was talked out of using it, but everybody wanted to yell about the incident. From what I could tell they were trying to convince each other they were the nastiest lot of people on the planet. Aguila was an exceptionally swarthy man, a guy with droopy ears and nose and a moustache that looked as if it were coated with shoe polish, who usually hung back from everything. But whenever he joined in the action, it was like throwing nitrate into a toilet bowl.

I didn't want a part of what was going on, but I didn't know what else I could do. I was drinking away my discomfort, pining for Starlene.

Eleven-thirty.

Twelve o'clock. She loomed in my mind like a big wave about to crash down. She wasn't there yet. I stared at the door as if it were my future, trying to understand what went wrong. Whenever I looked around at Los Huevos, all my eyes could see was their blood lust.

By one o'clock I was itching I needed her so bad. Then I heard the knock that would provide my salvation. The fiesta shut down in an instant. The Huevos hopped up, dug out their guns and knives. The atmosphere was suddenly pure poison.

"It's alright," I said with confidence. "That's a friend of mine."

She came through the door. Roy was with her. They were both going a thousand miles an hour.

"Roy, you skunk," I recall saying. "What the hell you doing with Starlene?" I looked at Starlene for an answer, but there wasn't much to see on her face. She was on the moon.

"She wanted company, man," Roy said. He was dirtier than me and without good reason. He had an outlaw face, stained moustache, bad teeth, patched bluejeans, odoriferous T-shirt. I hated everything about him now, even his long beautiful fingers that could play a guitar so fine.

"Don't say another word, Roy," I said. "I'm in a dark mood." I gave him a hundred dollar bill for fare back to Galveston and started to throw him out the door. He didn't resist. Roy had a big build and a lot of meanness deep in him, but I wasn't afraid. One of the Huevos moved up behind me. I looked at him and realized he was going to jump on Roy if Roy remained in the room another second.

"It's alright, it's alright," I said. "No problem. Just a friend who's leaving." I guess the Mexican considered Roy's presence a threat to their operation, especially after they saw how I behaved toward him.

Just as I had Roy outside, he squealed, "Starlene's gonna sing with the Brothers. Fuck you, Taylor." I knocked him in the side of the head with my fist and slammed the door on him. Starlene had been absorbed into the midst of the Mexicans. I forgot about Roy and went after her, grabbed her cold hand roughly.

"Is that true, honey?" I asked, tears forming in my eyes. The booze had gotten me into a terrible state of release.

"What?" she said thickly. "Oh."

"You singing with the band now?"

"I am?" she asked. She was all confused. No telling what Roy had gotten into her.

Lord, I didn't even know she could sing, just hum. Or maybe Roy was lying to aggravate me.

My heart was pumping strong for her. She was dressed in a dainty peach-colored sundress. Her curly hair frizzed out from under a sharp-looking straw panama. I wanted to be alone with her and cuddle, drop Roy from my mind. One of the Huevos grabbed her ass. I pushed him gently away. My adrenalin couldn't find its way through all the alcohol in my blood.

"None of that," I said. "Time to go. I'll see you boys in Galveston."

We reached the door right as Roy was coming back through it, talking a supersonic line of apology and regret. If he had had the time, I think his intent was to beg a ride with us back to Galveston, seeing as how Point Comfort is at the back edge of nowhere, but the world jerked ahead to his speed before he had the chance to make amends. Los Huevos came in on us before I knew what was happening. Roy fell dead or dying into the room, his neck opened by Mexican steel. A grinning Huevo swung his knife at me but then restrained himself, allowing the blade to penetrate my chest only superficially right above my heart.

He immediately threw his hands up in innocence. "Meestake, beeg meestake," he said, still grinning like he had only stepped on my toe. He pointed at the door and said "Gal-vees-ton."

I looked at the Huevos standing over Roy. Strange, but only Aguila hadn't been in on it. I stood up straight, feeling no pain, and went for the phone. Somebody put his hand on my shoulder, and Starlene began to scream.

"No policía," the Huevo with his hand on me said. It was the same guy who had just cut me.

"Right," I answered him. "No policía. Just an ambulance, that's all." I dialed the operator.

The Mexican took the receiver away from me, yanking the cord from the wall outlet. Starlene was still screaming. I turned in time to see Aguila lurch out of his corner. He was smiling wickedly. He wrapped a fat hand around Starlene's pretty lips, and they commenced to wrassle. I was a step apart from them but never made the distance. I felt no pain, only the blow from behind and my nose squashing as I hit the carpet.

This is the trouble that can visit a peaceful man sometimes.

The place was silent when I came to. The Huevos had cleared out of there. It seemed like I should have been dead, but I wasn't. Starlene was stretched out on the bed like a forsaken angel, her peach dress ragged up and blood-soaked, a tired smile locked on her bruised mouth. I bolted the door and went to her.

"Don't look at me so cold, Starlene," I said. "You know how sensitive a man I am."

I lay down next to her on the bed. I kissed her, squeezed her.

There was no smell of sweet lime on her like there always was before. It wasn't good, she wasn't for it any more. She was gone.

That fact grieved me deeply. I let her rise up to heaven on my grief. As I pressed her against me, my left hand caught in a hole just below her armpit. I pulled my fingers out of the chilly flesh and looked at them, then at her. She was slashed everywhere, as if the Huevos all needed to get inside her at the same time. Knife language—this was the only tongue the Huevos spoke fluently.

I reeled up from the bed and started drinking the liquor left in the room until I was as crazed as a man could get. Then I lay back down next to my love. I wept without shame. I cried, Don't leave me, baby. I lost consciousness. When I woke up it must have been hours later. The room was shadowy and smelled foul. I wept again. I cried, If you go, Starlene, you take too much of me with you. I gave you more than I knew I had.

The drunkenness had left me, but I had fallen into a delirious condition. There was a large pain in my chest, and I imagined it was the loss of Starlene's love. This was how it felt when two hearts were separated forever. I knew that if there was any love left, it would have to be located in her. That's where I would find it and restore myself.

I settled down and considered these thoughts. She had a long cut right below her breastbone. I stuck my hand in there and wiggled it up under the ribcage until I gripped her heart muscle. I just held it, waiting for something to run back into my veins. I fell asleep that way. The rest might be a dream for all I know. When I withdrew my hand I thought I had found what I was hoping for. In my palm was a hard little pearl. I studied it and thought, This is me, this is my part, what I gave her, the seed that got inside like a grain of sand in an oyster and grew to be love. I bit into it, believing I had to get it back circulating in my own flesh. I spit it out, it was such a sour thing. The agony in my chest remained unsoothed.

This is all I'm going to say about it. It's been bad enough already. I spent three days alone with her and my wretchedness until they busted the door down and dragged me out.

They tagged me for conspiracy to aid and abet the illegal entry of aliens. The mutilation charge that was finally dropped got a lot of attention from the press. I had to take the heat for Jim and Joe, although Los Huevos now conduct their business from behind bars.

My lawyer was expensive and encouraged the judge to show compassion in the end. I'm not in prison or the nut house but spending six months on a model farm with a high reform rate. Oh Starlene, I miss you sorrowfully.

Not too long ago this tweedy fellow drops by asking me if I've changed. Yes sir, I have, I answered him. I'll never do a foolish thing like that again, I swear. Do you regret your deeds? he asked. Mister, I don't, I said. Except in a legal way. He left and I went back to watching the soaps on teevee.

I stay up all night thinking things over. I'm not a bad man. I didn't hurt anybody, no one died by my hand. I guess I've been around the wrong sort of people too long. Somebody's been a poor influence on me. Maybe it was just her, the way she made you believe you were giving so much, and it was paying off, like you were making smart investment uptown. Isn't there a Mexican saying that goes something like, You eat the heart, or the heart eats you? Maybe I was thinking of that when I ate the damn thing.

I think somewhere there's a woman who'll understand what I did, the right and the wrong of it, and come to comfort me.

Honey, get in touch. I'm ready for love again.

In the American Society

GISH JEN

I. HIS OWN SOCIETY

When my father took over the pancake house, it was to send my little sister Mona and me to college. We were only in junior high at the time, but my father believed in getting a jump on things. "Those Americans always saying it," he told us. "Smart guys thinking in advance." My mother elaborated, explaining that businesses took bringing up, like children. They could take years to get going, she said, years.

In this case, though, we got rich right away. At two months we were breaking even, and at four, those same hotcakes that could barely withstand the weight of butter and syrup were supporting our family with ease. My mother bought a station wagon with air conditioning, my father an oversized, red vinyl recliner for the back room; and as time went on and the business continued to thrive, my father started to talk about his grandfather and the village he had reigned over in China—things my father had never talked about when he worked for other people. He told us about the bags of rice his family would give out to the poor at New Year's, and about the people who came to beg, on their hands and knees, for his grandfather to intercede for the more wayward of their relatives. "Like that Godfather in the movie," he would tell us as, his feet up, he distributed paychecks. Sometimes an employee would get two green envelopes instead of one, which meant that Jimmy needed a tooth pulled, say, or that Tiffany's husband was in the clinker again.

"It's nothing, nothing," he would insist, sinking back into his chair. "Who else is going to take care of you people?"

My mother would mostly just sigh about it. "Your father thinks this is China," she would say, and then she would go back to her mending. Once in a while, though, when my father had given away a particularly large sum, she would exclaim, outraged, "But this here is the U—S—of—A!"—this apparently having been what she used to tell immigrant stock boys when they came in late.

She didn't work at the supermarket anymore; but she had made it to the rank of manager before she left, and this had given her not only new words and phrases, but new ideas about herself, and about America, and about what was what in general. She had opinions, now, on how downtown should be zoned; she could pump her own gas and check her own oil; and for all she used to chide Mona and me for being "copycats," she herself was now interested in espadrilles, and wallpaper, and most recently, the town country club.

"So join already," said Mona, flicking a fly off her knee.

My mother enumerated the problems as she sliced up a quarter round of watermelon: There was the cost. There was the waiting list. There was the fact that no one in our family played either tennis or golf.

"So what?" said Mona.

"It would be waste," said my mother.

"Me and Callie can swim in the pool."

"Plus you need that recommendation letter from a member."

"Come *on,*" said Mona. "Annie's mom'd write you a letter in a *sec.*"

My mother's knife glinted in the early summer sun. I spread some more newspaper on the picnic table.

"*Plus* you have to eat there twice a month. You know what that means." My mother cut another, enormous slice of fruit.

"No, I *don't* know what that means," said Mona.

"It means Dad would have to wear a jacket, dummy," I said.

"Oh! Oh! Oh!" said Mona, clasping her hand to her breast. "Oh! Oh! Oh! Oh! Oh!"

We all laughed: my father had no use for nice clothes, and would wear only ten-year-old shirts, with grease-spotted pants, to show how little he cared what anyone thought.

"Your father doesn't believe in joining the American society," said my mother. "He wants to have his own society."

"So go to dinner without him." Mona shot her seeds out in long arcs over the lawn. "Who cares what he thinks?"

But of course we all did care, and knew my mother could not simply up and do as she pleased. For in my father's mind, a family owed its head a degree of loyalty that left no room for dissent. To embrace what he embraced was to love; and to embrace something else was to betray him.

He demanded a similar sort of loyalty of his workers, whom he treated more like servants than employees. Not in the beginning, of course. In the beginning all he wanted was for them to keep on doing what they used to do, and to that end he concentrated mostly on leaving them alone. As the months passed, though, he expected more and more of them, with the result that for all his largesse, he began to have trouble keeping help. The cooks and busboys complained that he asked them to fix radiators and trim hedges, not only at the restaurant, but at our house; the waitresses that he sent them on errands and made them chauffeur him around. Our head waitress, Gertrude, claimed that he once even asked her to scratch his back.

"It's not just the blacks don't believe in slavery," she said when she quit.

My father never quite registered her complaint, though, nor those of the others who left. Even after Eleanor quit, then Tiffany, then Gerald, and Jimmy, and even his best cook, Eureka Andy, for whom he had bought new glasses, he remained mostly convinced that the fault lay with them.

"All they understand is that assembly line," he lamented. "Robots, they are. They want to be robots."

There *were* occasions when the clear running truth seemed to eddy, when he would pinch the vinyl of his chair up into little peaks and wonder if he was doing things right. But with time he would always smooth the peaks back down; and when business started to slide in the spring, he kept on like a horse in his ways.

By the summer our dishboy was overwhelmed with scraping. It was no longer just the hashbrowns that people were leaving for trash, and the service was as bad as the food. The waitresses served up French pancakes instead of German, apple juice instead of orange, spilt things on laps, on coats. On the Fourth of July some greenhorn sent an entire side of fries slaloming down a lady's *massif centrale.* Meanwhile in the back room, my father labored through articles on the economy.

"What is housing starts?" he puzzled. "What is GNP?"

Mona and I did what we could, filling in as busgirls and book-keepers and, one afternoon, stuffing the comments box that hung by the cashier's desk. That was Mona's idea. We rustled up a variety of pens and pencils, checked boxes for an hour, smeared the cards up with coffee and grease, and waited. It took a few days for my father to notice that the box was full, and he didn't say anything about it for a few days more. Finally, though, he started to complain of fatigue; and then he began to complain that the staff was not what it could be. We encouraged him in this—pointing out, for instance, how many dishes got chipped—but in the end all that happened was that, for the first time since we took over the restaurant, my father got it into his head to fire someone. Skip, a skinny busboy who was saving up for a sportscar, said nothing as my father mumbled on about the price of dishes. My father's hands shook as he wrote out the severance check; and he spent the rest of the day napping in his chair once it was over.

As it was going on midsummer, Skip wasn't easy to replace. We hung a sign in the window and advertised in the paper, but no one called the first week, and the person who called the second didn't show up for his interview. The third week, my father phoned Skip to see if he would come back, but a friend of his had already sold him a Corvette for cheap.

Finally a Chinese guy named Booker turned up. He couldn't have been more than thirty, and was wearing a lighthearted seer-sucker suit, but he looked as though life had him pinned: his eyes were bloodshot and his chest sunken, and the muscles of his neck seemed to strain with the effort of holding his head up. In a single dry breath he told us that he had never bussed tables but was willing to learn, and that he was on the lam from the deportation authorities.

"I do not want to lie to you," he kept saying. He had come to the United States on a student visa, had run out of money, and was now in a bind. He was loath to go back to Taiwan, as it happened—he looked up at this point, to be sure my father wasn't pro-KMT—but all he had was a phony social security card and a willingness to absorb all blame, should anything untoward come to pass.

"I do not think, anyway, that it is against law to hire me, only to be me," he said, smiling faintly.

Anyone else would have examined him on this, but my father conceived of laws as speed bumps rather than curbs. He wiped the counter with his sleeve, and told Booker to report the next morning.

"I will be good worker," said Booker.

"Good," said my father.

"Anything you want me to do, I will do."

My father nodded.

Booker seemed to sink into himself for a moment. "Thank you," he said finally. "I am appreciate your help. I am very, very appreciate for everything." He reached out to shake my father's hand.

My father looked at him. "Did you eat today?" he asked in Mandarin.

Booker pulled at the hem of his jacket.

"Sit down," said my father. "Please, have a seat."

My father didn't tell my mother about Booker, and my mother didn't tell my father about the country club. She would never have applied, except that Mona, while over at Annie's, had let it drop that our mother wanted to join. Mrs. Lardner came by the very next day.

"Why, I'd be honored and delighted to write you people a letter," she said. Her skirt billowed around her.

"Thank you so much," said my mother. "But it's too much trouble for you, and also my husband is . . ."

"Oh, it's no trouble at all, no trouble at all. I tell you." She leaned forward so that her chest freckles showed. "I know just how it is. It's a secret of course, but you know, my natural father was Jewish. Can you see it? Just look at my skin."

"My husband," said my mother.

"I'd be honored and delighted," said Mrs. Lardner with a little wave of her hands. "Just honored and delighted."

Mona was triumphant. "See, Mom," she said, waltzing around the kitchen when Mrs. Lardner left. "What did I tell you? 'I'm just honored and delighted, just honored and delighted.' " She waved her hands in the air.

"You know, the Chinese have a saying," said my mother. "To do nothing is better than to overdo. You mean well, but you tell me now what will happen."

"I'll talk Dad into it," said Mona, still waltzing. "Or I bet Callie can. He'll do anything Callie says."

"I can try, anyway," I said.

"Did you hear what I said?" said my mother. Mona bumped into the broom closet door. "You're not going to talk anything; you've already made enough trouble." She started on the dishes with a clatter.

Mona poked diffidently at a mop.

I sponged off the counter. "Anyway," I ventured, "I bet our name'll never even come up."

"That's if we're lucky," said my mother.

"There's all these people waiting," I said.

"Good," she said. She started on a pot.

I looked over at Mona, who was still cowering in the broom closet. "In fact, there's some black family's been waiting so long, they're going to sue," I said.

My mother turned off the water. "Where'd you hear that?"

"Patty told me."

She turned the water back on, started to wash a dish, then put it back down and shut the faucet.

"I'm sorry," said Mona.

"Forget it," said my mother. "Just forget it."

* * *

Booker turned out to be a model worker, whose boundless gratitude translated into a willingness to do anything. As he also learned quickly, he soon knew not only how to bus, but how to cook, and how to wait table, and how to keep the books. He fixed the walk-in door so that it stayed shut, reupholstered the torn seats in the dining room, and devised a system for tracking inventory. The only stone in the rice was that he tended to be sickly; but, reliable even in illness, he would always send a friend to take his place. In this way we got to know Ronald, Lynn, Dirk, and Cedric, all of whom, like Booker, had problems with their legal status and were anxious to please. They weren't all as capable as Booker, though, with the exception of Cedric, whom my father often hired even when Booker was well. A round wag of a man who called Mona and me *shou hou*—skinny monkeys—he was a professed nonsmoker who was nevertheless always begging drags off of other people's cigarettes. This last habit drove our head cook, Fernando, crazy, especially since, when refused a hit, Cedric would occasionally snitch one. Winking impishly at Mona and me, he would steal up to an ashtray, take a quick puff, and then break out laughing so that the smoke came rolling out of his mouth in a great incriminatory cloud. Fernando accused him of stealing fresh cigarettes too, even whole packs.

"Why else do you think he's weaseling around in the back of the store all the time," he said. His face was blotchy with anger. "The man is a frigging thief."

Other members of the staff supported him in this contention and joined in on an "Operation Identification," which involved numbering and initialing their cigarettes—even though what they seemed to fear for wasn't so much their cigarettes as their jobs. Then one of the cooks quit; and rather than promote someone, my father hired Cedric for the position. Rumors flew that he was taking only half the normal salary, that Alex had been pressured to resign, and that my father was looking for a position with which to placate Booker, who had been bypassed because of his health.

The result was that Fernando categorically refused to work with Cedric.

"The only way I'll cook with that piece of slime," he said, shaking his huge tattooed fist, "is if it's his ass frying on the grill."

My father cajoled and cajoled, to no avail, and in the end was simply forced to put them on different schedules.

The next week Fernando got caught stealing a carton of minute steaks. My father would not tell even Mona and me how he knew to be standing by the back door when Fernando was on his way out, but everyone suspected Booker. Everyone but Fernando, that is, who was sure Cedric had been the tip-off. My father held a staff meeting in which he tried to reassure everyone that Alex had left on his own, and that he had no intention of firing anyone. But though he was careful not to mention Fernando, everyone was so amazed that he was being allowed to stay that Fernando was incensed nonetheless.

"Don't you all be putting your bug eyes on me," he said. *"He's* the frigging crook."* He grabbed Cedric by the collar.

Cedric raised an eyebrow. "Cook, you mean," he said.

At this Fernando punched Cedric in the mouth; and the words he had just uttered notwithstanding, my father fired him on the spot.

With everything that was happening, Mona and I were ready to be getting out of the restaurant. It was almost time: the days were still stuffy with summer, but our window shade had started flapping in the evening as if gearing up to go out. That year the breezes were full of salt, as they sometimes were when they came in from the East, and they blew anchors and docks through my mind like so many tumbleweeds, filling my dreams with wherries and lobsters and grainy-faced men who squinted, day in and day out, at the sky.

It was time for a change, you could feel it; and yet the pancake house was the same as ever. The day before school started my father came home with bad news.

"Fernando called police," he said, wiping his hand on his pant leg.

My mother naturally wanted to know what police; and so with much coughing and hawing, the long story began, the latest installment of which had the police calling immigration, and immigration sending an investigator. My mother sat stiff as whalebone as my father described how the man summarily refused lunch on the house and how my father had admitted, under pressure, that he knew there were "things" about his workers.

"So now what happens?"

My father didn't know. "Booker and Cedric went with him to the jail," he said. "But me, here I am." He laughed uncomfortably.

The next day my father posted bail for "his boys" and waited apprehensively for something to happen. The day after that he waited again, and the day after that he called our neighbor's law student son, who suggested my father call the immigration department under an alias. My father took his advice; and it was thus that he discovered that Booker was right: it was illegal for aliens to work, but it wasn't to hire them.

In the happy interval that ensued, my father apologized to my mother, who in turn confessed about the country club, for which my father had no choice but to forgive her. Then he turned his attention back to "his boys."

My mother didn't see that there was anything to do.

"I like to talking to the judge," said my father.

"This is not China," said my mother.

"I'm only talking to him. I'm not give him money unless he wants it."

"You're going to land up in jail."

"So what else I should do?" My father threw up his hands. "Those are my boys."

"Your boys!" exploded my mother. "What about your family? What about your wife?"

My father took a long sip of tea. "You know," he said finally, "in the war my father sent our cook to the soldiers to use. He always said it—the province comes before the town, the town comes before the family."

"A restaurant is not a town," said my mother.

My father sipped at his tea again. "You know, when I first come to the United States, I also had to hide-and-seek with those deportation guys. If people did not helping me, I'm not here today."

My mother scrutinized her hem.

After a minute I volunteered that before seeing a judge, he might try a lawyer.

He turned. "Since when did you become so afraid like your mother?"

I started to say that it wasn't a matter of fear, but he cut me off.

"What I need today," he said, "is a son."

My father and I spent the better part of the next day standing in lines at the immigration office. He did not get to speak to a judge, but with much persistence he managed to speak to a judge's clerk, who tried to persuade him that it was not her place to extend him advice. My father, though, shamelessly plied her with compliments and offers of free pancakes until she finally conceded that she personally doubted anything would happen to either Cedric or Booker.

"Especially if they're 'needed workers,' " she said, rubbing at the red marks her glasses left on her nose. She yawned. "Have you thought about sponsoring them to become permanent residents?"

Could he do that? My father was overjoyed. And what if he saw to it right away? Would she perhaps put in a good word with the judge?

She yawned again, her nostrils flaring. "Don't worry," she said. "They'll get a fair hearing."

My father returned jubilant. Booker and Cedric hailed him as their savior, their Buddha incarnate. He was like a father to them, they said; and laughing and clapping, they made him tell the story over and over, sorting over the details like jewels. And how old was the assistant judge? And what did she say?

That evening my father tipped the paperboy a dollar and

bought a pot of mums for my mother, who suffered them to be placed on the dining room table. The next night he took us all out to dinner. Then on Saturday, Mona found a letter on my father's chair at the restaurant.

> Dear Mr. Chang,
> You are the grat boss. But, we do not like to trial, so will runing away now. Plese to excus us. People saying the law in America is fears like dragon. Here is only $140. We hope some day we can pay back the rest bale. You will getting intrest, as you diserving, so grat a boss you are. Thank you for every thing. In next life you will be burn in rich family, with no more pancaks.
>
> Yours truley,
Booker + Cedric

In the weeks that followed my father went to the pancake house for crises, but otherwise hung around our house, fiddling idly with the sump pump and boiler in an effort, he said, to get ready for winter. It was as though he had gone into retirement, except that instead of moving South, he had moved to the basement. He even took to showering my mother with little attentions, and to calling her "old girl," and when we finally heard that the club had entertained all the applications it could for the year, he was so sympathetic that he seemed more disappointed than my mother.

II. IN THE AMERICAN SOCIETY

Mrs. Lardner tempered the bad news with an invitation to a bon voyage "bash" she was throwing for a friend of hers who was going to Greece for six months.

"Do come," she urged. "You'll meet everyone, and then, you know, if things open up in the spring . . ." She waved her hands.

My mother wondered if it would be appropriate to show up at a party for someone they didn't know, but "the honest truth" was that this was an annual affair. "If it's not Greece, it's Antibes," sighed Mrs. Lardner. "We really just do it because his wife left him and his daughter doesn't speak to him, and poor Jeremy just feels so *unloved*."

She also invited Mona and me to the goings on, as *"demi-guests"* to keep Annie out of the champagne. I wasn't too keen on the idea, but before I could say anything, she had already thanked us for so generously agreeing to honor her with our presence.

"A pair of little princesses, you are!" she told us. "A pair of princesses!"

The party was that Sunday. On Saturday, my mother took my father out shopping for a suit. As it was the end of September, she insisted that he buy a worsted rather than a seersucker, even though it was only ten, rather than fifty percent off. My father protested that it was as hot out as ever, which was true—a thick Indian summer had cozied murderously up to us—but to no avail. Summer clothes, said my mother, were not properly worn after Labor Day.

The suit was unfortunately as extravagant in length as it was in price, which posed an additional quandary, since the tailor wouldn't be in until Monday. The salesgirl, though, found a way of tacking it up temporarily.

"Maybe this suit not fit me," fretted my father.

"Just don't take your jacket off," said the salesgirl.

He gave her a tip before they left, but when he got home refused to remove the price tag.

"I like to asking the tailor about the size," he insisted.

"You mean you're going to *wear* it and then return it?" Mona rolled her eyes.

"I didn't say I'm return it," said my father stiffly. "I like to asking the tailor, that's all."

The party started off swimmingly, except that most people were wearing bermudas or wrap skirts. Still, my parents carried on, sharing with great feeling the complaints about the heat. Of course my father tried to eat a cracker full of shallots and burnt himself in an attempt to help Mr. Lardner turn the coals of the barbecue; but on the whole he seemed to be doing all right. Not nearly so well as my mother, though, who had accepted an entire cupful of Mrs. Lardner's magic punch, and seemed indeed to be under some spell. As Mona and Annie skirmished over whether some boy in their class inhaled when he smoked, I watched my mother take off her shoes, laughing and laughing as a man with a beard regaled her with navy stories by the pool. Apparently he had been stationed in the Orient and remembered a few words of Chinese, which made my mother laugh still more. My father excused himself to go to the men's room then drifted back and "dropped" anchor at the hors d'oeuvre table, while my mother sailed on to a group of women, who tinkled at length over the clarity of her complexion. I dug out a book I had brought.

Just when I'd cracked the spine, though, Mrs. Lardner came by to bewail her shortage of servers. Her caterers were criminals, I agreed; and the next thing I knew I was handing out bits of marine life, making the rounds as amicably as I could.

"Here you go, Dad," I said when I got to the hors d'oeuvre table.

"Everything is fine," he said.

I hesitated to leave him alone; but then the man with the beard zeroed in on him, and though he talked of nothing but my mother, I thought it would be okay to get back to work. Just that moment, though, Jeremy Brothers lurched our way, an empty, albeit corked, wine bottle in hand. He was a slim, well-proportioned man, with a Roman nose and small eyes and a nice manly jaw that he allowed to hang agape.

"Hello," he said drunkenly. "Pleased to meet you."

"Pleased to meeting you," said my father.

"Right," said Jeremy. "Right. Listen. I have this bottle here, this most recalcitrant bottle. You see that it refuses to do my bidding. I bid it open sesame, please, and it does nothing." He pulled the cork out with his teeth, then turned the bottle upside down.

My father nodded.

"Would you have a word with it please?" said Jeremy. The man with the beard excused himself. "Would you please have a goddamned word with it?"

My father laughed uncomfortably.

"Ah!" Jeremy bowed a little. "Excuse me, excuse me, excuse me. You are not my man, not my man at all." He bowed again and started to leave, but then circled back. "Viticulture is not your forte, yes I can see that, see that plainly. But may I trouble you on another matter? Forget the damned bottle." He threw it into the pool, and winked at the people he splashed. "I have another matter. Do you speak Chinese?"

My father said he did not, but Jeremy pulled out a handkerchief with some characters on it anyway, saying that his daughter had sent it from Hong Kong and that he thought the characters might be some secret message.

"Long life," said my father.

"But you haven't looked at it yet."

"I know what it says without looking." My father winked at me.

"You do?"

"Yes, I do."

"You're making fun of me, aren't you?"

"No, no, no," said my father, winking again.

"Who are you anyway?" said Jeremy.

His smile fading, my father shrugged.

"Who are you?"

My father shrugged again.

Jeremy began to roar. "This is my party, *my party,* and I've never seen you before in my life." My father backed up as Jeremy came toward him. *"Who are you? WHO ARE YOU?"*

Just as my father was going to step back into the pool, Mrs. Lardner came running up. Jeremy informed her that there was a man crashing his party.

"Nonsense," said Mrs. Lardner. "This is Ralph Chang, who I invited extra especially so he could meet you." She straightened the collar of Jeremy's peach-colored polo shirt for him.

"Yes, well we've had a chance to chat," said Jeremy.

She whispered in his ear; he mumbled something; she whispered something more.

"I do apologize," he said finally.

My father didn't say anything.

"I do." Jeremy seemed genuinely contrite. "Doubtless you've seen drunks before, haven't you? You must have them in China."

"Okay," said my father.

As Mrs. Lardner glided off, Jeremy clapped his arm over my father's shoulders. "You know, I really am quite sorry, quite sorry."

My father nodded.

"What can I do, how can I make it up to you?"

"No thank you."

"No, tell me, tell me," wheedled Jeremy. "Tickets to casino night?" My father shook his head. "You don't gamble. Dinner at Bartholomew's?" My father shook his head again. "You don't eat." Jeremy scratched his chin. "You know, my wife was like you. Old Annabelle could never let me make things up—never, never, never, never, never."

My father wriggled out from under his arm.

"How about sport clothes? You are rather overdressed, you know, excuse me for saying so. But here." He took off his polo shirt and folded it up. "You can have this with my most profound apologies." He ruffled his chest hairs with his free hand.

"No thank you," said my father.

"No, take it, take it. Accept my apologies." He thrust the shirt into my father's arms. "I'm so very sorry, so very sorry. Please, try it on."

Helplessly holding the shirt, my father searched the crowd for my mother.

"Here, I'll help you off with your coat."

My father froze.

Jeremy reached over and took his jacket off. "Milton's, one hundred twenty-five dollars reduced to one hundred twelve-fifty," he read. "What a bargain, what a bargain!"

"Please give it back," pleaded my father. "Please."

"Now for your shirt," ordered Jeremy.

Heads began to turn.

"Take off your shirt."

"I do not take orders like a servant," announced my father.

"Take off your shirt, or I'm going to throw this jacket right into the pool, just right into this little pool here." Jeremy held it over the water.

"Go ahead."

"One hundred twelve-fifty," taunted Jeremy. "One hundred twelve . . ."

My father flung the polo shirt into the water with such force that part of it bounced back up into the air like a fluorescent fountain. Then it settled into a soft heap on top of the water. My mother hurried up.

"You're a sport!" said Jeremy, suddenly breaking into a smile and slapping my father on the back. "You're a sport! I like that. A man with spirit, that's what you are. A man with panache. Allow me to return to you your jacket." He handed it back to my father. "Good value you got on that, good value."

My father hurled the coat into the pool too. "We're leaving," he said grimly. "Leaving!"

"Now, Ralphie," said Mrs. Lardner, bustling up; but my father was already stomping off.

"Get your sister," he told me. To my mother: "Get your shoes."

"That was *great,* Dad," said Mona as we walked down to the car. "You were *stupendous.*"

"Way to show 'em," I said.

"What?" said my father offhandedly.

Although it was only just dusk, we were in a gulch, which made it hard to see anything except the gleam of his white shirt moving up the hill ahead of us.

"It was all my fault," began my mother.

"Forget it," said my father grandly. Then he said, "The only trouble is I left those keys in my jacket pocket."

"Oh *no,*" said Mona.

"Oh no is right," said my mother.

"So we'll walk home," I said.

"But how're we going to get into the *house,*" said Mona.

The noise of the party churned through the silence.

"Someone has to going back," said my father.

"Let's go to the pancake house first," suggested my mother. "We can wait there until the party is finished, and then call Mrs. Lardner."

Having all agreed that that was a good plan, we started walking again.

"God, just think," said Mona. "We're going to have to *dive* for them."

My father stopped a moment. We waited.

"You girls are good swimmers," he said finally. "Not like me."

Then his shirt started moving again, and we trooped up the hill after it, into the dark.

Claire's Lover's Church

TERI RUCH

The city fathers did not like the church on the other side of the ditch by the welcome-to-our-city sign. They didn't like the dolls' heads with empty eye sockets in the churchyard dirt. They wondered about the midgets from out of town who appeared and disappeared at the rear of the church with stuffed duffel bags bouncing on their backs. They didn't appreciate the stained-glass windows showing naked women leaping around a handsome shepherd. And the glare of the church's gold front doors blinded people driving in and out of the city. The city fathers moved the welcome sign three feet to keep the church outside the city limits.

As a child Claire crawled down in the ditch, under the highway through the drainage pipe, and up the opposite bank. She pressed an ear to the glowing doors and listened to altos and sopranos hum the same three notes repeatedly. It reminded her of the chant she hummed herself to sleep with. The doors were always locked.

Rumor spread that a minister lived inside, that he kept many women with him. Claire started the rumor.

On Claire's twenty-first birthday, her mother gave her seven gilt-edged Bibles. "For your friends taking Philosophy of Religion 101 with you," she said. Her eyes were set so deep Claire wondered if she saw the edges of her sockets when she glanced left and right. Her straight thin lips reminded Claire of an equal sign.

By the gold doors of the humming church Claire dropped her seven Bibles. Twenty hands pulled her inside, ten naked women hugged her. "Remove your shoes," they said. "Shade your eyes. Overwhelming is the brilliance of our lover, blinding is the radiance of the women he has taught. Close your mouth, ye who would enter, for your gasp echoes. Close your mouth, be silent, our lover may soon utter. Unerring is his wisdom, unending is his grace."

They guided Claire to the organ bench and pressed her shoulders until she lay on her back. They held her hands and feet. "Where is the minister?" Claire asked. They opened their mouths then closed them. No words, just three notes hummed in harmony. They unzipped Claire's skirt, removed her blouse, unbuckled her sandals. Was it unreasonable of her, Claire asked, to demand to see the minister? A woman held her hand on Claire's lips while another, with a sponge, dabbed frankincense on her. Two women touched her nipples, another leaned close to her lips. Three slid their hands along her neck, her arms, her waist. One held Claire's thighs. Then they dressed her in a surplice and said, "You are prepared to meet our lover."

In the east Cry Room, the women sat Claire on the floor. Before them, a gold-skinned man in a large paper bag ate biscuits. When he saw Claire he embraced her and offered her, with the others, biscuits and beer. Claire could not look at him directly, but held the sleeve of her surplice before her eyes. Not even the bag could hide this man's beauty. He addressed the women:

A woman gave birth to a handsome boy at the same moment another woman gave birth to a headless boy. The handsome and the headless boys became best friends. One day the handsome boy's father fell in love with the headless boy's mother and the headless boy's father fell in love with the handsome boy's mother. The parents swapped. Now the handsome and the headless

boys had four parents. How happy and confused they
were.

The handsome boy grew up bad. He robbed rich families of their grandparents. One day he borrowed a baby.
This was too much. One of his fathers sought to whip
him. "Where's your mother?" he asked the kid. "Which
mother?" "My wife, your mother." "She's with my
other mother and my other father," he said. "Where?"
cried the father. "In bed," the bad kid said. The father
ran off with his whip and the handsome boy was never
punished for his crimes.

But the headless boy was not intelligent enough to be
bad like his handsome brother. He had no head, poor
bastard. His life was sad and uneventful.

All afternoon the minister spoke in parables. At sunset a midget
opened a duffel bag for Claire. The minister held her hands. "We
enjoy our evenings here," he said. "You're always welcome back."
She thanked him. Unwillingly she took her surplice off, dressed
again in her clothes and climbed inside the bag.

Wild women fill Claire's lover's church, leaping pew to pew and
laughing. "All women will be bad," the lover says. They are.
Hymnals show teeth marks from gentle gnawing and indented
spines from being thrown against the pews, the altar, hip bones.
Singing Glorias, the naked women flip from altar to organ, from
organ to altar. They make love to each other, then dress in robes
made from the paraments pulled off the altar and the pulpit. They
practice scandals with bad boys bagged in from nearby cities. The
women grin. They are bad, bad, bad, and love it.

None have seen the minister naked. He appears in the Cry
Room fully bagged for morning parables. Near noon he stands
behind the pulpit and guides the women in scandal practice. Late
afternoons he counsels them, on his knees. They kiss him and
each other.

Claire is not satisfied. She wants to see the lover bagless. In the men's room she lies on her back in a stall, peeking up as the minister looks in the mirror. He pulls her up beside him and points in the mirror. "Look how young you are," he says. He shows her his hands, says, "Old," and hits them against the wall. Claire slaps his golden ass and drags him to her mattress. She rips his paper off.

The minister can't get Claire off his back. She clings to his neck as he showers and shaves. While he bakes biscuits, she breathes in his ear and presses her breasts against his shoulder blades. She climbs off only so he can dress in his new paper bag and meet his women for breakfast parables and popovers.

He stares at Claire. He cannot concentrate on his parables. He wants her on his back again.

The minister rearranges his schedule to spend more time with Claire than with the other women. "We can't let them know," he says. "It will disrupt my ministry."

"Why do you teach us bad?" Claire asks. "Bad will be with us always," he explains. "We must be thoughtful so our bad behavior hurts as few as possible. My women will be bad responsibly." Claire requests a sermon on the relationship of bad to sad.

Outside, spitters gather on the premises. It must be winter now, Claire thinks. Standing in their steamy breath, the spitters stare in the Cry Room windows. In packs they glare at their spit as it freezes on a stained-glass shepherd spitting golden biscuits on naked women. The spitters are jealous of the minister. So is Claire. According to the laws he created, Claire should love each woman and the minister equally. But she prefers the minister. She writes a parable:

> A man had eleven wives. One loved the man more than the others and the man loved her more than he loved the others. He threw a party and invited ten men, hoping they would take away ten of his wives. The ten men raped the wife he loved the most and left her behind ten casks of sour wine.

Claire throws the parable away. Outside, the spitters comb their hair. They practice jumping jacks.

On Sunday, the minister repeats a sermon he delivered two months earlier. His congregation regards the large log in his eye. He writes a parable for Claire:

A married man sowed pennies in a supermarket parking lot. Some rolled into a drain. Others fell before the front tires of a Mack truck. Wedged in the tire cracks, the pennies were slapped against cement repeatedly before they flew in weedy fields beside the freeways. Still others were swallowed by hungry babies. But one a young woman found and, considering it good luck, she slipped it into her bra. She fell in love with the married man. But the penny, which the frugal girl hid in her bedroom closet, grew into a young, well-speaking and warm-hearted man who was not married. He and the woman fell in love. The married man swore never again to sow his pennies in a supermarket parking lot.

The parable disturbs Claire and the minister. Claire tries to write one:

A young woman kept tickets to Iceland in her freezer. Each morning she defrosted them and read the itinerary. Each afternoon she replaced the tickets underneath the trays of ice. Her lover asked if he could go with her. She bought him tickets, but had to sell the last of her goat milk to do so. Grateful, the lover moved in with her. This made the young woman happier than she'd ever been.

The minister interrupts Claire. "This parable is horrible," he says. "It rambles. What's the point?"

"The point," says Claire, "is that the minister does not stay with his lover and he never goes to Iceland, so the young woman stays on ice forever, fucking young, blond men."

"I don't think the parable as you stated it can hang together," he says. "And the relationship between the lovers isn't clear. What is it?"

"The man is interested in the woman's anxiety."

"Is that all? Does he love her?"

"It's not in the parable," says Claire. "That's all I know. It's not in the parable."

Claire writes another:

A greedy man took three fat women to bed. In the night, one stole his wallet. "Who's got it?" he asked at breakfast. None would confess. The women ate and ate—bacon, sausage, popovers—growing ever larger. The greedy man considered kicking them away, but he didn't want to sleep alone. He said, "She who confesses gets a foot-long ice cream sundae." The thief confessed and the greedy man gave her the sundae. She grew. Next morning the greedy man's gun was missing. Naked, he quaked. "Who's got it?" he cried. The women sat at the end of his bed gnawing on his feet. He offered them fried potatoes, shrimp and oysters. The villain pulled the greedy man's gun from behind her back. She ate, she grew.

All four hit the highways. This mobile mountain range struck terror in the hearts of hale pedestrians. The greedy man trembled.

Next morning he couldn't find his clothes. None of my ladies can fit into my clothes, he thought. He knew the evil in their hearts. "Ladies," he cried. "Why do you torture me?"

"What will you feed us?" they asked. He offered them fruit.

"No, no," they said.

"Celery, tomatoes."

"NO."

"Cheese cake?" The clothes fell on his face.

Now each woman measured fifteen feet by fifteen feet. The greedy man moved quickly, but not quick enough. Before the multitude of tow trucks came, the greedy women ate him.

In his room the minister tries to write his sermon on bad and sad. He's thinking of Claire. He wants to be with her, but the women would be upset. Why can't he please himself? Why does he have to be sad? Claire's parables disturb him. She says she has committed the worst bad yet, that she's in love with him. He tries to sleep.

Claire sits in the empty Cry Room. If the minister believes in bad, she thinks, why isn't he with her, now? He has responsibilities to his women. He promised he would train them in decent badness. Claire understands, but she does not feel loved. "Here is my body," she says. "Where is his?"

She looks outside at the spitters smearing each other's spit in their hair. Their primping disgusts her. Why is no handsome man among them, no man with heart and wisdom? Still, they are available. Claire undresses and steps outside. It's lovely weather here, she thinks. It's glorious to be in love, to fall in half-iced puddles, to grin in my sopping slip and bra, to freeze in my sopping slip and bra. I can even get a cold without worrying anyone. "Sick," Mom used to say. "Get ye the hell to bed then. Here's a box of tissues and a throw-up bucket. Best be well tomorrow. I'll have no messes in my house." And the teacher who wore elf-earrings isn't here to give me aspirin from the fat bottle she kept in her top desk drawer. Nor is my lover.

A horde of hungry spitters grab Claire, wrap her in electrician's tape and roll her behind a mound of dolls' heads. The spitters take turns raping her. At night they practice spitting by the fireside. Legs taped together, Claire tries to hop away. A spitter lassos her. "Where you going?" he asks. "Back to church," she says. "To praise your lord?" "To sing him hymns." "Sorry, sweetheart," he says. "Can't leave yet. Must pay for stepping out. I won't hurt you *too bad*. One bite here, a bit of blood, a bruise."

Three days Claire has been missing. The minister has not slept. He does not eat. At night he sees a body wrapped in silver, glowing in the light of the spitters' fire. He sends five bad boys out with duffel bags. The spitters toss the boys against the church walls.

They run back to the minister. Dare the minister emerge in person? Will the spitters laugh to see he cares so much for Claire? Will they think he is too old? The minister paces the pew ways, looks outside, paces. He leaves the church. He lifts Claire in his arms. Silent, the spitters stare. None try to stop him. The gold man carries his silver lover back to the church. Realizing they cannot penetrate, the spitters slink away in single file.

The minister unwraps his lover and lies beside her on her mattress. He kisses her bruises and anoints her cuts. She wakes ungrateful, with one eye open. "You've been sleeping with your women," she says. "A different one each night."

"Ritual," he says.

"Crap," says Claire. "It ain't all pain, this late night partaking."

"You should leave," he says. "This isn't good for you. I can't give you what you want."

"Your women need you," she says.

He nods.

The minister is not well. He has begun to disappear while he is speaking. Several of the women question his existence. One claims she walked through him twice—once in the transept, once in the narthex. "He was the scent of caramel," she says. Another says he disappears when the choir sings high E. Only Claire can reach the note and she refuses to repeat it. "He belongs in this world he created," she says bitterly. "He is the minister."

The women are jealous of the minister's distraction. They have begun to misbehave their own way instead of following the minister's instructions. Some have bitten the bad boys. The boys will not come back. Some women have stuffed biscuits in the organ pipes. The organ will not play on key.

Claire is losing patience. Why hasn't the minister addressed his congregation on the relationship of bad to sad? Why does he say he wants to sleep with her forever, but sleep with her only once a month? Why does he say she makes him happy, then tell her he's unhappy?

Claire leaves notes in her lover's Bibles asking him to meet her.

He doesn't. "The other women might . . ." "I know," says Claire. "They might get jealous." Claire has lost her patience.

Rumor spreads that those who enter a crack in the north wall of the men's room will be taken to a land where bad conscience does not accompany bad action, a land of no responsibilities. Claire started the rumor. One by one the women disappear.

The minister is depressed. He wants his women back. Claire hugs him. "Come to my mattress," she says. "You told me once you wanted to lie beside me forever, your left arm under my shoulder, your right arm around me."

The minister retreats behind his pulpit. "I am a minister," he says. "I need my women." He pauses. "And I need you."

"You're a bit too needy then," Claire says. "So am I." She packs her hymnal and her seven Bibles. She removes her surplice, dresses in the blouse and skirt she came in and steps outside in the dark. She hadn't realized it was night. In the church she lost her sense of endings and beginnings.

Beside the welcome-to-our-city sign, Claire watches the gold doors of her lover's church. She will give her lover three hours.

Where We Are Now
ETHAN CANIN

When I met Jodi, she was an English major at Simmons College, in Boston, and for a while after that she tried to be a stage actress. Then she tried writing a play, and when that didn't work out she thought about opening a bookstore. We've been married eleven years now, and these days she checks out books at the public library. I don't mean she reads them; I mean she works at the circulation desk.

We've been arguing lately about where we live. Our apartment is in a building with no grass or bushes, only a social room, with plastic chairs and a carpet made of Astroturf. Not many people want to throw a party on Astroturf, Jodi says. She points out other things, too: the elevator stops a foot below the floors, so you have to step up to get out; the cold water comes out rusty in the mornings; three weeks ago a man was robbed in the hallway by a kid with a bread knife. The next Sunday night Jodi rolled over in bed, turned on the light, and said, "Charlie, let's look at houses."

It was one in the morning. From the fourth floor, through the night haze, I could see part of West Hollywood, a sliver of the observatory, lights from the mansions in the canyon.

"There," I said, pointing through the window. "Houses."

"No, let's look at houses to buy."

I covered my eyes with my arm. "Lovebird," I said, "where will we find a house we can afford?"

"We can start this weekend," she said.

That night after dinner she read aloud from the real-estate section. "Santa Monica," she read. "Two bedrooms, yard, half mile to beach."

"How much?"

She looked closer at the paper. "We can look other places."

She read to herself for a while. Then she said that prices seemed lower in some areas near the Los Angeles airport.

"How much?"

"A two-bedroom for $160,000."

I glanced at her.

"Just because we look doesn't mean we have to buy it," she said.

"There's a real-estate agent involved."

"She won't mind."

"It's not honest," I said.

She closed the paper and went to the window. I watched a muscle in her neck move from side to side. "You know what it's like?" she said, looking into the street.

"I just don't want to waste the woman's time," I answered.

"It's like being married to a priest."

I knew why she said that. I'm nothing like a priest. I'm a physical-education teacher in the Hollywood schools and an assistant coach—basketball and baseball. The other night I'd had a couple of other coaches over to the house. We aren't all that much alike —I'll read a biography on the weekend, listen to classical music maybe a third of the time—but I still like to have them over. We were sitting in the living room, drinking beer and talking about the future. One of the coaches has a two-year-old son at home. He didn't have a lot of money, he said, so he thought it was important to teach his kid morality. I wasn't sure he was serious, but when he finished I told a story anyway about an incident that had happened a few weeks before at school. I'd found out that a kid in a gym class I was teaching, a quiet boy and a decent student, had stolen a hat from a men's store. So I made him return it and write a letter of apology to the owner. When I told the part about how the man was so impressed with the letter that he offered the boy a job, Jodi remarked that I was lucky it hadn't turned out the other way.

"What do you mean?" I asked.

"He could have called the police," she said. "He could have thanked you for bringing the boy in and then called the police."

"I just don't think so."

"Why not? The boy could have ended up in jail."

"I just don't think so," I said. "I think most people will respond to honesty. I think that's where people like us have to lead the way."

It's an important point, I said, and took a drink of beer to take the edge off what I was saying. Too much money makes you lose sight of things, I told them. I stopped talking then, but I could have said more. All you have to do is look around: in Beverly Hills there's a restaurant where a piece of veal costs thirty dollars. I don't mind being an assistant coach at a high school, even though you hear now about the fellow who earns a hundred thousand dollars with the fitness truck that comes right to people's homes. The truck has Nautilus, and a sound system you wouldn't expect. He keeps the stars in shape that way—Kirk Douglas, the movie executives. The man with the truck doesn't live in Hollywood. He probably lives out at the beach, in Santa Monica or Malibu.

But Hollywood's fine if people don't compare it with the ideas they have. Once in a while, at a party, someone from out of town will ask me whether any children of movie stars are in my classes. Sometimes Jodi says the answer is yes but that it would violate confidentiality to reveal their names. Other times I explain that movie stars don't live in Hollywood these days, that most of them don't even work here, that Hollywood is just car washes and food joints, and that the theater with the stars' footprints out front isn't much of a theater anymore. The kids race hot rods by it on Thursday nights.

Hollywood is all right, though, I say. It's got sun and wide streets and is close to everything.

But Jodi wants to look anyway.

Next Sunday I drive, and Jodi gives directions from the map. The house is in El Segundo. While I'm parking I hear a loud noise, and a 747 flies right over our heads. I watch it come down over the freeway.

"Didn't one of them land on the road once?" I ask.

"I don't remember it," Jodi says. She looks at the map. "The house should be on this block."

"I think it was in Dallas. I think it came right down on top of a car."

I think about that for a minute. It shakes me up to see a huge plane so low. I think of the people inside the one that landed on the road—descending, watching the flaps and the ailerons, the houses and automobiles coming into view.

"The ad says there are nice trees in back," Jodi says.

She leads us to the house. It's two stories, yellow stucco walls, with a cement yard and a low wire fence along the sidewalk. The roof is tar paper. Down the front under the drainpipes are two long green stains.

"Don't worry," she says. "Just because we look doesn't mean anything." She knocks on the door and slips her arm into mine. "Maybe you can see the ocean from the bedroom windows."

She knocks again. Then she pushes the door a little, and we walk into the living room. There are quick footsteps, and a woman comes out of the hallway. "Good afternoon," she says. "Would you sign in, please?"

She points to a vinyl-covered book on the coffee table, and Jodi crosses the room and writes something in it. Then the agent hands me a sheet of paper with small type on it and a badly copied picture. I've never shopped for a house before. I see two columns of abbreviations, some numbers. It's hard to tell what the picture is of, but then I recognize the long stains under the drainpipes. I fold the sheet and put it into my pants pocket. Then I sit down on the couch and look around. The walls are light yellow, and one of them is covered with a mirror that has gold marbling in it. On the floor is a cream-colored shag rug, with a matted area near the front door where a couch or maybe a trunk once stood. Above the mantel is a painting of a blue whale.

"Do the appliances and plumbing work?" Jodi asks.

"Everything works," the agent says.

Jodi turns the ceiling light on and off. She opens and closes the door to a closet in the corner, and I glimpse a tricycle and a bag full of empty bottles. I wonder what the family does on a Sunday afternoon when buyers look at their house.

"The rooms have a nice feel," the agent says. "You know what I mean?"

"I'm not sure I do," I say.

"It's hard to explain," she says, "but you'll see."

"We understand," Jodi says.

In the marbled mirror I watch Jodi's reflection. Three windows look onto the front yard, and she unlatches and lifts each one.

"I like a careful buyer," the agent says.

"You can never be too thorough," Jodi answers. Then she adds, "We're just looking."

The agent smiles, drumming her fingers against her wrist. I know she's trying to develop a strategy. In college I learned about strategies. I worked for a while selling magazines over the phone: talk to the man if you think they want it; talk to the woman if you think they don't. I was thinking of playing ball then, semi-pro, and the magazine work was evenings. I was twenty-three years old. I thought I was just doing work until I was discovered.

"Why don't you two look around," I say now to the agent. "I'll stay here."

"Perfect," she says.

She leads Jodi into the next room. I hear a door open and shut, and then they begin talking about the floors, the walls, the ceiling. We aren't going to buy the house, and I don't like being here. When I hear the two of them walk out through the back door into the yard, I get up from the couch and go over to look at the painting above the mantel. It's an underwater view, looking below the whale as it swims toward the surface. Above, the sunny sky is broken by ripples. On the mantel is a little pile of plaster powder, and as I stand there, I realize that the painting has just recently been hung. I go back to the couch. Once on a trip up the coast I saw a whale that the tide had trapped in a lagoon. It was north of Los Angeles, along the coastal highway, in a cove sheltered by two piers of man-moved boulders. Cars were parked along the shoulder. People were setting up their cameras while the whale moved around in the lagoon, stirring up the bottom. I don't like to think about trapped animals, though, so instead I sit down and try to plan what to do tomorrow at practice. The season hasn't started yet, and we're still working on base-running—the double steal, leading from the inside of the bag. Baseball isn't a thing you think about, though; baseball *comes.* I'm an assistant coach and maybe could have been a minor-league pitcher, but when I think of it I realize I know only seven or eight things about the whole game. We learn so slowly, I think.

I get up and go over to the painting again. I glance behind me. I put my head next to the wall, lift the frame a little bit, and when I look I see that behind it the plaster is stained brown from an interior leak. I take a deep breath and then put the frame back. From outside in the yard I hear the women speaking about basement storage space, and rather than listen I cross the room and enter a hallway. It smells of grease. On the wall, at waist level, are children's hand marks that go all the way to the far end. I walk down there and enter the kitchen. In it is a Formica table and four plastic chairs, everything made large by the low ceiling. I see a door in the corner, and when I cross the room and open it I'm surprised to find a stairway with brooms and mops hung above the banister. The incline is steep, and when I go up I find myself in the rear of an upstairs closet. Below me Jodi and the agent are still talking. I push through the clothes hanging in front of me and open the door.

I'm in the master bedroom now. A king-sized bed stands in front of me, but something's funny about it, and when I look closer I think that it might be two single beds pushed together. It's covered by a spread. I stop for a moment to think. I don't think I'm doing anything wrong. We came here to see the house, and when people show their homes they take out everything of value so that they won't have to worry. I go to the window.

Framing it is a new-looking lace curtain, pinched up in a tieback. I look out at a crab-apple tree and some telephone wires and try to calculate where the ocean might be. The shadows point west, but the coastline is irregular in this area and juts in different directions. The view of the crab apple is pretty, spotted with shade and light—but then I see that in the corner behind the curtain the glass is splintered and has been taped. I lift the curtain and look at the pane. The crack spreads like a spiderweb. Then I walk back to the bed. I flatten my hands and slip them into the crevice between the two mattresses, and when I extend my arms the two halves come apart. I push the beds back together and sit down. Then I look into the corner, and my heart skips because I see that against the far wall, half-hidden by the open door, is an old woman in a chair.

"Excuse me," I say.

"That's all right," she says. She folds her hands. "The window cracked ten years ago."

"My wife and I are looking at the house."

"I know."

I walk to the window. "A nice view," I say, pretending to look at something in the yard. The woman doesn't say anything. I can hear water running in the pipes, some children outside. Tiny, pale apples hang among the leaves of the tree.

"You know," I say, "we're not really looking at the house to buy it."

I walk back to the bed. The skin on the woman's arms is mottled and hangs in folds. "We can't afford to buy it," I say. "I don't make enough money to buy a house and—I don't know why, but my wife wants to looks at them anyway. She wants people to think we have enough money to buy a house."

The woman looks at me.

"It's crazy," I say, "but what are you going to do in that kind of situation?"

She clears her throat. "My son-in-law," she begins, "wants to sell the house so he can throw the money away." Her voice is slow, and I think she has no saliva in her mouth. "He has a friend who goes to South America and swallows everything, and then comes back through customs with a plastic bag in his bowel."

She stops. I look at her. "He's selling the house to invest the money in drugs?"

"I'm glad you don't want to buy," she says.

I might have had a small career in baseball, but I've learned in the past eleven years to talk about other things. I was twenty-three the last pitch I threw. The season was over and Jodi was in the stands in a wool coat. I was about to get a college degree in physical education. I knew how to splint a broken bone and how to cut the grass on a golf green, and then I decided that to turn your life around you had to start from the inside. I had a coach in college who said he wasn't trying to teach us to be pro ballplayers; he was trying to teach us to be decent people.

When we got married, I told Jodi that no matter what happened, no matter where things went, she could always trust me. We'd been seeing each other for a year, and in that time I'd been reading books. Not baseball books. Biographies: Martin Luther King, Gandhi. To play baseball right you have to forget that you're a person; you're muscles, bone, the need for sleep and food. So when you stop, you're saved by someone else's ideas. This isn't true just for baseball players. It's true for anyone who's failed at what he loves.

A friend got me the coaching job in California, and as soon as we were married we came West. Jodi still wanted to be an actress. We rented a room in a house with six other people, and she took classes in dance in the mornings and speech in the afternoons. Los Angeles is full of actors. Sometimes at parties we counted them. After a couple of years she started writing a play, and until we moved into where we are now we used to read pieces of it out loud to our six housemates.

By then I was already a little friendly with the people at school, but when I was out of the house, even after two years in Los Angeles, I was alone. People were worried about their own lives. In college I'd spent almost all my time with another ballplayer,

Mitchell Lighty, and I wasn't used to new people. A couple of years after we graduated, Mitchell left to play pro ball in Panama City, and he came out to Los Angeles on his way there. The night before his plane left, he and I went downtown to a bar on the top floor of a big hotel. We sat by a window, and after a few drinks we went out onto the balcony. The air was cool. Plants grew along the edge, ivy was woven into the railing, and birds perched among the leaves. I was amazed to see the birds resting there thirty stories up on the side of the building. When I brushed the plants the birds took off into the air, and when I leaned over to watch them, I became dizzy with the distance to the sidewalk and with the small, rectangular shapes of the cars. The birds sailed in wide circles over the street and came back to the balcony. Then Mitchell put his drink on a chair, took both my hands, and stepped up onto the railing. He stood there on the metal crossbar, his wrists locked in my hands, leaning into the air.

"For God's sake," I whispered. He leaned farther out, pulling me toward the railing. A waiter appeared at the sliding door next to us. "Take it easy," I said. "Come on down." Mitchell let go of one of my hands, kicked up one leg, and swung out over the street. His black wingtip shoe swiveled on the railing. The birds had scattered, and now they were circling, chattering angrily as he rocked. I was holding on with my pitching arm. My legs were pressed against the iron bars, and just when I began to feel the lead, just when the muscles began to shake, Mitchell jumped back onto the balcony. The waiter came through the sliding door and grabbed him, but in the years after that—the years after Mitchell got married and decided to stay in Panama City—I thought of that incident as the important moment of my life.

I don't know why. I've struck out nine men in a row and pitched to half a dozen hitters who are in the majors now, but when I think back over my life, about what I've done, not much more than that stands out.

As we lie in bed that night, Jodi reads aloud from the real-estate listings. She uses abbreviations: BR, AC, D/D. As she goes down the page—San Marino, Santa Ana, Santa Monica—I nod occasionally or make a comment.

When I wake up later, early in the morning, the newspaper is still next to her on the bed. I can see its pale edge in the moonlight. Sometimes I wake up like this, maybe from some sound in the night, and when I do, I like to lie with my eyes closed and feel the difference between the bed and the night air. I like to take stock of things. These are the moments when I'm most in love with my wife. She's next to me, and her face when she sleeps is untroubled. Women say now that they don't want to be protected, but when I watch her slow breathing, her parted lips, I think what a delicate thing a life is. I lean over and touch her mouth.

When I was in school I saw different girls, but since I've been married to Jodi I've been faithful. Except for once, a few years ago, I've almost never thought about someone else. I have a friend at school, Ed Ryan, a history teacher, who told me about the time he had an affair, and about how his marriage broke up right afterward. It wasn't a happy thing to see. She was a cocktail waitress at a bar a few blocks from school, he said. Ed told me the whole long story, about how he and the waitress had fallen in love so suddenly that he had no choice about leaving his wife. After the marriage was over, though, Ed gained fifteen or twenty pounds. One night, coming home from school, he hit a tree and wrecked his car. A few days later he came in early to work and found that all the windows in his classroom had been broken. At first I believed him when he said he thought his wife had done it, but that afternoon we were talking and I realized what had really happened.

We were in a lunch place. "You know," Ed said, "sometimes you think you know a person." He was looking into his glass. "You can sleep next to a woman, you can know the way she smiles when she's turned on, you can see in her hands when she wants to talk about something. Then you wake up one day and some signal's been exchanged—and you don't know what it is, but you think for the first time, *Maybe I don't know her.* Just something. You never know what the signal is." I looked at him then and realized that there was no cocktail waitress and that Ed had broken the windows.

I turn in bed now and look at Jodi. Then I slide the newspaper off the blanket. We know each other, I think. The time I came close to adultery was a few years ago, with a secretary at school, a temporary who worked afternoons. She was a dark girl, didn't say much, and she wore turquoise bracelets on both wrists. She kept finding reasons to come into my office, which I share with the two other coaches. It's three desks, a window, a chalkboard. One night I was there late, after everyone else had gone, and she came by to do something. It was already dark. We talked for a while, and then she took off one of her bracelets to show me. She said she wanted me to see how beautiful it was, how the turquoise changed color in dim light. She put it into my hand, and then I knew for sure what was going on. I looked at it for a long time, listening to the little sounds in the building, before I looked up.

"Charlie?" Jodi says now in the dark.

"Yes?"

"Would you do whatever I asked you to do?"

"What do you mean?"

"I mean, would you do anything in the world that I asked you to do?"

"That depends," I say.

"On what?"

"On what you asked. If you asked me to rob someone, then maybe I wouldn't."

I hear her roll over, and I know she's looking at me. "But don't you think I would have a good reason to ask you if I did?"

"Probably."

"And wouldn't you do it just because I asked?"

She turns away again and I try to think of an answer. We've already argued once today, while she was making dinner, but I don't want to lie to her. That's what we argued about earlier. She asked me what I thought of the house we looked at, and I told her the truth, that a house just wasn't important to me.

"Then what is important to you?"

I was putting the forks and knives on the table. "Leveling with

other people is important to me," I answered. "And you're important to me." Then I said, "And whales."

"What?"

"Whales are important to me."

That was when it started. We didn't say much after that, so it
wasn't an argument exactly. I don't know why I mentioned the
whales. They're great animals, the biggest things on earth, but
they're not important to me.

"What if it was something not so bad," she says now, "but still
something you didn't want to do?"

"What?"

The moonlight is shining in her hair. "What if I asked you to
do something that ordinarily you wouldn't do yourself—would
you do it if I asked?"

"And it wasn't something so bad?"

"Right."

"Yes," I say. "Then I would do it."

"What I want you to do," she says on Wednesday, "is look at
another house." We're eating dinner. "But I want them to take us
seriously," she says. "I want to act as if we're really thinking of
buying it, right on the verge. You know—maybe we will, maybe
we won't."

I take a sip of water, look out the window. "That's ridiculous,"
I say. "Nobody walks in off the street and decides in an afternoon
whether to buy a house."

"Maybe we've been looking at it from a distance for a long
time," she says, "assessing things." She isn't eating her dinner. I
cooked it, chicken, and it's steaming on her plate. "Maybe we've
been waiting for the market to change."

"Why is it so important to you?"

"It just is. And you said you'd do it if it was important to me.
Didn't you say that?"

"I had a conversation with the old woman in the yellow
house."

"What?"

"When we looked at the other house," I say, "I went off by myself for a while. I talked with the old woman who was sitting upstairs."

"What did you say?"

"Do you remember her?"

"Yes."

"She told me that the owner was selling the house so he could use the money to smuggle drugs."

"So?"

"So," I say, "you have to be careful."

This Sunday Jodi drives. The day is bright and blue, with a breeze from the ocean, and along Santa Monica Boulevard the palm fronds are rustling. I'm in my suit. If Jodi talks to the agent about offers, I've decided I'll stay to the back, nod or shrug at questions. She parks the car on a side street and we walk around the corner and go into the lobby of one of the hotels. We sit down in cloth chairs near the entrance. A bellman carries over an ashtray on a stand and sets it between us; Jodi hands him a bill from her purse. I look at her. The bellman is the age of my father. He moves away fast, and I lean forward to get my shoulder loose in my suit. I'm not sure if the lobby chairs are only for guests, and I'm ready to get up if someone asks. Then a woman comes in and Jodi stands and introduces herself. "Charlie Gordon," I say when the woman puts out her hand. She's in a gray pin-striped skirt and a jacket with a white flower in the lapel. After she says something to Jodi, she leads us outside to the parking circle, where a car is brought around by the valet, a French car, and Jodi and I get in back. The seats are leather.

"Is the weather always this nice?" Jodi asks. We pull out onto Wilshire Boulevard.

"Almost always," the woman says. "That's another thing I love about Los Angeles—the weather. Los Angeles has the most perfect weather on earth."

We drive out toward the ocean, and as the woman moves in and out of the lines of traffic, I look around the car. It's well kept, maybe leased. No gum wrappers or old coffee cups under the seat.

"Then you're looking for a second home?" the woman says.

"My husband's business makes it necessary for us to have a home in Los Angeles."

I look at Jodi. She's sitting back in the seat, her hand resting on the armrest.

"Most of the year, of course, we'll be in Dallas."

The street is curved and long with a grass island in the middle and eucalyptus along its length, and each time the car banks, I feel the nerves firing in my gut. I look at Jodi. I look at her forehead. I look at the way her hair falls on her neck, at her breasts, and I realize, the car shifting under us, that I don't trust her.

We turn and head up a hill. The street twists, and we go in and out of the shade from a bridge of elms. I can't see anything behind the hedges.

"The neighborhood is lovely," the woman says. "We have a twenty-four-hour security patrol, and the bushes hide everything from the street. We don't have sidewalks."

"No sidewalks?" I say.

"That discourages sightseeing," Jodi says.

We turn into a driveway. It heads down between two hedges to the far end, where a gravel half-circle has been cut around the trunk of a low, spreading fig tree. We stop, the agent opens Jodi's door, and we get out and stand there, looking at the house. It's a mansion.

The walls are white. There are clay tiles on the roof, sloped eaves, hanging vines. A narrow window runs straight up from the ground. Through it I can see a staircase and a chandelier. In college once, at the end of the season, the team had a party at a mansion like this one. It had windows everywhere, panes of glass as tall as flagpoles. The fellow who owned it had played ball for a while when he was young, and then gotten out and made big money. He was in something like hair care or combs then, and at the door each of us got a leather travel kit with our name embossed and some of his products inside. At the buffet table the oranges were cut so that the peels came off like the leather on a split baseball. He showed us through the house and then brought us into the yard. He told us that after all these years the game was still inside him. We stood on the lawn. It was landscaped with shrubs and willows, but he said he had bought the place because the yard was big enough for a 400-foot straightaway center field.

Now the agent leads us up the porch stairs. She rings the bell and then opens the door; inside, the light is everywhere. It streams from the windows, shines on the wood, falls in slants from every height. There are oriental carpets on the floor, plants, a piano. The agent opens her portfolio and hands us each a beige piece of paper. It's textured like a wedding invitation, and at the top, above the figures, is an ink drawing of the house. The boughs of the fig tree frame the paper. I look down at it in my hand, the way I used to look down at a baseball.

The agent motions us into the living room. From there she leads us back through a glass-walled study, wisteria and bougainvillaea hanging from the ceiling, down a hallway into the kitchen. Through the windows spread the grounds of the estate. Now is the time, I think to myself, when I should explain everything.

"I think I'll go out back," Jodi says. "You two can look around in here."

"Certainly," the agent says.

After she leaves, I pretend to look through the kitchen. I open cabinets, run the water. The tap has a charcoal filter. The agent says things about the plumbing and the foundation; I nod and then walk back into the study. She follows me.

"I know you'll find the terms agreeable," she says.

"The terms."

"And one can't surpass the house, as one can see."

"You could fit a diamond in the yard."

She smiles a little bit.

"A baseball diamond," I say. I lean forward and examine the paned windows carefully. They are newly washed, clear as air. Among them hang the vines of bougainvillaea. "But some people look at houses for other reasons."

"Of course."

"I know of a fellow who's selling his house to buy drugs in South America."

She looks down, touches the flower in her jacket.

"People don't care about an honest living anymore," I say.

She smiles and looks up at me. "They don't," she says. "You're absolutely right. One sees that everywhere now. What line of work are you in, Mr. Gordon?"

I lean against the glassed wall. Outside, violet petals are spinning down beneath the jacarandas. "We're not really from Dallas," I say.

"Oh?"

Through the window I see Jodi come out onto the lawn around the corner of the house. The grass is beautiful. It's green and long like an outfield. Jodi steps up into the middle of it and raises her hands above her head, arches her back like a dancer. She was in a play the first time I ever saw her, stretching like that, onstage in a college auditorium. I was in the audience, wearing a baseball shirt. At intermission I went home and changed my clothes so that I could introduce myself. That was twelve years ago.

"No," I say to the agent. "We're not really from Dallas. We moved outside of Dallas a while back. We live in Highland Park now."

She nods.

"I'm an investor," I say.

The Incorrect Hour
DEBRA SPARK

In the stone house, the clock runs backwards. When Yasmin thinks, "One o'clock, time for lunch," it reads, "Eleven o'clock, wait two hours and you can have breakfast." Everything else appears to be in sequence. The Tuesday newspaper comes on the day after the Monday newspaper. The digits on the calendar increase. In the morning, the sun tickles Yasmin's eyes awake through the east window. Evenings, the sun is where it should be, sitting like a pumpkin on the blue table of the sky.

Yasmin has been living for several months in the home of Ethel Melkney, a silent woman, when suddenly Ethel starts to speak. It is a peculiar thing. Ethel is a peculiar woman. Things in this house, Yasmin thinks, always seem askew. And she is not simply considering the woman's right hip which is jarred so that it seems to be supporting an imaginary laundry basket. Nor is she blaming the woman for her crooked nose. She is not even thinking of the land she is standing on, though that too is defective. She is referring to Ethel's clothes and her mouth.

Whether she intends to go to work or not, Ethel always wears pressed white nurse's uniforms. She is a medical secretary, not a nurse, so the uniform is a convenience, not an absolute requirement. Ethel has two of the stiff white garments and she washes one out every night. The woman's finances, it hardly seems necessary to note, are meager, though her home is on the grounds of an old estate and she eats paté once a week with dinner.

"Old Quiet Ethel," Yasmin writes to Eric in New Haven, "is spindly-armed and wiry-legged. Her mouth is acrid, but her eyes are sweet. I am sorry to say she went on a talking spree this morning. This is unfortunate because it ruins my name for her."

Eric's new job is to watch tapes at the Holocaust archives in New Haven. He is to watch all the films and write down what is in them.

"I'm not sure you want to do that," Yasmin said when he was hired. She is living in a sleepy Connecticut town and looking, half-heartedly, for a place for the two of them to live. For the duration of the summer, she has a job taking photographs for a summer theatre in town.

"Stupid job," Eric tells her.

"I hate your job," she says by way of response.

"Of course, you hate it. We all hate it."

"Of course, of course."

The way Eric has been instructed to do his job is designed to minimize pain. After two hours of viewing the Holocaust videos, Eric and Kyra, who works with him, have to take a break. It is part of the job description. Two hours of viewing and then one-half hour of coffee or tea. They are not permitted to cut their break short *by even five minutes.* Sometimes they go for a walk in New Haven, sometimes they just sit and talk but Yasmin advises against this. Kyra's mother has two red marks on her chest, right above her breasts. A Nazi slashed her there twice with a knife. If they talk, Kyra's voice starts to tremble. When this happens, Eric says he pats her hand but does not hold her. The boss for the project is a woman professor, a friend of the New York architect Eric will go to work for in the fall. She sits in a neighboring room and interviews survivors of the Holocaust. On bad days, she has everyone go home early.

First, they are indexing the events in the films. Later, they will put them together and write a narrative. If an actor is not hired to do the voice-over, Eric may opt to delay his move to be with

Yasmin, so he can do it. The professor thinks his voice, calm and serious, is well suited for the task.

The building that the Holocaust archives is located in is built of proud and private glass. It eschews transparency. Like the most nervous or the most polite of people, it chooses to mirror the appearance of its companions. The neighbors from across the street—a short brick building and a neo-Gothic structure—are encompassed in the building's facade. The weather is part of the building's personality. A grey building is an overcast day. A red building is sunset. Black building: eclipse of the sun, night.

Yasmin looks at Ethel's mouth and thinks, "Ach, American." Puritan ethics seem to gather in the wrinkles of that severe mouth. There, in the left corner are the words, "Lust is evil." A wrinkle, shaped like an S, at her upper lip cautions, "Temperance, restraint." And the right corner of her mouth knows whose side God is on. "God," it says, "God supports the wrinkles of this mouth."

Ethel begins speaking in earnest on a Sunday. Speech begins as it always does. There are sputtering sounds like the sound of a dust-filled needle on an old phonograph record. Then, a cough. A half-formed syllable. Finally, the word.

"Check-book," Ethel croons. She stands in the doorway of Yasmin's bedroom and dangles the item in front of her, as if afraid of contamination.

Yasmin leaps out of bed. She concentrates on the jump. "Like a gazelle," she instructs herself, "cover ground, stretch legs." She wants Ethel to notice, to think, "Yes, grace," instead of "Lazy child, in bed at noon."

"I am *so* sorry. I was paying my bills in the kitchen and must have left it there."

Ethel nods. Yasmin imagines she is thinking filthy words like "young" and "rich" and maybe even, "So this is it. This is how the world works out. In my later years, I have to support myself by having spoiled children clutter the house."

"Well," Yasmin says and pulls a grey robe around her thin, pink nightgown. The elastic has broken off the top and the gown keeps slipping off her shoulders. "I'll go and see if I left anything else down there."

Ethel follows Yasmin down the five stairs and into the kitchen. There is a folding wooden door at the entrance. It makes a loud, scraping sound as Yasmin slides it back to enter. There is quite clearly a rule concerning the opening and closing of this door. But it eludes her! It is part of an order she will never understand. She will leave it open after breakfast and hear Ethel rush down to correct her and close the door. Or she will close it, obediently, thinking, "Oh, I'm terribly good," and hear Ethel sliding it open.

Yasmin finds no more of her belongings in the kitchen. "I think I'll put some water on for tea," she says to Ethel. "Would you like any?"

Ethel shakes her head no, straightens the skirt of her nurse's uniform and says, "Before you, there was Amelia. If I am correct, Amelia came before you."

"How's that?" Yasmin says.

By noon, the light is always too bright in Ethel's kitchen. The room is like a slap of sun, a slap delivered directly to the eyes. The white of the appliances, of the walls and of the table disperse light all over the room. Bits of color intercede only at the window above the sink where there are red, yellow and blue barnyard animals on the curtains.

"I'm sorry," Yasmin says. "Did you say something?"

She is so in the habit of asking Ethel questions that she supposes she has asked her something and then forgotten the query in the lag time between question and response.

"Oh, nothing," Ethel responds and exits the kitchen for her bedroom. When Yasmin turns to the window, the breeze that is stirring the folds of the curtains make it seem as if the barnyard animals are laughing at her.

"What do *you* know?" she asks a blue pig near the hem.

In Ethel's house, the kitchen is considered common ground. The color of the room seems to require a change in behavior. The kitchen is the only room in the house that is not painted yellow. Taken as a whole the house gives the appearance of a confused egg, white in the middle, yolk all around. Usually Yasmin tries to stick to the yolk. One bedroom and the upstairs bathroom have been allotted to her. The living room, downstairs bathroom, other guest bedroom and master bedroom are Ethel's. Of course, the hallways belong to no one but they *feel* like Ethel's, so Yasmin is always running to avoid contact. If she could steer clear of the kitchen, she would be safe, for it is in the kitchen that her words have, over the past months, done their damage. When she is in the bedroom, she bites her pillow and thinks, "Stop driving me and this poor woman crazy with your questions, Cotton Mouth." More than once, she has resolved to be silent, a good lodger who comes and goes quietly, pays her rent and does not ask questions.

Yasmin makes her apologies to Eric rather than Ethel. "Dear Eric," she writes, "I think I bother this woman. I ask too many questions. I cannot seem to leave off."

In response, Eric writes, "If you don't want to talk to her, don't talk to her, I fail to see the problem."

This is just the sort of reasonable comment that makes Yasmin hate Eric.

It is difficult for people at the theatre to figure Yasmin out. Even her looks, compliments of a Scandinavian birth and grooming in a New York girls' school, seem different to Americans. She has the apple dumpling clean looks that are so common in her own country and so admired as beauty in the States. Men at the theatre find her attractive. Women say, "See, that's what Jews look like over there."

For her part, Yasmin thinks that what seems odd may be more than what is just typically Scandinavian. Things have been slightly wrong from the beginning. Her birth was an embarrassing event for all involved. No father was ever named. Whoever the man is, however, he is wealthy. He paid for her education. Now, he deposits two hundred dollars in her checking account each month. It is not a ridiculously high sum but, coupled with her

salary, it makes her comfortable. To a point, Yasmin appreciates
the money. Still, she faults her father for his initial error. It has
worked its way into her—the fact that her existence is somewhat
more accidental than the rest of mankind's and somewhat less
wanted. Frequently, she thinks, "But this is a mistake, I shouldn't
be here." She apologizes for herself too often but then she appears
to blunder on purpose. She knows, for instance, that she should
not press Ethel and yet she chooses to ask her, vacuously, questions about her life and family.

"I am sure," she writes back, "that everyone wants to talk
about their life. It is just a matter of coaxing the words out of her
warm throat, past her leathery lips."

Of course, Yasmin knows this to be entirely untrue.

"Who's Amelia?" Yasmin asks while washing her dishes for the
third time. She is stalling.

"Oh, Amelia," Ethel says, "Amelia was the daughter of Judy
Fabel. Do you know her?"

Yasmin wants conversation. She wants to shriek in gleeful surprise, "Know her? Know her? Why she's my own mother." Anything to keep Ethel talking. Instead she shakes her head.

The fact that Fabel was an actress neither impresses Yasmin nor
does it ring bells in her brain. This is sure conversational defeat,
this admission to a lapse in knowledge of the theatre.

Yasmin shakes her head and says, "Sorry." Her dishes are
cleaner than clean. It is time for an exit.

This is how she leaves: she smiles uncomfortably, she wipes her
damp hands on her black skirt and mumbles the word, "Good-
bye." She walks the length of the kitchen in three very long seconds, she pulls the folding door back with a screech, goes up the
stairs. At the top, she sees Jesus at the Top of the Stairs. It is her
nickname for the crucifixion figure, centrally located in the house.
She looks at it and thinks, "Not me, I'm a Jew and an atheist, I
don't believe in you on two counts, so enough of those disapproving eyes." She brushes past the figure into her bedroom. Even

with the photographs she has hung on the walls, it is not a pretty room.

"Ug-a-lee," Eric whistled the first time he saw it.

"Not that ugly," Yasmin had said, considering the big bed, the chair, dresser and closet. The entire room was the color of cheap mustard.

"Life inside a hotdog bun," Eric remarked.

"Well, you don't sleep here so don't worry about it."

"I don't sleep here?"

As long as she is in a Christian woman's house, Yasmin will agree to a reverence that is respectful, if not pious. She does not, for instance, say, "Oh, Jesus Christ," when she is in the house. No man sleeps with her here. This is not a difficult situation. When Eric visits, they go to the beach then come home late. She puts him in the guest bedroom and says, "Stay." He objects, he licks her face. Yasmin, however, has studied the figure at the top of the stairs long enough to know what is expected of her. It is an American Jesus. This is old-time American morality. Hard work and clean living are expected.

"Why should she care?" Eric had asked.

"It's her house, that's enough. She does not even want me here. I mean, she doesn't want to have to take in boarders."

"I can see that, but what you do shouldn't bother her."

"Goodnight. Kiss me goodnight."

He had licked her face.

"Dis-gusting," she said and closed her bedroom door.

Yasmin cannot remember how she met Eric. She cannot remember the first time she touched him. This bothers her. How could she forget such a thing? Of course, it happened sometime when he was finishing his graduate degree in architecture and she was taking photographs at the local theatre. But when? It is confusing.

She has an early memory of him, but it may be a fiction. She sees Eric and herself walking out of the Holocaust archives. They are arguing, she pushes him and he tosses his blond hair, with a jerk, out of his face and stumbles several feet backward. But she would never do this! She never fights with anyone. True anger frightens her. In her memory, she backs him against the wall of the building and kisses him. It is sunset. She is not holding him, she is *at* him. The building looks lurid. "People," he starts to say, "people will . . ." "See us," Yasmin finishes in her mind but will not free his mouth to let him get the words out.

Sometimes Yasmin imagines that this was the first time she touched him. But this is impossible. She knew him for a long time before he took the job at the Holocaust archives. If Yasmin could remember how she met Eric, she would remember how she was before she knew him. And this, too, she cannot do. It is as if prior to knowing him she had not comported herself to the world in the correct way. Now that she is not in New Haven with him, she feels that she is living in a peripheral town.

Yasmin has a theory about life and living—she will start both tomorrow. This is to say that she lies around in bed a lot. Sometimes she mutters to herself, "So this is what life's like." She is not sure she has a handle on the whole process yet. Life is what is lived by American mothers and fathers, Swedish townspeople, European cityfolk—but she is none of these. What little family she once had, a mother and a grandmother, is gone, and while she does not feel sorry for herself, which is to say she is not burdened by grief, she does miss the instruction in how it is one is supposed to go about living. Her work commands a good price and she shoots fast, makes prints quickly. There are small towns with small theatres throughout the Northeast where she can get work. The photography is an avocation for her, not a passion. Her efficiency leaves her with a great deal of extraneous time during which she wonders whether her life is, in fact, real life or some fake and rarefied version of the genuine article.

Ethel, Yasmin thinks, knows what life is and she is through with it, though life is not yet through with her. Life may go on for another thirty years. The only reason Ethel has any patience with this long epilogue is that she is Christian. Still she opposes life on every front. Speech is kept to a minimum. She has no interest in attracting anyone. She has already married, had children and divorced. That was life and that is over.

What Ethel wants most now is to hit fifty-eight. When she does, she can move out of Connecticut into a retirement community in West Virginia. She will be rich. Her small house will go for almost ten times the amount her husband paid for it years ago. For Ethel, the years go slower rather than faster. She is afraid she will never age the necessary two years and make it to fifty-eight.

On a Thursday evening, Yasmin finally asks, "Did Amelia Fabel board here last summer?"

"Oh, yes," says Ethel. "She was a lovely girl. In the acting part, at the theatre. She was apprentice to someone important. But I can't remember who it . . . oh, yes . . . no, I can't remember who it was, but it was a very famous man."

Often, when Ethel talks to Yasmin, she looks at the refrigerator instead of Yasmin. At times, Yasmin wants to lean over and instruct Ethel in what's what. "Refrigerator," she will say and point at the appropriate object. And, then, kindly, pointing to herself, "Person."

"Yes, such a lovely girl. She really was."

"What's she doing now?" Yasmin likes to think that all the people at the theatre go on to successful careers in New York.

"Poor girl," Ethel says, "she died."

"Oh, my God," Yasmin says. It is an honest slip-of-the-tongue. "What happened?"

"You didn't read about it in the papers? Her mother was a well-known actress. Rich and famous."

"I've never heard the name before you mentioned it."

"Well, it seems," she says, looking briefly at Yasmin and then turning to the refrigerator, "that she fell out of a window."

"A suicide?" Yasmin asks.

"It could have been." She pauses. "It could have been that someone pushed her."

"Oh, that's so ugly. That's awful."

Around Ethel and Yasmin, the earth's crust is giving way. It crumbles for several acres in every direction. The two women are on the Baron's land, though there is no Baron. Years ago, the cellars had been dug and the stones partially laid for a large estate. There was to have been a greenhouse, a manor house, a carriage house, a potter's shed and a barn. Only the potter's shed was completed before stocks and the Baron crashed. Local legend has it that the Baron, deep in worried thought, thrust his hands into his pockets and went for a walk to think about the land he was hollowing out on credit. He ambled for hours till his foot caught on a low-lying log and his body lurched forward. His hands were too deep in his trousers to be pulled out in time to brace himself. A large rock was ahead of him on the walk. The Baron's demise was, quite literally, a fall. Now, the children in the town have named a certain rock which has a deep red ore, running like a giant tumor over the face of the stone, as the deadly rock. The red ore is commonly identified as a stain.

Ethel's house was not meant to have boarders. It was never meant to be a home. It was to have been the potter's shed. The fact that the shed housed, for years, the whole of Ethel's now dispersed family gives one a sense of the grandness of the proposed design for the estate. Surrounding the shed, the earth is striated. It looks as if the demands on the earth's crust were too much, as if the surface was pulled too tight and tore in several spots. There is a deep rectangular hole for the greenhouse, a giant square for the manor house. There are holes for no apparent purpose—perhaps a fountain or a tool shed was meant to be placed on top of the smaller holes. None of the holes in the earth have been taken care of. At night, Yasmin can hear the crash of rocks falling from the sides of the holes where the foundation has given way. Squirrels, rabbits or mere gravity upset them.

"At last," Yasmin breathes jealously in the dark, "they are at the center."

If Ethel and Yasmin have to communicate and there is no prospect of a kitchen encounter in the near future, they deal with each other by bathroom note. They leave three-by-five slips of paper on the right hand side of the bathroom sink. The bathroom notes are letters without salutations, without loving closures. It has to be an "Ethel dash" and a "dash Yasmin." It is important that they have no relationship, sincerely, truly or otherwise. They are never "yours" or "dear." Ethel set the precedent and since Yasmin is young enough to be Ethel's daughter, she feels obliged to follow suit. One day, when Yasmin comes back from the theatre, there is a note that says: *Eric called. Is that your bike in the garage?*

Yasmin assumes that it is her bike in the garage. She takes it every day to work, but she is frequently gone before Ethel. It is possible, though not likely, that Ethel has never seen the bike before. Yasmin goes to check and, yes, it is hers. She goes up to her yellow bedroom and calls Eric.

"What's up?" he says. His call had been a return call.

"Come visit me," she says. "I'm as lonely as any human being deserves to be."

"Oh, I can't. I'm going sky-diving this weekend. I started lessons. Every Saturday."

This will, Yasmin thinks, certainly cut into his weekend visiting time or kill him.

"Why do you want to do that?"

"Oh, Yasmin, it's great. It's such a thrill. I was telling my father the other day about it. There's nothing like it. It's even better than sex."

This is no small statement out of Eric's mouth. Eric thinks sex is the land's offering to atheists, its absolute spiritual fulfillment.

"My father said I was underestimating sex."

"I'm with Pop," Yasmin says.

That night, Ethel says over her toast and tea, "So that's your bike?" Soon, Yasmin has to go shoot a romantic comedy.

"Yes," Yasmin says.

"Would you like some jam?"

Yasmin is touched by the offer. It sounds like kindness.

"No, but thank you for offering."

"Well, I hope you are careful on that bike."

It is a clunker of a bike. A one-speed. She could not go quickly if she tried.

"Oh, I'm careful. It's a wonderful place to ride. This town is, I mean. Not too many hills." Yasmin knows she is frequently stupid when she tries to be sweet. It's as though genuine sympathy and intelligence exclude each other.

"Still, all those cars," Ethel says.

"Hardly any."

"Well, I don't know," Ethel starts slowly. Yasmin sees her head edging toward the refrigerator.

"Sarah was the one before you."

"I thought Amelia was."

"Oh, yes, but before Amelia was Sarah Tayles and she had a terrible accident."

"Yes?"

"A car hit her while she was riding her bike. Right here, in this town. Maybe half a mile from here."

"Was she O.K.?"

Ethel looks up, as if surprised by the question.

"Of course she wasn't."

Eric and Yasmin have a pattern for their weekend visits. After dinner, they go for a long walk on the Baron's land. Then, they go to a beach and make love. By dusk, the beach is deserted.

Eric likes the Baron's land. It appeals to the architect in him. He imagines structures above each hole. The land appeals, too, to the one thought he has had about American history that does not relate to the Second World War. He thinks the stock market, pre-crash, was a modern-day tower of Babel.

Around the hole for the manor house, Yasmin and Eric are considering rooms.

"Here!" Eric shouts from the south side of the hole. "Right here is a parlor with wooden paneling. It is octagonal. No windows. One day you and the Count . . ."

"The Baron, the Baron," Yasmin corrects him.

"Okay, one day you and the Baron are shooting the breeze in the parlor. The Baron, goblet in hand, leans back against the wall and disappears!"

"No!" The two of them are always imagining miserable fates for the Baron.

"And where has the Baron gone to?"

"Don't know."

"Guess," Eric insists.

"Spontaneous combustion."

"No, no."

"He was a mystic but a messy one. He accidentally levitates himself out of the state."

"Good, but no. Sliding doors in those wood panels. A trap room. When he gets bored at a cocktail party, he just has a wall swallow him up. The entire room is made of these mysterious sliding panels. The Baron can become bored on *any wall in the room!*"

"The Baron thinks I am dull?"

"That's not the point."

"I have become a bore."

After considering the manor-house hole, they consider the greenhouse hole and the rock on which the Baron supposedly fell.

"If a Baron," Eric says, "falls in the woods and no one hears him, does he make a sound?"

"No good," says Yasmin. "He left a stain."

After they walk, they go to the beach, which lies a quarter of a mile to the south of Ethel's land. The spot they pick is right where the water hits the sand. "It seems darkest here," Eric says.

"Seaweed," says Yasmin.

At night, the ocean's water is black and unappealing. Neck to neck, chest to breast, thigh to thigh sounds like the slap of the water against the sand. When Yasmin's back arches, Eric puts his wrist with its cold watch at the small of her back. It feels like a sea creature. This is not an altogether pleasant feeling.

Always someone is sinking under.

Monday nights are opening nights at the theatre. Yasmin goes to the opening-night party and shoots patrons with gold snakes running up their arms, actresses sipping wine, producers offering food, drinks, cigarettes to people who look important.

At two in the morning, after a party for the opening of a bedroom farce, she returns home. She is careful as she opens the front door. Walking through the living room, she notices that the kitchen light is on.

"Oh," she jumps as she goes to hit the light.

Ethel is sitting at the kitchen table with a mug of warm milk.

"Oh, you frightened me. You're up late."

"I couldn't sleep so I got out of bed to make this cup of milk." The way Ethel states this it sounds like a question and Yasmin wants to reassure her: "Yes, yes, that's exactly what you did."

"Would you like some? There's plenty in the pot."

"Oh, no . . . well, yes, I would. I haven't had warm milk since I was a kid."

"It's good with a little cinnamon."

Yasmin goes to the stove and pours herself a mug of the milk. It smells good. The heat was lowered just at the point of boiling and the milk has the smell of something that was almost ruined but saved at the last minute.

"These cast parties," Yasmin starts to say as she sits, "these cast parties that I have to shoot are so miserable. Such conspicuous consumption."

"Are they all very rich?" Ethel asks in an angry yet eager manner.

"Well, you know, like most of the people who live here."

Ethel is, in fact, the only person in the town who seems to need money. The want is visible in her demeanor. Sometimes the S-shaped wrinkle at the top of her upper lip will look, to Yasmin, more like a dollar symbol than anything else.

"That's not your style, is it? Though it could be, but it's not."

"No," Yasmin says, "no, it's not."

"You know," Ethel says, and this time she does not look at the refrigerator, "you remind me of a girl who used to live here in the winter. Laura Storey from a good Boston family. She was smart.

A little younger than you. Still in college, though," Ethel smiles, "she was not as well-mannered as you. Too wild and a smoker."

"Her fate?" Yasmin asks. She senses that, for Ethel, the lives of her previous boarders are like practice pieces of knitting. To be pulled out.

"What?"

"And what is she up to now?"

"Well, she's in Boston, last I heard, recuperating from a sledding accident."

"Of course." Ethel does not appear to hear Yasmin's words.

"She was in a tobogganing accident, two towns over. Her leg caught in a tree on the way down and she could not get herself untangled. It was a mess. Her leg snapped over her head and all."

"Of course," Yasmin repeats, "of course." Perhaps Ethel, Yasmin thinks, could do the voice-over for the Holocaust films. She likes to narrate disaster.

It is early Monday morning and Eric is getting set to drive back to New Haven.

"Don't drive yet. You're still too sleepy." Driving scares Yasmin. She doesn't have a license and imagines messy accidents for people who don't have the good sense to use public transportation.

"I'll be fine, I told you."

Destruction, Yasmin knows, has this virtue—unlike love, it is close at hand. It is inevitable, while love is only possible.

In the kitchen, Eric is dressed for work. Yasmin sits on a kitchen chair in her pink nightgown, which she keeps pulling up over her shoulders. She is stirring a bowl of oatmeal for Eric.

"I don't eat breakfast," he says. "I never eat breakfast."

"Neither do I. It's good for you. Come here."

She pulls him over to her and he places his hand under her hair and runs his fingers up and down her neck. His lips follow his hands over her neck, her shoulders. She stops fussing with her nightgown and he starts pushing it down so its pink folds lie in a puddle at her waist and wrists. Eric runs his tongue over her collar bone, across the base of her neck and her chest to her breasts.

There is the harsh, shrill cry of the folding door. "Oh! I . . . ," Ethel says. "You two." Or maybe, "You, too." It is impossible to tell as she puts no inflection in her voice. She slides the kitchen door shut quickly and there is the sound of her feet going quickly up the stairs.

"Oh, this is terrible. This is terrible. Who would know she would be up at this hour." Yasmin is shaking her head. "This is terrible."

Eric is quiet. Yasmin cannot look at him.

"She'll hate me now. Like the others."

"Don't be ridiculous," Eric says and puts his hand back on her neck and leans to breathe hotly in her ear, "Fabel, Tayle, Storey." For her, his words are like faulty revelation. At the moment of understanding their meaning, she understands their falsehood. She knows he wants her to see that Ethel's little horrors are inventions. But the past contains more than three wealthy boarders.

"No," she says, "history."

"No," he says, pulling away, "her-story."

But this is just his version of things. Yasmin suspects that he sits at the Holocaust archives thinking fact to fiction, reality to film. She imagines, and this thought appeals to her, that he will remain at the archives to narrate the films. He will stay there for a long time and when he finally phones to say he is ready to join her, Ethel will say, "You want *who?* Yasmin? Oh, she's gone now." The thought pleases her into confrontation.

"History," she insists and feels giddy. She hears the barnyard animals on the curtains crowing and oinking the word. She hears the clock strike the word as it rings the incorrect hour. She hears a boulder outside fall from its spot in the foundation and strike bottom, echoing the word. Even the earth, it seems, will not bear up under the grievances implied in that word.

Conviction
TAMA JANOWITZ

The eviction notice said I had a week to get my things out. How they could do this to me, Marley Mantello, a sensitive artist and a skinny guy, I couldn't understand. Okay, so I hadn't paid my rent in months: why should I, when there was no heat? But I wasn't about to waste my energy on trivialities such as this. I called up my sister. "I'm moving in with you," I said. "Is that creep husband of yours gone yet?"

"Oh yes," my sister Amaretto said. "He's gone. You know what's strange? After all those years, of him saying he'd kill me if I ever left him, he was the one to go. Just because he thought I was taking too much cocaine. But really, he didn't seem very upset to leave at all."

I told my sister I was sorry about this, though frankly I couldn't even remember what the rat had looked like. But my sister, busy at her studies—for she had dreams that she could pass the medical school entrance boards simply by studying hard—didn't seem in the least bit sad about their break-up. Well, she had always had that ability to discard her previous lives like the skin of a snake and slither on to something new.

Since she didn't put up any protest about my moving in with her, I decided I'd go up there right away, to scout out the situation, so to speak. I wanted to see where I'd put my canvases and paints, where I'd sleep, and so on and so forth. I just shut the door to my place and took the subway uptown.

Amaretto's apartment had basically been stripped bare by her husband. On his way out he managed to walk off with a lot of the antiques. Without much furniture, the place for some reason looked smaller. And my sister had never been much of a housekeeper, her clothes—soiled black lace underwear, Day-Glo green lace socks, a shawl made from strips of leather—were strewn all over the place.

"How are you, Sis?" I said. "Hungry?" She was busy at her desk and didn't look up. So I went into the kitchen and looked in the fridge, where I found nothing but some old paté: canard with orange, I thought. Or maybe it was pork with refried beans. Paté is often hard to determine. Anyway, it smelled okay. I dumped some of it on a piece of French bread and then made myself a cashew-butter sandwich to go alongside.

"You know what, Marley?" my sister said. "I'm really glad you've decided to move in with me. Also, make me one of whatever it is you're eating. I just realized I haven't eaten since last night. I had three jelly donuts."

"Why are you glad I'm moving in with you?" I said suspiciously, for I have always suspected anyone who was too glad to see me.

"Oh, I did something stupid," she said.

"I could have told you that," I said. "What did you do now?"

"Well, I answered an ad—a personal—in the paper," she said.

"Smart girl," I said, sitting on the edge of her desk and handing her a hunk of paté. "What did you do that for?"

"Marley, don't be judgmental," she said. "If you don't want to stay over here to protect me, at least I have Cassie."

Which was true: Rafe had not taken the dog with him. Cassie lay under the desk and tried to make love to my leg. Amaretto handed me a page torn from *The Village Voice.*

WOMEN OF ALL AGES. GET WHAT YOU REALLY
want from a man. 28 year old single male, goodlooking,
seeks same in female for sexual relationship. I am honest
and sincere. If you have not answered an ad before, try this
one. It is sincere.

"You answered this?" I said.

"That and the other one I marked."

> CONSERVATIVE CATHOLIC SWM, 5'7", 127 lbs,
> seeking F with similar attributes and
> philosophy for lasting relationship.

"But Amaretto, you're not Catholic," I said.

"Yes I am," she said. "Remember, I had to when I married Rafe."

"Well, you're not conservative Catholic and you're five foot nine."

"Yeah," she said. "But I figured that guy wouldn't quibble over a few minor points. He put an ad in the paper, he had to be pretty desperate."

My sister had a point. But how could I best relay the information to her that she sorely needed psychiatric help? "Amaretto, you're really sick," I said, "You better see a shrink. Did you give these guys your address or anything?"

"Actually, I did," she said. "I wrote to them and told them my name was Petunia. See, I figured when they called up I'd tell them I charge money for my services. I'm really broke, you know; Rafe didn't give me much money, and if I get into med school it's really going to cost."

"You fool," I said.

"Well, I did change my mind since writing to them," she said. "That's why it would be good to have you around for protection. I don't need their money now, I found a part-time job."

"What kind of job?" I said. Already I was thinking maybe I should fight my eviction notice, and then Amaretto could give up her apartment and move in with me: obviously my sister needed constant supervision.

"I'm going to work for a place called Linda's Phone Fantasies," Amaretto said. From her desk she took out another clipped ad.

> HOT HORNY LADIES
> will help you live out your every fantasy. Linda's Phone
> Fantasies, American
> Express/Visa Charge accepted.

"You actually took a job with this outfit?" I said. Oh, I was furious with her. "I absolutely forbid you to do this!" My stomach was churning around in a rage: I took the cashew-butter sandwich off the plate and bit into it. "Do you really think I'm going to let you sit there in some crummy room with a bunch of girls with Brooklyn and Queens accents filing their nails and jerking strange men off over the telephone?"

"Mmm," she said. She ignored me and picked up one of her Stanley Kaplan Course study books. "Twenty-five bucks an hour, more if I develop my own regular clients. I need the money. Now let me study, I have to take the med entrance exams tomorrow."

"Well goddamn it, take out a student loan or something!" I said. "You really make me sick, with your warped way of thinking." And I stared around me: at the long, narrow living room, almost empty, and my sister sitting hunched at her desk like St. Jerome in his study, only beardless. "Supposing I straighten out this business with my landlord and you move downtown with me?" I said. "Then you wouldn't be paying any rent, things would be easier."

"I like it here," my sister said. "If you want to move in, fine. If not, let me get back to cramming."

Well, where was I going to paint in her tiny apartment? It was a dark, gloomy place: through the dirty windows came a sooty light, nearly edible in appearance, a thin paste seemingly squeezed from a tube. Which led me to think about color, especially the color of light. Newton, as everybody knows, has said that light consists of seven prismatic colors. And if you put these all together, you supposedly get white. This is what the scientists of today all agree upon.

But Goethe, thinking sensibly, said this can't be true. Why? Because every light that has a color is darker than colorless light. He said that white light is simple and homogeneous, and becomes colored only when it is passed through something opaque like cigarette smoke in front of a dark background, or the blue sky, which is only a great amount of atmosphere in front of total darkness.

I would have preferred to believe in Goethe—the painter Turner went for his theory, rather than Newton's. But hell, who was I to disagree with modern science? Not that twentieth century technology had made any lasting imprint on me: if I got stranded on a desert island tomorrow, I wouldn't even be able to reinvent gunpowder, let alone the stereo system.

While I was thinking all this, by accident I kicked the dog under the table, he let out a yelp. "Leave my dog alone!" Amaretto said, without looking up from her book.

"I didn't mean anything by it," I said. "I just can't understand how you messed up so bad: twenty-four years old, in the process of divorce from a nice, if a trifle creepy, kind of guy—and now simultaneously deluding yourself that you'll get into medical school and be able to support yourself by working for a Phone Fantasy sleaze operation."

"Do you remember the time you got all the chihuahuas drunk?" my sister said. We grew up in a house of chihuahuas— my mother supported us by raising and breeding them. What my sister was referring to, I suppose, was the time I swapped the dog's water for vodka, and pretty soon all of them were staggering around the kitchen, thirty drunken chihuahuas. Amaretto cried and cried; I told her the dogs were always going to stay that way.

"I remember," I said. "What are you trying to tell me? That I was a rotten person, who should have done a better job being a brother to you?"

"No," Amaretto said. "That's not what I was thinking. I was just thinking, it's funny how the younger brother or sister always adores the older one so much. I wanted to be exactly like you, but I could never paint pictures, and there was nothing else I could think of doing to impress you. And honestly, you never had anything but contempt for me."

Was this true? I couldn't remember. Maybe she was just nervous about her upcoming test, otherwise she would never have been so cruel. Anyway, I figured I'd go back downtown and pick up some of my things, then I'd bring them back here so I could protect my sister in case one of the lunatics called looking for Petunia. "Come here for a second," I said.

"No," she said, "You're going to spit on me!"

"Amaretto, we're not eight and twelve any more!" I said. "I'm not going to spit on you, I promise. God, you're paranoid. I just want to give you a hug." Which was true: but when she stood up for a minute and made as if to hug me, God help me, I could not help myself, and gave her a few fast nuggies on the head. So maybe she had a point.

"God damn you, Marley," she said.

"Hey, I didn't spit on you, did I?" I said. "Anyway, I'm going to go home and get some things to wear, and some small water-color stuff I can work on here until I get the walls knocked down. Then I'll be able to move the big painting up here." The big painting—the fall of the House of Atreus—was twenty feet long, there was no way I was going to be able to work on it in this cramped apartment unless I tore down the walls between the second bedroom and the living room.

"Knock the walls down?" Amaretto said.

"Don't answer the door for anyone while I'm gone, but give me the keys so I can let myself back in."

"Marley, wait just a minute," my sister said. "Knock the walls down?"

"You said that already. Just give me the keys."

"I may not be here when you get back," she said. "I'm going out for a little while, I'm going to meet Jane for a cup of coffee."

"You better not go out for long," I said. "You have to study, what time is your test tomorrow?"

"Early," she said. Jane was Amaretto's creepiest friend, why she would want to spend time with her I could never figure out. Jane was a woman who used to be a man—a transsexual, now in her forties. Jane had never recovered, apparently, from the sex change—her weight zoomed up and down depending on her mental state. Sometimes Jane was a giant, 250 pound lobster, at others a small, flaccid elderly child. Well, she never appreciated this when I pointed it out to her—old Jane didn't have much of a sense of humor. What never changed about her was her red face; an accident on the part of a dermatologist who had removed the top layer of skin to cleanse and purify, and had walked off with a few layers too many. Why my sister cared for her so, I don't know. With all Jane's problems she was lucky she had found a job selling advertising for a gay men's magazine. She didn't need to work—Jane was fabulously wealthy, and she lived with her parents in their mansion. But how her parents felt about their only son being a woman I never found out. Well, Jane refused to speak to me, and this sort of thing didn't interest Amaretto.

I went back outside and took the subway downtown, thinking of all the paintings that I wanted to paint: the First Astronaut to Meet an Extraterrestrial; the Ode to the Baseball Hero of the Future; the painting of the Raising of Lazarus as an *hommage* to Raphael in honor of his 500th birthday.

But when, a few hours later, I returned to my sister's with some paints and some underwear, she wasn't home. This didn't trouble me, not for a while. It was good for her to go out with her friend, however creepy, so that she didn't worry too much about these med school entrance exams she was going to have to endure the next morning. I didn't think I could stand it if she flunked. Honestly, I could tolerate failure in myself, but in my sister it would have been devastating. She had gotten this idea of going to medical school, why I couldn't figure out. She had never done well in college, in this day and age she had majored in Home Economics, learning to make Jell-O and balance a checkbook, two lessons which didn't help to keep her marriage together.

Anyway, the afternoon dwindled into twilight. I was busily occupied, I got out a hammer and tried to figure out how I could dismantle the wall without forcing the collapse of the entire apartment building. As long as I could get one continuous wall twenty feet long, that I could get back from far enough to look at, I would be fine.

While I was occupied with this pastime, the phone rang. "Is Petunia there?" a low, menacing voice said.

"I don't know any Petunia," I said.

"Petunia," the voice said.

Then I remembered my sister's alias. "My mother can't come to the phone right now," I said. But this didn't discourage him.

"Hey," the voice said. "Petunia said in her letter she wanted to meet me. I'm coming over."

"You come over, I'm calling the cops," I said, and hung up the phone. Well, I knew what would probably happen. You see, I have never thought I had very long to live. Probably I would be tragically murdered. Such is the fate of artists in this world. Look at Gérault, who might have been a truly great artist, but who destroyed himself by the age of thirty-three. And Degas, who lived but who went blind and couldn't even see to paint a picture. Well, it wouldn't surprise me if I was bumped off by a Personal Ad lunatic. Then my work would be of interest, at last, to the critics. And this was what I had always dreaded, for I have always loathed and despised the critics, who to me were the scum of the earth. They would not look at my paintings, but would simply state that Marley Mantello had idolized the past. They would make no attempt to see that my art was a balanced, interesting art that attempted to speak to all and created a personal, universal language.

Because critics spent a lot of time getting money for criticizing, and they preferred it that nobody produce any new creative works. Then they could go on talking about the stuff that was dead and gone, and yakking among themselves, and maybe talking about how criticism was more important than art itself. That way they could feel good about themselves. *They didn't want anything new and original.* So my paintings would be stashed away someplace, like Turner's greatest hits, not to be discovered until years after my death. At which point I would be dead: it wouldn't make any difference to me.

Anyway, the evening passed with no sign of my sister. About seven that night my mother called. She was surprised to hear my voice: she was calling to wish my sister good luck on her exam in the morning, and I told her Amaretto had gone out with Jane and should be back soon. "I'm going to move in with Amaretto, Ma," I said.

"Is something wrong, Marley?" my mother said.

Well, I didn't want to worry her by telling her that I had been evicted and that her daughter was busy answering personal ads in the paper and was about to go to work for a Phone Fantasy joint. Mothers are not equipped for the truth: they live in their own world, concerned with their children getting a balanced diet and receiving enough vitamins; there was no use in telling her life was otherwise. So I merely said that I was frustrated in my work: I should have been getting much more acclaim for what I was doing, the fact that I was being ignored made me unhappy.

"I have heard many people speak of happiness," my mother said. "But I myself have rarely experienced it. Perhaps only for brief seconds, and then only while indulging in fantasy. Or at times I've been happy when it's gone unnoticed—while eating malted milk balls and lying in bed after a rainstorm, for example. And by the time I realized that I was happy, it's too late: I've already returned to that state of normalcy known as misery."

"But Ma, you know, sometimes I think: what if I'm not a great artist? This scares me."

"Marley," my mother said. "In ten years after you're dead, they may say that you're the greatest, but you'll be dead."

"That doesn't make me feel better," I said.

"The truth is, Marley, on your deathbed, looking back, you're not going to get a grade, you're not going to get a mark 'Could Have Done Better.' If you can't have fun along the way, why bother?"

"Forget it, Ma," I said. "There's no use my trying to communicate with you." All I had wanted was a little reassurance: to be told that I was indeed the best artist in the world. Instead, she had to give me her usual lecture. I heard the buzz of the doorbell; maybe it was Amaretto, returning at last, having forgotten her keys. "I have to go," I said.

"I'm not keeping you," my mother said. "By the way, I'm taking up horseback riding again: a woman has offered to trade me her palomino pony for two of the chihuahuas. I think you might come up and repair the old fence by the shed—I'm turning your studio into a stable."

"Yeah yeah," I said. "I'll speak to you soon." And I went to the door. Who or what was on the other side of the chain? A small, mousey creature, practically bald, who I presumed was selling Girl Scout cookies loaded with razor blades, or Fuller brushes. "What do you want?" I said.

"Petunia!" the man said.

"I'm Petunia," I said. "And you know what I'm going to do with you?"

An alarmed look crossed the little geezer's face. "What?" he said.

"I'm going to tie you up to the radiator and leave you there for three days."

The man let out a little squeak. "You lied to me!" he said. "You said in your letter that you were a tall redhead. You answered my ad pretending to be a woman."

"That's right," I said. "What kind of creep would put an ad in the paper saying he's a sincere person looking just for sex? I'm going to tie you up to the radiator and make you drink out of a dish."

"I didn't say that! I said I was a conservative Catholic, you invited me over for coffee at five o'clock!"

"Oh," I said. Well, I did invite him in for a cup of tea; but he acted sulky and went off. Anyway, he wouldn't have been right for my sister—when I looked at my watch I saw it was nearly nine-thirty, the guy was late and hadn't even bothered to call.

I spent the rest of the evening working on my watercolors and attempting to dismantle the living room wall. Finally, around two in the morning, I fell asleep during a rerun of the Mary Tyler Moore Show; Mary was having a fight with Lou Grant. And I didn't wake up until ten o'clock the next day, to the sound of that doorbell.

I went to the door, still in my sleep-ridden state. "Hey, you creep," I said, figuring this one must certainly be the sincere sex-lover. "Get lost! I've got a Doberman pinscher in here, he likes to knock creeps like you onto the floor and rape them!"

"It's me, Marley," my sister said. "You want to let me in, I don't have the keys."

I opened the door. There was Amaretto, bleary-eyed, her hair like a big rat's nest, all snarled on top of her head. "Where have you been?" I said. "You missed your goddamn test, didn't you? What happened, you went out with Jane and took coke again?"

She didn't speak, but ran to the bathroom, where I could hear her brushing her teeth. In this respect my sister was like me: she brushed her teeth as much as seven times a day, we both had this fear that our teeth were going to fall out. Chunks of ivory wiggling loose, bloody gums, and a hatred of dentists, that subspecies of human beings who spend their lives looking into people's mouths.

"This does it," I said. "I was worried sick about you, don't you have any feelings?"

My sister came back into the living room, pulling at her hair with a long pick. "Hi Marley," she said. "Got anything to eat?" I figured I was right, she was indeed stoned or something.

"No," I said. "Nothing to eat."

"You know what?" she said, and burst into giggles. "I got arrested."

"Arrested?" I said. "What for? Jesus Christ, why didn't you call me? Where were you?" It was hard for me to feel compassion for her at that moment: her self-destructiveness rendered me hostile toward her.

"I was in jail overnight until Rafe's lawyer could come and get me out," she said. "That bastard made me wait overnight."

"But why didn't you call me?" I said.

"I could only make one phone call, I knew you didn't have any money, so I called Rafe."

"What happened?" I said. "Not that I'm sure I actually want to know . . ."

"I met Jane, as we planned, and Jane said, listen, you're all wound up from studying, why don't you come over to my house —she lives with her parents in a big house out on Long Island, you know—and take a sauna. So that sounded like a good idea to me, I mean I was just going to go out for the afternoon, it's not that far away—and we got my car out of the garage, and went out there. Anyway, Jane's father has been sick for a long time, and she was depressed and on these happiness pills, and I thought it would do her good for me to spend some time with her."

"Oh yeah," I said. "The blind leading the elephant."

"Anyway, I was taking a sauna with Jane. I really like being friends with her. I feel as comfortable around her as I do with men, but I can joke with her like a girlfriend. She combines the best of male and female, at least to me."

"You would pick a lunatic for a best friend."

"Anyway, Jane got up to take a telephone call. She was gone a long time, and I was half asleep there in the steam. I had nearly nodded off when I heard someone screaming. I guess maybe I really was asleep, for I had no memory of where I was, but when I heard this high, girlish scream, I ran tearing down the hall. Someone was being hurt, or something. I had nothing on but a towel I wrapped around myself. Oddly enough, in my panic I didn't think to find my clothes, I just ran to help. On the way I was congratulating myself—what a fine doctor I'd make, with this immediate, unconscious response in myself."

"Yeah, but now you missed the goddamn test," I said. "Which you probably would have flunked anyway." I was so mad at her that this is what came out of my mouth: not the kindest thing to say.

"The sound was coming from a room with a closed door. I burst in. There was an old man lying on a hospital bed, a tiny man curled up in the fetal position, his mouth open in a cavernous gape. He was all attached to IV tubes. And the room stank. Oh god, I thought, I had walked into the father's sick room. Jane hadn't told me that her father was on the brink of death, just that he was sick. No wonder she didn't want to go home alone. But you know how famous Jane's father is, don't you, Marley?"

"No, how would I know who he is?" I said. "Who is he?"

"Well, he started this huge cosmetics company, back in the thirties. Anyway, he must have made millions from it, though he retired a long time ago when Jane was still in her twenties. Ryder Cosmetics. Next to Revlon, it's one of the biggest companies."

"Never heard of it," I said, though actually I had seen those goddamn ads on the TV, with the slinky girl anointing herself with some perfume that must have smelled like horseshit, judging from the romping white horses in the background.

"Well. I couldn't take my eyes off Mr. Ryder, Marley. His face was all planes and angles, he didn't look like a person—from his throat came this thin, bubbling sound, an inhalation, and then once again that involuntary high scream. I had left the door open behind me and didn't hear the nurse come in.

" 'It's all right,' the nurse said, 'It's just time for him to have some more medication.' She was a little chocolate-colored thing— she smiled at me with white and gold teeth. A wonderful Jamaican accent, sounding like coffee percolating early in the morning. I instantly felt a little calmer. 'Here, just a minute,' she said, paying no attention to the fact that I was only wearing a towel. 'I'll fix him up and then you can say hello. He likes to have visitors.'

"She went over to the bed. 'Don't hurt me, Claire, don't hurt me,' Mr. Ryder said. The nurse gave me a look. 'I'm not Claire, Mr. Ryder,' she said. 'Your wife will be here in a little while. I'm Linda, remember? I'm going to give you your injection now.' But still Mr. Ryder kept whimpering, 'Don't hurt me, Claire, don't hurt me,' until the nurse gave him the shot.

"I felt ashamed that I had raced into the room only to feel totally helpless and sick to my stomach . . . the nurse pulled me over to the side of the bed. 'Mr. Ryder likes to have visitors,' she said, as if Mr. Ryder wasn't there. 'Take his hand now.' I found I was shaking all over; the nurse practically had to force my hand onto his. The hand was emaciated and cold. But his fingers wiggled just for a second. I could see his cold, hard eyes, the lids half closed. And it was as if his hand was his only remaining connection with the world around him, a hand that had been well-cared for, with smooth, polished nails, a clean hand with the vague traces of power still in them. Then his mouth fell open all the way. Maybe because he had no teeth left I was afraid. That horrible black hole, with stubs of ivory like an old lion . . .

"Mr. Ryder wasn't letting go of my hand, finally the nurse pried me loose and took me out into the hallway. I realized then that there was no way I could be a doctor. I just looked at the nurse, so relaxed, such a warm person. She just emanated warmth. And I knew that if I became a doctor, I would always be a cold and businesslike one, hating my patients and afraid of them too.

"I just had to say something to the nurse. 'You must be a great person,' I said. I know this sounds dumb, but she was the sort of person you instantly wanted to say something like that to. 'Are you a full-time private nurse?' I said.

" 'No," she said, 'Just during my vacations, and weekends. The rest of the time I work in a state home.'

" 'You mean to say this is your vacation now, and you're working as a private nurse?'

" 'Well, the state home doesn't pay enough to keep a chicken alive,' she said. 'But I want to work there. It's this way, you see— when I was ten years old my sister was born, she had only one leg and a congenital heart defect that could have been operated on, but my mother didn't have the money. She had to put her in an institute, and that's where she died, no one was looking after her. She was four years old. So I made up my mind then, I was going to work in a state home when I grew up.'

"I didn't have anything to say. If I had had money, I would have given it to the nurse, but she probably would have been insulted. I just knew I wasn't fit to be a doctor, that the only reason I was studying to get into med school was to prove to Rafe that I could be good at something. And the world doesn't need any more doctors like that."

"Aw, Amaretto, you're overreacting," I said. "You'd make a good doctor."

"No," she said. "Anyway, I went into the bathroom and I found a bottle of Dalmains and I took four. Then I told Jane I was going back into the city."

"And you got arrested for drunken driving," I said. "So now what's going to happen to you? They won't let you be a doctor, not with a police record."

"I told you, I'm not going to be a doctor," she said. "I understand now that I'm not cut out to be one. Anyway, I won't have a record, I'll just get a warning on my license provided that I sign up for an alcohol abuse class. They thought I was drunk, they didn't know I was on pills. Anyway, the police officer was very nice. I gave him my phone number."

"That reminds me," I said. "A lot of men have been coming over here looking for you. One, anyway."

"Don't bother me," my sister said, "I have to go lie down now." And she went off into her bedroom. But from there she called out to me, "Marley, would you go out and buy us some stuff to eat? Take ten dollars from my wallet."

What should I be, if not a slave to my sister whom I had always ignored? But on the way to the store I was angry with women—in particular, with my mother and my sister, who had always given me such a hard time and were no doubt helping to shorten my life. Certainly they didn't appreciate my genius. But then I remembered Bach, with his twenty-one screaming children, working and working on into his sixties. His family life could not have been easy.

I stopped off at Gristede's, purchasing ground lamb, canned cheese dip and spaghettini; but when I got back home I went into my sister's room and found she had fallen asleep in a bed full of books. I took the books off the bed and piled them up carefully next to her on the floor. Maybe she would change her mind, she could always take the test at a later date. And I pulled some of her rat-nest hair away from her face, and shut the curtains before going out of the room.

But my sister was not completely passed out. From the other room I heard her weakly speaking. "Marley?"

"What is it?" I said. "Go to sleep."

"Marley? I just wanted to say, I love you."

At this I was very pleased, a sister is not obligated to say such a thing. "But what do you think of my work?" I said.

"It's brilliant," my sister said in a muffle. "I think you're a brilliant painter and a misunderstood genius."

"That's right, baby," I said. "You got it. I tell you what. I'll wake you up in a while and help you study. You can always take another MCAT, you know."

"But Marley," she mumbled. "I really don't want to be a doctor. If there's one thing I can't stand, it's sick people. I was thinking, though, of what I wanted to be. I'm going to study modern dance."

Well, how could I be expected to understand that for my sister this was only the beginning of slipping from one dim fantasy into the next. That for her from now on life was going to be a series of dreams: in some she learned to fly without a plane, others in which she played the piano upside down on the ceiling. How different was it for me, after all, I who merely painted these dreams but understood they were not for the living? I went into the living room and once again began hammering at the walls.

Sparks
SUSAN MINOT

Okay, so I met this guy the other night.

I can just hear Duer saying—if I ever told him—*That's great.*
Can just hear it, all the way from California after he's gone into
the other room and shut the door so she can't hear. I can picture
him exactly—his sneakers up on the desk, wearing shorts, acting
as if he's having a perfectly normal conversation even though it's
me. Out the window are the palm trees they have out there, the
round and bristling kind that look like they've had the living
daylights scared out of them, but he's not looking at them. Instead
he is lifting his shirt, keeping the phone tucked by his chin, to see
if he's getting fat.

Whoever she is anyway.

But the other night I did meet this guy. I don't know. I mean I
didn't know *what.* It got me rattled. He was an actor, okay? with
cheekbones and a chin and this direct soulful gaze and I thought
forget this. Needless to say . . .

The only reason I went in the first place was Stacey. I made
lame excuses. She said, "It's just dinner at Jenny's, Lil," using her
fed-up-sister voice. "You're coming."

Half of Jenny's penthouse is an art gallery. Voices were coming
from the kitchen and we walked in and right off I saw him, this
guy in black pants and boots, talking to Jenny. His hips were at a
certain angle, a curious face. I couldn't look. We gave kisses to
Nita and Lex, smiling with their suntans—Lex had on a faded

green shirt he'd been wearing since high school and around Nita's throat hung her usual gold chain with the charm and the dangling fist. Duer wears a chain, a plain one. Out of the corner of my eye was the guy leaning to look at Jenny's earring, she with her jaw tilted up. His profile was interested—it unnerved me—was he *really* interested? I escaped into the gallery.

The walls were white. In one corner was a fellow covered in chalk. We pretended we weren't aware of each other and looked at the pictures: scowling teenagers with smoke drifting from their mouths. A famous writer, scowling. Trees in Central Park in the dead of winter looking like nerve explosions. New York pictures. One of a girl in an empty bathtub had her giggling, the man's shirt on her unbuttoned all the way down. From what I hear of Duer, he has girls like that, one after another, undoing them like buttons.

We sat on the floor. The only piece of furniture was a square red leather chair and Stacey was in it. The lilac barrettes in her hair matched the lilac colors of her skirt; things on Stacey usually matched. So in walked the guy holding his beer bottle with two fingers, Mr. Casual, strolling in not the least bit self-conscious at all. Stacey was finding out things, like that the fellow with the dust was a carpenter from Brooklyn but a sculptor really. Another fellow in a tie and blazer as if this were a real dinner party had three names. One of them was Pierpont. Jenny had shrugged and said he was just a friend of the family. The actor, it turned out, had just made a movie. Stacey asked him about that. He launched into a detailed plot explanation.

Duer says, "Maybe I'll try the movies," half kidding but really not kidding at all.

"But you can't act."

"You don't have to," he says, meaning he has the looks. We go to the movies a lot—we see the one about the woman psychiatrist who has her own nervous breakdown and after when I'm dissolving again, he says, "I told you we shouldn't have seen that one."

Everyone tilted forward politely, listening. In the middle of the floor like a centerpiece were Stacey's red plastic shoes and during pauses in the conversation we'd look at them. The guy had a lot to say, sitting there with his boots crossed at the ankles, cheerful, clasping his knees. He was talking about his bike being stolen. His face darkened for a moment, then, as fast, became bright again. The carpenter muttered so we could barely hear. "We all get burned," I think he said.

There was one ashtray and I leaned over to it and suddenly the guy is two inches from my face, asking me, close up, "What do you do?" He was good-looking, all right? and it was too obvious. He had this eager, obvious expression. It's trouble when they're handsome, I'm not kidding.

I asked did anyone want another beer and fled to the kitchen.

At a party Duer walks straight up to the best-looking girl and plants himself an inch away from her. Or at a restaurant if he sees a girl going by, he'll bolt out in pursuit, his napkin in his hand. After she disappears, he stops, out of breath in the freezing cold, laughing, tapping his cowboy boots, letting the other girls get a good look at him.

"You could not believe it," Nita was saying and Lex finished her sentence, "There were fifteen bridesmaids." They watched Jenny shake lettuce at the sink; her shorts reached to the backs of her knees.

"You're kidding," Jenny said, not surprised. Jenny acts like everything is perfectly regular.

"Her dress had wings on it," Nita said.

"And there were fifteen ushers." Lex looked at Nita even though he was telling Jenny.

"You are kidding," Jenny said.

"Did her father give her away?" I asked and they all looked uncomfortable. Lex fidgeted with a corkscrew. The guy walked in, swiveling his head as if to ask why there was a dead silence.

"I'm sorry I'm such a black cloud," I say to Duer. He's gotten me out of bed for a walk by the Charles. The world, Spring, is melting. I wear my nightgown under my beige coat and lean on his arm. The breeze bats itself mild over my face, feeling light and heavy at the same time.

"You are not a black cloud," he says.

"Oh I know . . . but I am. I really am a black cloud."

"You're not. Stop saying that."

The river is swollen and moving fast. "Isn't the air something?" I say and tears fill my eyes. Duer's face is close, listening.

"You are not a black cloud," he says after a while.

"But I don't believe . . . in this life . . ." I say and press my mouth against the corduroy of his sleeve to stop it and try to think of other things to say and try to keep breathing.

"To top it off," Nita was saying, fending off Lex at an arm's length. "We had to stay with his old girlfriend."

"We did not *have* to," Lex said, annoyed.

"Well we did."

"She's not even an old girlfriend," he said. "I went out with her when I was fourteen."

"Sixteen more like," Nita said and crossed the kitchen to stand next to Jenny. She watched her chop red peppers.

Lex headed for the door. "Whatever," he said.

Everyone drifted in and out. Stacey made a clatter searching for a pan. I found the beers in the freezer stacked like torpedoes.

The actor was saying to Jenny, "She moved out." He held his bottle at his hip like a pistol and stared angrily, suddenly in a sulk. Jenny nodded, counting napkins.

Duer has no problems whatsoever getting girls. His girlfriends are the types that flirt with waiters, or who will dance with anyone who asks them, looking straight into the other person's eyes as if it were no big deal. Once at Café École a girl comes up to our table, hands Duer a note and leaves without a word. The note has her name and telephone number. He laughs and blushes and cranes out the window to see her cross the street. She's wearing bright red tights. Now, when he calls from California, he'll say, "I met this—ah—person," not daring to say girl to me. "Do I want to hear about it?" I say and wreck the conversation.

The guy had decided to explain his whole love life. He spoke to Jenny but everyone in there was listening. ". . . So wouldn't you think? After three years?"

"Sure," Jenny said matter-of-factly. She was banging a chicken with a wooden club.

"Not her. She won't speak to me."

"At all?" Nita said. This was her favorite topic of conversation, love difficulties.

The guy turned to her gratefully. "Don't you think that's strange?" Nita nodded and thoughtfully began picking at the label of her beer bottle.

Out the window above the sink I could see sluggish pleasure boats way out on the river. The water moved like lead, swirling and thick and opalescent. It was taking a long time to get dark.

"So now I've been going on dates," the guy was saying, "and they are the worst." I wandered out to the terrace where the carpenter was standing in the hot wind. He considered me from under his brow, expecting annoyance. I asked him how he knew Jenny. He'd been to college with her, he said, and now five years later had run into her coming out of a movie.

"Which one?" I asked, figuring I'd seen it.

"University of Montana," he said.

I heard the guy's voice reverberating in the kitchen. Duer always—no, forget it.

* * *

Typical actor—instead of remaining on the roof with the rest of us, he had to climb the water tower. Nita was shrieking at him, shrieking to be up on the roof in the first place. We'd gone up to see the sunset smudged with haze. The actor struck a pose like some swashbuckler, his shirt rippling in the wind. Lex crossed his arms and regarded the guy.

"Why don't you go up?" I asked.

"I'm chicken," he said proudly.

There was no guard wall. At the edge you could look past your toes to the street thirty stories below. Some kids were setting off firecrackers; they broke from a huddle. There were flashes, popping and crackling.

"Lil," Stacey said. I turned around. She was standing in the middle of the roof. "That's not funny," she said.

Jenny was showing the carpenter a pier that had burned for two days. Did you get any smoke? he asked softly. You're not kidding, Jenny said with no surprise in her voice. The guy on the water tower was pretending to fall, giving Nita a complete heart attack. Please! she screamed. I myself was wondering about the girl he mentioned, the one who wouldn't talk to him.

Then it was dark and we were the last ones left up there—me and Mr. Casual—he was chattering away about some book he'd just read, about astronauts and rockets. It was rigorous, he said, made him want to start boxing or something. You know? he said. I sort of nodded. Who was this guy? I could hardly make out his face in the dusk but when he gripped a sooty pipe right near me I could see his hand and something about his hand made me dizzy. Jesus. He told me he ran four miles a day. I wanted to tell him this didn't feel like a normal conversation, to tell him, I'm sorry, I'm not really normal, I'm—

"You're too hard on yourself," Duer says. He's watching himself in the mirror, putting on cologne, using mine.

"Hard on myself?" I give a pathetic laugh. I've got sweaters on and a shawl and around me is a sea of sheets. I haven't moved from bed for three months. It's like being stranded on an island, seasick.

He says maybe I should see the doctor again. "You can't take everything so seriously," he says. He rubs my knee under the covers like absentmindedly polishing a doorknob. Later, when he gets home from night classes, he kisses me and I taste beer.

There was a long thin whistle, then crackling, then way across the water we spotted the fireworks, way over New Jersey, so far away and so quiet, like flint being struck. They burst here and there like dodging artillery fire.

He came close. He leaned against the tar-black wall and his pants blended in. He apologized for being from California. The fireworks were recalling some childhood tragedy, a short circuit with Christmas lights. I pictured the holiday frazzle in the LA sun, he reimagined his own scene, staring off toward the river, his profile inches away in the dark. His mother still lived out there, he said, his voice going louder when he turned, which threw me off. What was that? I reached for the loop of the ladder to steady myself, wanting to explain, I haven't been well. My eyes felt hollow from trying to see in the dark and I stepped down the ladder, silently apologizing, shaky, one rung then the next, you see, I'm not completely—

"Come on," Duer says, long-distance. "You're fine."

When I got to the bathroom I could hear Stacey and Jenny near the record player. "Lil seems fine," Jenny said in her regular voice.

"No," Stacey said, meaning no to something else, "she's much better."

I looked into the mirror to see if I could tell. When I put my fist to my chest, I could feel my heart up close to the skin like an ear up close listening at a door.

The chicken got burnt. "I think it's better that way," said the shy carpenter. The table was out on the terrace, curved glass tubes around the candles. The flames gave everyone animal eyes.

I sat next to him. I know it was brazen of me. I'm sure everyone noticed. I was perfectly nonchalant then suddenly felt utterly stupid, exposed. Not that he wasn't used to it, I'm sure, I'm sure it was perfectly normal for girls to seat themselves brazenly down, squaring their shoulders, settling their laps next to him. I banged my elbow and my fork went flying. Everyone politely ignored it. The actor, my dinner partner now, bent to retrieve it, twisting in his chair so that his black pants brushed against my leg.

"Whoops," he said in this eerie whisper.

The family friend in the tie and blazer, being conversational, said, "Jenny says you're a painter." I must have given him an odd look because he blushed behind his horn-rims. "Aren't you?"

Stacey said, "She is. And if she'd only do it more, she'd be good." Her eyes were warning me, her warning-sister eyes.

My dinner partner's plate was piled high with food. He hadn't touched it because he was talking so much. He cracked a joke. Everyone laughed. Nita kept laughing by leaving her mouth open, closing her eyes, and not making a sound. I was cutting my food. Suddenly he turned his chin my way. "Do you like to go dancing?" he said.

Eat your supper, I wanted to say, or Take me home and make me better, but instead I nodded and looked—I don't know— away.

Across the courtyard was an identical building with identical penthouses. The lights went on in one of them. Everyone hummed and nudged each other like this was going to be good, the window the size of a movie screen. It looked creepy over there, the light a weird topaz, the two people walking with bullet-shaped heads.

"Who is it?" Nita said and she leaned heavily against Lex. As if he'd know.

Jenny was picking cucumbers out of the salad bowl, not at all interested. "It's the bedroom," Lex said, which got even more hushed attention. Stacey had paused to look over her shoulder and her knife and fork were held in suspension over her plate.

Lying in bed, Duer and I can see the red neon sign across the river snaking forward like a fuse, blinking *COCA-COLA*.

He lit my cigarette. Not with a match like a normal person but with a whole candle, lifting it from the jumble of baskets and dishes and glasses, pretty damn suave, so the tube didn't wobble or make a sound. He held it. What could I say to that? How was I to respond?

I wake out of nightmares and Duer puts himself around me, holding my arms down, *Ssshhh,* he says as if he can hear the engine between my ears. Other times there are other sounds: wings flapping, as if a bird were trapped in my skull, or a distant throbbing, someone *else's* heart beating far off.

Mr. Entertainment was telling another story, about a bum in the back of a bus singing at the top of his lungs, booming out a baritone. We heard an imitation of it.

"My brother was a bum for a while," said the carpenter softly. "After his girlfriend left him. He used to sleep in front of church vents."

Stacey looked at me with a face that meant Uh-oh.

Duer isn't the type to worry. After school is out he takes me to Maine. He practically carries me to the car, my hair matted in an old braid, my face swollen. I talk a blue streak asking nonstop questions keeping the conversation going. He answers driving along perfectly normal, staring ahead.

That night in the middle of the night he comes into the bathroom with a towel around his waist.

"What is it?" he whispers. His eyes are in a tortured squint against the light.

I'm in the bathtub with my arms out over the edge, watching my hands dangle. "I think," I start but my voice is like static. I try again.

"What, Lil?" he says, begging, his hand clutching the towel in a fist.

"I think I've blown a fuse," I say.

In the morning on the phone with Stacey, Duer holds my foot in his lap and touches it like testing a peach for bruises. They discuss doctors; Duer looks at my perfectly calm face and his eyes glaze over. My own are as dry as sockets.

It's Stacey who drives me to the hospital. "I just want to rest," I tell her and just saying it makes me start to shake like a car going over potholes. When I finally talk to Duer four days later, I'm standing in the hall at the pay phone. In the background his record player is going pretty loud.

"I'm not supposed to come," he says. "They don't think it's a good idea."

Other patients are hanging around in the corridor trying to eavesdrop. "They don't?" I say.

I hear him bite into something like a carrot. He says he's still going to California for law school. "I know, Duer," I say. As if I've forgotten that. Then I simply don't see him again. The other person who doesn't visit is my father, but he doesn't know what to do either.

Jenny got up. "Prepare yourselves," she said in her deadpan way, "for a surprise dessert."

"Goodie," Nita said, eying Lex like she'd like to eat him.

We carried out the dishes into the bright kitchen. Jenny ordered us, "Get out," waving us away. "Just sit out there and wait."

"Okay, okay," laughed the actor, his hands fluttering up near his ears.

One time that Jenny comes to the hospital with Stacey, she asks me, "Are you getting shock?" Direct question. I've brought her into the bathroom so we can smoke. Her cigarette pack has a bull's eye on it.

"Why, do I look it?"

"No," she says, puffing away, perfectly comfortable leaning against some washroom sink.

"But I have to talk to the doctors," I say. "Which is worse." The doctor wants to know about Duer. He peers down from a height. I look small to him, a wreck. He wants to know—sex, obviously. He wants to know how old I was.

"Fifteen."

"That's quite young isn't it?"

"Maybe."

"What did your parents say?"

"To what?"

He is specifically blunt, trying to shock me. I say, "That was hardly a topic of conversation."

"I see," he says, taking in a distant landscape.

"No," I say. "My father wouldn't ever say anything. He'd let Mum handle it."

"And what did she say?"

She whispers through the crack that it's time for church and Duer freezes under my quilt. She is gentle, a gentle mother, shutting the door. "Did she see me?" he whispers, his face appearing with the covers like a kerchief. His body is a huge lump in the bed and I give him this look. "What do you think?" I say.

I tell the doctor, "Nothing."

"And the time you had that trouble?"

By now I'm sick of this and exhausted. "Which time?" I ask him back.

"What the hell is she doing in there?" Lex said, listening for something in the kitchen.

"Cool your jets," Nita said.

"Patience, patience," muttered the carpenter happily, a little drunk.

The fellow in the tie tried to brighten the conversation. "Has anyone seen the movie about—?"

Then right in my ear this guy started whispering maybe we should all go dancing somewhere or maybe he and I could get a— I looked down and watched his hands pick apart one of the little carnations Jenny had in the vase, his fingers slowly and deliberately shredding the whole thing. Or else, he was saying, I could get your number—

It was too much; I panicked. "What are you doing?" I said, interrupting him and trying to joke like someone else might, pointing to the flower to tease him.

His face jerked away as if he'd been stung and a rash spread down around his eyes and his cheeks went haggard. My own face dropped, idiotic and speechless and ashamed. He had dropped the ruined flower to pick his fingernails and was staring at the rim of his wineglass, thinking of something else entirely.

The blood came roaring up past my ears and darkened my vision. I tried to stand up but the dizziness got worse. Suddenly out of nowhere everyone was roaring and hooting. I gripped the table and managed to push myself up into that loud, mottled air. Something bright flashed in front of me, there was a hissing and gentle flames and Jenny's startled eyes.

I almost knocked her over. She was holding the dessert platter high as if it had taken flight. The baked apples on it started to roll and in my daze I saw one go over the edge and then it thumped, still aflame, like a beanbag onto me. Embers stuck. Everyone shot up and flapped around and batted at it. I couldn't remember the last time I'd been flapped over, much less handled at all so when two hands fastened onto my upper arms I didn't think of what I was saying—with all this trying to stand up, trying to connect, trying to put out sparks—and just exploded with, "Duer—"

I know. But that's what came out.

The hands let go and I was plopped back in my chair. The bustling settled and went quiet. Stacey's face appeared concerned in front of me, looking this way and that, assessing from different angles.

Jenny said, "So much for pommes flambé." She picked up the fallen apple and lobbed it over the terrace wall.

"Did it burn through?" Nita whispered with fascination and her head came close. Over her shoulder I noticed the lights, noticed the city for the first time all night, the dots zigzagging everywhere. There was a yellow glow like you get from a bonfire. Nita's hand hovered over the singed place on my shirt, feeling for heat. In the candlelight Stacey was thoughtfully pressing the base of her wineglass, turning it slightly, adjusting it. Behind her, the tiny lights dazzled, flung like sequins across the dark blocks. In each window, a TV probably, with snowy reception or a radio picking up airwaves, crackling like me, and beside the icebox vent a bowl of cat food set out, waiting. Lex said something about still hoping for the dessert anyway. Jenny brought the coffee cups all shaky across the terrace. In the opposite apartment the lights had gone out and the windows were dark like dark mirrors. It's always seemed odd to me, and wrong, that the lights far away are the ones which sparkle most quickly, flickering, like the currents of the heart, the distant tremblings felt more urgently sometimes than the ones near at hand. The quiet carpenter, hunched, struck a match and held it lingeringly to his cigarette. Jenny spooned out the apples and the hum going around the table was low and appreciative. Then he—the guy—got up.

He was leaving. His metal chair scratched the brick when he pushed it back and he stood up, preparing to go. I didn't look. His hands pressed the back of his chair. "I wish I could stay," he lied, "but I have to be heading." He switched boots. "Time to hit the road." Some cowboy pulling out of town.

There was a sigh and everybody's shoulders rose up a little. No one wanted him to go. *Awwww,* they said. For an instant he looked as if he might change his mind, reclaim his chair, have another beer to please his audience or maybe a little more—he took in all the rosy faces—wine. Seeing mine no doubt decided him. To protect myself against further shock, I was concentrating all my attention on a flame's stray flirtation with a mild draft. So he left.

I reached for Stacey's lit cigarette, the rattle mounting again, took a second nervous drag then looked for one of my own, knowing I'd done wrong again and sorry. I went for the candle which, despite the glass tube had—served me right—gone out.

I sank back exhausted and inside the apartment heard the elevator humming down. I fumbled the cigarette at my lips, quite ashamed of myself when suddenly there was a mild glow from all these matches being struck and all these arms came forward, each cupping a tiny flame. They'd been there all along and were only waiting—five, even six—so all I had to do whether I deserved it or not was to lean forward into their light, my cheeks ablaze, and take my pick.

Last Night

DENNIS McFARLAND

Since her divorce, my wife's younger sister Sharon has conducted a two-year death march through three different men. The first was a druggie type with a motorcycle, a man who was about as jaded as you can be and still get out of bed in the mornings. The second was more decent, but scarred from a failed marriage of his own; he had difficulty with the smallest decisions, and would occasionally disappear for two and three weeks at a time, turning up later with a fresh suntan. Then came Howard, a deeply disturbed painter whom Sharon met in a jazz loft somewhere near the Lincoln Tunnel. Sharon once told my wife Marilyn that she and Howard were extraordinary in bed together; this may be true, but it seemed that each time we saw the two of them, they were exchanging hateful glances across a room.

Last night, Marilyn and I went to the theater and stopped in afterward at a place near the shipyards in the Heights, a wharfy-looking pub with planked floors and rusty lanterns on the tables. We had Fiore with us, a friend of Marilyn's, a very tall, good-looking man who runs a ticket agency in town; Fiore had gotten us the tickets. I wish we had chosen a different bar. This one was a neighborhood spot we go to often, and Howard, the disturbed painter, was sitting at a big round table near the front door.

Howard's face is dispiriting to me. There's something reptilian about the man's mouth, and about the way his eyes hold still for long periods of time, then dart back and forth mechanically for no reason. He sat with a noisy group of people, and to his immediate left was a black girl with her hair in about a thousand braids and with bright, red-painted lips. Marilyn and Fiore walked in ahead of me, apparently not noticing Howard, and momentarily, I hoped I could get by, too. But already Howard had grabbed my arm.

Without a word, he held out both upturned palms to me, an invitation to slap hands. It was all the more rankling of him to try this chummy tactic since he knew very well that I didn't like him. Before I could say anything, the girl next to him reached for the collar of my shirt, pulled me forward, and planted a juicy, lip-sticky kiss on my mouth. I felt the tip of her tongue on my lower lip as I drew away.

"Do I know you?" I asked her.

"I don't *care,*" she cried—a statement that didn't seem intended solely as an answer to my question.

"Don't pay any attention to her," Howard said. "It's been snowing in here all night."

This was Howard's way of letting me know they'd been doing cocaine. He stood and walked partway with me through the bar. He asked if Sharon was with us.

"No," I said. "We haven't seen Sharon in over a week."

"Are you sure she's not with you?" he asked.

"I think I'd know if she were," I said and began looking around for Marilyn and Fiore.

"She's supposed to be meeting me here for a drink," he said.

I repeated that I hadn't seen her, and Howard blinked his eyes several times as if he were trying to clear his vision. "She'll turn up," he said and returned to his table.

Marilyn was waving to me from a corner near the stairs that led to the basement of the place, where there were restrooms and telephones. As I reached the table, Fiore got up and headed for the jukebox, jingling coins in his hand.

"I know," Marilyn said as I sat down. "Howard. I saw. Who's the kisser?"

"I haven't the slightest idea," I said. "Guess who's meeting Howard here any minute for a drink?"

"Not Sharon . . ." Marilyn said. "Now I know I'm having a martini."

We understood that Sharon had broken off with Howard some three weeks earlier. Sharon had been out twice during that time with Fiore, whom she'd met one night at our place. I liked the idea of Sharon and Fiore together. Fiore has a feminine side that I thought would be good for her. All the others, including her ex-husband, burnt out as they were, were breast beaters and swaggerers. Three weeks ago, when Sharon supposedly broke off with Howard, we learned that he'd hit her in the face. Sharon was the first to say he hadn't hit her badly. Only blacked an eye and caused her cheek to swell to the size of a softball.

When Fiore returned from the jukebox, he put his hands on the tabletop and said, "What are we drinking?"

"Lots," Marilyn said. "As much as we possibly can."

I knew what she was feeling. We'd hoped to relax, and now, added to our disappointment over Sharon's still seeing Howard was the fact that Fiore was with us. I asked them to order me a beer, said I would be right back, and went downstairs to the telephones. I dialed Sharon's number and let it ring eight times. I'm not sure what I would have said had she answered. Just that we were there . . . had Fiore with us . . . maybe we should go somewhere else. But of course we could have done that anyway; there were two or three other places nearby. I think that sometimes, when you're able to predict trouble, there's a perverse curiosity to see if you've predicted correctly.

When I went back upstairs, Sharon was standing at our table, wearing a pea coat and a long skirt. She had her hair piled on top of her head in a messy way, and she looked beautiful. Sharon *is* beautiful, the kind of woman who, as Marilyn says, doesn't have to try. Marilyn says this despite the fact that their physical features are very similar; but not since our college days has Marilyn dressed the way Sharon does now. Sharon always gives you the feeling she's playing everything down. She always moves languidly. Marilyn once said that nothing good would ever happen to Sharon as long as she went around with "that black cloud over her head." What she meant is that Sharon is without hope—that two minutes into a conversation with her, surrender creeps into each sentence. The languor that's initially attractive turns to lethargy, a kind of dullness you sometimes see on the faces of unhappy teenagers. Sharon will soon be thirty.

As I rounded our table, she's just kissed Fiore, and I could tell from the way her eyes lingered on him that she was glad to see him. She hugged me and said into my ear, "Don't say it. I know."

"I wasn't going to say anything."

"Marilyn's already told me you ran into Howard," she said. "It's only a drink. It means nothing."

"You don't have to justify anything to us," Marilyn said, and for a second, I thought she meant it.

"Yes, I do," Sharon said.

At that moment, all of us, including Fiore, turned and looked across the room at Howard's table; he was craning his neck, staring in our direction.

"I have to go over there," Sharon said. "I wish I'd known you all were here."

I smiled and nodded, watched her walk through the bar, her hands in her coat pockets. Marilyn pulled gently on my sleeve. "Sit down," she said. "Your beer's getting warm."

"It's awful to feel so disapproving," I said. "To be made to feel it."

"Believe me," Marilyn said, "it's worse for her."

We both looked at Fiore, who crossed himself, Catholic-style, shrugged his shoulders, and downed his drink.

Fiore had ordered another round, our third. Marilyn was getting more and more animated. She and Fiore were—of all things —exchanging ghost stories. It was like being at camp. I excused myself and went downstairs again, this time to the restroom.

As I started back up the stairs, Sharon was coming down. She put her arms around me, resting her head on my shoulder while standing on a step higher than mine. We stood there for a minute in silence, and I thought of the night she introduced us to Howard. It was in October, after the weather had turned cool, but before it had turned cold. We'd driven to the beach together, which was a dumb idea; not only did the wind at the beach cut to the bone, but once we were there, no one talked much. A tall wire fence stood at one end of the beach, a boundary line for a beach-front nursing home. Sharon and Howard had strolled some two hundred yards ahead of us. The moon was almost full, and as we approached the fence, we saw the two of them kissing. Howard had Sharon pinned with her back against the fence. He stood before her, not with his arms around her, but with his hands on either side of her head, fingers locked into the wire of the fence. It was erotic and untender enough to make Marilyn call to them before we got any closer: "Hey, you guys—we're both freezing!"

Another night, some weeks later, when we had Sharon and Howard to dinner, Sharon left the dining room where we all sat talking, and after some time, I began to miss her. When I went looking for her, I found her in our bedroom, sitting on the window seat with her legs crossed. She hadn't turned on a light, but there was snow in the garden, and she was silhouetted by the white glow in the window behind her. When I asked Sharon what she was doing, she straightened the pillows in the window seat, looked around the nearly dark room, and said, "It's so pretty in here, isn't it? Even when we were girls, sharing a bedroom at home—somehow, Marilyn's side of the room always looked better."

I asked her the same question now, on the stairs at the bar, as she leaned her full weight against me: "What are you doing?" I whispered.

"How can you love such a crazy person?" she said, pressing her cheek against mine. At first I thought she meant Marilyn, because Marilyn was being loony upstairs with the ghost stories, but I realized that she meant herself.

"Because I don't meet any sane ones," I said.

She lifted her head, leaning back far enough to look at me. "Things are going to change," she said. "I know it."

It was a child's voice, made timid by both a need to believe and a need to convince. She released me and continued down the stairs.

We didn't leave the bar when we first started to, because just as Marilyn was wrapping a blue cashmere scarf around her neck, Sharon showed up at our table and sat in the chair next to Fiore. "Are you going already?" she asked.

"No," Marilyn said. "My neck was just getting cold." It was stifling in the bar; sometimes Marilyn isn't as funny as she thinks she is. "What did you tell Howard?" she asked Sharon.

"I just said I was going to sit at your table for a few minutes," Sharon answered. "He doesn't mind. He's having fun."

"He doesn't look it," Marilyn said.

Following Marilyn's gaze, I turned and saw that Howard had left his table and stood at the far end of the bar, his forearms resting against the bar rail. He seemed fixated on something in the grain of the wood. At first, he was hanging his head, then, his shoulders still hunched, he glanced blankly around the room. I gave Marilyn a look, a warning to let up.

"If you want to know the truth," Sharon said, "he's a little depressed tonight. Which is why I met him for a drink."

"Oh," Marilyn said, crossing her legs. I'm pretty sure she had some comment ready about depression and brutality, and she would have said it had I not been glaring at her. She had an impatient, almost spiteful look in her eye—a look I'd noticed more and more frequently when she was around Sharon. Since the divorce, Sharon has visited us often, and poured out the details of the messes she's gotten herself into; quite some time ago, I sensed a gradual withdrawal on Marilyn's part. When Sharon would come to dinner, Marilyn would clear the table and spend the better part of the evening washing the dishes and cleaning the kitchen—a thing she hates doing. And soon after Sharon took up with Howard, Marilyn withdrew further and became only barely friendly. I don't know the particulars, but I think she and Sharon had one of those arguments that seems to be about one thing and is really about another. I wasn't there, at Sharon's apartment, the afternoon it happened; all Marilyn told me at the time was that

Sharon had become unreasonable because Marilyn didn't care for the painting of Howard's hung over the mantel.

At our table, Sharon soon turned all her attention on Fiore. They angled their chairs slightly away from the table, and before long they were leaning their heads close together, talking quietly. I overheard Fiore say ". . . thirty dollars a plate and we had to soothe the ego of the maître d' besides," and then he leaned back in his chair and laughed so loud that I turned and looked toward Howard. Howard's attention, like half the people's at the bar, was directed at our table.

When it seemed that, under the table, Sharon had placed a hand on Fiore's knee, Marilyn said, "Well—I think I'll go downstairs and powder my body."

As she rose from her chair, she leaned over and said to me, "I want to get out of here. I don't like this one bit."

After she went downstairs I felt awkward sitting there, ignored by Sharon and Fiore. I went to the bar and ordered a last beer from the bartender. In less than a minute Howard was at my elbow. His face was miserable, blotchy-looking, slits for eyes. I don't know what he was drinking, but the glass he banged on the bar was half full of something straight, no ice.

"I know she doesn't give a damn about me," he said, "but I never thought she'd rub my nose in it like this."

"If you know that, you shouldn't see her anymore," I said. I might as well have quoted Howard the Pythagorean theorem.

"If she wants to pick up guys I can't stop her," he said. "But why does she have to do it right under my fucking nose?"

I hated to, but I felt sorry for him. His faculties didn't seem sufficiently intact to perceive the obvious—at least that Fiore was a friend of ours, had arrived with us. I said, "Look, Howard, Sharon's not picking up anyone. This is really none of my business, but I think you should know that he's a friend of ours and someone Sharon's already been out with a couple of times."

This was not a good move on my part. I'd thought it might help him to know that Sharon hadn't simply strolled through the bar and lit on the first good-looking man she saw. But the part of this that had sunk in was the last part, the part I should have withheld.

He gulped his drink. "I feel like busting a chair over her head is what I feel like doing."

"Where would that get you?" I said.

"It wouldn't be wrong," he said. "What she's doing is worse."

Marilyn was back at the table, peering in our direction. "We're going to leave now," I said to Howard, "and I think you should, too."

The look he gave me then was utterly vacant—the same look Marilyn had once described as "out there where the buses don't run." I left the bar and returned to the others. At the table I said quietly to Sharon, "I think you should go. Howard's angry and I don't like the things he's been saying to me at the bar."

Sharon stood. Marilyn was next to her, and I faced them both. Marilyn dropped one of her blue cashmere gloves to the floor, I bent to retrieve it, and just as I straightened up, Sharon suddenly fell forward against my chest. A figure quickly disappeared down the stairs to my left and behind me. I should have known instantly, but it wasn't until Sharon said softly, "Howard," that I understood what had happened: He'd clipped her with his shoulder on his way to the restroom.

I went to Howard's table, where the black girl was now sprawled with her back against a man's stomach, her eyes closed. I found Sharon's pea coat and brought it to her. "Get out of here," I said. "Before he comes back. Get in your car and go home."

She took the coat, sliding from under the arm Marilyn had put around her, and started for the door.

I asked Marilyn, who was already gathering her hat and scarf from the table, to bring my jacket. "I'm going to make sure she gets out," I said. I noticed Fiore still sitting in his chair, looking as if he were in a daze.

When I reached the vestibule at the bar entrance, Sharon stood there dropping coins into a cigarette machine. "I'm just getting cigarettes," she said.

I pulled her hand away from the machine. "Go," I said. "I'll *bring* you cigarettes. Get out of here now."

"I'm only—" she started to say, and I felt something brush my shoulder from behind. This time Howard had shoved her hard against the door, which flew open, and we were all three on the sidewalk outside.

The next four or five minutes went by very quickly, and this is less an account of what happened than what was perceived: My hands on Howard's shoulders, shoving him to the pavement. Sharon's scream. Howard, flat on his back in the street, legs scrambling over the curb. Sharon in her car, staring at me through the windshield, then bent over the steering wheel, sobbing. My own words: "If you don't start the car and get out of here now I'll—" Knuckles cutting up one side of my nose. Heat spreading through my face, both my ears popping. A ship in the harbor, sounding its fog horn. Lines of light—streetlamps—sideways across my vision. Howard, pounding on the roof of the car, then kicking the fender as it pulled away from the curb, chasing after it, shouting at it as Sharon made a U-turn and drove away.

I heard Marilyn's voice. "My God," she said, pressing a handkerchief against my upper lip. Fiore was standing on the sidewalk behind her. I turned and saw Howard on the other side of the wide street, walking away, head hung down, weaving side to side a bit, bawling. A blinking neon sign over a closed delicatessen lit him red, then he disappeared around a dark corner, toward the bridge, the opposite direction from Sharon's.

A few feet away from me, a cab pulled to the curb. Marilyn was holding the door for Fiore. I walked to the cab, and as Fiore climbed in, bending his long legs behind the front seat, he said, "Let joy be unconfined. Let there be dancing in the streets, drinking in the saloons, and necking in the parlors."

I recognized the quotation from "A Night at the Opera," and I suddenly hated him. He now seemed effete to me, willowy. As the cab left, Marilyn said, "Well, I guess *he* won't be seeing her again."

"Just get the car," I said. "I think my nose is broken."

"We should go to the hospital," Marilyn said.

"We have to go to Sharon's first," I said, leaning into the center of the car, turning the rearview mirror so I could get a look at my nose. Already, it was approaching the size of a small avocado.

When we reached the corner of Sharon's street, Marilyn pulled the car to the curb and stopped. "I don't think I can do this," she said. "I'm afraid of what I might say."

"You have to," I said. "She needs us."

"She needs you, you mean," Marilyn said. "She doesn't need me. I can't feel any sympathy anymore. After tonight, I'm really finished. There's nothing more I can do. I'm not sure there's anything anyone can do. What have you really accomplished tonight? Besides getting your face smashed?"

When she said "face smashed" the whole upper half of my skull began to throb. I looked at her and said, "I don't know."

One thing about Marilyn: When you refuse to argue with her, she'll most often argue with herself. A slightly guilty look crossed her face, she shrugged her shoulders, and said, "Well—at least it must have felt good to punch him."

I smiled, which hurt.

"I didn't punch him," I said. "I only pushed him, and it didn't feel all that good."

Marilyn reached toward my face, as if she were going to touch me, then thought better of it, and put her hand back on the steering wheel. "That's the sad part," she said. "Nobody gets to feel good."

She put the car in gear and turned the corner. The bare trees on Sharon's block, lit by the pink light of the streetlamps, cast quivering, crosshatched shadows over everything. As we drove slowly down the street, I thought of something my father had once said to me when I was a teenager—that busybodies are people whose hearts are usually in the right place and whose noses seldom are.

Sharon's car was parked in front of her building. She was still in it, resting her head against the steering wheel. As Marilyn backed into a space some four cars away, on the opposite side of the street, our lights fell across her car, and she lifted her head. She got out and walked down the middle of the street to us. She kept her head down. I heard her boots on the pavement. She went to Marilyn's side of the car, and Marilyn rolled down the window.

"Please go home," Sharon said. "I want you both to know that I'll never see him again. I want you to know that. But now I want to be by myself."

She pulled her coat tightly together, crossed her arms over it, and walked across the street. Without once looking back, she went to her door, opened it, and was quickly inside.

Marilyn stared at Sharon's building. We were both stunned by this abrupt ending. Marilyn looked at me and said, "She'll probably call you tomorrow." Then she added, more softly, "I know she will."

"You're more concerned about me than you are about her," I said.

"You're my husband," she said, angling the car out of the parking space. "I have a sense of priorities even if you don't."

Marilyn said this rather coldly, but I could see, even in profile, a kind of hopelessness on her face. As we drove past Sharon's building, a light went on inside her apartment—in a window on the second floor—then went off.

Out our bedroom window, the sky was dimly lit, blanketed with nearly white, shapeless clouds, cold and diffuse, dulling all colors in the room. I sat in the window seat and saw a huge bird—an owl, I think—fly from our neighbor's mulberry tree, up, over, and behind the wall of the nearby schoolyard. In this light, our privet hedge looked frozen, smooth and gray on top, as if you could skate on it. I heard Marilyn's breathing from the bed where she lay sleeping a few feet away. I went into the bathroom and found the small white envelope of codeine tablets they'd given me at the hospital. I swallowed another of them, and as I returned to the bedroom, I glanced at Marilyn; she lay on her back, her hair strewn wildly on the pillow beneath her head, and I was struck—

as I have been from time to time—by the resemblance between her and Sharon.

I recalled the fragile look on Sharon's face when, earlier, standing with her arms around me on the stairs at the bar, she told me that things were going to change. And I recalled a time, long ago, when Marilyn and I had rented a small house on the Jersey shore, and Sharon visited us just weeks after her divorce. We spent the day at the beach, swimming in the nearly too-cold water and playing backgammon in the sand. In the late afternoon, after Sharon had lost at backgammon, repeatedly, to both Marilyn and me, she sauntered rather morosely toward the water. Marilyn and I continued playing, and after a few minutes, I heard Sharon's scream. I leapt from the sand and ran into the water, swam to the spot, chest-deep, where Sharon struggled to gain her footing; "Help me," she said, and I caught her up, one arm behind her neck, the other in the bend of her knees, and floated her into the shallow water near the surf. She was crying, real tears, when I put her down. She'd been stung, badly enough to raise a considerable welt on her thigh, by a jellyfish, though by evening, all evidence of the injury had disappeared. Back at the house, sunburned and thirsty, we finished off most of a bottle of gin during and after dinner. There were meteor showers that night, and late, after eleven, we went outside and lay on the cool grass of the lawn behind the house. We cried out at the lengthy, most brilliant shooting stars like children at a display of fireworks. Afterward, when we'd gone to bed, when Marilyn and I were making love, I looked into her face, and Sharon passed through my mind: Sharon, in the water, saying, "Help me. . . ."

Looking at Marilyn now, I thought how different these two women were from each other, and how their physical resemblance seemed to heighten this difference. I went to the bed and got in under the covers beside her. She stirred, rolled onto her side, facing me; drowsily, she whispered, "Can't you sleep?"

"I only half tried," I answered.

After a moment of silence, I whispered, "Do you suppose it's possible that we have owls in Brooklyn Heights?"

She opened her eyes for a second, then closed them and said, "No." Then, as an afterthought, she added, "Did you see one?"

"I think so," I said.

"Well," she said, her eyes still closed. "Maybe . . . I suppose anything's possible."

And I supposed that anything was. Possible, I supposed, that Sharon's life would change, as she predicted on those dark stairs last night. Possible, too, that I was not in love with my wife's sister, but only attracted to her desperation, to her obvious need. Marilyn moved closer to me now, in bed, and we held each other until the room was almost bright.

In Christ There Is No East or West

KENT NUSSEY

In California they come at you on their bicycles, the white-shirted boys with their ties flying over their shoulders: Mormons or Jehovah's Witnesses or Young Republicans for Christ. I'm walking down a narrow suburban sidewalk, between the palm trees and the rock gardens, when they come at me from the street. Their eyes are beads of black light set in pink masks, American cupid faces, round and blemishless and perfectly naked.

"Hello there!" one shouts, like a war cry, and they shoot around me, one on either side in a slap of sharp air and light.

For a moment I stand and watch them pedal away. I take a step, and another, and I'm walking again, toward home on the dark side of town. These young missionaries have ridden their bikes from the bad heart of my neighborhood where they spend their days. They see it unraveling from month to month. They thrill in the absolute proof of God's plan, history's inevitable slide. They do not believe in gentrification or government aid. Instead, these boys laugh at the citizens whose indifference has handed them the power. They are the stumbling block that was not seen. Tonight, in a clean motel, they will sleep on the lulling hum of a tremendous power, on the certainty of their stock in a great destructive machine and their status in what comes next.

Home, I smoke a cigarette on the back porch which I share with the college girl next door. Our kitchen doors are side by side. We enjoy living on the second floor, above the dust and rowdiness of the street. Liz regards me as a kindly but eccentric uncle or older brother. Her comings and goings are refreshing to me. She is busy and intelligent, a dark blonde who wears men's T-shirts and unfashionably tattered jeans. She understands music. She reads Camus and Cyril Connolly and loves the idea of culture's richest veins opening for her here, in the midst of these squalid facts. Our building, for instance, is a four-unit stucco affair surrounded by half a dozen trees gone rank and jungly; between the road and the front entrance there is no lawn, only weeds and old newspapers and the dank carpet of dead things from the trees. The building faces a long, yellow complex of garden apartments inhabited by illegal aliens and bikers. The street is lined with abandoned cars up on blocks and overflowing dumpsters. On weekends Liz rushes up and down the back stairs with cameras around her neck and skinny, half-frightened university boys in tow. She says she came here to escape the high rents, but I wonder: she drives a brand-new Saab, white as a scoop of ice cream, and once a month she flies to Los Angeles.

What happens on the street interests her. She isn't afraid.

And despite all this unsavoriness, our back porch is not a bad place to be on an autumn evening. The moon catches between ragged eucalyptus branches; the cold menthol air carries the muffled roar of coastal traffic and the classical music on Liz's stereo. I'm grateful for her healthy presence after the hysterical couple that lived there last year. The woman moved out after the police took her husband away in handcuffs. That was on Christmas day. Jessica was with me then; we were eating turkey when the cruisers pulled up outside. We saw everything from the front window, with wineglasses in our hands.

I snub out my cigarette on the plank railing and knock on Liz's door. The music, Mahler or Brahms, is loud and she doesn't hear me. For a minute I wait, then go inside my place, turning off lights and undressing as I move toward the bathroom. There I draw a hot bath and lower myself into the tub. For an hour I soak in the dark. I light another cigarette and watch the vague smoke rise with the steam. My mind is stuck in neutral and my body is falling away.

I hear myself snoring lightly through clenched lips. The cigarette is drooping and I start awake when hot ashes hiss in the water around my neck. In the steamy dark I get out and towel off. I pull on a sweatshirt and boxer shorts and walk from room to room turning on lights. I sit at the portable typewriter and start a letter to my father. He lives in another part of the country. Mostly, this is helpful, but sometimes I'd like to see him, if only to remind myself of who I am.

As I type I notice that my fingernails need clipping; they're growing like crazy these days. Toenails, too. My body is a cosmos out of control, an ecosystem in anarchy; its chaos intersects and coincides with the confusion of our planet. It puts me in mind of the question I asked in seminary school: Is apocalypse personal or historical? The professor, a man renowned for his randy jokes and unoriginal thinking, replied, "Both, but that doesn't stop the world from starting over again."

> Dear Dad:
> Thanks for the cognac and playing cards. How did you know? I read the Emerson piece you suggested, the one about the Transparent Eyeball. Damn good. Highly excellent. I couldn't find the Johnny Hodges record but I came across an Art Pepper reissue that is truly fine. Did you see the Rangers beat the BlackHawks in Chicago? That goalie is a miracle, smooth as oil. I saw the last period at the bar. Still no work, but I'm playing better than ever. Don't forget what we talked about your checks and call me collect next month.
>
> Your son,
Vincent

As I seal the envelope I realize that I'm wearing my father's underwear, hand-me-down shorts with little red scimitars and swastikas across the waistband. This cheers me and I go to the kitchen for the cognac that came UPS two days ago. Already the bottle is half empty, but I fill the bottom of a tumbler and toast my father, who has all his marbles and gets thrown out of nursing homes for practicing the clarinet and riling his cronies with talk about Gray Power and sex after seventy. He is a liberal of the old school and will not allow his heart to be broken by donzels and fools. He did not discourage my theological ambition, but clearly my father was pleased when I went back to the trombone.

"There's still a place in this country for a sharp bop trombonist," he said.

I don't believe this, but still, I play.

I toss off the cognac and step outside again. All's still next door. I knock briskly and this time she opens, smiling and blinking as if she's never seen me in my boxers before.

"There you are," says Liz. "How was the audition?"

"Fine, but these people want someone to fill in the spaces. They want sandwich sound. Anybody can do it. They know I'd be tempted to show off if I got the job."

She opens the fridge and hands me a bottle of beer.

I say, "Thanks. Could I borrow those piano concertos?"

"Concerti," she says. "Sure, but the recording isn't great."

We wander into her living room. Its primary furnishings are a spineless couch and a wicker armchair. A string of tiny blinking lights hangs from the ceiling, sparkling across posters of foreign cities and Diane Arbus photographs.

"Your posters are better than mine," I say.

"Here it is," she says, handing me the album. "Take these, too." And she hands me two more. I look at the jackets: *Einstein on the Beach* and a spanking-new press of Beethoven's sonatas with Emanuel Ax and Yo Yo Ma. Liz's taste and knowledge are astonishing. Her blood is rich with culture. It seems to promote her complexion and the sunny burnish of her hair. She is twenty-one and I am thirty-four. We are on opposite ends of the supply and demand. She takes photographs and buys records. I play trombone all day. She says she can hear it through the walls.

She flashes a magazine in front of me and says, "I've been

reading this article on the eugenics cult of the first half of this century. Amazing."

"I don't even want to know," I say. "That stuff frightens me plenty."

She laughs. She says, "But it's interesting. There's so much talk about race these days."

"Let's talk about something else."

We step back to the kitchen. I study the dinner plates in her sink. I sniff the air.

"There's a smell like dogs coming up through my pipes," I say.

"It's the spaniel downstairs. I bet it died and the old lady hasn't noticed."

Liz shrugs.

"Why don't you stop over later on?" she says.

As she closes the door she smiles as though she'll laugh the moment it clicks shut. I stand on the porch in the dark, the chill coming through my shorts. I hear Liz inside; she moves a chair and almost immediately her telephone rings. It chirps like a bird and she answers it cheerily. Below me, in the driveway, the moon floats like icebergs in the black puddles. Liz's voice moves around her apartment. She speaks rapidly and each silence is followed by bright laughter.

In my own kitchen, I put the beer in the refrigerator with the others. The middle level is almost full of frosted, amber bottles.

That night, I dream of Jessica, who shared this bed only five months ago; I dream we're in an Italian restaurant and there's a bad scene between us. I shout and throw my water glass against the wall. Two men, one tall and the other short, appear behind me. Both are balding and wear red flannel shirts with diamond studs in the cuffs and collars. They work for Mr. Polara, Jessica's boyfriend. They say he wants to see me, outside. I shake my head but they lift me by the elbows and usher me around the corner. I try to scream. I know Polara will break my arms.

I wake with the blankets around my head. I catch my breath and feel my way to the living room to sleep on the couch. Back East, right now, Jessica will be starting her day, leaving the house of a man I've never seen, whose name is not Polara. A man who knows, perhaps, of my self-pity and absurd rages. Or maybe she tells him nothing. That's what I'm hoping as I slip back into sleep.

A fervent knocking rouses me from the couch. The drawn curtains are full of sunlight. I groan hell and damnation and, cinching my robe tight, I fumble toward the front door.

The man on the landing is not unnerved by my appearance. Squinting in the sun I see that he's tall and black; he wears black clothes and shoes that shine like black paint. His hand proffers some kind of pamphlet. I can't read the print but each black finger is studded with a silver ring.

"No," I say and I start to close the door.

His hand moves fast, fingertips pressed firmly to the door, just enough to keep it ajar. He looks hard into my eyes—not asking, staring for time—but he doesn't speak a word.

"Sorry," I say, and I shut the door.

For a moment I hold my eye to the peephole. He's still out there with that same look of righteous incredulity, his hand still stretched toward me, as if he's looking right back at me through the peephole.

Back on the couch I stretch out and sigh. Five minutes and I'm almost asleep, when he knocks again, louder this time.

"Honestly," I say and I rush the door, throwing it open to the clean-cut young man, handsome and straight and definitely white, who flashes me a smile as though a haggard face in a bathrobe is precisely what he's been waiting to see. He extends his hand.

"Mr. Pomeroy," he says. "It's a swell morning."

"Who are you?"

"I'm here to talk to you," he says.

He stands in the brightness of the new day, smiling. I lean out the door and look from side to side.

"Where's your friend?"

"I work alone," he says. "I stopped by yesterday, but you were out."

"Yesterday?"

He nods and once again offers his hand. He wears a white shirt with half sleeves and a tasteful blue tie. A good smell, like soap and rubbing alcohol, comes off him and suddenly it hits me that he's a dead ringer for Liz. A taller, male Liz with black hair. But the face is hers, line for line.

"It's for a good cause, Mr. Pomeroy. I'm here to talk to you about your future, and the future of this town."

I don't want to, but I shake his hand. He has light in his eye and when he smiles all his teeth show. They're good teeth, white as pearls and regular as bathroom tile.

"You can trust me," he says, and then, laughing: "By the way, I like your robe. What color do you call that?"

I look down at my robe. "Yellow," I say. "I call it yellow."

"Or goldenrod. That's a good name for a color."

His smile isn't the least indulgent. He reaches out and touches my sleeve. There's some dried ketchup near his finger and suddenly I'm embarrassed in front of this proper young man.

"All right," I say. "Come on in. But make it brief. This goes against my better judgment."

He shows me his teeth, his innocence and zeal, and he darts through the doorway with surprising quickness. Before I can fix the latch he's getting comfortable on the couch, dropping my blankets in a heap on the floor.

"Thanks, Mr. Pomeroy," he says. "You have a real nice place here. I like the arrangement."

I say, "Talk. You've got five minutes. I have a mid-morning appointment."

"What about coffee?" he says. "Have you had coffee yet?"

I frown at him and tug my robe at the shoulder.

"You make coffee and I'll talk," he says. He grins with an earnest eye.

"Okay, let's hear it," I say, and I move into the kitchen and put the kettle on. He's quiet out there. I fix the filter in the cone and I step into the living room with pot in hand. His eyes are closed, his clean hands folded; his elbows are planted on his knees. He looks up and smiles.

"How's that coffee coming?"

"What did you say your name was?"

He shakes his head and folds his arms. "You don't trust me, do you? You really can't let go of your suspicions."

"I trust you," I say. "I trust everybody. Now please leave."

He's still shaking his head.

"I'm not getting through, am I?" he says. "Mr. Pomeroy, I'm here for a purpose, and you owe it to yourself and your neighbors to hear me out. There's a change coming, and you have to face it."

He's planted behind the coffee table, as if daring me to come after him.

"Listen," I say, "don't start with me. I spent a year in seminary. I've read the Bible the way some people read *TV Guide.*" I could feel myself getting mad. "I see you guys working this side of town. Why don't you walk a few blocks and try that line on those rich people. Tell them about this big change."

While I speak he smiles at me, beatifically, tolerant.

"What difference east or west?" he says. "The work will go on where it will."

I point at the door.

"Out," I say. "Now. Please."

"Mr. Pomeroy, what's wrong? You've got trouble, am I right? A woman maybe? Where is she now? You can trust me."

The kettle starts to whistle. I press my palm against my forehead.

"I'm sorry," I say. "I have work to do. I need to be alone."

"Sure," he says. "Not to intrude. A quick cup of java and I'm gone. Relax now."

"All right," I say, and I shuffle out to fill the pot.

Sometimes I get confused. I forget that I have specific goals on earth. I forget that there are people out there who understand my frame of mind. But the way this boy says my name makes me want to renounce all the old ways, the old music, and begin again.

I return with two cups and set one down before him on the low table. He's sitting on the edge of the couch, arms crossed on his knees, leaning forward eagerly.

"Have any cream?" he says.

"No cream."

"Half 'n' half?"

Our eyes meet for a moment.

"Black is fine," he says and he lifts the cup to his face and breathes in the aromatic steam. He sips from it. "Good," he says. "You make a wicked cup of coffee, Mr. Pomeroy. You're not drinking."

"I will," I say. "After you leave."

I settle in the armchair and watch him drink.

When his cup is half empty he looks around the room. He nods at the trombone case in the corner.

"You're a musician," he says.

"That's right."

He says, "May I?" And he springs across the room and crouches over the case, working the clasps with his hands.

I open my mouth, but I don't protest. Deftly he puts the trombone together and makes a breathy sound in the mouthpiece.

"It's a fine instrument," he says and he raises the bell toward the window and runs through a couple of scales. Without breaking stride he launches into song. He plays tunes I recognize: "Stardust" and "On a Clear Day." He plays the Johnny Carson theme and "A Taste of Honey." He plays effortlessly; his hands know the positions as if this were as natural as eating with a fork and spoon.

He lowers the trombone and smiles at me, a little sheepishly. I sit there with my hands spread on the armrests, the full cup of coffee on the floor between my feet. I feel shabby and not young. This boy can play.

"Don't stop," I say. "Let's hear more."

He smiles and hefts the instrument. He plays a sweet, liquid tone; I don't know the titles but these are old hymns, melodies my father played at weddings and funerals. The room seems to fill with golden light and the boy plays as if he's been sent from God to take me home.

He finishes and looks at me over his shoulder, triumphantly.

"That's good," I say.

"Consider the future. My advice is make your peace with this world," he says. "Don't sleep on enmity."

And then, quickly, he disassembles the trombone, carefully

placing each part in the case's red plush grooves. He snaps it shut and steps over to my chair. Before I can rise, he leans over and pumps my hand.

"Thank you, Mr. Pomeroy. Thanks for the coffee and your time. Remember what I said. Don't sleep on it."

He smiles and withdraws his hand and almost instantly disappears behind the door, closing it softly after himself. I'm in the chair with my fingers locked on the rests and I'm listening hard, listening for the music he made in my living room's stale, morning air.

Later, I hear Liz climbing the back stairs. Her door slams. I pull on a clean shirt, lace my sneakers, check in the mirror. I step out and tap on her door. She calls from the other room and I open the door. In the living room I find her sprawled on the chair, her legs in blue pedal pushers stretched toward me. Her face seems pensive, abstracted. With my eyes on her white ankle socks and red moccasins I say hello. I stare and she doesn't speak.

At last she says, "Well?"

I shrug. I say, "I like your shoes. How was your day?"

"Awful," she says. "I'm angry. You want to know what about? I'm angry at myself, for being lazy. I'm angry at how easy it is for other people to paint pictures and write books. I want to *make* something."

"So make," I say.

She grimaces and sniffs. "Easy for you to say. I heard you playing over there this morning. You were really making music over there. I heard you."

I look at the posters on the wall behind her.

"It takes practice," I say.

"But still, to rip through a dozen songs like that. You made it sound easy. I'd give anything to play like that. There's more than talent or practice involved. It takes a state of mind."

I shrug. She looks at me, brows contracting.

"Are you all right, Vincent? You don't look right. Are you ill?"

"I haven't been outside today. I need fresh air, that's all."

She sighs and runs her hand through her hair. Her nails are pink and shapely.

"To tell the truth," I say, "I've been thinking about Jessica back in upstate New York. I've been thinking how important it is to have one person who sees the world the same."

Liz looks away, frowning slightly.

"You asked too much of her," she says. "You expected too much."

"What do you mean? You never even met her."

"But I know you."

"I screwed up, sure. But I never lost faith."

Liz looks at me and shakes her head. She says, "Faith? Faith in what? The poor woman needed some stability. You play the trombone, for God's sake. It's not complicated."

"Wait a minute. A moment ago you were telling me how much you wanted to play. You wanted music in your life."

She stretches in the chair, arms splayed over the sides.

"That's got nothing to do with it," she says. "All this talk about faith isn't going to solve your problems. You've got to take care of yourself. You've got to live in the world."

I shake one of her Marlboros from the pack and roll it between my fingers. "Just the same, when the world comes apart you need one person to see it through with you."

Liz says, "But it's you that's coming apart, not the world. You know what I'd do if I were you? I'd get a loan and buy a car. That's Step One to living in the Twentieth Century."

She dangles a red moccasin from her toe. Her legs are full and not long and suggest a contour of rich, physical life. Her legs are celebrations, like Christmas in a wealthy house.

The next afternoon I'm walking home from another audition, taking my time along the quiet side streets with their well-tended homes. All last night the rain fell and the lawns are electrical green; the trees and gardens full of a dark potency. In front of a low sweeping house of crystal and stone an old Chinese man is cleaning out the pedestal birdbath. He wears a plaid flannel shirt and a porkpie hat. His face is white and faded. He works meticulously, with expressive white hands, as if he were concerned with the happiness of birds rather than the order of domestic landscape. And I think of my father, that hot old man, playing Sidney Bechet on a phonograph that looks like a battered typewriter case. His room has a window that opens on an eastern city where it might be snowing, blue snow falling drowsily against gray brick walls.

The light jumps and tears; the missionary boys on their bikes fly over pavement as if they've been flung from the sky. In a moment of ideal geometry I'm caught between them and the gardener. He steps into a shadow and the boys swoop in, shoulder to shoulder, their bright faces growing larger, brighter.

My will dissolves and snaps back solid.

"Come on," I say, and I level the trombone case at my hip, holding it as though it were a lifeline, a rocket, an engine that will pull me through the clean, white space between their hearts.

The Things That Would Never Be Mine

MICHELLE CARTER

This time, I'm not letting him go on about it.

"Just because we're not kids anymore," he's saying, "doesn't mean we should let our lives get cluttered, that we should stop moving, *seeing.*"

I usually let him carry on, whatever's on his mind, while he slices the roast or irons his shirt. But tonight, it doesn't seem fair for him to start in on Sarah and how she's been weighing me down. Though he hasn't yet said her name, though I could change the subject or leave the room, I hold up my hands and say: "Listen."

He looks up from button, needle and thread, shirt pocket. I tell Peter about all I've seen:

Now thirty-seven, I've migrated the length and breadth of California like a cut-rate local airline. As a kid in Bakersfield, I thought the city got its name because the sidewalks looked dusted with flour. As a co-ed in Santa Cruz, I braided scarves into my hair, went to poetry readings, and seduced my linguistics professor. As a graduate student in Berkeley, I roomed with women called Zoomer and Ariel, and ran down Telegraph Avenue with dogs named Barbara and George. These years of moving and no clutter have led me to San Francisco, to writing freelance articles,

often about my own husband's photography. My leisure time
tends to sitting crosslegged on the bed, coaxing air into my asth-
matic lungs, while Peter photographs highway dirt with a telephoto lens. Yes, we're free, we can pick up and move with the best
of them. With asthma and highway dirt we can travel light.

"Joan," Peter says, "we've worked in Paris, Berlin, Boston,
New York—now, the University of Connecticut calls. Look at it
this way: it's how we live." He looks back to his shirt and draws
the needle through the button.

"Those are locations," I say. "I thought you were talking about
seeing."

He pulls the thread taut in one brisk tug.

I watch Peter sew, his movements smooth, capable. Other people's pulses quicken while arguing—voices tremble, eyes moisten,
blink. In our eleven years, I've never seen Peter reveal an ugly
emotion in a gesture. Peter is a man who runs water in the ice tray
after using three cubes, who would never leave a grocery cart in
the middle of the parking lot or eat the chocolate vein out of the
Fudge Ripple. It's as though he was born with eyes clear, hands
ever steady for lifting the camera, pressing the shutter.

"Sarah is eighty years old and she's just had a stroke," I say. He
won't accuse me of changing the subject; we both know we've
been talking about Sarah all along. Throughout the three years
we've lived in San Francisco, Peter has resented Sarah and the
demands she makes of me. She's changed things, he says, she's
thrown off the balance. But what will he say now, to this, to a
woman growing near to the end of her life?

"Joan," he says. "She has family coming out her ears. Tell her
we're moving. Tell her tomorrow."

I first met Sarah two weeks after we moved to San Francisco.
I'd gone to meet her husband at the Medical Center, to interview
him for an article I was doing about surrogate mothers. Adam
killed himself six months after our interview, after suffering an
embolic stroke. Though it seemed arbitrary and grim that the
same quirk of the brain hit both of them, their strokes were as

different as their responses to them. For Adam, the physical effects had been minimal; it was his memory that suffered more than anything else. Sarah said he could still recall the obscurest of details about their courtship and marriage, their children and their pets, parties they'd given and the meals they'd served. But he lost all memory of decades of research, nearly everything from fifty years in the medical profession.

The day of the interview, I knocked on the door once, twice, no answer. I was rummaging through my purse to double-check the appointment time when the door opened just enough for Sarah to peer out.

"I'm looking for Professor Ludlow's office," I said.

She opened the door and retreated inside, dropping herself into the leather chair behind the desk. All the lights in the office were out, and the curtains were drawn over the window. Even in the darkness of the room, I could see the silver in Sarah's hair and how elegantly it was styled in soft waves around her face. But she was looking off in the distance at nothing, her stare blank, unselfconscious. And was that a quilted housecoat she was wearing?

"Will the professor be back soon?" I asked.

She spoke slowly, still staring toward the bookshelves. "He's removing the wire to the coil in my Buick. He always says the same thing, that I've no business driving like this. He thinks I charm a different mechanic every time into slipping another wire into that coil." She stopped, shook her head. "I've a stock of those silly wires—me putting them in myself, you see, he's never considered that."

I nodded. "Well," I said. "Maybe I'll wait out in the hall."

There was something about the way she shifted her gaze to me, something in that one smooth motion, that made me finally realize: this prim old lady is drunk. Sarah quit drinking after Adam died. I was never sure whether his death had made her fear for her own life, or whether in his absence there was merely less reason to drink.

"Julie called last week," she said, resting her elbows on the desk and her chin in her hands. "Ruth's middle girl. I told her I just wasn't going to that wedding. What a fuss she made."

I peeked into the hall. No professor in sight. "That's relatives for you," I said, and tried to laugh.

"Well," she said, lifting her eyebrows, "I just felt terrible about it. So I called her back this morning. 'Julie honey,' I told her, 'I've changed my mind.' "

"That was nice," I said.

"Nice," she said. "Julie didn't say it was nice. She said, 'Changed your mind about what, dear? What day was it you said you'd be coming?' "

I leaned in the doorway, yearning to dash away. But there was something about this sad lady—it was as if she needed something very badly but was accustomed to going on without it.

"So Julie just hadn't taken no for an answer," I said.

Sarah drew her legs under her, like a little girl. "She didn't remember," she said. "She'd forgotten everything we said."

Sarah stares straight ahead as I walk into her room at the hospital.

"Sarah?" I say.

She doesn't flinch.

"Hey." I touch her arm, then realize it's the one with no feeling. "You okay?"

When she turns to me, I realize that her face is almost back to normal. Her stroke was far less severe than Adam's had been; the effects were largely physical, and remediable with therapy. Three weeks ago, the paralyzed side of her mouth curved down comically, like a mouth painted on a sad clown. Her eyes had seemed to be rimmed with blood. Each day, her face and mouth look less distorted. But it's still something of a strain understanding what she says, which never fails to make her angry.

Sarah is speaking without inflection, like a robot in a science fiction movie. "The nurse says that if I speak ver-y slow-ly and e-nun-ci-ate each sound, it might be less dif-fi-cult to un-der-stand me."

I fight back a smile and pull a chair beside the bed, on her good side. It's a relief to see her cranky, spunky, rebellious. "You're sounding more like your old self," I say.

"Old self is right," she says. I see that her eyes are wet; she seems to know that I've noticed, and turns away sharply.

Sarah looks off in the direction of the dresser, which is covered with the family photos she had me bring over. One night while eating cake in her living room, we counted the faces in the photographs—fifty-three, not counting the repeats. She had five brothers, three sisters, four children, nine grandchildren; the nieces, nephews, and extended cousins seemed to span the globe interminably. Allow me to count out my relations, I told her that night: Mother, father—divorced; Peter; me.

"Did you hear from any of the kids today?" I ask her.

She doesn't answer.

For two days after the stroke, all the children and many of the others called; a week of cards and letters followed. The doctors reassured everyone that Sarah's life wasn't immediately endangered, that she'd most likely hold steady for the time being. A few days ago, a cousin came by with flowers. Other than that, as far as I knew, not a single relative had considered boarding a train, bus, or plane to come be with her. This confirmed my worst prejudices about relatives, families: Sarah's stroke wasn't worthy of inconvenience.

"So," I say. "Congratulations on your first day in physical therapy." I pull my purse to my lap, take out the things I've brought her: the foam toy football, the rubber ball and paddle, the plastic Slinkie. I read an article that recommended these kinds of toys for stroke victims, to help restore muscle control and motor coordination.

"So," I say again. She doesn't turn to look at me, so I rest my presents beside her on the bed.

"Okay," she says. "Let me tell you about physical therapy." She has stopped the robot talk and her speech is clear, though the slur is still pronounced. "They sat me at a desk with a young nurse behind it—a Chinese nurse, a Genghis Khan. She gave me a test where she'd hold up pictures—a tomato, a dog, a little girl. 'Identify each subject,' she said. 'Person, animal, or thing.' She yelled the instructions, Joanie, as if just because you're old and dying you're automatically senile and deaf."

My lungs are tightening—the hospital air.

Dying, I want to say. Cut it out.

We sit for a long time, not talking. When an orderly comes to dim the lights, I'm embarrassed by the toys and put them back in my purse.

I feel the bed dip as Peter sits beside me. Eyes closed, I'm imagining that my lungs are party balloons, that each breath pushes the walls open easily, gorging the sacks with air.

"You hungry at all?" Peter says.

I shake my head, cough for a good minute. "Damn it," I say. "It's not fair, a person going through life not being able to breathe."

He lifts my hand to his lap, pats it. He's heard that line before. What a silly thing marriage seems at times—a mutual tolerance of repeated, unanswerable complaints.

"You should come out to the living room and help me with the slides," Peter says. "I did a show for this group last quarter, so I've got to change things around."

Peter is giving a slide show at the university tomorrow, sponsored by a campus program called "ArtThrob." He prepares meticulously for shows, regardless of the audience. Peter's care and planning afford him the luxury of composure in front of strangers, the appearance of casual, indifferent, spontaneous charm. This is one of the things I work hard not to hate in him.

"You go ahead," I say. "I don't think I've got the oxygen for it."

Peter kisses my cheek, stands up, still holding my hand. "How did Sarah take the news?" he says.

I squeeze his hand, let go, turn onto my side.

"Joan," Peter says.

"Joan what?"

He sits on the bed again, exhales a heavy sigh I envy him for.

"Sarah"—I suck in a thin, deep breath—"is busy being chided

for not enunciating. She spends her afternoons taking flash-card tests for the first time in seventy years. I don't think she should have to think about me moving right now."

Peter shakes his head. "It's just that I don't understand," he says. "You have to tell her sometime. You've always pampered her, and now you're being cruel by not telling her."

I sit up, scoot back to lean against the headboard. "Don't tell me that I'm being cruel to her."

He holds up his hands. "Sorry." We sit in silence, listening to my lungs wheeze.

"I don't mean to be hard on you about this," he says. "I just never understood, that's all. I never understood you running over to see her all the time. Letting her down like this was inevitable—you had to know that."

I turn away, swing my legs over the side of the bed. "I don't know so much, really," I say. "You don't know so much either. And that's the way we like it, after all."

Peter laughs, then stops abruptly. He looks at me for a long time, then leaves the room; I know he's decided not to probe. Soon I hear him back at his slides, clicking from one to another, too fast.

One of the things I've always loved about Peter is the value he places on privacy. He is loving, affectionate, genuinely interested in me and my happiness; but at a certain point, we don't push. We have matured beyond needing to turn ourselves inside out for each other, exposing every sinew, each deep, irrational need and motivation. In 1974, when we married, our vows included the lines: "To love you is to respect your right to remain separate from me. There are things about you I will never know."

We lived near Boston in our second year of marriage, in Hingham, just south along the coast. Peter planned to have his students meet at the house once a week. Once classes began, he decided this wasn't practical, though we had a huge den and rooms to spare. He started coming home after midnight at least twice a week; their workshops had gotten crazy, lively, too spontaneous and unpredictable to cut short. At the end of the semester, the students held a party for Peter in one of the dorms. He insisted that I'd find these undergraduates silly and trivial, but I wanted to go get a look at this stimulating group that excited Peter so.

I felt the heat of her interest the second we walked in the door. The lounge was carpeted wall to wall with a barbecue-sauce-colored shag, and there was furniture to match. Peter disappeared into a group of tall boys who'd applauded as we entered. I headed for the chips and dip, which was where she set upon me.

"Ms. Mason?" she said.

"Yes," I said. "I'm Peter's wife, but I use my own name, Lesh."

She smiled uncomfortably, looked away.

"You did pretty well," I said. "You got the 'Ms.' right."

We both laughed. "I'm Lisa," she said, and held out her hand.

"I can call you Joan, then?"

"Of course." When had I said Joan?

She squeezed my hand, shook it, covered it with her other hand. There was something terribly earnest about this young woman, dressed as I might have dressed as a sophomore at U.C. Santa Cruz—hair bound in a batik scarf, Indian skirt, sleeveless black leotard. That was what I was thinking as she took my hand: how much she reminded me of me. It was also then, in the way she squeezed my hand, held it, and looked into my eyes, that I understood her message, meant not unkindly: I'm fucking your husband; it's the way of these things.

"She has nothing to lose," I told Peter at home that night. "That's what's not fair. She has nothing to lose, and I don't."

"Don't what?"

"Don't have nothing to lose," I shouted. I ran into the bathroom and slammed the door, burning with jealousy, hatred, fear, every childish emotion we had worked to rise above. I threw water on my face, looked up at the mirror. I looked at that moment, of course, visibly older: the skin seemed less taut around the mouth, under the eyes, along the line of the jaw. I'd stood like this in many bathrooms, scrutinizing my features, back when it was me wearing the leotard and the scarves in my hair. The things in older women's bathrooms had always seemed like trinkets, toys— a little shell to hold your rings while you wash your hands, bundles of straw flowers hanging upside down, a matching brush, comb, nail file, mirror. I'd look these things over, sometimes picking them up and replacing them carefully; then I'd rejoin the party, heading, always, straight for the women. I would make them know me, those women with the wedding bands. I'd meant no harm, and I would take nothing from them.

That night in my bathroom after crying about Peter's student, I dried my face, combed my hair and wrapped it in silk. I put on green eye shadow and dabbed some red on my cheeks. Yes, I hated that girl in the dormitory, but not for screwing Peter. I hated her holding my hand, her speaking my name. Her watching me from across the room, knowing me in secret.

I'd found Peter in the living room, sitting in the dark.

"I don't want to be in our house tonight," I said. "Let's go somewhere. Let's go out dancing."

When he turned to me, his eyes were wet. "It's how we'd planned to do it," he said, "this marriage. Just keep outside things from each other, remember? And don't let anyone else become more important?" He looked away, started shaking his head. "You know I never want to hurt you. So I'm asking, really asking: What do we do?"

I opened the coat closet. "The paper said there'd be snow flurries tonight."

"Joan," he said. He walked over to me, closed the closet. "I love you, you know—but there's more to it than that. There are reasons we're together, you and me."

I nodded, he was right, there was something the same in us. His hand was pressing the closet door as if something was pushing from the other side.

"There's this arts center," he said, "in Paris. The art department has decided photographers are eligible for fellowships there. Anyway, well, they nominated me to go—I mean, us to go."

That was the first of our moves, prompting our first declarations of freedom, rootlessness, our never-ending commitment to no commitments. We made plans, packed, spent a year in a tiny flat at the Cité Internationale des Arts, where I started getting my periodic asthma attacks. Then there was Berlin, then Freiburg, New York, Washington.

Now San Francisco, en route to Connecticut.

From the hallway, I watch the screen. A slide comes on, muted black rivulets—Peter clicks it away and the screen goes white. Another slide, then the white screen, then another slide, another. Peter knows the slides, doesn't need to scrutinize them now. That happened long ago, when the photographs were new:

He'd call me into the room. He'd be standing near the screen, a few feet from the new shot. I'd join him, he'd put his arm around me, kiss my hair. What do you think? he'd say.

I'd squint at the screen, move a step closer.

Stop, he'd say, then take hold of my shoulders and pull me back to just the right distance.

The nurse at the desk tells me that Sarah can go home. She is to take her medication faithfully; part of its job is to thin the blood, so she's to be very careful to avoid bleeding. She ought to go to Physical Therapy once a week, as she feels the need. But she can go home.

I walk into her room and bend down to kiss her. She throws her good arm around my neck, magazine and all.

"Let's get you out of here," I say.

A nurse helps bundle her into her housecoat while I pack her things. As I'm arranging her photos in a box, spreading tissue between the frames, I feel Sarah's hand on my shoulder. "Just stack 'em up," she says.

In the car, she's retelling her Physical Therapy stories. She's barking out the words like the Chinese nurse. " 'Listen and think *hard,*' shouts Genghis Khan, holding up a coloring-book tomato. 'This is green vegetable? Or this is red vegetable?' "

I've been out of breath during most of the drive, but from laughing, not asthma. This is the first time since the stroke that I've heard her carry on as she used to.

"So I ask her," Sarah says, "how ripe she likes her tomatoes—

which, I add, are not vegetables, but fruits. 'Mrs. Ludlow,' she sighs. *'Concentrate.'* "

I carry Sarah's suitcase and the box of photos into the family room. Sarah refuses, as always, to sit on the couch, which she says is too rigid and uncomfortable for human behinds. I lower her to the floor, her favorite sitting place, and she rests her back against the couch.

"I'll take the suitcase on up to your bedroom," I say.

She pats the floor next to her. "Sit," she says.

I put down her things and sit beside her on the floor. She rests her head on my shoulder, and I wrap my arm around her and hold her against me. If I wait too long to tell her about us moving, she might think I've been deceiving her, or that I haven't cared enough about her feelings to bother to mention it. I wish I could see her face. Holding her close without being able to look at her makes me feel as if somehow she knows about everything.

"You know," she says, her head still resting on my shoulder, "you're the only one who's any damn good."

I laugh, which surprises me, but then Sarah laughs too.

"Stay and have dinner?" she says. "Help me open some cans?"

"The slide show." I've almost forgotten it—I look at my watch. "Peter's slide show's at seven. I should leave in a half hour."

Sarah sits up. "Slides!" she says. "Wonderful!"

"Wait," I say. "You just got home, you're supposed to take it easy, be careful—"

"Joan, honey, I've had three weeks of careful."

"You're on that medication, and the doctor said—"

"It's funny . . ." She frowns and pauses, as if she's only broken a silence. She turns to look at me. "When people talk about dying, they go on and on about pain, fear, loneliness. You know what it is more than anything? It's boredom, pure and simple. Long, dull, empty time."

I get up, mostly to make her stop. "Let's open some of those cans," I say.

"You don't want to talk," she says.

"About dying?" I say. "I'm always up for a good chin-wag about dying." I cross the room, look down at a stereo console that hasn't been opened in years. There are outlines in the dust where some of the family pictures used to stand.

"Anyway," I say, "you're not dying. You're getting better."

"Better than what?" she says. "I'm eighty-five years old."

"Eighty-*five*?" I say. "You just had your eightieth birthday, remember?"

Sarah shrugs. "Some people turn thirty over and over—me, I've been hanging onto eighty instead."

I sit on the couch she's leaning against. She's eighty-five years old.

Sarah slaps her good hand on her thigh. "Do you know what that means? We've missed out on *five birthdays.*"

"Creative reasoning," I say.

"So! We're entitled to a celebration—a quintuple celebration."

I laugh. "Okay," I say. "We're entitled."

"Perfect," Sarah says. "Now go over to the bookshelves. There." She points to the shelf of encyclopedias. "Feel behind, toward the right—around 'R' and 'S'."

What I pull from behind the books is not a surprise: Jameson Irish Whiskey.

"Sarah—"

"Don't even start," she says. "I'm a grown woman. I'm old enough to be four grown women."

Sarah tells me to get the crystal glasses. I sit back on the couch, and we toast each other's health. Sarah downs most of her drink in one swallow.

There will be no good time, and now is better than most.

"There's something I might as well tell you," I say.

"It's Peter again, isn't it," she says.

I let out a sigh. "I guess." But it isn't just Peter. It isn't fair of me to say so.

"I knew it," she says. She reaches with her good arm, stretches, grabs the bottle. "You ought to go ahead and let him have it once in a while. He's kind of a cold customer, you know."

"No," I say. "That's not really it."

Sarah pours herself another drink. "Peter has never liked me," she says.

I laugh. "It's not your fault," I say. "He knows I come here to relax, to sit and talk and just be easy. Peter doesn't know how special that is. For Peter, just about everything is easy."

Sarah sips from her glass, then holds it in the air as if putting it down would be too much of a gamble. "Well I don't like him, either," she says. "I'll never forgive him for how he's treated you —dragging you from city to city, staying out half the night with all his pretty little friends."

I want to say, stop—I've only told you half of it. I would have told you everything but I was afraid you wouldn't understand.

"He's damn lucky to have you," she's saying.

"Wait," I say. "We're both lucky, Sarah."

"Ha!" She sits up, stiff, indignant. "Bad luck. He says he loves you, but he's no real husband. The man has no feelings, Joanie."

"Feelings." I shake my head. "He feels a lot, too much maybe."

"Too much of what feeling?" she says. "Name one real, human, too-much feeling."

I look at her sitting up tall, trying to make me feel stronger by lashing out at Peter. But it's not so simple. I smile, shrug. "I don't know," I say. "Looking at the same person, the same house, the same place over and over. That can give you that kind of too-much feeling."

"Too much of you?"

"Too much of one thing. Too much of the same day."

Sarah puts down her glass. "I suppose I just don't understand."

I touch her arm lightly, run my fingertips along the skin that hadn't been able to feel. "You understand," I say. "Long, dull, empty time."

She finishes her drink, pulls the bottle toward her.

"Are you wondering how I know so much about why Peter's like he is?"

Sarah fills her glass and holds it to her chest. I close my eyes and say, "Let me tell you a story."

I run into one of Peter's students in a bookstore downtown. He's a tall, slim boy with dark features, the kind of boy I always wanted when I was in school. We talk nervously for half an hour in the fiction aisle—we pull books from the shelves when we run out of topics. He doesn't know many writers, he says. Professor Mason's sure a kick, he says.

Professor Mason, I say.

I pull my fingertips across the spines of the books lined up on the shelf we're leaning against. He make you call him that? the boy asks me. I laugh and the boy trails his fingers along the books, the way I've been doing. Maybe just in public, he says, then I say, Or just in private. We laugh, both of us taken off guard by the word, what with the two of us leaning together, shoulders touching, feeling the warmth of each other's skin through the fabric of our shirts.

When we leave the bookstore, an alarm goes off. The boy stops, dumbstruck, looks down at the book he's carried out of the store. He sprints back inside, straight for the cashier. I watch him through the storefront window—waving his arms, rolling his eyes, laughing too heartily, too much. I realize, watching him, that he didn't take the book out of absentmindedness alone; it was the sheer, honest excitement of my inviting him out for a beer. I think how there's nothing on earth like the excitement of very young men. It's determined and obsessive; it's sweet and childlike and plainly vulgar.

We walk to the sprawling old tract house he shares with six other students. He leads me by the hand down a dimly lit hallway, through a kitchen that smells of hamburger grease. Lying back on the foam mat that serves as his bed, I listen to the blending of bass lines from two stereos somewhere in the house. My mind isn't cluttered with the things I'd have expected—the looseness of the skin at my thighs, the stretch marks on my breasts. I feel only the power of his blood as it pulses, I hold his mouth against me to feel the breath come hot and quick. Later, when he's drifted into sleep, I turn on the desk lamp and twist the hood against the wall. I move around the room, touching books, records, photographs, guitar, loving the smell and sound and feeling of things that will never be precious, mine, familiar.

When I open my eyes, Sarah has turned around, is watching me.

"When did you do this?" she says. "Who is this boy?"

"Who?" I say. "I don't know who. He's from Boston and Paris and Freiburg and Washington. San Francisco. Storrs, Connecticut."

She frowns, looks away. "When was Connecticut?" she asks, though I can tell I needn't answer. We're quiet for a long time, and I'm afraid to guess what she's thinking.

"But why?" she finally says. "It's pretty and exciting, all of it, everything we've done—but so ugly, too, and there's nothing to count on."

She looks so tiny in her robe, her hair so soft, her eyes darker than I'd ever realized. Eighty-five years old and nobody knew. "Our secrets aren't so very different," I say.

Sarah smiles and twists the cap back onto the bottle. We lift our glasses and toast every birthday ever.

By the time we eat some soup and Sarah dresses, we've barely enough time to get to the gallery. She takes uncharacteristic care in choosing what to wear, as if the simple beige slacks and sweater could come to matter.

I park in the red zone near the gallery entrance so Sarah won't have far to walk. My lungs have tightened and I'm wheezing lightly, so I'm happy to move at Sarah's pace. I know I should find Peter before the show and reassure him that I've come. But tonight I won't leave Sarah's side until I tuck her into bed.

Most of the seats in the gallery are taken, but we find two in the second-to-last row. The gallery holds about fifty chairs; a dozen students are roaming about, looking at the landscapes hung on the stark, white walls. In front of us, a blond boy in a pin-striped shirt has twisted around in his chair to talk to the young woman next to me. A hole is ripped in one of the shoulders of her T-shirt, and her black hair is cut above her ear on one side, chin-level on the other. When she catches me looking at her, she smiles sweetly, her braces catching the light.

"How soon will you be moving?" Sarah asks me.

Peter comes in the side door and everyone applauds. He stands in front of the blank screen, waits for the applause to die down. The dimples in his cheeks deepen when he smiles.

"Three weeks from tomorrow," I tell her. She takes my hand and holds it in her lap.

"I'd like to thank all of you," Peter says, "for braving this seventy-degree evening to be here tonight."

The crowd laughs warmly. Peter continues, delivering his usual for-those-of-you-who-don't-know-my-work opening remarks. There is talk of focus, of finding one's material. His eyes scan the crowd as he talks, but I don't make a move to help him see me.

The lights go out and Peter retreats to work the projector. I have to breathe through my nose to quiet the wheezing.

The first few slides are crowd pleasers I took a few years back: Peter asleep in bed, the camera next to him on the pillow; Peter in the bathroom with the camera hanging from his neck, one hand brushing his teeth and the other brushing the camera's; a candle-light dinner between Peter and the camera; the camera in a highchair, Peter lifting a spoon to its lens. Though we used these shots to get people laughing, there was something about them that made us furtively proud: So many people were fooling themselves; those people might as well have married cameras.

The first shot of Peter's work is red at the core, with waves of violet dissipating into black. He talks about developing techniques, while students nod smartly in response. The second shot is wavy too, in blacks and grays. A young woman shouts a question about f-stops. Peter flips back and forth between that slide and the first, illustrating his answer.

I suck in a long, slow breath. There isn't enough air in this room.

The second set of shots is gritty and sharply focused. Peter talks about the power of texture and there are questions about the lenses he used. Sarah leans forward, squints, nudges the boy in the pin-striped shirt.

"But what do you think it *is?*" she asks him.

The people around us laugh. Peter pauses and looks in our direction.

I helped Peter take this photograph. We had gone to his sister's house to borrow her highchair for a shooting. When Peter's brother-in-law answered the door, he was out of breath and his eyes were wet. "Did we come at the wrong time?" Peter said. Then his sister came to the door, embarrassed, combing her hair through her fingers. "I forgot you were coming." She laughed nervously. "It's in the garage. Could you go around to the side door?"

We could hear almost every word of their argument through the thin garage wall. We found the highchair under a tool shed.

"Look at this," Peter said, moving the highchair aside.

"You think you're the only one?" Peter's brother-in-law was shouting. "This hurts, you goddamn moron," he yelled.

"What are you doing?" I whispered. Peter was running his fingers along the oil-stained rug, getting his camera out of its case.

"Damn right it hurts," Peter's sister was screaming.

"If I had just a little more light," Peter said. I found a flashlight and shined the beam on the rug while Peter held the camera very still.

Even in the dark of the gallery, I can tell that Peter has spotted me, that he knows I'm listening. Sarah straightens up, still holding my hand in her lap, and asks Peter loudly, "What is this a picture of?"

I sense Peter's horror at hearing Sarah's voice. The crowd laughs, and he has to laugh along.

"Don't you think," he finally says, "that the shot isn't really *about* that thing, whatever it might be?"

We thought we had it figured out. We thought we saw things that other people didn't.

"A gravel road, maybe," says the young woman next to me. Someone in my row says, "A towel—terry cloth."

My lungs seem to be shrinking into themselves. I lean close to Sarah and whisper, "It's indoor-outdoor carpeting."

The boy in front of us hears, turns to nod. Peter puts on another slide.

"A brick in our chimney," I whisper. And next: "Our sidewalk." "Upholstery." "Birch bark." "Salt."

Snake Head
LYNDA LEIDIGER

The whole snake-head business began, of course, on Halloween.

I had seen it in the window, weeks before, on the shelf with a gorilla, Richard Nixon and an old man with one bloody eyeball hanging down over his cheek. The snake was a king cobra, emerald green, a proud hood splayed behind its head. Its flat black eyes stared arrogantly above me. I loved its milky fangs.

The night before the party, my husband took me to buy a mask. "What do you want that for?" he said when he saw it. He was trying on a Jimmy Carter mask and chuckling at himself. The clerk told him they had just sold the last Menachem Begin.

"I don't know," I said. "It's me."

I slipped it on. It was very dark and I could hardly see out. My eyes were focused through two small holes in the roof of the cobra's rubber mouth. It was like tunnel vision, the clerk's face looming toward me as through a fisheye lens.

"It's very unique, dear," she said, squinting at me. "I only had half a dozen of these, and I had to order them back in January. This is the last one."

Some other customers started to gather around me, pointing and snickering. I made hideous faces at them, testing the mask. They didn't see.

"I'll take it," I said. My voice bellowed in my ears behind the thick rubber walls.

"Isn't it awfully hot?" my husband said. He peered in at me

without meeting my eyes and nodded in satisfaction, as though he had paused at the entrance of a haunted cave and found it empty.

I wore the head all the way home in the car. I could see only straight ahead; palm trees waved like giant feelers at the edge of my vision. I had the odd sensation of being brought home from the hospital. Instead of taking the freeway, my husband drove slowly down Ventura Boulevard all the way from Tarzana to Studio City. Although it was early afternoon and the car window was rolled down, nobody seemed to notice my head. I could tell he was disappointed.

"And they say people in *New York* are blasé," he muttered.

For the party, I put on a strapless gown of purple velvet, swarming with seed pearls and rhinestones. I also had black-velvet gloves to my elbows, a rhinestone bracelet and black-patent-leather shoes with straps around my ankles. Finally, I draped a fawn-colored rabbit-fur jacket around me. The jacket felt odd; my husband had given it to me and I had never worn it. The thought of the dead rabbits was still faintly sickening.

My cobra eyes stared at me from the mirror. A golden reptile throat rose from my shoulders. I was magnificent.

"It's a shame you don't have some green body paint," my husband said. He was angry because he wanted to go as a gypsy and I wouldn't let him take my violin. He thought he had a right to it because I hadn't played in two years. He grumbled as he cut a hole in my throat so I could drink through a straw without taking off the head.

It turned out to be one of those Hollywood parties. I'm not sure how we were invited, but we went because my husband thought he might make some connections. Someone told him Ralph Bakshi might be there. A Doberman in a feather boa lunged for me at the door, barking and frothing. Fidel Castro slapped the dog's snout until it was quiet, and handed me a joint.

"Charmed, Fidel. I'm Joan Crawford," I said, holding out my velvet hand to him. He looked pleased to be recognized. Nearly everyone laughed. My husband beamed; he hadn't been so proud of me in years. I held the joint to my throat and watched in the mirror as the smoke slid out over my black tongue.

We went out onto the patio and stood, smoking, under the cardboard skeletons hanging from the eucalyptus trees. Their feet scraped loudly against my head. I could tell that Ralph Bakshi wasn't going to show up there. I got myself a glass of wine punch.

"Hey, what do you look like under that mask?" some guy asked. He wore a tweed cap and there were several pipes in his pockets. I tried to decide whether or not the pinkish-purple blotches had been painted on his cheeks. "I bet under that mask you've got blond hair. Am I right? The coat's the tip-off; if you had dark hair, you wouldn't wear a coat that color."

"If she had, like, black hair, the contrast would be too much," someone else agreed. He was an actor from Phoenix. He told us several times that he had just arrived in L.A. yesterday with two dollars and eight cents in his pocket. His shoes didn't match and his eyebrows were drawn so that one went up and the other down.

"I bet she's got blue eyes, or maybe hazel, and high cheekbones. And very soft skin," the guy with the pipes said suggestively. His acne glowed eerily under the patio floodlights.

My husband smirked, pleased.

"Just pretend I'm not here," I said, and had another hit.

A girl with pigtails and white knee socks came bouncing out of the house. Under one arm she carried a cloth doll in a bonnet. "I heard there was something to smoke out here. I haven't moved so fast all night." She giggled.

"It's harsh," the actor said, passing her the joint.

"Harsh. It's nice to hear *harsh*. I mean, people say *raspy*. *Raspy and dusted!*" She tossed her pigtails and took the joint in long, noisy gasps. "It's flippy. Hey, you're a soldier," she said to Fidel.

He took the cigar out of his mouth disgustedly. "Exactly what are you supposed to be?" he said.

"I'm four years old," she said, cradling the doll.

"I'm twenty-one, going on a thousand." The guy with the pipes kept trying to look in at me, but he was having a hard time standing up. I was having a hard time trying to figure out why no one seemed to have come in costume.

"God, aren't there any potato chips? Raw vegetables give me ulcers," the actor said and wandered off.

The guy with the pipes poked the girl's doll. "That Raggedy Ann?"

The four-year-old scowled, crinkling her painted freckles. "This is *Holly Hobbie.* Her friends call her Hobbie; I mean, *Holly.*" She dissolved in giggles.

I found that I could push pretzel sticks through my throat.

"I want to show you something," Fidel whispered. He led me up to his room. Over his bed was a huge oil painting of a Venetian canal. He told me he had painted it himself in 20 hours. It wasn't badly done at all. Somehow, he had put a small light behind it so there was a sun in the sky, which he could make brighter or dimmer. The sky was a kind of faded amber color and the crumbling buildings were dried caramel. He turned the sun low for me. "I knew you'd like Venice," he said, fingering my purple velvet.

Just then, the four-year-old came in. "Wow. What color is it?" she said.

Fidel let go of my dress and put the cigar back in his mouth. He looked as though it didn't taste particularly good. "There are twenty-two colors in it," he said. "I have them written underneath."

The four-year-old bent over him to get closer to the painting. It was getting hot inside the head; I felt like going out again. As I left, I heard her telling Fidel that she could see a little blue. I met the Doberman on the stairs. He quietly showed me his teeth but didn't bark.

My husband scarcely took his eyes off me all night. He devotedly brought me carrot sticks and slivers of zucchini to push through my throat. Once or twice he pressed against me behind the punch bowl.

Two more people came to the party, a cop and his girlfriend. They came as each other. The guy who thought I was a blonde had taken over the stereo and was playing two lines of a Dylan song over and over again.

" 'Oh, Momma, can this really be the end?' " he sang mournfully, waving one of his pipes.

"Oh, let's go," my husband said. "Everybody here is still trying to break into commercials."

As we left, the guy stopped singing Dylan to whisper to me, "I've voted you beauty queen of the night."

I turned to glare at him, but the snake head stared straight ahead, haughty and indifferent, as we swept past.

At home, I took off the purple dress and touched the emerald scales of my face.

"Leave your shoes on," my husband said hoarsely.

He pushed me onto the bed, grabbing my breasts and pulling himself into me, a climber gaining a momentary hold on an impossible cliff. I dug my nails into the meat of his broad back and spurred him on with my shiny heels. He came within seconds, as always.

"That was wonderful," I said, as always. I touched the cobra head gratefully and cried until my tears welded the rubber to my skin.

I wore the snake head to work on Monday, with a new dress in a soft, wine-colored material that clung to me. I felt sleek and shapely, but it was the cobra head that made me feel beautiful.

"What are you supposed to be?" Rosemary said. She was a stupid, unhappy woman, just smart enough to be perpetually suspicious that people were making fun of her. She had been a secretary with the company for 28 years.

"Happy Halloween," I said, sitting at my desk and uncovering my typewriter.

Rosemary frowned at me. "You watch it," she said. "Mr. March said just the other day he thought you had some kind of rebellious streak. But *I* stuck up for you, *I* said you were *maturing*. You're going to ruin me," she hissed.

There was a stack of work in my basket. I crumpled the vinyl cover of my IBM and shoved it into a drawer. "I'm getting a cup of coffee," I said.

Going down the hall to the coffee machine, I saw my lover. He was lean, forest-eyed, wheat-haired. Seeing him always took my breath away, made me weak in the knees. I was a fool, an embarrassment to myself.

He smiled at me. His eyes slid up the forked tongue and found me right away. He shook his head. He thought I was beautiful.

Safe within my rubber fortress, my slack idiot's face melted for him. I have known you 100,000 years; we were dinosaurs together, I told him soundlessly.

Mr. March saw us in the hall. He bent toward me, trying to look down my dress. "Don't we look yummy today?" he leered, looking to my lover for agreement, but he was gone.

"Do we?" Fuck yourself in the ass, I mouthed gloriously.

His lean brown vulture's head bent farther toward me. "Who are you supposed to be?" he said. His wrinkled tie dangled obscenely outside his vest.

"I'm supposed to be a secretary," I said.

Still bent over, he said, "Why are you afraid of me?"

"I'm not afraid of you." I hate you, I said.

His face constricted with pretended concern. "Why don't you open up to me?" he said, very low. "You mustn't be afraid. You won't get the reaction you expect. Think about that." He wagged a finger at me, brushing my breast.

"I'll think about it." You asshole, I said.

When I got back to my desk with my coffee and my straw, Rosemary was typing furiously. "You're cute" was all she would say.

My lover came by to take me to lunch. We went to his apartment. He is a writer; his four unpublished novels, neatly bound, stand next to his bed. They are all about a woman he loved in Paris eight years ago. He does not expect to love again.

The early afternoon sun, filtering weakly through the vines, dappled us like lepers. He stroked my proud hood with one hand as he undid my dress. I writhed beneath him, then over him, my hidden face contorted into molten curves of longing. I felt my lips curl past my teeth; sweat drizzled down my cheeks. There was a downpour in my head, dim memories of an ancient sea.

Afterward, he gave me some Perrier to sip through a straw. He

put on an old record and sang to me, his voice flat and husky as
the November wind. He was wishing he was in Paris.

I cut tiny slits between the scales to make the head more comfortable and stopped wearing make-up. I took off the snake head
for a few minutes every night and washed my face in the dark
bathroom. Once I turned on the light and nearly screamed. The
head in the mirror was pale, grotesquely small. The face quivered
stupidly, a weak, pitiable, unsafe face. A face that I had tolerated
despite nearly 30 years of consistent betrayals. Of its own will, it
would blush and snarl and yawn and weep and look alternately
sad and foolish. It had no interest in protecting me. I had given it
many chances, I thought, as I put the snake head back on. It felt
so good.

After I had worn the head for a week, Mr. March called me
into his office. He liked to sail and there were models all over his
desk and credenza. "Don't you think you're carrying this thing
too far?" he said, staring in at where he thought I was.

I said nothing. A cobra says nothing.

"You're not in college anymore. This kind of prank won't go
over here. You've got to think of your career," he said. "You're a
bright girl, but you've got to start watching your step. We can't
have this. Besides, it must get terribly hot in that thing," he added
hopefully.

I reminded him that I was always on time, that I was the best
typist in the office, that my work was always in compliance with
company standards. I casually mentioned discrimination and the
Equal Employment Opportunity Commission, which was already
handling several suits against the company.

He blanched under his Sunday-sailor's tan, then tried to look
hurt. "I don't know why you're afraid of me."

I left him jabbing his pen into the rigging of an old whaler.

Drinking all my meals through a straw was beginning to make
me thin. For the first time in years, I liked the way I looked. My

lover ran his tongue along the clean blades of my hipbones and pressed his face against my flat belly. He murmured that he thought his French was beginning to come back.

He puréed oysters for me in the blender and made me duckling *à l'orange,* frogs' legs *provençale,* poached salmon with chestnuts. He sautéed tiny carrots and crumbled dillweed into the melted butter. He tenderly fed his creations into the blender and I drank them with a straw.

My husband complained, "Your tits are too small." He said it was like screwing on box springs without a mattress. He had lost his hold. He bruised the span of his chest against my knees night after night. He never wanted me to take off the snake head.

Sometimes, after he was asleep, I'd sneak into the kitchen and put something into the blender for myself, a *taco* or a bowl of Cheerios, and drink it through my cold sleek snake throat. Once I stole a page of my lover's latest manuscript and tried to drink it, but Paris was a pulpy gray paste that stuck in the straw and had to be scraped out of the blender.

I began playing the violin again. I crouched in the closet and played while my husband slept. I began memorizing arias from Bach's *Passion According to Saint Matthew* and singing along quietly in melancholy German. I cried happily in the dark, under the coats.

After a while, Mr. March wouldn't even look at me, no matter what kind of dress I wore. I licked my lips at him invisibly as he shrank against the wall, clutching his attaché case, his bald brown head smooth with revulsion.

Rosemary no longer confided what she and Mr. March said about me. They went to long lunches together; she'd come back flushed and self-righteous.

She rarely spoke to me. One day she said fiercely, "Why don't you just go home and have some kids? Or are you afraid they'll hatch?" Her sneer was so ignorant that it needed no reply.

My husband bought me an imitation-leather bra and garter belt. He went to Frederick's of Hollywood, I suppose. He also bought me some absurdly pointed imitation-snakeskin boots. Luckily, I never had to walk in them. It must be like making love to a La-Z-Boy recliner, I thought, smiling while he grunted and battered himself against my Naugahyde thighs.

One night, when he was through, he told me about a bad dream he'd had.

"You burned the house down," he said. "You meant to do it. You said we could only take a few things, to make it look like an accident. Then you sprinkled gasoline around the house and we lit it. I helped you." He shook his head slowly and said again, "I *helped* you."

"Why did I do it?" I said.

He looked at me, his eyes searching the cobra cavern. He looked puzzled, then annoyed and sullen, like someone trying to scrape mayonnaise out of an empty jar that he could have sworn was full. "I don't know," he said. "It wasn't in the dream." Moments later, he was asleep.

A few nights after that, he got up for a glass of water and heard me in the closet. I was playing *Come, Sweet Death,* sobbing blissfully. He grabbed my arm and yanked me out into the light. He was shaking. Slowly he reached for me and, with both hands, tore off my head and ripped it up the back. He looked at it for a moment, lying in his hands. Then he threw it into the bathtub and started lighting matches. The scales began to smoke and melt, oozing across the pink porcelain. The smell was nauseating.

He carefully turned over the head so that I could see the emerald hood darken and fall away. The black cobra eyes rolled upward in despair, the soft fangs flowed like marshmallow cream over the forked, hot tar tongue. I pressed my violin into my chest until the strings groaned.

The room was filled with fetid black smoke. My husband was crying, too, tears cutting grimy ditches through the soot on his face. For a long time, he watched the feeble, smoldering thing that had been the snake head; he couldn't stand to look at me. Finally, he got himself a glass of water and went back to bed.

Jillie
EHUD HAVAZELET

I have a photograph of Jillie from that summer. Lank blond hair
and the thin angling legs of a girl not quite thirteen. One hand up
against the sun, her eyes blur into shadow and her lips are just
opening, to smile or to speak. It is an old photograph and I have
not kept it well. In the background, the top of the garage has been
sheared away, and cracks run crosswise throughout the print. The
scar on Jillie's face looks remarkably like one of these, a pale blue
seam reaching from the wisps of hair by her ear to the delicate
curve of her jaw and disappearing.

It was taken the day of a barbecue. The plates were not yet
gathered and my father announced he would take pictures. My
mother bent over Grandmother and began fixing her face. Sandra,
Jillie's mother, took a mirror from her purse and dabbed at the
cocoon of hair piled above her head. Jillie was standing in front of
the garage when my father called her name. Lifting a hand to her
eyes, she turned into the sun just as the shutter snapped.

Sandra was my mother's sister, younger by six years. She met
and married Pete, over my parents' objections, while living in
their house, in what was to be my room. They simply came in one
night and announced they were moving to Ohio, where Pete had
landed a job. Sandra was wearing a pearl necklace and a new coat.
They hadn't meant not to invite my parents, Sandra said. It had

just been one of those spur-of-the-moment things. Pete stood by
the window drinking a beer as Sandra showed them her ring. He
was a tall sturdy man with thick red hair down to his shoulders.
His blue eyes were lively, except when he was drinking, and they
gave him an expression of almost constant amusement. When my
mother walked up and told him he had better take care of her
sister, he smiled at her and said he guessed he could do that all
right.

Pete worked in auto parts in Youngstown. When Jillie was born
they sent pictures, and for my arrival, a miniature leather football
with my name tooled across the stitches came by parcel post.
They were supposed to visit Christmases, and one year, a joint
vacation on the Gulf of Mexico was discussed, but the plans never
came through. Sometimes, my mother had long conversations
with Sandra on the phone.

Jillie remembered the first time Pete hit her mother. She heard
the arguing from her bedroom, the voices rising to such a pitch
that she sat up in bed. When the sound of Pete's hand on her
mother's face stung in her ears, she held her breath and pulled up
the covers. When the door slammed and she knew her father had
gone, she stayed under the blanket anyway, feeling her breath
warm the air around her.

The summer before Jillie was thirteen, Pete and Sandra had a
fight. On the second day of a drunk, Pete grabbed Jillie and put
her in the car. He drove fast and talked about Sandra in a way
that made Jillie close her eyes and try not to listen. She did not see
the swerve of the front wheels, or the fence they broke through, or
the tree. Pete was unconscious for twenty-four hours with a con-
cussion and broken ribs. Jillie was not seriously injured, but glass
from the windshield sliced into her face.

Sandra took Jillie from the hospital before the plastic surgeon
could examine the girl, and drove eighteen hours to my parents'
house. When my father opened the door onto a mild summer
night, she was shaking. "I'm not going back this time," she said.
"I swear I'm not." Jillie stood behind her, her face swollen and
discolored under the bandages. She hesitated on the threshold for

several seconds before coming in and letting my mother embrace
her.

That summer, I don't think I knew I was in love with Jillie. I
was a shy twelve-year-old. But I knew a center had come into my
world. I spent hours looking at Jillie when I thought she didn't
know; I found myself thinking of how she would react before I
laughed or grew angry. And I stared at her scar, which flared red
and seemed to divide her face in two.

I showed Jillie my secrets. I showed her the hole toward the
back of the garage ceiling, hidden by the dark and planks of wood.
We climbed through and sat by the small window in the garage's
peak. I took her to the blue house, where birds lived in a pipe by
the roof. We waited in the bushes and counted eight birds one
after another—squeeze out, flutter and fly—like pinwheels in the
wind. In the park, I showed her the painted outline of a body on
the asphalt and we stood for some moments in silence, staring at
the place a dead person had lain.

In the afternoons, our mothers would go shopping, or to the
beauty parlor to lift Sandra's spirits, and Jillie and I would stay
with Grandmother. After her second stroke, Grandmother could
move nothing except her eyes. The doctor told my father it was
questionable if she even saw with those eyes anymore; it might be
a passive response to light and shadow, the doctor said.

Some days, we put Grandmother in her wheelchair and took
her to the back porch. Jillie said she liked it in the sunshine and
the air, and I was always ashamed to say I thought the doctor was
right, that she didn't know what she liked or disliked anymore.
There were cherry trees in the yard, and in late summer, robins
pecked among the black hulls of decomposing fruit, and the air
was heavy and sweet.

One day, Jillie put a basket of cherries in Grandmother's lap.
After a few moments, a robin landed on the gate in front of her
and then hopped into the basket on her knees. The bird wrestled
with a bit of fruit and stretched a thin white worm from it. I
giggled and looked nervously at Jillie.

"We shouldn't do that," I said.

"She likes it, can't you see?" Jillie said, not turning from Grandmother. There was now a bird in her lap and another on her shoulder. "She's the kind of lady who likes the birds."

Other days, we stayed with Grandmother in her room. Jillie sat on the large four-posted bed and took one of Grandmother's hands, turning it over, stroking it, running her fingers up the raised blue veins. "Look. Aren't they beautiful?" Jillie would ask me. Jillie would say, "Do you want me to dance, Grandma?" and I would look closer at Grandmother's face because Jillie said she would answer, though I never saw how.

Taking a shawl or the frilled coverlet off the bed, or sometimes just wrapping herself in and out of her long bright hair, Jillie would dance. There was no music as Jillie wove her arms slowly through the air or whipped them about in wild leaps; just Jillie's feet on the wooden floor and her quick hoarse breathing.

She never asked me if I wanted to dance, though I'm certain I wouldn't have. As she veiled fingers across her face or flung her legs before her, she kept her blue eyes on Grandmother: watching. She was dancing for the old woman. And those other eyes, faded, pendent with tears that would not flow—I came to believe those eyes saw Jillie dance.

In the loft over the garage, I would rub Jillie's back until we were called to dinner. At midday, the sun burned at the holes in the roof, but toward evening, light angled softly through the dusty window and the world looked muted and far away.

Jillie lay on her stomach and I pulled the sweatshirt up, over the downy groove where the skin was softest, stopping at the rounded slopes of her shoulders. I brought my fingers up slowly, rippling the flesh and then passing. Sometimes I would rest my hand on the small of her back when her breathing became still, and sometimes I lay down beside her and stared at the roof, pierced by tiny spots of sun.

"When we live together," Jillie said, "it won't be any place like this."

"Where will it be?" I asked.

"Someplace high up, in the snow. Someplace it would take days to get to and most people wouldn't even try. It would be white, like the snow, and you couldn't even see it except for the smoke from the chimneys."

"What would we eat?"

"Whatever we found. We would trap things and kill them."

"Rabbits? Squirrels?"

She nodded. I looked up at the rafters and tried to picture what was in Jillie's mind. I tried for the snow; the cold sharp air; the building, white against white, vanishing into itself. The image shimmered in my mind and faded. I felt lonely.

"And will we come back here at all?" I asked her.

Jillie turned her head toward me. Her eyes reflected the sinking light like an animal's in the dark.

"No," she said. "This place will be gone."

On the day Grandmother died we sat in the kitchen while the doctor drank his coffee. He was a small man in a dark suit and he held the coffee cup inches from his face, as if wanting its warmth.

"You like to see them go that way," he said. "They don't even know it at the end."

In our holiday clothing, Jillie and I sat with Grandmother. The light was dim through the drawn shades. I sat in a chair by the bureau, conscious of the pressure of my necktie. Jillie stood by the bed, the heel of one black shoe on the toe of the other, her white dress faintly luminous in the midday twilight.

"Do I look like her, you think?" she asked me. I was startled by her voice. I rose. From closer, I could not make myself suppose Grandmother was resting. She seemed impossibly heavy, skin sagging in folds against her face. I saw no relation between the body in the bed and Jillie, white dress and shiny shoes, leaning forward as if she might, at any second, begin to float.

"No," I said. "She's old."

Jillie moved closer and tried to hold one of Grandmother's hands. She could not move it. "Jillie," I said. She reached out a hand, rested it on Grandmother's forehead, and pinched an eye open with her thumb. The skin pulled away and the eye—solid, dry and lusterless as bone—stared in fixed surprise at the ceiling.

I heard myself say Jillie's name, and felt her shoulder warm beneath her dress.

On Jillie's birthday, we had a party after dinner. My mother baked a chocolate cake with Jillie's name on it and my father bought a bottle of champagne. Sandra gave Jillie a pair of turquoise earrings and promised to take her downtown to have her ears pierced the following week.

Sandra drank a lot of champagne and when my father put a record on the phonograph, pulled me into the center of the room to dance. She pressed my head against her dress and the sweetness of her perfume mixed with the sour smell of the champagne as she sang into my ear. Her breasts were heavy against my cheek and I was embarrassed to be considered so young that I could be held to them like a child. After the music, we sat at the table. Sandra was still singing. She put her arms around Jillie.

"Oh, honey," she said, "you're getting to be so beautiful, your own mother will be jealous soon." She smiled. "When I get the money, baby, I promise. We'll fix that horrible thing on your face."

The phone rang in the kitchen and my father talked in a low voice. Sandra was winding Jillie's hair above her head when his voice became louder. "I'm not sure she *would* like to," we heard him say.

Sandra's eyes, which had been wandering, became alert. "Who is that?" she said to my mother. "Who's on the phone?"

My father came into the room. "It's Pete," he said. "You don't have to talk to him."

Sandra rushed past him into the kitchen. We could hear her sobbing. Jillie picked up one of the earrings and rubbed it between her fingers. Sandra hung up the phone and walked in.

"Pete's in town," she said. "He's coming over."

"We won't let him in the house, Sandra," my mother said.

"He wants to see Jillie. It's her birthday."

Pete arrived in a sport jacket and tie. His hair was in a neat ponytail and he carried flowers and a six-pack of beer. He stood in the doorway smiling. Sandra stood at the table.

"Sandy," Pete said.

She ran to him and they kissed. Pete walked in with Sandra on his arm. My father nodded stiffly at him and my mother went into the kitchen.

"Honey," Sandra said. "Say hello to your father."

"Hello, Daddy," Jillie said.

Pete said, "I've come for your birthday, baby. Did you think I'd miss that?"

Jillie walked over and Pete put his free arm around her. Pressed into his large body, she looked very young. Her eyes, clear and insistent, seemed to focus on something far away.

In my room that night, I heard the sounds of an argument. There was my father's voice trying to remain civil, my mother's with a shrill note of pleading, Pete's casual drawl, always as if a laugh were gathering just below the surface, and Sandra's wail, lifting slowly.

The front door slammed and Sandra began to scream. My father shouted and I heard my mother breathing as she climbed the stairs to her room. My father said something to Sandra, and his tone had a finality that prevented any answer. I heard his heavy feet on the stairs, and as I fell asleep, Sandra's whimpering into silence, alone.

In the loft the next day, I found Jillie with a sleeping bag and a basket of food.

"She's going back to him," she said. "They want to take me with them."

I looked at her face. In the shadows, the scar reached out of her hair like a long bony finger. I looked at the sleeping bag and the food, and nodded.

"I'm staying here. You'll bring me food and empty that can at night. You can only come up here at night."

"It'll get cold, Jillie."

"I took your father's sleeping bag. They don't know about this place, do they?"

"I don't think so. Nobody uses the garage."

She looked around. The events of the night before and Jillie's announcement upset me more than I could tell her, and in any case, I knew I would help.

"How long will you stay here?" I asked.

She was startled. "I don't know," she said. "A few days." She sat on the sleeping bag.

"I have something for you."

She smiled. "What?"

"A birthday present." I handed her the album cover I had brought with me. Inside was a collage cut from magazines and travel posters. A white wooden house with light blue shingles sat on a snow-covered mountain. There were fruit trees and sea birds and a pointed sun-face wearing dark glasses. To the side, Arctic hares ate leaves and brambles. "Our place," I said.

"It's perfect," she said. "I'll look at it all the time."

That evening, Jillie did not come home for dinner. Sandra kept lighting cigarettes and leaving them unsmoked all over the house. I had already said I knew nothing, but when my mother walked in to say the last of the neighbors had not seen Jillie, Sandra looked wildly at me. "He knows," she said. "He knows where she's gone. Make him say."

She grabbed my shoulders and shook me, her fingernails deep in my skin. I remembered Jillie saying if you're going to get hit, start to cry, and they'll feel sorry for you. It's not hard, she had said. Crying is a lot like laughing. To my surprise, a thin cry escaped my mouth and tears started down my cheeks.

"Leave him alone, Sandra," my mother said. "Can't you see he's as upset as we are?"

Sandra called Pete at his hotel and they drove around the neighborhood together. The police came and my mother gave them the photograph of Jillie in front of the garage. I was sent to bed.

At breakfast, Pete was in his undershirt, making a list of the people Jillie knew. He asked me where we used to go, if we had any favorite spots. I told him we didn't. He looked at me, and I felt a pressure build in my throat. It was harder, somehow, to lie to Pete. I thought he would accuse me right then, but he looked away and asked for more coffee.

All day, my parents were on the phone. I looked around for things to bring Jillie that night and tried to draw as little attention as possible.

Jillie was wrapped in the sleeping bag. I could barely make her out.

"How's it going?" she asked.

"Okay. They're upset. I'm worried about your father."

"Is he drinking?"

"A little."

My eyes grew accustomed to the dark. I had never been in the loft at night before.

"Spooky in here," I said.

"No, it isn't. It's nice. Look." She pointed at one of the walls. Halfway up, wedged between two nails, was the picture I had given her.

"It's kind of cold," I said.

"Come in here."

We sat under the sleeping bag for a few minutes and then Jillie said I should go. They might wake up and look for me.

"Where's the can?" I asked.

"Near the hole. You probably stepped in it."

"I see it. You want anything special?"

"Yeah. Peanut butter."

I stood up.

"Thanks," she said, and stood near me. She leaned over and kissed my cheek.

"You're a dumb bitch," Pete said, looking at Sandra blankly.
"You never should have been a mother."

"Me," Sandra said. "Who do you think she's running from?"

"She's crazy as you are. Two crazy bitches."

Pete had been drinking since early morning. He sat at the table
pouring whiskey slowly into a water glass, holding it momentarily
before his lips and then drinking it down in big unhurried swallows. He had been silent an hour before speaking to Sandra.

"Well," he said. "We find that kid and I'll fix her."

Sandra stood in the doorway to the kitchen. "Yeah, Pete," she
said. "You fix her. Why don't you take her for another ride?" Pete
filled a glass with whiskey. "Big fucking guy," she said. "Why
don't you finish your bottle and beat me up? My sister's never
seen you do it. Why don't you beat her too? Beat up everyone and
then disappear for a month." Sandra's voice was getting higher.
She leaned against the door frame and her head bobbed with the
force of her breathing.

"You better shut up now," Pete said.

My mother took Sandra by the shoulder and led her into the
kitchen. My father sat down opposite Pete.

"What a dumb bitch," Pete said, looking away.

It had been a chilly day, gray clouds hanging flat against the
sky, and toward evening it began to rain, a steady careening rain
that hissed off the sidewalks. When I went to bed, it had not let
up. I waited two hours and slipped out, carrying a blanket and a
large poncho.

I climbed into the garage by a side window. Water fell steadily
from the ceiling and collected on the cement floor. I climbed
through the hole, almost losing my balance on the slick wood.

"Jillie," I whispered.

"Hi," she said. I sat without moving, waiting to see. Rain
whipped at the roof above and the air smelled of wet dust and
rotting wood. After a few moments, I could distinguish the out-

lines of the walls, and here and there, a downward shimmering where water slid on them in sheets. Jillie was in the far corner, wrapped in the bag. Her hair hung in limp strands.

"Are you all right?"

"Yeah," she said. "I got a little wet."

I had to slosh through an inch of water to reach her. The sleeping bag oozed like a sponge.

"It's freezing in here, Jillie," I said. "Maybe you should come down." She didn't answer. "I brought a blanket," I said, "and a poncho. Is the sleeping bag all soaked?"

"Just the bottom. It's dry up here."

We listened to the rain. There was a clarity to that sound I have not forgotten—each drop sharp against the shingles, distinct, though identical to the rest. It was soothing.

Jillie said, "Help me. It was so hot before, I let my clothes get wet."

She folded the sleeping bag in half and lined it with the blanket. She draped the poncho over the bag. The spot she had chosen was the highest on the floor, the roof above it nearly whole. The makeshift bed would be relatively dry.

"There," she said, when she had finished.

She stood up and began taking off her clothes. I could almost feel the shiver as her skin opened to the damp. Her clothing slapped to the floor. Moving fast, her pale body shifting before me like clouds before the moon, she crawled into the bag.

"Is it okay?" I asked.

"Oh, it's warm."

I sat by the edge of the bed. The rain seemed to be subsiding. It rose and fell against the roof, breathing, almost.

"Jillie," I said. "I want to stay."

"All right," she said. "There's room."

My clothes were slimy with the muck I had crawled through. I pulled them off quickly and slipped in beside Jillie. Her skin shocked against mine, first cool and smooth, then warmer. She pulled the bag over us and turned toward me. There was room enough only if we pushed together. We put our arms around each other and my hands, as if automatically, began stroking her back.

Her fingers drew me close lightly. My lips brushed her face and I began kissing her, softly, as if I would never stop, her nose, her cheek, her mouth, her eyes. I heard the rain moved by the wind and my short breaths between kisses.

It was just light. The rain had ended and isolated dripping sounds mingled with birdcalls. I felt sweat on Jillie's skin and her face was warm. She sneezed, and from the slight glaze in her eyes, I could see she was feverish.

She made me hurry. I dressed and looked at her shuddering in the bag.

"You're sick."

"Hurry," she said.

I don't know if my decision was made then or if it formed slowly through the morning. I have never been able to conclude that I even made a decision, with the weighing of choice, of consequence. But I know that Jillie's face was in my mind all morning.

My mother stood by the window in the kitchen, drinking coffee.

"She's in the garage, Mom."

"What?"

"Jillie is."

"What are you saying? Where?"

"In the garage. She's sick."

I sat at the table and heard the noises and shouting. When Pete carried Jillie in, Sandra walked up to me and slapped me hard across the face.

My ears filled with ringing and I turned quickly toward Jillie. She was looking at me. I felt my mouth opening, and then her eyes became dull, solid. She looked away.

Jillie was in bed three days and she didn't want to see me. The night after she was found, Pete and Sandra and my parents had a long talk. By the end, both Pete and his wife were crying.

When Pete loaded the car to leave, Jillie was on the sofa, wrapped in a blanket. She still had a fever, but they wanted to get her home. I had climbed up to the loft before my father boarded it shut and taken the collage of the house in the snow. I gave it to Jillie.

"What's that?" Sandra said brightly.

"It's just a place," I said, looking at Jillie. "A house."

"Oh," Sandra crooned. "Did you make it?"

"Yes. For Jillie."

"That's nice," Sandra said. "I'm sure she's very grateful."

Jillie did not look at me. Pete came in with a box of candy and a huge rag doll. There was kissing and hugging and talk about Christmas. Pete gripped my shoulder and gave me a steady look by which I suppose he meant he forgave me. Sandra rumpled my hair and left a waxy imprint of lips on my cheek. We went out to the car and waved until it turned the corner. In the house, Jillie had left the collage on the sofa.

Some time later, the police returned the photograph of Jillie to my parents. For years it has been bundled, along with the snow collage, in a box full of poems, love letters, and other tokens which are supposed to stay forgetfulness.

I have seen Jillie since. Though we did not see her family, over the years, I heard news of her: Jillie had moved away without finishing school, had wired from Mexico for money, had been in trouble with the law. When I was eighteen, she was to have come to the wedding of a distant cousin, and I took the train overnight to Buffalo, but she had called to say she couldn't make it. My cousin didn't know why.

I had heard of her marriage and, vaguely, of children. When my job required that I drive out West, I realized I would be passing the town in which she lived. I resisted all thoughts of a visit. That summer was long past, but it was still familiar to my mind, sometimes as if I could accommodate only that single memory.

But, on the day of the drive, something in the late-afternoon light moved me. It was summer again, and the sky ahead threatened rain. I had been driving since early morning, and suddenly, the thought of driving through the night in another rainfall to another motel was too much to bear. A quick phone call, a short detour, and I stood in Jillie's home.

Her blond hair was clipped and she wore sunglasses like her mother's. A surgeon had repaired her scar and her young woman's face was without blemish, though more sharply angled than I remembered it. The children were away, she told me. They would be so disappointed.

We sat in the living room and drank beer. I met her husband, whose resemblance to Pete was so strong that I found it hard to look at him. From the way he grasped my hand and said, "So here's the famous cousin I've heard so much about," I knew he had never heard a word about me.

We talked briefly about that summer, and Jillie's husband loosed his hearty booming laugh several times at our adventure. They asked about my business; they expected a wedding invitation soon. When they invited me to stay for dinner, I said no, I had friends awaiting me on the Coast.

Before I left, Jillie kissed my cheek and said, "You know, I could have killed you that day, I was so mad. Still, I should thank you. I mean, what would have happened if they'd left us up there?"

The three of us laughed and I got into my car. As I pulled away, I looked back at Jillie and her husband on their doorstep, arms raised in farewell. I thought I would remember them that way. But when I try, the details don't mesh. Each time, something more is missing—the shape of the house, or the tree I'm certain grew in front of it. Last time, I forgot the sunglasses, and I've changed the husband's hair several times, and soon I'm certain I won't see anything at all.

Hands

GREGORY BLAKE SMITH

Here in New England we sit in chairs.

It's from my porch rocker that I watch the raccoon. He usually comes at dusk, that time of day half dog and half wolf, when the downturned leaves seem to glow with the sunset and the upturned ones glimmer with moonlight. I watch him pad through autumn weeds while the sweat of my chairmaking dries on my skin. He lingers in the shadows, still woodside, the sun falling further with each moment, and then waddles onto my lawn. He looks like a house cat, once the woods are behind him. He tosses a wary look at me and then slowly disappears behind the chair shop. After another minute I hear the enormous crash of my garbage can lid falling on the stones. He doesn't even bother to run off as he used to, dawdling at the wood's edge until it's safe to come back. He seems to know I won't leave my chair.

"A twenty-two," my neighbor Moose says while I pare stretchers. "A twenty-two and then we won't blow the b'Jesus out of the pelt."

I take a few more cuts with my gouge and then ask him how he thinks the raccoon has missed his trap line all this time. He peers at me with that cold menace of old age. He has a white beard that rims his chin like frost.

"It probably don't run my way," he says. "But if you want it trapped I can trap it. It's just a pissload easier to shoot it if it's coming every night like you're ringing the dinner bell. Right here," he says and he goes over to the window just above my workbench and taps at a pane. His fingers are scarred with patches of old frostbite. "We'll take this here pane out. I can rest the barrel on the mullion. If it's close enough I'll get it clean through the head and I'll be richer one pelt and you'll be poorer one dinner guest."

I tell him I'm not sure I want to kill him.

"*Him?*" he says. "How d'you know it's a *him?*" And he spits on my woodstove so the cast iron sizzles and steams.

Outside, my moaning tree sends up a regular howl.

"*Please* cut that tree down, Smitty," my sister Jaxxlyn says every weekend when she comes up from New York. "It's driving me positively psychotic."

I tell her it's a poplar. I can't cut it down. I don't use poplar in my chairs.

"But you heat with wood," she says. "Don't you? Don't you heat with wood?"

Not poplar wood I don't, I say. Too soft.

"It's driving me positively psychotic, Smitty."

I say what about New York. What about the car horns and the sirens. She says they don't have trees that moan in New York, Smitty.

Smitty, she says.

My name is Smith. I'm a chairmaker with a tree that's grown itself tight around a telephone pole and a raccoon that's taken a fancy to my garbage. I've never minded the name Smith. I like the ancestral whiff of fashioning and forging in its single syllable. And I don't mind the moaning tree and its outrage over the telephone poles that have been stabbed into the landscape like stilettos, rubbing its insulted bark in the slightest breeze and howling when the wind blows in earnest. But the raccoon has unsettled me and I don't know why. My sister—who hates her last name and is being driven psychotic by my moaning tree—is not bothered by the raccoon.

"I think he's *cute,*" she says, sitting on my porch with me as the fat creature moves from shadow into moonlight and back into shadow. "My friend Flora in the west seventies has a skunk for a pet. You should see him, Smitty! His little claws go clack-clack-clack on the linoleum, you know? Of course he's been desmelled or whatever they do to them. Oh, Smitty!" she says as the garbage can lid crashes on the stony ground. "Isn't that the cutest thing? How does he do it? Just *how* does he do it? Do you leave the lid on loose for him? Is that how he does it?"

Hands, I tell her, and I feel a faint panic at the word. They've got hands. And I hold my own hands up in the gloom, the backs reddish with dusk, the palms silver with moonlight.

When Monday comes I try tying the lid shut with mason's twine. That night there is no aluminum crash and I think: so much for hands, so much for raccoons, so much for half dog and half wolf! The next day I start in on a set of eight Queen Anne chairs, carefully designing the *S*-shaped legs to Hogarth's line of beauty. But that evening the raccoon comes trotting along the forest floor, hiking up onto my lawn behind the shop. It takes him a few minutes longer, but eventually the harsh, bright crash shatters the dusk. I sit in a stupor. In ten minutes he emerges from behind the shop trundling happily along. He pauses partway to the wood's edge and tosses me a scornful look over his shoulder and then vanishes into the now-dark bushes.

"You might open up a motel," Moose suggests, "seeing as what you already got yourself a rest'rant."

My cabriole legs aren't right. I can't strike the balance between knee and foot. It's never happened like this before. I get out Hogarth's *Analysis of Beauty* and look his *S*'s over, and I print *S S S S S* on my graph paper, write my own name: *S*mith, *S*mith, *S*mith, *S*mith, but when I go to draft my Queen Anne leg I can't balance the knee to the foot, the foot to the knee, the *S*'s top orb to its bottom. I spend a whole day at my drafting table, trying, and end up tossing a sheaf of rejected legs into the stove. That night the raccoon dines on pumpkin and old cantaloupe.

I get my bucksaw and my knapsack and my spool of pink ribbon. If I can't work I'll hunt wood, do the felling now and wait until the first decent snow to find the marker ribbons and sledge the logs out with Moose's snowmobile. I plan on a two-day roam, bringing my sleeping bag and some food. At the sight of my bucksaw, my moaning tree groans.

I'm going to forget about raccoons.

I poach my lumber, and maybe that's why I have a feeling of trespassing when I go into the woods, of being where I only half belong. There are stone walls everywhere, built in earlier centuries and now running mute and indecipherable through the forest. Walking, I try to picture perfect S's in the air, but the stone walls distract me. They are like hieroglyphs on the land. From time to time I come across an old foundation, a sprinkle of broken glass in the weeds and a small graveyard a ways off. I find a bottle or two, an old auger, but they look as alien there as I do. Farther on, the stone walls are so tumble-down they have ceased to look like walls. There is a feeling of low menace all around.

I mark my wood as I go, but on this trip I keep my eyes open for hollowed trees, for trees with holes, a cicatrix, disease. I climb up several and look inside, peer up the trunk of one, but there's no sign of habitation. That night, lying on dark pine needles, I have a recurring picture of the raccoon back at my house, sitting at the kitchen table in one of my chairs, with knife and fork in hand— perhaps a napkin—eating.

By noontime on the second day I've swung around to where I know there's a stand of tiger maple near a marshy pond two miles from the house. I spend the afternoon carefully harvesting the rare, figured wood, dragging the delimbed trunks down to the pondside and stickering them off the ground so they won't rot. The work puts the raccoon out of my mind. I feel healthy, feel the steel teeth of my bucksaw sharp and vengeful, the rasp of the sawn wood like the sound of defeat. But after the last haul, just as I sit content and forgetful on a stump, I catch sight of a tiny footprint in the soft silt that rings the water. Farther on, there's another one.

There's a hush over the pond. The marsh reeds stand like pickets along the shore. Across the way the shadows between the junipers and low laurels seem to breathe in and out. I have a feeling of having been tricked, of having been watched all along.

On the water the whirligigs hover like spies. A scarlet leaf flutters through the blue air and lands a foot or so from the raccoon's footprint, then cartwheels slyly until it covers the print. But it's too late. In the west, where my house is, the sun is kindling nests of reddish fire in the blue tops of the spruces.

You've got yourself a comfy den, I'm saying half an hour later after I've found the raccoon's beech tree. I've brought a crotched branch from the pondside for a leg up, and I'm peering into a yawning hole maybe ten feet off the ground. I say it out loud. I do. I say: leaves and dried reeds, decaying wood for heat, some duck down. You've done all right. Yes, you have. You've done all right.

The trees seem to stir at the sound of my voice. I pull my head out and listen. They sound baffled, outraged. I want to say to them: "Do you think so? Do you think so? So *I'm* the intruder? Do you think so?" But I don't. I just look at the hasty illogic of the shadows. Trees don't come on all fours and pry your garbage can lid off, I say. Even Darwin can't see to that, I say, and I go back to looking inside the raccoon's den.

I'm not afraid he's in there somewhere. I *know* what time of day it is. I *know* where he is. But off to the side, in a decaying burl, something has caught my eye, something shiny and unnatural. I look closer and realize he's got himself a cache of junk, bottle caps and aluminum can rings. Then in the next instant I recognize a piece of old coffee cup I'd broken in the summer, and then, too, a router bit I'd chipped and thrown out, then an old ballpoint, a spoon, screws.

Are you a user of spoons, too, raccoon? I finally say out loud. And screws? And pens? Are you a writer of sonnets? I say.

But even as I talk I hear footsteps behind me on the leaves. I pull my head out and look around, but there's nothing moving, just the vagrant leaves falling. I listen again, hear them coming closer. Is it the raccoon returning? I hang fire a moment and then start hurriedly down the trunk. But before I do I reach in and steal back my old ballpoint. I hide the crotched limb in some bushes nearby.

For the next few days I wonder just how much the raccoon knows. There's no new contempt evident in his regard as he bellies up out of the woods onto my lawn—but he may be a master of his emotions. Jaxxlyn has put a bowl of water out for him. She says she's going to move it nearer to the house each day until the raccoon gets used to being with us. She wants me to do the moving on the weekdays.

My West Hartford client calls and asks how her Queen Anne chairs are coming. I start to tell her about the raccoon. I start to tell her about William Hogarth and beauty and order, about how a man can't work when a raccoon's eating his garbage, about how I've allowed eagle's claws for chair feet in the past, lion's paws too. But this raccoon is asking too much, I tell her. There's a silence on the line when I stop—and then she asks again how her chairs are coming.

"Six inches each day," Jaxx tells me as she gets into her car. "Six inches, Smitty."

Monday I can't work. Tuesday I can't either. Tuesday evening I wander off into the woods again, walk the two miles to the raccoon's tree. Somewhere on the way I know we cross paths. I get the crotched limb out of its hiding place and steal back a screw.

The next morning I get the mating *S*'s of the cabriole legs down perfectly in ten minutes, and by sundown I have all sixteen legs squared up and cut. That night I take the router bit back.

Thursday it's another screw. Friday a piece of china. I'm going great guns on my chairs.

Jaxxlyn doesn't understand why the raccoon won't drink her water. She asks if I've moved it each day. Then she talks to the raccoon from the porch, talks to him so he pauses in his jaunty walk and looks our way. She alternates from a low, cooing voice to a high, baby voice. The raccoon and I exchange looks. He knows, I think to myself. He knows. He can hardly cart things off as fast as I can steal them back. He knows.

For the next week I am a maker of chairs in the daytime and a sitter of chairs at night. I'm a happy man. Only during the in-between hours do I venture through the woods to the raccoon's house and then venture back in the near-dark. I've taken to putting my booty back in the trash can.

My West Hartford lady drives cross-state to see how her chairs are coming along. I let her run her wealthy fingers across the soft wood, up and down the smooth legs. She shivers and says it feels alive still. "Doesn't it feel alive still?" she says.

Back in the woods I take a different route to the raccoon's tree. I figure I might catch him out this time, but it turns out we've merely switched paths, and he's trying to catch me out. I round the pond quickly, the last fall leaves floating like toy boats on the water, and hurry to the bushes where the crotched branch is hidden. The trees are quiet. I throw the crotch up against the tree-trunk, climb quickly up, and in the half-light see that the raccoon has taken the ballpoint pen back.

Still writing sonnets, raccoon? I say and I reach in and take the pen back. But just as I do the den bursts into a flurry of fur and claws and teeth. I hear a hiss, a growling sibilance, and just before I fall see two leathery hands gripped around my wrist and a furry mouth set to bite. An instant later I am lying scratched and hurt in the laurel below. Above me the raccoon peers fiercely down at me from his hole. His eyes are black and fanatical, and he seems to say: "All right? All right? Understand? All right?"

Violence! I spit through my teeth, stumbling back through the woods. I don't even try to stanch the blood coming from the punctures on my wrist. *Violence! Violence!*

Moose laughs. He laughs and asks how much the first of my rabies series costs. I'm sitting in his living room feeding bark into his stove. I don't answer him at first. I'm sick and I ache from the shot. Finally I tell him twenty dollars.

"Well, let's see," he says and he sights down the barrel of his twenty-two. "A raccoon pelt brings thirty dollar nowadays. You already used up twenty of them dollars on that shot. But I figure my half is still fifteen. So I figure you owe me five dollar."

I muster enough character to tell him he's getting a little ahead of himself, he's getting a little eager.

"No eagerer than that raccoon's getting," he says. The frostbite on his face crumples with his laugh, as if the skin there were half alive. I sit sullen and witless. I feel wasted. I don't know what to do. The raccoon comes and ravages my garbage.

I lie in bed for two days. When I'm up again I ask Moose for one of his box traps. I tell him I don't want to shoot the raccoon, I want to trap him. And once I've trapped him I want to let him go. He looks at me like this is confirmation of some suspicion he's had about me all along, never mind raccoons, some suspicion he'd had since he met me and my chairs.

"I ain't altogether sure a raccoon will trap so near a house," he says. "Raccoons ain't dumb."

This one will, I say. He's a modern raccoon.

But that night, sitting in my warm chair shop on a half-finished Queen Anne chair, I watch the raccoon stop and inspect the trap, puff at the acorn squash inside and then waddle over to the garbage can. He knocks the lid off with a professional air, but before he crouches into the garbage, he tosses a disdainful look through the windowpane at me and my chair. Behind him the trap sits in a state of frozen violence.

Beauty is the visible fitness of a thing to its use, I say to the raccoon in my dreams. Order, in other words. In a Yale-ish voice he answers back: "Not entirely different from that beauty which there is in fitting a mortise to its tenon."

I wake in a sweat. My wound itches under its bandage.

On the second night, kneeling on the wooden floor in my shop, the chairs empty behind me, I watch the raccoon sniff a moment longer at the squash but again pass it up. This time it's contempt in his face when he catches sight of me through the windowpane. That night the air turns cold.

What do you want? I whisper to the raccoon in my sleep. *What do you want?*

"What do you want?" the raccoon whispers back. *"What do you want?"*

On the third night I forsake the chair shop for the junipers, hiding myself long before dusk in the green shrubbery that skirts the forest's edge. It's snowing. The flurries make an icy whisper in the trees overhead. I watch the sun fall through autumn avatars and set in blue winter. The snowflakes land on my eyelashes and melt New England into an antique drizzle. I blink my eyes to clear them and wait with my joints stiffening, my toes disappearing.

By the time the raccoon comes I am iced over, a snowy stump among the evergreens. He pads silently through the snow, leaving tiny handprints behind him on the slushy ground. He doesn't see me. I watch him with frost inside me, my breathing halted, my hands clubbed. He looks for me on the porch, in my rocker, then tries to spy me through my shop window. For an instant he seems stunned by my absence, by the change in things. He turns and peers straight across at where I sit in the frozen junipers. I am certain he sees me, even nod my head at him. For a moment we are poised, balanced, the one against the other. He blinks, acknowledging my presence in the snow, and then with an air of genteel reciprocation, turns and walks straight into the trap.

When I reach him he has his paws up on the trap's sides, the fingers outstretched on the fencing. He peers up at me as if to see if I'll take his hands as evidence after all. There are snowflakes on his eyelashes. When I bend over him our breaths mingle in the cold gray New England air.

Cuisinart
FRED LEEBRON

She knocks on the door and says, "Honey, can I borrow your Cuisinart?"

"Sure," I say.

"Honey, I got a date." She's got her hair dolled up in a platinum pile. Her fingernails are lacquered orange.

"What are you making him?"

"Carrot soup and shrimp casserole."

She takes the Cuisinart and leaves. It's an old Cuisinart, a heavy one. I don't help her.

We used to make dinner a lot together. We'd take off our work clothes, put on shorts and T-shirts, and cook up meals from a book we got at the library: *Food for Two*. Curried egg salad, chicken salad, beef bourguignon, stroganoff, chicken in white wine sauce, cacciatore.

Now we're having one of those modern relationships where we see other people. She sees more. I don't see much. She sees a different guy every weekend. He's usually over six feet with curly brown hair. He's usually got wrists that are bigger than my biceps. But he's usually a pretty nice guy.

I don't worry about these things. Sometimes I look in the mirror and I go, "Honey, you're boring." Sometimes she'll come over —she's still got her key—and climb into bed with me at three in the morning. Sometimes these modern relationships are pretty nice.

Tonight's a little different, though. It's the same guy for the third weekend in a row. I think she calls him Chop. He's a familiar guy. I've played basketball against him in the gym on Sunday afternoons. He's got that curly brown hair that she likes so much. And freckles. Freckles kill her.

She lives right down the hall, and now I hear Chop clomping down there in his work boots. He always wears these muddy tan work boots and a flannel shirt that hangs out of the back of his trousers like a warning flag. Chop's pants are always jeans, and his hands are always stuffed in the pockets, so the pants grab his thick legs and the swoop of his buttocks. He's got a good outside jump shot; and when he drives the lane you generally get out of his way.

The Cuisinart starts whirring soon after she shuts the door behind him. She never starts cooking until Chop comes. "It's something sexual. It's always something sexual. You make food together and then you make love together. That's the way these things work out."

The Cuisinart goes for a time. Maybe he's grabbing her around the waist and she can't concentrate. Maybe she's rubbing his shoulders and doesn't care. Maybe they're screwing standing up in the kitchen.

They're still not finished with the Cuisinart. You can do a lot of things with a Cuisinart. There's six or seven different blades that you can use. It's a cylindrical machine, but it can dice, slice, mash, whip, chop or scallop. It can make onions into little crescents and carrots into long, thin hairlike strands. When you really whip up stuff it'll stick to the sides of the Cuisinart, and you have to take a rubber spatula and scrape it clean.

"Occasionally, it'll break down on you." That means you didn't screw on the blade tight enough, or the little rotor down in the engine is burnt out or busted or just loose. Lots of people have these Cuisinarts. It means you like cooking and don't mind cleaning up afterward.

I don't use it much these days. I eat frozen meat pies from Mrs. Swanson, or I grab a bowl of chili at the bar. I drink a lot to keep my weight up, but it doesn't seem to be working. She says you can only put on so much weight by drinking, but you've got to eat. I don't feel much like eating.

But this is my drinking year. Okay, so it's been longer than a year. I drank before I met her and I drank more when we went out, when we were more than modern but less than old-fashioned, when we loved each other without being in love, when we lived together without being married. She's a good drinker and she made me a better one. When we cooked those meals together, we drank a lot, too. I always drank a lot with her. I'm a boring guy, I've got nothing to say, I might as well drink and cover it up. Lots of people are that way.

It got bad when she was working and I wasn't. I'd walk over every day at noon to meet her for lunch. We'd split a pitcher or a carafe. Then I'd go home and pass out. She'd come in and wake me up at six. We'd start drinking and making dinner, and by the time I had the last bite of stroganoff, I'd be ready to pass out.

"Honey," she'd say. "What's wrong with you?"

"I'm afraid I might bore you to death," I'd want to say. "So I'm going to pass out first."

Anyway, about two months ago she said she was tired and worn out. She said she wanted to freshen up our relationship. I asked her what that meant. She said it meant seeing other people.

"What do you mean, 'seeing other people'?" I said. "You mean going out on the street and taking a look? Or you mean going out on the street and bringing these other people back and—"

"Shut up," she said. "Just relax." She poured me another drink. I think it was a scotch and soda. Then she sat down and crossed her legs and folded her arms across her breasts. I was beginning to get the picture.

And she said, "Honey, I'm moving back to my place. We might work out. We might not. But I'll just be down the hall. Can you handle it?"

I downed my drink in one slug. I eyed the Cuisinart; it was the only attraction in the kitchen. Then I poured myself another drink. I tried to stir it with my finger, but my hand kept shaking. A puddle spread on the counter as if the glass were leaking.

There was another thing, too, that hurt us. Back when things were as good as they were going to get, we had gone and taken the blood tests. They said we didn't match. We weren't even sure we were going to have kids, but the results did something to her.

So "Of course I can," I said. And she moved out. She piled all her things in empty beer cases and old milk crates that she swiped from a grocer's. For weeks there were all these cases stacked high against the walls of this apartment. She's just moving down the hall, she said. It felt like she was moving to Australia.

Well, so she moves out, and of course it changes a lot of things. Her hair, for instance. Almost every week it's a different color: purple or orange or green streaked with black. It used to be just a plain, thick brown, but now she says she wants to "cut loose."

At first she let herself in a lot, made love with me when I was least expecting it. But I didn't have a key to her place, so I could never do the same thing to her.

After a while, though, these surprises dropped from three times a week to two times a week. Now it's barely once a week. In the past three weeks Chop has been over ten or twelve times. So she wants me only occasionally.

It makes me feel like basketball. When I was in high school I was a pretty fair basketball player. But not great. I was second string. But I had a good outside jump shot and when the opposing team filled the lane against us, I'd be sent in. It was only in tough games when we were almost losing. And I would salt away a couple jump shots and be taken out again. That was my basketball career. After my last game, I wanted to cut up everything. I took my sneakers and my uniform and ran a power lawnmower over them. The rubber of the sneakers got tangled in the blade. It took me a long time to want to play basketball again.

Now take this thing with her. She's got a pretty good deal going. Chop is hot stuff. I can see that. But, hey, when she wants me, she calls me off the bench. I rise and whip off my warm-ups, enter the court to the roar of the crowd, hit my jump shots and sit back down again.

That Cuisinart's finally stopped. That was a long spin. Carrots do that, though. They make the Cuisinart work.

You think of how Cuisinarts work and how they blend things

together. Carrots and potatoes and apples, for instance, can be pureed together until they all feel the same way on your tongue. And they're perfectly balanced, happy, with each other. That's quite a thing that the Cuisinart does.

There's a knock on the door. The clock says it's three, but I don't believe it. Sometimes you lie in bed for so long it feels like you've been trying to fall asleep your whole life.

"Come in," I say.

"Hi, honey." She's wearing a bathrobe with nothing under it. "I'm bringing back your Cuisinart." She struggles with it to the kitchen counter.

I climb out of bed. "Chop go home?"

"Of course not," she says. The kitchen light stuns me for a moment, so I don't see her blinding smile until it's too late.

"What's going on?" I say.

"Oh, honey," she says. "I think he's the one for me. I really do."

"Oh, Christ," I say. I sit on the kitchen counter beside the Cuisinart. I look down at its open face.

"He moving in?" I plug in the Cuisinart. It's got on its puree blade. All I have to do is flick the switch. This is the kind of thing you think at three in the morning on another sleepless night.

"Yes," she says. "You're not hurt, are you? We weren't working out anyway."

"No." I take a deep breath. It feels like my whole heart is shaking. How can I love this person? is all I want to know. Her hair's always a different color and all she does is make me drink. What's the matter with me?

"Good," she says. "That's my honey."

"Come here," I say. She looks so good, her platinum hair now hanging in bangs, ringing her face. She must be fresh from bed and wanting to gloat. People are like that when they find the right person. They just want to tell everybody.

She walks over to me and smiles.

"I hope you'll be very happy," I say. There's a fine ringing in my ears, the roar of the crowd. I take hold of her hand.

"Oh, honey," she says. "You're so sweet." She smiles sweetly at me. I have her hand and together I plunge us down into the Cuisinart, trying to flick the switch on the way. The roar is thrilling. I'm coming off the bench and I'm putting up my shot. Both of us are in there together, and we are finally blending. Yet even as she struggles and even as she screams and even as the Cuisinart shrieks us all together, I can hear Chop pounding down the corridor, coming to pull us apart, coming to take me out.

Then I look down and I've got my hand in there alone. The Cuisinart isn't even on.

But "Honey," she says. "Honey, are you all right?"

View from Kwaj
PATRICIA MACINNES

In 1954 I didn't believe that World War Two was really over. The navy was still pulling up the remains of Japanese soldiers from the bombed tunnels on Kwajalein, an atoll in the Marshall Islands where we were stationed. My father used the half skull of a Jap as an ashtray in his office and loved to tell how they found the soldier holding a bottle of sake between his skeleton legs. "Hell, the booze was still good—we finished it off for him." He'd grin as he leaned back in a rattan chair at Com-Closed, the officers' bar, while a couple of his friends sat around the table. They wore short-sleeved khaki shirts and shorts that flared a little like skirts. Their hats with gold eagles and spit-clean patent-leather bills were always placed squarely in front of them, as if for inspection, while they drank from kelly-green tumblers.

The whole family could go into Com-Closed. My father ordered Shirley Temples for my mother, my brother Jimmy, and me, and we ate greasy peanuts while the battles of the Pacific were recounted. My mother would fume, push back her fire-red hair, and look across the bar as if she didn't know my father as he got drunker and the stories louder.

We first heard about the hydrogen-bomb testing on Bikini at Com-Closed, and from the start Jimmy wanted to photograph it. He usually took underwater snapshots of killer clams, exotic fish, and coral when he went skin diving. He'd also gotten every teenage girl on the island to pose for him. Jimmy was almost 16, skinny and redheaded, and he looked as young as me. My father called him "Bubble Eyes" because he spent so much time reading.

"All girls want to be photographed," Jimmy told me. "You wouldn't believe what they'll do in front of a camera." He kept a scrapbook of snapshots with the girls' names in quotation marks. There was "Carol" in a bathing suit alongside a bird of paradise. "Shirley" bending over in shorts. "Barb" in a prom dress stretched out on his bed.

Jimmy got the idea to photograph Bikini when Max Knudson said we might be able to see the fireworks from our own back yard. "Biggest one ever in the Pacific. Only 150 miles away," he told us. Max was dark with thick thighs, a chin that reminded me of the end of a potato, and a perpetually horny look on his face. I even spotted him eying my mother's legs once when she came into Com-Closed in bermuda shorts.

"A thousand times more juice than the one we dropped on the Japs," Max went on. "And the 'A' sure made them sit up and whistle *Dixie.*"

I waited for Teddy Banks, the harbor pilot, to say something. He didn't look up. He was rolling a swizzle stick around in his mouth and scratching his German shepherd, Major.

Teddy had been 15 miles from the first H-bomb blast on Eniwetok in '52. My father said Teddy could go to prison for discussing what he'd seen. But sometimes after a few drinks he'd talk. "We did our time in hell," he said. "Like worms squirming in a blaze when that fireball went up. I'll tell you one thing I'll never forget. After the blast. The damnedest thing. Fifteen, 20 minutes after everything calmed down, we look out in the lagoon and the water's moving backwards in this wave. We start seeing sunken PT boats on the bottom and fish flopping around. I swear it. We just stood there watching until we got hit by the winds again from the shock wave. Knocked me flat. I look up and notice the lagoon water. The goddamn thing's a frigging tidal wave by then, and it starts coming straight at us. I'll admit it—I peed in my pants. I thought for sure that was it. You never seen me run faster. We'd a been pounded to shit, but sandbags piled on the beach what saved us. The wave hit them and sprayed up like a demon. We wiped one of the islands off the map during that test. Nothing out there now but a pit a mile wide."

My father told us about the scientists on Eniwetok holding a fish up to some film and the thing photographing itself. When I asked Teddy, he wouldn't talk. "Get Jimmy to figure it out," he said. "He's the genius. What the heck do I know?"

Jimmy said something about radiation.

"Hell, radiation," Teddy said. "What does anyone know? The military keeps upping the rads that are safe. Can't argue with the experts. I'm healthy. That's all I know."

From the beginning, I was convinced that the testing on Bikini meant another war coming that only we knew about. Or maybe everyone in the States knew something we didn't. We had no TV or phones, only limited radio—some half-sloshed sailor playing *Throw Mama from the Train* 50 times a day—and newspapers and mail took a week from Honolulu. "Face it," my mother said, "we're living in the outer reaches of the solar system."

Anything could be happening. But no one seemed worried. Maybe it was the tropical heat or the fact that most people stayed drunk. Gin, whiskey, whatever you wanted went for a dollar a fifth.

Maybe after not hearing from the outside world, everyone just lost interest. Service people were used to secret tests on remote bases. You didn't ask questions. Besides, the testing meant security. Even Jimmy said that when I asked if it worried him. "Don't be a dummy," he said. "The bomb's so we'll never be the ones to get creamed."

"The military, what a hell of a life," my mother used to whisper to me in the kitchen. My father always accused her of turning us against his profession.

"For God's sake, Lee, don't go running off with some sailor," she told me.

"Where am I going to run?" I asked. The "rock" was only six square miles. Besides, I wouldn't have anything to do with sailors.

"Just make damn sure you know what you're getting into when

you get married," she said. "Don't let anyone talk you into anything." It was a story I'd hear often. When she was 19 she had a
job at Woolworth's, where my father bought candy bars. Back
then any man in a uniform was A-OK and service life meant
travel. She never dreamed of the places they'd stick bases.

"Pestered me until I said yes. All he really wanted was to sleep
with me," she said. They were married in five months.

Besides my father, what made her mad were the geckos in the
house. Under the rugs, in shoes, in the toaster. They'd lose their
grip and drop from the ceiling. My mother would scream and try
to suck them up in her vacuum.

Boredom and sweat. That got to a lot of people. Brackish,
brown drinking water and surplus meat frozen over a year. Nothing was ever fresh by the time it was shipped to us. Like the firs
sent for Christmas—somebody's idea of a joke. They were a pile
of brown needles when they arrived.

I was 14, and unlike my father, who thought civilians and natives were inferior, I'd begun to feel there was something less
about us. Something as second rate as the olive-green cans of
surplus food we got in the commissary, the standard-issue sheets,
the silverware stamped U.S. NAVY. I wanted to live in a tract
house and stay there for more than a year. Buy floral blankets and
towels. Get name-brand food with colored labels in grocery stores
called Piggly Wiggly or A & P. So what if things cost more in the
civilian world? Everything has its price.

I felt lonely, sorry for myself. But I would have anywhere at
that age. I made up melodramas about dying and worked myself
up for a cry. I stood in front of the mirror wishing for somebody
else's legs and chest.

I was also in love. Kilimej was Marshallese and exotic. He came
from Ebeye every day with the other natives who worked on
Kwaj. I fantasized about his fleshy lips, his faint mustache with
light sweat. He had a tattoo on his arm—"E" for his island—that
he had made himself with a black pen.

"Kilimej" wasn't his real name, but I didn't know it then. Another native called him something like that. I found out later that
it meant "Black Dog."

Kilimej boxed groceries in the commissary, and I used to take the rusted island bus there and buy one thing just so I could go through his line. He never looked up, but flipped items from his left hand to his right, and when he got going, they became almost a blur. I'd always tip him 50 cents from my allowance. He didn't say much. I asked how he liked his job and he only shrugged.

"Not one of those natives became a doctor, a lawyer, or anything," my mother said. "They're still living in the Stone Age. Who could have ambition in this heat?"

We took the boat to Ebeye, three miles away, just to get off Kwaj and to buy things like shell jewelry and fans made of pandanus and feathers. Ebeye was the inter-island trading post, and even offshore you could smell the rancid copra, the drying coconut they traded for soy sauce. Skinny dogs and chickens ran loose, and five feet of empty soy sauce bottles were piled on the beach. The natives lived in shacks and didn't use furniture. "Lazy slopeheads," my father said. "You'd think they'd get sick of living like that."

I wanted to take Kilimej to the States, where he could go to school and get a good job. I wanted us to adopt him like the family who tried to take their cleaning girl back with them. It was never allowed. Not one native made it out of the islands.

That didn't stop me from thinking about babies. Call it hormonal pull. I pictured scenes of squatting in the sand and giving birth. I was more than happy with the idea of suffering. Even then I suspected that it had everything to do with love.

My father tried to tell Jimmy that there wouldn't be anything to photograph of Bikini. "Hell, Max doesn't know what he's talking about, Bubble Eyes," my father said. "Bikini's at least 300 miles from here. You'll be waiting around for nothing."

It didn't stop Jimmy. He got a telephoto lens and bought every roll of Kodacolor film in the exchange.

The bomb was scheduled to go off before dawn on the first of March. The day before, Jimmy set up a tripod on the northern end of Kwajalein and camped out. He tried to talk Barb into bringing her sleeping bag, too, promising that she could be in some pictures. When she didn't go for it, I was second choice. "I guess you can stay with me tomorrow night if you want," Jimmy told me when he came home to pack sandwiches. His freckled arms and face were sunburned and his legs were scraped up.

"These pictures will be worth money someday," he said, biting into a cheese sandwich. "You can say you saw the bomb. Once-in-a-lifetime chance." Then he smiled. He knew how to get me. "You better hope you see it only once. The Russians have one, too, you know."

"How about if I brought someone?" I asked.

Jimmy rolled his eyes. "Who? That hood from Ebeye?"

"Forget it," I said. "You don't know who I mean." But it was exactly who I meant. I'd been thinking about it for days. The problem was the Marshallese weren't supposed to spend the night on Kwajalein. "The navy doesn't want any hanky-panky with the natives," I'd heard my father say. But sailors would stay on Ebeye after the last boat and walk the reef back when the tide was low. I decided that Kilimej could do the same thing.

I lay on my bed looking at the white tiles on the ceiling planning it. No one would see him on the beach, and in the morning he could hide out. I could even sneak him into my room.

I thought of us staying up all night together, and I had to do it. I put on a pair of shorts and a T-shirt with a bleach spot so Kilimej wouldn't think this was any big deal for me, and I got to the commissary for his two o'clock break.

Since he didn't know much English, I wasn't sure how I'd explain. He was behind the building drinking a Coke and smoking, and when I walked up, he smiled. I smelled Aqua Velva on him. Up close, I was as tall as he was, maybe taller. His white shirt was unbuttoned to the middle of his chest, and his skin looked so smooth that it seemed poreless.

I knew he didn't have much time, so I jumped in about Bikini. I threw my arms around to show an explosion and he laughed. "The biggest ever," I said. "Tomorrow night. I'm going to stay on the beach and wait for it."

It suddenly occurred to me that he could see the same thing on his own island, but then I thought of my father's binoculars. I held my fists up to my eyes to show him. "You want to come? Stay on Kwajalein tomorrow night?" He looked confused. "Just come over on the reef like the sailors," I said, pointing to the water and moving two fingers like legs. "Hide out until you go to work."

Two box boys walked by and spoke to Kilimej in Marshallese. He said something back and they laughed. I was beginning to feel embarrassed. "I don't know. It was just an idea," I said. "It's only my brother and me. He won't be around much," I lied.

"You have beer?" Kilimej asked.

"Sure," I said. "Whatever you want. You name it."

Oil glistened on his hair. He ran his hand over loose strands. "Maybe I come," he said. "The beach tomorrow?"

"By the fire rings," I said. "Would it get you in trouble?"

"I do what I want," he said. He didn't smile, but winked when I turned to go.

I couldn't stand it. In less than 24 hours we'd be together. I started making plans to ditch Jimmy. It wasn't as if he hadn't done it to me before.

That night I cleaned my room, just in case Kilimej needed a place to hide. I hid stuffed animals and put out the baskets and pandanus bird figures from Ebeye. Then I sliced up my legs shaving with my father's razor and tried on a grass skirt. It didn't fit, but I kept looking in the mirror.

I went to the dock the next day when the work crew was about to leave for Ebeye. I spotted Kilimej in the group, but I didn't say anything to him. He pulled out his knife and played mumblety-peg with some of the boys.

There were about 200 Marshallese. The men wore khaki pants and T-shirts. The women had on loose print dresses. Some had sunglasses and purses, and one held a pair of red high heels.

Before they got on the boat, a sailor checked to see if they had stolen anything. Kilimej jerked his arm away when the sailor looked him over. Then he stalked up the ramp and gave a hand to

Stella, the old woman who did ironing for the lieutenant's family. I watched him lean against the side of the boat and spit in the water. As they pulled out, I called his name and he waved. "See you," I yelled and pictured him walking back over the coral to be with me.

At home I hid beer and a bottle of Black Velvet whiskey in my beach bag. I threw in a couple of cans of root beer as a mixer.

Jimmy was fidgeting with the tripod when I found him on the beach. I rolled out my sleeping bag and roasted hot dogs, leaving a few for Kilimej.

Jimmy and I weren't saying much. He didn't run his mouth a lot anyway and it drove my mother nuts. "A house full of damn introverts. Why doesn't someone talk?" she'd yell now and then.

But when Jimmy did say things, they were unexpected. "For Christ's sake, you're smart," he said when we were lying there watching the waves. "Go to college and do what you want. Don't end up like Mother."

"What makes you think I'm so smart?" I said. I should have known I wouldn't get more.

"Put it this way. You don't seem as asinine as most girls your age." Then he tossed sand on my sleeping bag. I was glad he didn't know.

Night was setting in, so I took a walk down the beach. Kwaj was crescent-shaped, and the airstrip and buildings dotted with lights looked small surrounded by the dark water. A warm wind started up and blew sand in my eyes. I felt the grit in my hair and under my nails. The tide was still low; I could see the reef.

I went back to Jimmy and lay down on my bag like I was going to sleep. I closed my eyes and pretended that Kilimej would be there when I opened them and I would act surprised. I did that for a while. I counted the waves and knew each one took the possibility of him farther away. It was late now. He wasn't coming. I threw the extra hot dogs in the fire and they sputtered.

He probably knew from the beginning that he wouldn't come. I saw myself standing behind the commissary asking him, waving my arms around to describe the blast. Those box boys laughing.

"What's got you?" Jimmy asked.

"How about a beer?" I said. The wind was dying down. You could taste salt in the air. It was thick enough to cure a ham. We went through the six-pack and I kept looking for Kilimej in the shadows until Jimmy asked why I was jerking around.

"Things never turn out the way you imagine them," I said. "You know?" Jimmy knew what I meant. Like at Christmas. After the presents, my mother would always say, "Is this it? Thank God it's over for another year." And the tree came down by the end of the day.

A lot was like that, I decided. It was better just to think about things. I'd pictured Kilimej's arm around me, his high-school ring on a chain around my neck. But he didn't have a high school; he hadn't even shown up. There it was. Nothing ever matched a fantasy.

Maybe getting pictures was just a daydream of Jimmy's and we wouldn't see a thing. The night was calm and I couldn't believe there would be an explosion in a few hours. Teddy called it almost holy when the water shot up in the air and mushroomed out with white halos of electricity around it. He told us that during the flash he saw the bones in his hand, even with his eyes shut tight and his head buried in a trench.

I thought about the men out there sitting on top of a bomb that was like nothing ever before, and I didn't blame them if they got mindless drunk that night.

For years Jimmy would describe the blast as the sun rising in the north that morning. He woke me up screaming, "Jesus Christ almighty!"

The whole sky lit up a brilliant whitish-yellow, brighter than day. A second later it changed to yellow, red, and green. Then the sky flamed in twisted shapes, and we saw the fireball blaze like a small sun for a moment just above the horizon.

Jimmy was going crazy with the camera. "*Life* magazine's going to be begging me for these," he yelled.

In a few minutes, the color was gone and it was dark again. Jimmy put down his camera. We thought the whole thing was over when a wind suddenly swept the island and bent the palms down so far that the fronds almost brushed the ground. Garbage cans clattered over. Then the whole island shook and the sound came from below and above, louder than thunder, pressing us down to the sleeping bags. We held our ears, but I could feel the sound in my stomach and wanted to throw it up. I thought about the men on Eniwetok who'd been tossed around in their trenches with electricity crackling through them.

The vibration crawled up the buildings and we heard the windows rattle, then pop and shatter. I got scared. An atoll is only a honeycomb of coral, and I imagined the island splintering and getting sucked below the water.

People were running out of their houses, thinking there was an earthquake. The waves broke closer. Jimmy jumped up and grabbed the tripod. He was dripping sweat and kept wiping his hands as he tried to hold the camera.

Finally the shaking stopped. We didn't move at first. We didn't talk.

The sky was getting light and people stood around in their bathrobes pointing at what looked like a thunderhead in the distance. The dark billows were rising, spreading out. Jimmy took pictures of me with that in the background. Then we watched through the binoculars as the smoke moved slowly eastward along the horizon.

I wondered if Kilimej was watching. Maybe he had been stopped coming to Kwaj. I decided I'd try to talk to him. Learn his language. I wanted to tell him about the testing and what it was like on Bikini.

Jimmy was still taking pictures when I started home with a headache from the beer.

I saw my father, Teddy, and a couple of Waves come out of Com-Closed. One pretended to kick Teddy in the butt, then the two women walked off to the barracks laughing. My father had spilled a drink on his shorts and his usually Brylcreemed hair was rumpled. I noticed the wrinkles around his eyes and in his tan face. He was still handsome.

"You missed it," I told them.

"Scared the piss out of Major and broke some bottles of damn good Scotch," Teddy roared.

"I'll be a son of a bitch," my father said, looking at the sky. "Let's go see Bubble Eyes. I don't believe it. Bless his little old heart." As they walked off, Teddy was singing *Shake, Rattle, and Roll.*

At our house the light bulbs had broken out of their sockets. My mother was sweeping them up along with some dishes. "I thought the damn walls would go next," she said, swatting at a gecko with her broom.

The place was steaming. She'd closed the windows and had even pulled sheets off the line. My father opened the windows as soon as he got home. "For Christ's sake, the blast was miles away," he said. "We'll suffocate in here."

They argued about it, and the windows were opened, then closed, again and again the rest of the day.

Two days after the blast, a destroyer brought in 82 natives from Rongelap Atoll. "Dusted," Teddy told us. "A hundred miles east of Bikini and the wind dumped two inches of fallout on those poor bastards. On Utirik also, 300 miles away. More Marshallese are due in tomorrow. Christ, kids were out playing in the ash and it was falling in the food and water. Now everyone's got bleeding burns and they're puking their guts out. I don't know what happened. Those islands are downwind. We got the natives out during other tests. Didn't even warn these people. What were those assholes at headquarters thinking?"

I watched from a distance as the natives were helped off the ship. No one on Kwaj was allowed near. The Marshallese were taken to the hospital and checked over with Geiger counters. Doctors were flown in from the States. "No significant danger," they said. Teddy told us they were having the natives wash off in the lagoon a few times a day with special soap. "What do you do?" he said. "There's no medicine you can give. We'll keep them off their islands for a while. Just have to wait and see what happens."

The next day, I went to the dock to look for Kilimej. I was going to talk to him about the blast and find out what had happened to him the other night. I took beer along in my beach bag.

The ship from Utirik was in with 157 natives aboard, and they were still coming down the ramp when the work crew lined up for the ferry. The Ebeye people stared at the other islanders in the distance, pointed, and talked in Marshallese.

I wasn't sure how much Kilimej or any of them knew. A tent city was just being set up on Ebeye for the Utirik natives. The area was roped off and a marine would be guarding it, not letting anyone in or out. I didn't think I could ever tell Kilimej what had happened. If it could ever be explained as "just an accident." Jimmy said it looked to him like the natives had been set up as guinea pigs, although nobody in the military would ever admit it in a million years. We didn't want to believe it, so we just didn't talk about it.

I finally spotted Kilimej on the wharf. He and a boy in a ripped T-shirt were sitting apart from the work crew. The boy saw me first and said, "Here comes that girl."

Kilimej was wearing a thin blue-green shirt, the color of a Coke bottle. His arms appeared hard and strong in the short sleeves. He never looked better.

"Kilimej," I called out. I held up the beer to show him. He glanced at me and I started to walk over. Then I stopped. He was whispering something to his friend.

"Hey, kid, you brought us beer?" the friend said to me, stuffing gum in his mouth.

I looked at Kilimej. He got up and started throwing his knife into a wood barrel. I stood there, waiting for him to come over, wink at me, explain why he hadn't shown up that night. I watched the quick jerk of his wrist, the black handle of the knife, and the blade flipping into wood with a whack.

"What's wrong?" I asked him. "Why didn't you come to Kwaj? We watched the blast through binoculars. You could have really seen fireworks." I wanted to make everything sound okay.

Kilimej kept throwing the knife. Each time he went to get it, I thought he'd say something. The rest of the wharf—the sailors and natives and kids, the people coming off the ship—all of it disappeared. I waited.

"Why don't you talk to me?" I finally said.

Kilimej's friend said something to him in Marshallese and cracked his gum.

"What is it you want—a beer?" I said to Kilimej. I brought out the bottle of beer and walked over close to him as he pulled the knife from the barrel. I could see the muscle in his arm tighten and the sweat on him. I knew his skin would feel soft and damp. I touched him gently on the shoulder with the cool beer. Instantly, he shoved my arm away and knocked the beer out of my hand. The amber bottle shattered on the dock. People looked over at us.

"Get away, girl," Kilimej snapped. "Get out, navy girl. Get out of here." Suddenly he spit on the ground. He looked at me and he spit again. He spit with hatred and as if he could rid himself of all the spit inside him.

All I could do was hate him—the sweat on his upper lip, the blackness of his hair, his eyes that turned me into nothing but spit. Even though I always swore I'd never sound like my father, I said it: "Slopehead." Then louder. "Slopeheads. You wouldn't have anything, not a thing without us. You'd still be living in the Stone Age. Stupid slopeheads."

Kilimej raised his knife to his cheek. His eyes fixed on me as if to aim. Then his eyes sent me out of my clothes, shoes, anything mine. Down to the Jap tunnels where I was nothing, absolutely nothing. His eyes held me there until his friend laughed. Then Kilimej turned abruptly and walked away, as if suddenly I no longer existed.

Later, I went over and over that scene. I saw his eyes and prickled with sweat, felt it down my back. For two days I didn't come out of my room, and I never went near the commissary or dock again.

The 239 natives were shipped out in May. The ones from Utirik were sent back home. The Rongelap natives went to another island to wait until it was "safe" to go back.

No one had been allowed near the natives. But one time from afar I saw some of them rinsing off in the Kwaj lagoon. The navy had supplied American bathing suits. I got a glimpse of a man in baggy tropical-print trunks with gauze over his eyes. A woman in a green bathing suit with no hair on her head.

We left Kwaj in October and were transferred to "another hell hole," as my mother put it. China Lake, a base in the Mojave. Almost 30 years in the navy for my old man by then. He began scratching on the bottom of each new can of shaving foam the number of years, months, days he had left to go.

He'd kept snapshots of his favorite bars to remember every town where we had lived. Some time between moves my mother tore each one out of the album. All my father had then were the names—THE BOTTOM'S UP CLUB, SAN PEDRO; ACEY-DEUCY, PENSACOLA; COM-CLOSED, KWAJ—printed in white ink on the black album paper.

We kept in touch with Teddy after we moved. In 1957 we heard that the Rongelap natives were returned to their island. "The year of the animal, the natives call it," Teddy wrote. "They say the babies aren't human out there ever since we set the world on fire. They look like monkeys, octopuses, bunches of grapes, jellyfish. One was brought to the Kwaj Hospital—born without skin. The only good thing is they die right away."

Ten years later, Teddy was dead of cancer. The natives on Rongelap and Utirik were suffering from tumors, cancer, thyroid disease, and cataracts.

There are still pictures in my father's album of the blast. The smoke looks like a smudge above the water and the colors of the sky like they aren't showing up true. Jimmy wrote on each one BIKINI H-BOMB, VIEW FROM KWAJ.

There's also a picture of me that Jimmy took in front of a lean-to on Ebeye. I'm wearing a broad-brimmed straw hat to cover a frizzy home perm, and I have on a black bathing suit that looks as if it's made of vulcanized rubber and has what my mother called "bones" in the top. I've got a hibiscus in my hair, and I'm posing like Veronica Lake. In the background are some natives, one girl in a white cotton dress. I was almost 30 before I noticed the cast of that peculiar island light over us all. And that girl. Her hands on her hips, staring me down with everything she's worth.

Ten Cents a Dance
JOSEPH FERRANDINO

Lola had tattooed feet. Tattoos on her feet, I mean to say. And when she wore spiked heels, the ones with those little straps across red-painted toes and around her ankles, you could see the bright blue eye on each instep spooky peek up her skirt. She told me the women she worked with called her "four-eyes" behind her back. Called her "four-eyes" and snickered.

She explained Lola was not her real name. It was Mayvis, like the song thrush. Mayvis Plaiben from Terrebonne Parish, close enough to New Orleans to use it as her name.

"I call myself Lola from Nola," she said once while we were eating in that little Italian restaurant near where Lola worked. It had a white tile floor with squares of red and green. Lola liked to touch the fresh-cut flowers. They had them on every table in a small vase with painted flowers on it.

She ate ravioli. I don't remember what I had. But Lola looked lovely.

"Lola DiNola," she said, almost singing it. "I like the sound. Don't you?"

I nodded. I think my mouth was full.

"I like the sound and it's easy for men to remember," she said.

I agreed. Anyone would.

I think it was that night, in the small restaurant—yes, I'm almost sure of it because there was Italian music, some familiar Mario Lanza love songs, playing on the jukebox—and that night I thought to myself she was a woman with a name that wasn't hers from a town she'd never been to. Things like that mean something to me. I realized as we ate in the candlelight Lola was not as old as she looked, or as old as I had thought at first. Her hands were young. Her fingers long, well-formed and muscular almost, each like a dancer or a cat.

It was a show to watch her eat. She made everything look so good.

That night she told me things about herself and Terrebonne Parish. Things I never could have imagined. She answered a lot of questions for me, but I don't think she knew she was. I remember being surprised because she made more sense than I thought she would just judging from her appearance. I mean she wasn't so spaced out as she seemed. But maybe I'm getting ahead of myself. Ahead of where I should be to make you understand. Let me start at the beginning.

It starts, of course, when we met.

I worked in a ladies shoestore, you see. I have for the past three years. I was a social worker before that, but I just couldn't handle working with the terminally ill any longer. After a while it gets to you. I mean it really *gets* to you.

At first I thought it was noble, helping those poor people out. I felt like what it was I was doing, you know? But how many times can you look into the sunken eyes of the almost dead and tell them to cheer up? But it wasn't noble, you see. That's my point. I could not fool myself any more. Could not believe I fooled them any more either.

So I quit to sell shoes. At least I don't feel guilty like I did peddling false hopes. Now I simply give them what they want. It's honest for a change.

It's funny, my selling shoes. I can't really call it coincidence. When I was a kid, eight or nine I guess, anyway before I lost my hair, I was in love with my baby-sitter. Her name was Anne, beautiful Anne with long black shiny hair and eyes that sparkled when she looked at me. She was eighteen, and whenever I saw her feet, like when she kicked her slippers off, I felt my body change inside. I mean in my stomach and in my chest and how it tickled

down there and got stiff, stiffer than from the pictures in my
father's magazines. She was beautiful. The most beautiful I've
ever seen. And in my fantasies when I could do anything I wanted
to her and make her say anything I wanted her to say to me, she
said:

"Henry, rub my feet. Do my feet, Henry."

And I hold them in my hands and rub them gently. The toes,
the arch—that's the most sensitive—Anne doesn't have calluses
on her heels. They are smooth and dry.

So when I saw the ad in the *Times* for a shoe salesman I
thought of Anne and took the job. Anything to get away from the
basket cases. Now I tend to their vanity instead of the instinct to
live. It's more difficult at times, but so much more rewarding.

It was a humid August day, the kind when my toop curls up at
the edges and the mesh shows, I just know it, and the adhesive
runs down past my ears from the temples in streams of thick gray
sweat. But inside the store the air conditioner was blowing cold
and I went into the bathroom to rearrange my piece and blot the
wet. I felt I looked okay when she walked in.

Andy, he's the other salesman, was busy with an Eastside type
and her snotty little brat. Andy jumped me for that one, and after
seeing the hassle they gave him, I was glad he did.

I pretended to read the *Times*, but I listened to what went on.

"Mommy, they pinch. Oh, they hurt, Mommy," the brat cried.

And Andy was up to his eyeballs in opened shoe boxes.

"Do you think cookie pads will help?" the Eastside type asked.

"That depends on which shoe you buy, ma'am."

"I want red," the brat said.

"You need white . . ."

"With buckles, Mommy. Please."

"With laces, dear."

Andy came out from the back with several boxes under each
arm, tripped over one on the floor and dropped everything over
the seats.

I read the obituaries and laughed to myself.

Lola walked in wearing a white T-shirt and a short denim skirt.
Her breasts were small but the nipples erect like someone dropped

an ice cube down her back. I wondered if the air conditioner did it after the wet heat outdoors. She had very nice legs, though a purist might say she was knock-kneed. But I am no purist. She was wearing white tennis shoes.

I folded the paper and dropped it to the floor. Stood and smiled. She smiled back and sat in the same seat I had just gotten up from.

I thought her smile seemed kind of forced. She pulled her upper lip tight over her teeth. She was pretty anyway. Just nervous, I guessed.

"I'd like to see style ten-fourteen in black," she said, almost in a whisper. I had to lean forward.

"In what size?" I asked.

"I'm not sure," she replied. "You'd best measure my foot."

She placed her right foot up on the angled board of my stool. She pulled the hemline of her skirt higher to free her leg.

I glanced up while I untied her sneaker. I learned from experience how to do it without getting caught. Following the smooth tanned line of her thigh, I shot a white cotton crotch edged with red lace. It appeared to be red in the shadow. I had her pegged as a silk or satin type. You know, frilly and lacy. Lots of plain dressers wear silk underneath against their skin. But cotton? On her I didn't expect it.

I got an even bigger surprise when I slipped off her terry-cloth anklet. A blue eye, bright and big around as a quarter, looked up at me from the top of her foot. A fine dark line, almond-shaped with lashes that seemed to flutter, held the staring blue eye in place as it looked me over.

I don't think I smiled. I tried not to react in any way, because, to tell you the truth, I did not know what to say or do.

She placed her foot on the sizer.

"Ohhh. That's cold," she said.

"Size six," I said.

I tugged at the sizer as a hint to move her foot. She kept it firmly pressed in place, smiling with the two blue eyes in her head. I slipped my fingers under her arch and slowly lifted her foot. She laughed a low, throaty laugh.

"I'm ticklish," she said. Her eyes were almost closed.

"I'm sorry," I said.

My glasses are heavy because they're so thick, but I don't notice them until I get nervous. Then they get so heavy on my nose I can't breathe.

"Don't be," she whispered.

I had to breathe through my mouth.

I squeezed my hand gently, the hand holding her foot. She wiggled her toes. With two fingers I touched the tattoo, rubbing small circles on her instep. The top of her foot was tanned. Even her toes were acorn brown. Except where the nails were painted red. And where the toes curved under, the skin faded lighter to almost white. No calluses. No rough skin.

I avoided looking into her eyes. I told you my glasses are thick. My eyes seem like pitted California Colossals when someone looks at them. I see it in the mirror all the time, so I avoid making direct eye contact like that. I looked into the eye on her foot. I did sneak a glance, though. I took the chance and her eyes were closed. Her head kind of moved back and forth. I started to sweat.

Before I pulled the ten-fourteens in a black size six from the shelf I popped into the bathroom. I could not breathe. My glasses crushed my nose. I washed my face and checked to make sure no mesh was showing at my hairline. None was. But the edges were curling just a little. I knew I'd have to be cool.

She placed her foot in my hand when I returned. This is how we should greet one another. Men and women. Lovers, that is. Like a secret handshake, members of the same subcultural order. I eased the warm foot into the shoe. She ran her fingers down the side of her throat in sort of a stroking motion.

"They look fine," I said.

"Do you really think so?"

"Yes I do. Believe me. They'll be fine."

After I helped her into the second shoe—there was a tattoo on that foot too—she stepped across the carpet, her legs sexy and exciting in the forced posture. She pranced to the mirror, turning from side to side. She walked away from her image, then stopped to admire herself.

She tried on two dozen different pairs that day. She bought the ten-fourteens.

"My name is Lola," she said. "What's yours?"

"Henry," I replied.

I noticed one of her teeth was missing. Up top, next to the front ones. She was still pretty. Although, by my standards, they are all pretty. My older brother used to tease me about that all the time.

"She's got legs just like you like 'em, Henry," he'd say. "Feet on one end and snitchet on the other." Then he'd slap his knees and snot up the front of his shirt. I hated him. Still do. But he was not far from right. I mean, it's all relative. When you're half blind and don't have a hair on your body, well, women just aren't attracted to you. So anytime I could get one I tried my best. Lord knows it didn't happen often. God. Not near often enough.

So when Lola seemed friendly, what could I do?

I knew I was sweating, that maybe mesh was showing or the adhesive melting, but I didn't care. I mean, I cared, but not enough to leave her and get fixed up in the bathroom. I was afraid, afraid she'd leave and I'd never see her again. I even tried a Valentino move—I know you have no idea how hard that was for me—and God how I regretted it while I was doing it, but I made the move. And you know what? I stared right into her eyes and we locked in for a few seconds and she didn't laugh at my pitted olives and the goddamn milk bottles crushing my nose so I had to breathe through my mouth.

When she paid for the shoes she handed me a card from some dance hall downtown.

"That's where I work," she said.

I still have that card. I keep it in my dresser, in the top drawer right under my clean hankies. It reminds me of the start.

I guess I should tell you more about Lola and shoestores. I hadn't known this on the day I'm telling you of. I found out later on.

That day we met, on that day she'd been to a half-dozen shoestores before walking into the one I work in. Browsing, that is. She rarely bought anything. What she liked to do was shop for shoes. Try on pair after pair. Examine the stitchwork. "Are they leather uppers? . . . The heels—nailed or glued? . . . Patent or vinyl?" . . . She'd walk slowly on the carpet. Admire herself in the mirror. Let herself be looked at. And then with a sigh she'd say:

"They're just not quite right."

And hope, as the salesman slipped off the rejected shoe, he would cradle her foot, just for an instant, in the palm of his hand. Stroke, as if by accident, her sole with his fingertips. And she told me she had her favorites. I was one of them before other things happened. Lola knew which of us fondled, discreetly, her feet.

She had her way of rewarding her favorites. Though when she did it to me—or maybe it was when she told me what it meant, I'm not sure—anyway, she said she enjoyed watching them react when they discovered her without panties one day exposed with her leg upraised on the angle-boarded stool.

"With an innocent look on my face, of course. As if I really forgot to put them on," she said with a smile revealing the toothless space.

It was one of those things I took the wrong way, I guess. I mean there's a limit to being open-minded. So I made her promise to cut that out. She said she has. And I believe her.

I felt uncomfortable going to see her where she worked. I'd never been to a place like that before. I had heard of them, but somehow I always associated them with World War Two; with my father and my uncles.

The hallway was littered by handbills and reeked with piss. Paint hung from crumbling plaster walls. The rotting stairs creaked under cracked linoleum. I walked in and went directly to the booth to buy my tickets. Then I was allowed on the dance floor.

I saw Lola rubbing her nose with the back of her hand as she leaned against the worn-down wooden railing. Starspecks of light spun quick then slow on the rough stucco ceiling. Lola told me later that when she was not dancing she liked to watch the light bounce from the mirrored ball.

I saw her dancing with someone else once. She held on limply and looked up as she danced. Not with her head tilted back. Only with her eyes, way up, like this, eyes straining almost rolling over to look inward. And in those eyes she spun quick then slow with the stars.

Another record started to play. Somehow that surprised me. I really expected a band. Lola's knit dress was snagged on a splinter in the rail at a spot not yet smoothed by the sweaty hands of the hopeful or the callused backs of the shipwrecked.

It was hot in there. Like a sauna. I reached up carefully to make sure the toop hadn't shifted on me. Boy, that is the worst. Worse even than curled-up ends, exposed mesh, or melting adhesive. There was no air up there. Only the slow music and the smells.

Lola turned to get a view of the problem. Stretched her chin, pushing it past her shoulder as if to hook it there. It slipped. Her makeup left a smudge. She froze when she felt the cloth pull, reaching blind with her hand to free herself from the rail without further damaging her dress. She was wearing the ten-fourteens. They sure looked good on her.

I walked up behind her, sucking on a butterscotch, and tapped her twisted back.

"Would you like to dance?" I asked, feeling stupid. Stupid for being there; stupid for what I said. I felt I had to make up for that. I wanted to impress her.

"Would you care to dance?" I repeated.

"As soon as I get free," she said.

"Can I help you?"

"I don't know. Can you?"

She tugged on the thread. Something gave. Lola did not know if the splinter pulled loose or if the yarn separated. I couldn't see in that light. She straightened her dress over her hips—her hipbones really stood out—and took my hand. I wanted to apologize for its being so wet. Before I had time to say it we were out in the middle of the floor dancing close to one another under the spinning star-specks.

"I like your aftershave," she said.

"Thank you. Your perfume is really nice," I replied without having noticed whether she wore any.

"It seems all the men I liked back home used to wear that kind."

"It used to be a lot more popular," I said, thinking it through for a minute. I decided it was encouraging.

Lola held me tighter. She pressed her lips close to my ear so that I felt her breath on my cheek.

"Usually they smell of stale closets and cheap cologne," she said.

"Who?" I asked.

"My dancing partners."

She laughed suddenly. It was unprovoked. I didn't know it then, but I learned later on she did this often. Not only laughed when she remembered something funny; sometimes, if she thought of something sad, she'd cry. Just bust out crying for no reason at all except she thought of something sad. It was the same for anger. And jealousy. And sometimes she'd just really get the urge to do it out of the clear blue. Know what I mean? Let me tell you, I like that a whole lot.

But this first time she laughed.

"I was thinking," she said.

"About what?"

"Nothing."

"It was something."

"No . . . I'm sorry."

"It was something made you laugh. What was it?"

"Well . . . no . . . I couldn't."

"Sure you can."

"I couldn't. You see, it's funny now but it sure wasn't funny when it happened."

"If it's funny now, then it's funny. Tell me . . . Please."

"Oh Lord it's so embarrassing . . . Ever go to a dance when you were in high school?"

"Yes," I said.

But I hadn't. I was too young to wear a toop back then so I went all through school being called "Mr. Clean." I hated to go out. In the winter it wasn't too bad, because I could wear a hat all the time. It was worse in warm weather. I mean I looked like a piglet. No, I didn't go to school dances. Or to gym. Or swimming. Or anything everybody else did.

"My breasts were always small," she said.

"I hadn't noticed," I replied. But they were small. Like fried eggs. I thought of that in the shoestore. But her nipples stood up like thimbles on a pincushion.

"You saw them, all right. In the store. Anyway, when I was in high school I wore falsies. You know, those foam-rubber cup things."

"I guess so," I said. I think I saw a pair once in a novelty shop.

"I had to wear them. Lord. They were smaller than they are now."

I almost pulled back to look at them.

"Believe it or not," she said. "Why, when I was a girl Daddy and my big sister Donna, she has some pair, boy, my big sister, anyway, Daddy and Donna both told me if I wanted them to get bigger I'd have to rub chicken poop on them. Donna said that's what she did and boy does she have some pair, let me tell ya."

I smiled. Big boobs are all right, but I've always been partial to legs. I wanted to tell her that. I didn't. Not then.

"One day they peeked in 'round the henhouse door and caught me rubbing it on while I was fetchin' eggs."

I thought it made sense. If someone told me chicken crap would grow hair I'd swim in it. I didn't see the joke until she told me.

"I gave Donna a bottle of coke syrup and gasoline. She didn't pull no more tricks after a couple swigs from that jug. No sir."

"But what does that have to do with going to a dance?" I asked. For some reason I really wanted to know. It was more than just pretending to be interested.

"Nothing really. Except that I was at a dance with Ol' Buster Rohr one night when I was wearing those rubber cups. He used to splash that same aftershave as you and it was what put me in the mind of the dance and made me laugh."

"And?" I asked.

"Well, we were dancing, Buster and me. Close. Real close. Like this." Lola jerked me against her body. I felt her ribs rubbing mine. She was strong. Stronger than I thought she was. I liked that. "And one of my false titties pressed up against his cigarette pack. A circle formed around us with people yelling "Poke it out! Poke it out, Baby!" at me. It looked like I stuffed half a lemon in my bra flat side out."

We danced until my paper chain of tickets disappeared. While I was buying more at the booth, I watched Lola dance with someone else. I don't know why but I just turned and walked down the filthy stairway and out the door into the hot street.

Two days later she came into the store. To say hello, she said, and give me the reward I already told you about. We met that night and went out together. Dinner and a movie. I forgot what we saw. It was the first time we talked outside of her job or mine.

The discomfort and tension I had felt earlier I had blamed on being in the store or in that dance hall. You know, in a "situation." But that night, alone with Lola in the restaurant and again in the theater, or in the street walking; in the cab; on her stoop: I still felt tense. I wanted to know why she was being so nice to me. She seemed to like me and I couldn't deal with it. Hundreds of women a thousand times less lovely than Lola would not even look at me twice—unless it was to mock me—let alone actually listen to me and smile at me and laugh at my stupid jokes.

"Look. What's going on?" I asked. I must have shouted it, because people at the other tables turned around to look. But I was used to that. People always turned and stared at me wherever I went. Sympathy. Sympathy means better you than me.

"Do you feel sorry for me, Lola? Is that your game, Baby?" I tried to sound tough. God I wanted to cry, to fall to my knees and kiss those tattooed feet and beg her to act as if she liked me for the rest of my life.

"It's not that way, Henry."

"Bullshit."

"It's not like that at all."

"Then just how is it? Can you tell me how it is?"

"I'll try."

And she did tell me. That night, after the ravioli, in her apartment she told me how it was.

Her favorite high school teacher, a man who wore the same aftershave as I wore, did more than just teach Lola about art. His name was Mr. Holsclaw and he called Lola "Circe."

"And I called him Mr. Coleslaw," she said. "But only when we were alone."

She told me he was totally bald. Not a hair anywhere on his body.

"Not on his chest or his legs. No eyebrows, even," she said.

It's funny, but when she said that I didn't cringe or feel uncomfortable. I mean, if someone, another woman, had said it, I'd know for sure she was talking about me. I'd die. I'd sweat and the edges would curl and the mesh would show, I just know it. But I don't think Lola realized I was totally bald too. Had the same problem as Coleslaw. Slick as a dumb head of cabbage. But I don't know if Lola saw I was bald that night. My toop, when I wasn't in a sweat, fit me pretty good. And my glasses covered where my eyebrows should be, and besides, my eyes looked so big and buggy through the milk bottles, nobody could stare at them long enough to see there wasn't any lashes around them.

"Like an amphibian," someone said to me once. I think it was my grandfather.

Lola was the first person I met whom I could stand to hear talk about it. Even my mother couldn't bear to be in the same room with me, especially on weekends after an appointment with her hairdresser. But with Lola I could deal with it.

Anyway, that night, if she had noticed she kept it to herself. Later on she really seemed surprised to find out. But I think she knew all along, she just didn't make the connection.

Lola told me about a place, a roadside clump of slat-board cottages with peeled paint and rain-stained walls. She never did know where it was.

"The room always smelled mildewy," she said. "Like my Daddy's shoes. We lived near the river."

Coleslaw took her to this place, this mildewed room where he called her Circe and she laughed. She always laughed, she said, because he had told her Circe turned men into swine. And ever since, she had an image of him with a curlicue corkscrew tail. She saw him with pig features and it always made her laugh.

And I could not blame him. Lola was truly beautiful when she laughed, because she did it with her eyes. They sparkled, seemed to spin, cradled in wrinkled corners. The skin pulled tight over her cheeks, and her lips, her full lips, danced.

I faded as she spoke. I saw a hairless Coleslaw, sweating through his tongue, rooting on the bed like a fat hog in a mudhole oinking snorting sniffing at her body. And Lola, her laughing eyes and dancing lips, her head upon a pillow.

"Play with my feet," she said.

And I would play.

"I never told my folks who made me pregnant," Lola said. "I just left home. Had the baby in Mobile."

She followed the smoke from her cigarette bend around the room. She looked as if she wondered where it went.

"I left it there for adoption," she said after a while.

She moved up to Charleston, because the war in Asia was hot and there were lots of young soldiers all over town away from home with money in their pockets lonely and afraid to admit it.

Her roommate Rikki had a bright red arrow pointing upward tattooed on each thigh. She also made one-reelers with the midget who wore a black mask and support socks. Lola liked the tattoos. Got a few herself. But she kept away from an acting career.

"Folks back home might a seen me," she said. "Daddy goes to watch 'em at the Moose Lodge."

She told me about the pickup bars in Charleston. They didn't serve liquor by the drink, so a guy had to buy a bottle for three times the regular price. Then he could take the girl out after making a deal with her.

Lola and Rikki used their apartment for out-of-towners to cut down on expenses. Most of the guys never knew where the cab let them out. They wouldn't be back in town anyway. The girls paid the weightlifter next door in skin to listen in for trouble. There rarely ever was.

I was never in the Army. My eyes kept me out. But I had bought it plenty of times. I mean, how else could I get it? So I knew what Lola was talking about. And it didn't really bother me. Later on I told her it didn't matter, that I could overlook it. As long as she stopped shopping for shoes. But that night I almost blew it. I almost offered to buy it from her. And if I had had more money on me I would have. God. I'm glad I didn't.

And not because she gave it to me free.

Not free, of course, counting dinner and the movie. Andy, he's the other salesman, and I used to argue about that all the time. About how it costs him more to get it free because of dinners and tickets and presents and such. He even worked it out on a calculator. His free dates cost him more than the women I paid for it. And sometimes he didn't get anything. But I always told him his way was better. I don't know why, really. It just seems to me that it should be. Andy said I was crazy, that he was going to do it my way: it was cheaper and less of a hassle.

After that night with Lola I knew I was right. I even know why now.

You know, I haven't worn my toop in so long I forgot where I put it. Mayvis—I call her Mayvis now, she asked me to and I like it better—Mayvis says I look nicer without it. And I tell you it's a relief. Now I get a kick out of getting on an elevator, let's say, and running into a guy who's wearing a rug. You should see them squirm and turn away. They always stare at my pink head with the wrinkles in the back when they think I can't see. It fascinates them. And I know they say to themselves, "God that guy's got guts."

We laugh a lot, Mayvis and I. And I'll tell you how I get her started. One night, while I was rubbing her feet, I put my chin between her ankles. She said I squinted. I don't remember. She looked down at me.

"What's got eyes but can't see?" she asked.

"Me."

She laughed. "What else?"

"Your feet."

"And what else?"

"I give up."

"A potato, silly."

Sometimes when we're quiet, watching TV or something like that, Mayvis will just bust out laughing aloud. When I ask her what's so funny she rubs my head and says, "A potato, silly."

And that's how it is.

I'd like to tell you more. Believe me, there's plenty to tell. But Mayvis is out playing bingo with my brother John's wife, Mary Lou, and the baby is crying in the next room.

Oh. I drive a cab these days. I don't sell shoes any more. It was part of the deal.

Three Maids' Children

MONA SIMPSON

Our mothers cleaned other people's bathrooms and scrubbed floors, but we had plans. We wanted college, scholarships, big-name schools, the works, and we weren't trusting to luck or chance or talent or ourselves. We cheated.

We sat on the concrete steps outside the chemistry room at the end of the hall in the new building. This was Beverly Hills High School in 1975. At our feet, a patch of grass began between here and the old brick typing building. No one came around this small yard, there wasn't any reason. Maybe smokers occasionally, you could see the twisted butts in the soft dirt. Neat girls in skirts and short-sleeved blouses went into the typing building and came out, girls you never saw anywhere else on the campus. We heard the clatter from the patio inside and the zoom and thug of cars racing down the ramps of the parking lot. The new building also housed its own four-story garage.

Ellen and I copied algebra problems with soft dull pencils. Kevin had taken the test that morning. He had written down the questions on a spare page in his notebook. Ellen figured them out and I memorized the solutions. We would get the same test later this afternoon.

"Whoa," someone shouted in the distance. You couldn't quite

forget it was lunch hour. The cafeteria was on the fourth-floor patio.

Kevin stood over Ellen's shoulder fighting about a sine wave.

"No," she kept saying. "Look. It's simple."

He clapped a hand on his forehead, seeing. "I should have known that. I do know that." Kevin had to study algebra more than we did. He was in the early class.

"Okay, now English," Ellen said. We ripped our essays out of our spiral notebooks and handed them to Kevin. Ellen's was one neat brief paragraph. Mine was four sloppy pages, back and front, held together with the left corner folded down. I could never find a paper clip when I needed one. Kevin went over our essays, crossing things out, rewriting. In the quiet of his pencil, noise from the patio rose, like different colors on a plain sky. Ellen and I hugged our knees. We were far away. We planned and plotted, but mostly we just waited. I bit my knee. Lunch hour was spending itself away again.

Ellen tugged at her shoe, a kind of sandal she wore with navy blue knee socks. She was picky about shoes. None of us dressed well; we couldn't. Not everything we wore was our own. But Ellen took care with shoes. I could go into Judy's, a shoe store in Century City with about eight hundred different styles and point to the one Ellen would buy. One summer I did, and we came to the first day of school wearing the same shoes.

Then Ellen stood up. She opened the old wooden door to the chemistry room where the empty chairs sat waiting as it seemed they had since the beginning of time, watching the half-full beakers. Ellen walked to the teacher's lab and opened his notebook. I went to stand watch at the other doorway, the one on the hall. She copied his notes for our write-up next week. She didn't even seem to hurry. I watched the big round clock on the wall for all of us. It stuck still where it was and then it jumped.

Finally she was done. We walked, free, through the slow air back to the steps, where Kevin still hunched over, finishing our papers. He took these stupid things seriously, as if our weekly English essays were the great American novel.

Ellen shrugged and bit her thumb when Kevin gave her back

her paper. Then came the rip from her notebook again and she
started copying the paragraph over in clear, up and down cursive.

"Why did you change that?" I said, pointed. Ellen always did
just what he said. I always fought. They told me I was like that
anyway, with teachers, and it got me in trouble. But I didn't even
know when I was doing it.

"It sounds stupid—'centuries of oppression breeds an inner
sense.' For one thing it should be breed."

Ellen shrugged. "Why bother."

I always accepted Kevin's verdict anyway, in the end, and then
I felt dumb for even piping up if I wasn't going to stick to it, and I
wasn't. We all settled down to work. I had the most to copy and
the clock was stuck at four minutes to one but I could tell it was
about to jump.

When the bell rang, I sighed and stumbled up. Ellen creased
her essay in half; mine was another not-finished messy paper with
cross-outs, stuck in a disheveled notebook.

"Okay," Ellen said, to nothing in particular.

We cheated every day, swapping the questions before tests. I'd
seen Ellen a hundred times step up to a teacher's desk during
lunch hour, open the drawers, then leafing through notebook
pages as innocently as if they were the pages of a dictionary in the
library and she was leisurely flipping through, looking for a word.

Kevin rewrote all our essays. He put in special things for us, he
said he was giving us each our own style. And Ellen did math and
science. I wasn't especially good at anything that we could tell.
That was part of my problem. But it was all right. The three of us
managed. And I had a job. I was the only one with a job.

"Here," Ellen said, stuffing a black sweater in my hands. Ellen
was the most organized person I ever met. She always carried a
huge purse with pockets on the outside. She stuck her arm into it
and extracted things, like rabbits from a hat, only things we could

use. Ours was a pragmatic relationship. This sweater was for tomorrow.

"So we'll meet at nine o'clock," she said.

I gave Kevin five dollars for tennis. It was his turn to buy balls. I was glad to give him money. I had cash from tips.

We weren't the only maids' kids in Beverly Hills High. We were just the only goody-goods. In the advanced placement track, the nearest to us was the French teacher's daughter. She wasn't rich and she lived outside the district. She got to go to school here because both her parents were teachers in the system. You saw them at the end of the day. The mother's skirt hung down unevenly, a run in her stockings, as she bent over, loading files into the trunk of the Chevrolet. The tall, awkward daughter climbed into the backseat and all around them sixteen-year-olds in sports cars streaked out loudly, with four o'clock exhilaration.

Beverly Hills minded a tight district. People were always trying to sneak their kids in. Every year, three or four were caught using false addresses and thrown out. There was a guy I knew, Les. I didn't find out until a decade later that he had lived in Fairfax. There were all these parents doing it, trying to sneak their kids in. And our mothers didn't care at all. Beverly Hills was just where they worked.

We knew who the other maids' kids were. We kind of watched them, followed what they did. We knew when one of them started sleeping with a student-body officer and when one of them got into trouble.

The next morning at nine o'clock the three of us met in the park on Little Santa Monica in front of the Catholic church. Jerry Ortiz had walked off the roof of the high school on acid. We didn't talk to our friends about it and we didn't tell our parents, either. Drugs scared our parents. I was wearing Ellen's sister's picky black sweater. Kevin had on a suit he looked ridiculous in. The cuffs and sleeves came inches too far up.

"We better go," Ellen said. We slid into the last pew. There weren't many people there, only scattered clusters. Candles burned on the sides of the church the way they always burned, it could have been any day, really. We knelt as the priest walked out and began. Ellen flipped through a prayer book.

Near the front was a full row that was probably Jerry's family —a grandmother, a mother, a father and three little girls. In the row behind them, a white woman stood alertly, holding the hands of two children. That woman was wearing a linen hat.

Kevin and Ellen and I—none of us touched drugs. We were probably the only three kids in Beverly High who hadn't tried marijuana. Maybe the French teacher's daughter, too. It bothered me sometimes, being so straight. It was one of the things about the three of us. We didn't excite each other. There was a girl in a coma. Her cousins, her brother, everyone whispered about her and worried. That rocking—you could be wild, you could hurl off, fall, if there was a net to catch you and rock you and whisper you well. The thing about us was, we knew it: if one maids' kid blasted his lights out with drugs and never went anywhere, nobody would even know it. They wouldn't miss us. Only our mothers, in still moments, private in a hallway, stalling a minute with the vacuum cleaner running; they would remember us with no one to tell, no one to believe they had lost, that we could have gone somewhere.

We put my tip money in the offering and filed out into the sunlight.

"Well, we did that," Ellen said. We sat on a bench, traffic on Little Santa Monica roaring by. Back under the trees a cluster of people stood. I pulled the picky sweater off my head. Kevin loosened his tie and stood up, falling into a cartwheel. Kevin had grown taller this year and he had a fuzz of blond hair on his upper lip. Looking at him, Ellen shuddered a little. He leaped through the dry leaves, experiencing his physical being.

"What are you wearing tonight?" Ellen said.

We were both invited to Isabel's party and Kevin wasn't, but that figured and we didn't feel bad about it. Anyway, we said anything in front of Kevin. We didn't worry about his feelings.

"I don't know yet. What about you?"

"Maybe a red skirt."

"Did you get something new?"

"No, my mom's." I could see Ellen doing what I was doing, going silently through every closet in every room of her house, assessing each garment, could it work? She had sisters, that helped. I had just my stuff and my mom's. What to wear. It was as necessary and important a problem to us as how to score on our achievement tests. (That day, months later, Ellen pulled her hair back in a ponytail while the proctor passed out the sealed booklets.)

It was Saturday. We'd each go home and change into our after-school clothes and help our mothers around the house. Kevin picked up handfuls of leaves and threw them into the air. Kids in Beverly Hills had great clothes. Most sixteen-year-olds here didn't have after-school clothes. They just had clothes. Clothes, clothes and more clothes. We saw their discards. In some households, they were kept as rags. Our mothers picked through them, plucking out what might fit us, holding it across our shoulders, measuring, deciding it was perfectly good. We had had fights with our mothers over these clothes. We didn't want to wear stuff other people had thrown out.

Ellen stared at the traffic. She picked up a hand and bit her nail. "I'm sorry, I'm preoccupied," she said. "Jeff."

"Are you going to see him this weekend?"

"At Isabel's party, but it doesn't have anything to do with him and me." The skin of Ellen's fingers was puffed and pinkish around ridged nails. Her hands looked old. It was the only thing wrong with her.

Kevin came up behind us and smashed dry leaves into our hair, down our shirt backs.

"Kevin," Ellen yelled, standing up. "This is a good dress! Dammit. We better get going."

We lived far apart. Ellen lived in the hills, up in Trousdale Estates. The Criers, people in the big house, had always hired Japanese help. Her father gardened and all her mother did was iron shirts in the front house. They had their own cottage in a eucalyptus grove on the back of the property. Kevin lived alone with just his mother. Kevin and I could walk to school. Ellen had to carpool.

Today, she stood on the corner for the bus. She shook her sister's sweater out against her lap, then folded it neatly in thirds and put it in her bag. Buses hardly ever came in Beverly Hills. Kevin and I left her standing there. Sometimes it seemed like we didn't know each other that well. When we walked away, I looked back at her standing there, reading a book. There were things I didn't understand about her. Every day, she went home after school, lay on her single bed and did all her homework.

At Isabel's party, two girls dropped acid. While they were upstairs and we heard them giggling through the bedroom floor, some of their friends solidified into a circle. They disapproved.

Abby was the first one to come down the stairs. It was quiet now up in the bedroom. Missy must have fallen asleep on top of the coats.

"Have you heard what happened to Abby?" one of the boys in the circle said. "She died last week."

"I know," said a droopy, red-headed girl. She was a cousin of the girl in a coma and she seemed to thrive on sorrow.

Abby stood with one hand on the banister, pale as a ghost, two sheaths of heavy dark hair on the sides of her face.

"It's really too bad, she should have been more careful," another boy said.

Those people in the circle had only been sitting there before, but now they lifted their hands and joined.

There were more of us who hadn't said we'd do this. We were in corners of the room, pressed against walls.

Then Abby took another step down, her legs, in black tights, as fragile and tentative as a deer's.

"I'm not dead, I'm here," she said.

No one in the circle moved. "It's really too bad," the red-headed girl whispered, later.

The rest of us stood holding our plastic cups, hesitating. We hadn't agreed to do this. We hadn't gone in the circle. But we were quiet anyway. I looked around at the people near me, they weren't moving either. It was as if from that moment on we all held still and looked wherever we'd been looking before. It was like a game we'd played as children; if you moved, you were out. We froze and stared into the plastic cups as Abby ran around the circle touching her friends, stumbling and screaming. The circle changed. They all looked down now. But no one had the nerve to stop.

"It's too bad," a boy said.

Then Abby ran upstairs yelling, "Mis-sy." We heard her fall on the landing. Then the circle broke up and people started shouting at each other. I saw Ellen across the room standing in front of a dark glass door. She was wearing her sister's black pants and a shirt I didn't recognize. We were both uncomfortable seeing each other. We compromised ourselves all the time to have these friends. But we usually didn't have to watch each other do it.

Later, I found her in a bathroom, splashing her face with cold water. "Jeff and me broke up again," she said.

The next day, Kevin and I walked home together. We usually did.

"Did you read *The Great Gatsby?*" Kevin asked.

"Mmhmm." I was thinking of other things. It was always that way with us. There wasn't much romance or even fun between the three of us. Mostly, we exchanged information and goods, things we needed. We were like family except, for what we needed now, we could help each other more than our families could. What did our families know of Ivy League colleges? Our mothers were maids. They weren't educated.

"Remember how Gatsby always watched the green light. For her. Look." He pushed me around, tugging my hand. His physical being again.

"So?" There were two lamps on either side of the high school steps. One was burned out, the other was sort of yellow. The high school was pink stucco. Sometimes it seemed majestic and imposing, other times it sat on the tiered lawns like a huge, ridiculous cake.

"The green light! I can't believe that lamp—doesn't it look green to you? It had to be green. I think of him in love with Daisy and waiting for her and I watch it. God."

"Are you in love, Kevin?" It was an absolutely new thought. I turned to him. I had been thinking of silver high heels Ellen and I had seen at Judy's. It had never occurred to me that Kevin might be in love. Now that I considered it, it began to seem funny.

"Yes," he said.

Then, I can't say exactly why, but I had the feeling he was going to tell me it was me. I cupped my elbows in my hands. I kept looking at Kevin. He was white and pasty, gangly, soft. Nothing. I couldn't fall in love with him. I already liked Les Kaplan. Kevin, Kevin was outside that altogether. Kevin wasn't what Ellen and I wanted. He never could have been. He was what we had.

He and I kept walking. I cradled my books.

Then Kevin couldn't stand it anymore, he spun off, sashaying on the grass, his long arms out to the winds.

"It's Ellen," he yelled. "Ellen, Ellen, Ellen."

I shook my head. "I don't know, Kev." I looked at him again. He hadn't changed.

Ellen was in love with Jeff, Jeff Gunther. Jeff was the kind of guy who, if you knew him and I told you Ellen was in love with him, you'd shrug and say, Well, who wouldn't be? And when he left her, no one really felt bad. Everyone shrugged like, Well, what did she expect?

When they'd gotten together, the summer we were fourteen, they had both looked better, all of a sudden. I hadn't seen Ellen in a few weeks and then when I saw her, she'd lost weight and she was tan and her hair had grown longer. A piece was caught and twined around her gold hoop earring. Parts of her were just a little different but she ended up prettier than I'd ever thought she could be.

I saw them on a summer evening in the little theater at the high school. The repertory class was performing *Anything Goes*. Ellen sat on Jeff's lap and she'd slipped off her sandals so her long feet moved on his thighs. Jeff looked better too. His acne had cleared and his hair had grown down into a swoop that touched his eyebrows.

I had never seen her that happy before, but then who wouldn't be and who normally is anyway? I went up to them in the auditorium—everyone who knew them did, and people who didn't I bet wanted to. They mostly ignored me while at the same time being elaborately and even patiently kind.

It wasn't that I expected much from Ellen; we all understood that when we were doing well, we left each other alone. It was how they were. I looked down at Ellen's hands. The nails were still bitten and ridged, the cuticles puffy. She slid one under Jeff's thigh.

I sighed. Kevin and I were walking past the concubines' houses on Beverly Drive, little cottages built in the forties by the movie moguls for their mistresses. I'd never been inside one, but they were supposed to be no kitchen and all closet, kidney-shaped pools in the backyards. While Kevin ran onto one of their lawns, pretending to chase a fly ball, then to miss it, groaning, full of the thrill of effort and longing, Ellen was biting her nails in a carpool, settling in the far back compartment of a station wagon, trying to think in a clear line over the noise of the Crier boys.

Things were no longer good with Jeff. The fall of our sophomore year, when the football season began, Jeff had broken up. That year, he'd come to a New Year's party with a blonde from another school. Ellen accepted his verdict silently, keeping her movements to a minimum. She didn't say anything about the blonde. She figured they'd broken up, it was fair. And so it went with them. Summers, they drifted together, spending long hours in his bedroom and long winters of work, they talked only in school, the smartest two in math and science. Jeff couldn't help noticing Ellen. She always made the highest mark in the class. Once Kevin stopped in front of her desk in AP Physics. "You got a hundred on *that?*"

"She always does," Jeff growled, somewhere behind.

Last year, she'd tried calling Jeff in November. It didn't work.

Ellen was the best student in our seven-hundred-eighty-five-person class. She would have been even without cheating, but we weren't taking any chances. We wanted college more than we wanted to know we could do it by ourselves. We figured there would be time for that later. Ellen's homework always looked clear and simple, with no erasures. She seemed to do everything right the first time, the opposite of me. There must have been some pleasure, not only in seeing the small single line of As on her computerized report card every semester, but also in turning over a page, finishing it and adding it to the stack on her desk, problems worked out every day between the hours of four and six. I was thinking that as Kevin and I walked home, up the wide streets.

"Do you think I have a chance?" Kevin asked.

I shrugged. I would be home for an hour and help my mom fix dinner, but before they all sat down to eat, I'd be off on my bike to the ice-cream store. Ellen's mother came and knocked on her door at six o'clock to call her to supper. Ellen and her sisters sat at the table with their hands folded and their hair pulled back from their faces while their father took off his high gardening boots and hung them up behind the door. Ellen's father said he liked to look at their faces.

I made myself a dinner at the ice-cream store. I got so I made special combinations, things customers had never tasted. I made milk shakes with chopped walnuts and jimmies and swirls of hot caramel laced through the ice cream. And I ate leaning against the front window by the street. I loved doing that. I held the tin container with a towel and ate slowly, with a long spoon.

"I read today in the paper," Ellen's mother said, "that in *China* during their Cultural Revolution . . ."

"What's that?" Ellen and Kevin and I were sitting with our

notes spread out on the kitchen table. Ellen's father had picked us up at the UCLA research library in his gardening truck. Her mother bent over four identical pots on the stove.

"Don't they teach you kids history? I've told you, Ellen, about the Gang of Four and how they sent people to the fields. A big mistake, they're learning it now. It says all over in the papers. But I read today something in the E section. See, it pays not to just stop at the front page. You have to follow it to the back. I learned that when they sent an office or a factory where the people worked or a school, they sent them all to the same farm. Now, isn't that something? Because that's just what they did with us. We'd all lived nearby each other before. In the old house on Colby Street. I knew lot of lot of people. And those houses are worth a pretty penny now." She shook her head over the pots as if she were scolding children. "If you'd go every Sunday, you'd know some of these things."

None of us really fought with our parents. Ellen's only quarrels were over church on Sundays. Ellen liked to stay home on Sunday mornings. She said it was her only time alone in the cottage. The women from the parish referred to people not only according to the name of the camp but also to the wings and corridors they'd lived in, as if their memory of those twenty-nine months in Utah was as alive as their own children today. The women at church exchanged recipes. They were up on the congressional passage of laws for compensation and they talked about them hopefully. At that time, Ellen didn't talk about those things at all. And when she did, years later, she was rueful—so unlike her parents. I went with them all one Sunday. Most of the women and girls in the church were dressed in fluffy, pastel-colored dresses. After the service they served light, thickly frosted cake. The atmosphere was happy and affluent, like a wedding, though, at that time, few of those families were truly prosperous. It was as if they could see ahead to their children's lives.

In the closet of Ellen's cottage, there was a shelf of tidily wrapped presents. Ellen's parents would have never dreamed of visiting their church friends without a wrapped gift in their hands. All their church friends did the same. But Ellen's parents didn't even open the presents they were given. They put them on the shelf in the closet and recycled them, the next time they paid visits. This required bookkeeping and, on the inside of the closet door, was an elaborate chart of whom each gift had been received from and to whom it was therefore safe to give.

"Japanese," Ellen said with her particular shudder, as if it were a generational affliction.

Ellen's father was kind. The thing about him was, he was happy. He felt he owned three acres of gardens and he knew every pond and tree. He'd built it all. He had a library of catalogues in his work shed and new ones came in the mail every day. Seed catalogues. Bulbs. Saplings. For a while he'd raised orchids. The people in the big house, the Criers, they paid for it all. He had his own gardens, by the cottage. He raised hybrid chrysanthemums. He entered them in shows, each season he won some prize. The year we graduated, he was elected president of the LA County Chrysanthemum Society.

By the time Ellen was a junior in high school, her parents had saved up money. Her mother stopped cleaning the front house. She worked part-time in a bakery coffee shop opened in the new, tiny Japantown by two women she knew from church. She wanted to move nearer the parish. She wanted to buy a condominium. But Ellen's father couldn't bear to live away from his trees. It wasn't a sorrow between them. She teased about it, sitting in the kitchen talking to her friends on the phone, her nylon-stockinged feet smooth and plump on another chair.

That spring, Ellen was going to a prom at another high school, with a boy she'd met from the church. She was clear about her intentions with Dave. "It's better than sitting around at home." But a prom was a prom and a prom dress a prom dress and so I had to come and see it. Ellen and her mother had sewn it together over the course of evenings in March. It was totally Ellen. More simple and straight-lined than you would think possible and still a fancy dress. I helped her into it. She was most pleased about the shoes. They were another girl's—some girl I didn't know from the parish—with tissue paper stuffed in the toes. The girl wore a size 8. Ellen got flustered and started crying because her hair wouldn't dry and her sisters and mother followed around in the excitement, tripping and giggling. The inside of that house belonged to the women.

Just before she was going to leave, her mother told her to go out and find her father so he could see her. I watched them from just outside the house. It was still daylight and he was across the garden, holding a hose loosely, watering. Ellen was walking over the grass and stone, wobbling on her pumps in that cream, petal-colored dress. He turned.

I called in sick to the ice-cream store. People would be walking down Beverly Drive to fancy restaurants. I didn't want them coming from proms and looking in the window and seeing me. I had to keep my hair back in a rubber band while I worked.

I ran out the door after dinner. I couldn't bear to be home. There was a movie on TV Kevin and his mother were watching. I brought along the SAT practice book too. We lived a walking distance apart. It was April and the northern streets of Beverly Hills were full of limousines and voices.

Kevin's mother always seemed old, decades older than my mother. She had gray hair she kept braided up around her head in a twirled bun. She wore a uniform but, with Mrs. Sutter, you couldn't be sure she had to. It really could have been her idea. Mrs. Sutter was a pastry chef, and the Berringers, people she worked for, praised her lavishly for her everyday creations. People always told her she should open a store. She and my mother sometimes talked about it; my mother was going to be the business manager. But they never did.

Mrs. Sutter folded and pinched intricate turnovers while Kevin and I sat at the kitchen table, passing the SAT book back and forth. There were proms all around us. Even the smell of magnolia from the open kitchen window, like perfume, made me feel younger, that and having tall glasses of icy milk at our sides and a plate of cookies between us.

"So what did her dress look like?" Kevin asked.

"Yellowish white."

Kevin nodded and swallowed as if this were serious information. Mrs. Sutter asked, "Who is this you are talking about?" She had some kind of lisp.

"Ellen."

"Your friend Ellen? What is this dress?"

"Yes, my Ellen. My Ellen's going to a prom with another guy!" Kevin's arms shot up in extravagance and I saw how much his mother liked him. She smiled as if she wasn't supposed to smile.

"I feel like a little drink!" she burst out, her flour-coated hands clasped in front of her apron, in her voice the pure lilt of inexperienced mischief.

This vision of her was so startling, Kevin and I both looked up. She walked on the balls of her feet in the sturdy, gray, crepe-soled shoes to the cupboard and put her finger to her lips. She took out three fancy tiny crystal glasses and a bottle of sherry. She poured each glass half full, looking over her shoulder to make sure no Berringer could see.

We refilled our glasses many times that night. We toasted, crowding next to each other on the sofa in the TV room, the apple turnovers with their warm threads of white frosting cooling in the clean kitchen. We were happy enough.

But that look over the shoulder—that was as common to us as washing our faces, something we did every day.

Kevin walked me home. It was late for us; the movie was over; Mrs. Sutter had fallen asleep with an afghan on her lap. But it was still early outside, with the screech of brakes on beautiful cars and a spill of girls in dresses and fragile, tippy shoes and the stomping class of boys behind.

It was strange for me, being walked home. I didn't know what to do with my hands. Three times a week I closed the ice-cream store. I was the one the owners trusted. So I stayed after the others left and cleaned the glass cases, back and front. Then I sat in the last booth with the radio blasting and counted the register money. I put the bills in order, clipped twenties, then tens, fives, ones. I laid them in a brown plastic zip-up bag with an accounting slip. Every time I walked outside down two blocks to the bank deposit chute. The street was always deserted and windy that time of morning. I walked with my bike handlebars in one hand and the plastic bag under my shirt, then I bombed home pedaling standing up the whole way. I was afraid someone would hold me up for the money.

Kevin didn't know I did that. He was carefully walking on the outside of the sidewalk and it was only a little after midnight. I didn't tell people things about the ice-cream store. Kevin and Ellen were home in bed at two or three in the morning on school nights and I was embarrassed not to be.

Kevin walked me to the back door, where my mother and I went in the Hanners' house. Cars scraped down the alley behind us. He kissed me then, his face and teeth pushing against my cheek so for a second I felt I couldn't breathe. Then it was easier. We stopped and he was looking down at me. I wiped my mouth off with the back of my cuff.

"I like somebody," I said. Les Kaplan. I didn't know if anything was going on with us, it probably wasn't, but we walked around almost every day at school. Les always remembered everything I told him, even things I forgot. Things I mentioned liking —something to eat or a book I read or something, all of a sudden, he had it. But he never saw me, hardly ever. He got picked up after school and he never asked me over to his house. He called me sometimes but he never gave me his phone number. Once, he came into the ice-cream store. I gave him a free dish at the counter and he just sat there for a long time. I didn't like him seeing me like that with my hair back.

"Les Kaplan? You just like it that he follows you around. That guy. You just like being worshiped." I must have blushed and Kevin cuffed my shoulder. "You little goon." Then he kissed me again and ran his hand from my throat to my belt.

My mother was up that night when I came home. She was in the screening room with a movie running and an old scrapbook album on her lap. "Look what I found," she said when I walked in. No where-have-you-been-until-one-in-the-morning. My mother wasn't like that. But when she patted her hand on the leather sofa, you wanted to sit there next to her, you wanted to rub near the satiny fabric of her robe.

The scrapbook was old newspaper clippings of Elaine Rogers, the former MGM starlet we lived with. The movie was her movie, *Tennessee Rose.* My mother had started the archive of Elaine's life. "Two letters came from Germany this week," she said, "And one from down there. Argentina. She's still getting royalties from Argentina."

Fifteen years ago, Elaine Rogers was driving a red convertible on Sunset Boulevard when her radiator overheated. The car stalled at Sunset and Doheny and a short man in tennis clothes parked on the rounded corner and jumped out to help her. This was Manny Hanner, the game-show producer she married.

They found us five years later when they already had their two children, Roger and Tammy. It was a great house. We were amazed when we first moved in. At night, when everyone was asleep, we used to get up and open the refrigerator. The little light was the only light on in the house. We'd just stand there in our nightgowns and stare.

I was eight when my mother and I moved in. Those first few years, we were alone with the kids most of the time. The faded cover of the Sunday supplement from one year says, "Elaine Rogers on Return Visit to New Jersey Hometown." We got used to the house. We could walk anywhere around in it. Manny and Elaine went away a lot, to New York, to London, Saint Moritz. My mother ruled the house then or at least she was supposed to. She had about as much authority as a substitute teacher.

To my mother, Tammy and Roger were both perfect-looking kids: they had freckles and naturally curly hair, blond and red-headed. But as soon as Elaine and Manny left in the car to go out of town, pipes broke, fuses blew and my mother and I were chasing screaming naked children down the long tiled hallways, trying to catch them the way you'd try to catch butterflies. Nothing seemed to work. My mother wore a white uniform then that was tight-fitting, like a nurse's. I remember both standing in the breezeway once, against the tiled, echoing wall, heaving. She put her hand over her belly. We both looked at each other and at the still empty living room, like a ruin, furnished in beige, dim in the curtained light. We sighed. It was amazing, the way these people lived.

Later, doctors explained Roger's problem and the Hanners stayed home more. But I never could have guessed it at the time. Then I felt like we'd discovered the real inside of mansions. It was loud and mean and screaming and nothing ever worked. Long days while their parents were in Switzerland, Roger and Tammy peed on the floor, threw eggs in the pool and screamed, "You just work for us, we can *fire* you!" Then, stuck there, the muscles in the backs of my eight-year-old knees hurting, scrubbing the clay tiled floor, I swore I'd never forgive them, ever. But luck, ours and theirs, determined what we could forgive, more than anything that happened then.

There is something I haven't told, a part of my life. I had my own forays into the rich world. Most of us did. It was compensation for the others of us who lived there. My mother saw movie stars in Gelson's. She and Mrs. Sutter compared guest lists for the Hanners' and the Berringers' parties. Ellen saw Jeff's house, touched Jeff's things, all infinite sources of privilege and mystery.

I had Sharon, the granddaughter of a wealthy industrialist. I use the word industrialist now. Then we never thought about how or where or when rich people got their money. They just had it. They were it. I had heard of Leonard Mayer. Leonard Mayer was famous. It was a name you knew, like a brand of something. A wing of the Art Museum was named for him.

Sharon and her brother Howard lived with their mother and their maid in a twenty-two-room house. Their maid spoke no English and she walked through the silent house silently, always carrying a vacuum cleaner or a mop. I took my shoes off at the door there. Everyone seemed to go lightly through that house.

There was something funny about Sharon. I never really understood what it was—but my knowing her was kind of a secret. Her own mother seemed to see it. She gave Sharon hints, telling her how to sit. Boys in ninth grade stuck a razor in her homeroom desk. But Sharon just stared back blankly. People gave up.

Even when Sharon was a little girl, all the other children at school would have known that she was Leonard Mayer's granddaughter. Beverly Hills children were that way. They wouldn't have liked her or disliked her for that. But it was something they would have all known, a fact, like the color of her hair. Their affections were founded on other things, qualities that must have seemed ineluctable and elusive to Sharon, when she tried to decode the systems of popularity. They were mysterious to me, too, but after a while I made friends and Sharon never did. The girls were generally polite to her, it wasn't that. In fourth grade, we would all be standing together in a circle for a game of ball at recess, the girls shouted to her equally, the ball came her way and in the exhilarated happiness of hearing her name, she kicked with all her might. They cheered. She sighed, her chest filling from the bottom with contentment, a candy of belief that she was all right after all. But when the bell rang and the girls drifted naturally in pairs walking to their lockers, Sharon would find herself alone again. She told herself, It is my own fault. I have to keep up, she thought, and dashed into a run, breaking between two girls; she heard their voices hush and saw their eyes turn down. Around her she heard references to afternoons, evenings together, a life outside school. So it was true, what she most feared. In her heart, she knew that she had no friend and that it was unfair—she had done nothing. But though she knew this, she didn't remember it most of the time and she could be quite noisy and boisterous, always trying. In class, raising her hand, straining out of her seat, she often seemed conceited.

She decided that the other girls' sneakers were whiter than her own and she tormented her mother in the evenings. Her mother made poor Manuela put the sneakers through the wash machine four and five times with bleach. Still, they didn't seem to Sharon like the others'.

I was new in the third grade. On the playground once, girls said to me, Her grandfather is Leonard Mayer and then went on with our game. Sharon was the first person to invite me over after school. Walking for the first time through the house on North Alden Drive, the ordinary touches surprised me. The kitchen had gingham curtains. It also had three ovens and four sinks. I counted the sofas in the living room: eight. Each chair had a curtain of pleats. It was as if someone had taken the old Elks' auditorium and its huge industrial kitchen and hung up tiny framed pictures and pot holders. It was the second mansion I'd been inside. The first was the Hanners'. Before that, we'd lived with my mother's family in Silverlake.

By the time we were in high school Sharon didn't expect anything from me. She was grateful whenever I saw her. But I needed her, too. It's hard to explain. I didn't mention her to my other friends. Ellen and Kevin knew, the way they knew most things about me. But they looked funny when they talked about her too. I was like a man having a secret affair.

We lay on Sharon's pink and white princess beds and talked about important things that didn't seem important then. We talked about how we were going to live. We determined not to waste time worrying about makeup. We talked and talked for hours, the hours other girls must have sat on closed toilet seats in front of mirrors, learning how to draw on eyeliner. We lay with our arms over our heads, hands useless, gesturing, theorizing. Sharon promised that there were places we could go when we were eighteen, department-store palaces where we could pay once and women would teach us everything. "And we won't have wasted all that time now, when we can be learning things!" Sharon cried.

I am thirty-one years old. I still can't properly apply eye makeup.

Even then, I wasn't so sure about learning things and catching up on being pretty later.

"And when I'm grown up, I'm never going to waste time cooking and setting a table for a man. I can eat a carton of yogurt for supper and I'm perfectly happy," Sharon said.

That seemed to me mostly what they did eat there for supper. Yogurt or one slice of cheese. Their maid couldn't cook at all. She tiptoed through the huge house and unobtrusively fried her tortilla and heated her can of beans. Sometimes I wondered about Manuela. She wasn't old, but then she wasn't pretty either, and from what I could tell she never spoke to anyone. I knew Spanish. I could have talked to her. But I never did.

At the Hanners', we ate a good dinner every night. My mother and I had to fix a healthy meal for them. Every night, we made a protein and a starch, wild rice and a vegetable. I wouldn't have wanted strawberry yogurt and that's all for dinner.

But I couldn't bring up my mother as an example. My mother was a maid. Sharon wanted to be a big career woman. And so did I. I spent time at the Mayers', giving up my mother's good dinners for yogurt and old pickles. Sometimes my mother called me there, talking politely with Mrs. Mayer for a few minutes and then, when I came to the phone, asking me to come home because she was lonely.

Ellen and I each threaded our lives through those mansions, all so different from our families, but Kevin really didn't. He played after-school tennis and switched back and forth novels with other boys from the honors class. They read Salinger, Forster and, of course, Fitzgerald and swooned. The other guys accepted him, but it was different than with Ellen and me. He didn't try. He just liked the guys who liked him.

And his mother minded more. He was friends with a guy named Andy whose family hiked to the top of a mountain for Thanksgiving and roasted a turkey there. Our sophomore year, Kevin went along and left his mother at the Berringers'. She had to bake pies for their Thanksgiving. And anyway, can you see

Mrs. Sutter in a parka on top of a mountain? But Kevin couldn't sleep all night. He hiked back down alone as soon as the sun rose, leaving while the others were still in their tents. He hitched on the highway and made it home by suppertime on Friday. And he seemed to know then that he would never try anything like that again.

He never fell in love with a rich girl. Not one. Not one of the pretty, silly girls caught his eye. There were nice girls too, and he talked to them in school, but he always preferred our company, Ellen's and mine. He stayed home most nights, reading in the same room where his mother embroidered or studying at the kitchen table while she baked.

Ellen and I knew, as deep as anything we were, we wanted to leave—what? Something. Now we would call it the class we were born in. And that seemed a good thing to us, and to our parents, too. I think we both wondered if Kevin was different because he was white. It was a different thing for a white woman to be a maid.

Leonard Mayer was a small mostly bald man who had tufts of white hair on either side of his head, just above his ears. He spoke with a grandiose, English-sounding politeness, elaborately pronouncing the consonants of my name as if I were some sort of fancy cake. Amanda.

I was invited to his seventieth-birthday party as the best friend. When I came to the door in an ironed blouse with a ruffled collar, my mother's blue velvet skirt and color around my eyes, Sharon glared at me as if I were a traitor. She picked up the careful gold chain from my neck and then dropped it back. "You look like a package," she hissed.

I hooked some hair behind my ear. I was wearing Ellen's glittery earrings. "My mom," I said and rolled my eyes.

Sharon went to France for her junior year. She sent me long dreary letters which I hardly ever answered. I didn't miss her.

Without the house on North Alden Drive and her family, she didn't seem like much to me. I didn't remember what I'd liked about her. I was closer to other girls now, girls I could talk about with each other. Sharon said in her letters that she was assigned to an awful French family in Rennes, which sounded like an industrial city.

In spring, she came back, fat and fluent. Really, she'd gained at least forty pounds. She said she rode a bicycle to school every day and stopped on the way back in a warm bakery for two pastries. But you'd have to eat more than two to gain that weight.

She stood at the teacher's desk, speaking to our French class. "So how was Mayer?" Kevin asked us, later. Kevin took Spanish.

Ellen shrugged. "She sounded exactly like Mayer but in French." She was fluent but it didn't make anybody like her more. Those years, I never really saw what it was in her nobody liked.

That was May. In June, something strange happened at the Mayers'. It seemed Mrs. Mayer didn't want her children living there in the house with her anymore. She arranged for Howard to go to boarding school and then she drove Sharon to the Claremont Valley. They found out that with Sharon's grades and scores and the Claremont College's generally failing finances, they would accept her without her senior year.

She decided to do that. She'd said before that she knew she could get into Stanford because her grandfather was a trustee. But who would give up Stanford for Pomona? Who cared about a year early? I didn't get it. Stanford was the rest of your life. Sharon called Pomona the Harvard of the West.

She left in September while Ellen and Kevin and I were working on our college applications. I told them what Sharon was doing. Ellen shrugged, "Good. One less person."

Knowing what we know now, we could have played up our poverty, written our essays about being maids' children. But we didn't know that yet. We learned that in college. We were still trying to be like everybody else. For parents' occupation, Ellen put "horticulturalist." I said my father was "deceased." I pictured a funeral, a stern day beside old trees, the ground frosted over, my mother in a hat, a little girl in a coat with a ponytail.

A few years before, sometimes, a man came at night and picked my mother up in a battered truck. His headlights flooded the kitchen and she would rush out in a whisper. She wasn't exactly allowed to be gone all night. But she was back in the kitchen before anyone was up, wiping down the counters. The man always came in the patched battered truck in darkness and I never got a look at his face. But I always thought he could have been my father.

Kevin was the only one who told the truth: "domestic house-keeper and pastry chef." Ellen and I winced looking at the top sheet of the application forms, where we couldn't check "Caucasian."

One night in autumn my mother and I sat in the dark at the Hanners' kitchen table. We were eating a pie Mrs. Sutter had sent home with me, a cranberry torte. All the Hanners were gone and we were alone in the house. They were driving Roger to a special school not far from where Sharon was in Claremont.

Since the Hanners were away, we didn't cook. We sat with mugs of coffee eating the pie one thin slice at a time. My mother had begun to take a nervous interest in my future. I told her about Sharon giving up Stanford.

"Stanford," my mother said, shaking her head so her hair fell over her cheek. Of all the colleges I talked about, Stanford was the name that stuck with my mother. I'd heard her whisper to Elaine Hanner, "She thinks she wants to go to Stanford." They had both looked at me then, with a mixture of doubt and awe, wondering if I'd get in. Manny Hanner had gone to The Farm, and Elaine, my mother and I once sat on the sofa looking at his old pictures. Going there would be like joining a private club. I would be allowed to use everything.

"Sharon could have had him help her. He's a trust*ee,*" I said. "I wish he'd help me. I need it."

"Maybe he would. Do you think he might?"

I shook my head. Rich people were busy. I thought of him sitting at a fine desk in a silk robe and slippers, making decisions about erecting and demolishing buildings. "He'd never think of it. He only met me that once.

"Yeah." The smell of jasmine and eucalyptus came in strongly from outside. I sliced another piece of pie and ate it off my hand. Can you smell more in the dark or do trees let something loose at night? Mrs. Sutter was a brilliant cook. The filling was airy. The crust was a dream. And nobody would ever know it. Only the Berringers.

"Maybe I should call him or write him a letter." I sighed.

"Would he know you? Who you are?"

"Yes. But still."

My mother cut another slice, eating with concentration. "When do you have to get that paper in to Stanford?"

"December."

"December. Maybe we should bake something for Thanksgiving. Why don't we get this recipe from Jean Sutter and we can bake one for him. So then, after that, when he's got you in mind, you can write a note and ask him.

I didn't know and my mother didn't understand about college admissions either. We were sitting in a kitchen in the dark. Stanford. The letters, like on Manny Hanner's old sweatshirt, seemed printed somewhere on the dark.

My mother talked on the phone with Mrs. Sutter. "She said she wished she could get Kevin to do something like that. She says he admires you two—you and Ellen, but that she can't get him to stand up and go for things for himself. He is a bit of a dishrag, isn't he? He's sort of timid, waiting all this time for Ellen. I don't blame her, either, I can't see them together. She wants too much for him. 'Course, maybe that's better for a boy. To be like Kevin." Her eyes smoked over then. She was thinking of Roger, who was never timid. She frowned. "Should we call Ellen? We can all bake together."

"Ellen doesn't need any help." Ellen didn't. And if I was going to cheat, this time I was going to do it alone.

Ellen and Jeff were together again, the first year during school. Kevin and I hardly saw her. She and Jeff decided on everything jointly now. There were school-wide achievement tests you didn't put your name on. They mattered for the district, not for us. Ellen and Jeff figured out the right answers and filled in the wrong circles, to bring down the Beverly Hills score. But they wouldn't have done that on anything that counted for them.

We baked in chaos. By Thanksgiving week, Roger was already expelled, chasing Tammy under the kitchen table while my mother and I read the steps of the recipe. I washed cranberry filling out of Tammy's hair in the maid's tub, off the kitchen.

My mother drove me to Leonard Mayer's house. The trees looked black and solid that night, the sky shone navy blue. The moon, covered with mysterious clouds, seemed a waxy yellow. It was the kind of night when things seemed ominous, for the good or for the bad. My mother stayed in the car when I ran out over the lawn, carrying the pie covered with tin foil. A Chinese butler in a blue suit took it from my hands.

I'd rested my note on top of the pie.

A week later, we were eating supper. The Hanners' house, as usual, was a zoo, Elaine in ribboned pigtails chasing Roger around the table, Tammy crying, having spilt milk on her dress, my mother springing up for a towel. It occurs to me now that perhaps my whole friendship with Sharon had to do with the silence of her house.

Manny Hanner walked in, sprightly, in green tennis clothes, slapping a fan of mail down on the table. "Two letters for Elaine from Argentina and a letter for a Miss Amanda Soto from Leonard Mayer. What's this all about?"

I grabbed it and ran to the kitchen and ripped open the envelope. It was a carbon of a letter to Stanford's admissions office. "I would like to recommend Amanda Soto. She is an excellent student and a fine girl and she would make an enthusiastic addition to your student body." I held the letter in both hands and read it again and again. I still know it from memory. His penmanship was fancy and his secretary appended a note complimenting my

grammar: "Your letter was refreshing. Almost no one knows to
put the comma inside the parenthesis anymore. People just don't.
Excellent, for a twelfth-grader."

The next day Sharon called from Claremont. "I heard you
asked my grandfather to help you get into Stanford. They'd probably let *me* in because I have his same name and they'd hope he'd
give them money for a building or something. But it wouldn't
work for anyone else. It would have to be me. I wanted you to
know that, because I don't think there's much he can do for you."

On April fifteenth, Ellen and I stayed home from school. At the
Hanners', mail came through a slot in the front door. When I
heard it drop onto the terra-cotta tiles, I ran and then closed my
eyes. Once I felt the first thick letter, it was all over. I got in
everywhere. Ellen did too. Kevin got in everywhere but Princeton.

Ellen wanted Radcliffe. She always had. And now Jeff was in
Harvard and he was going. But Ellen and her father spent a long
afternoon walking over the Criers' grounds, around and around.
Ellen knew by then that she wanted to be a doctor, needed to be,
and she had a fat scholarship to the seven-year medical program
at Northwestern. Her father would have been gentle. "We could
pay for four years of Harvard and you still may not get in. And
this way, you know you're in. You can relax and have a little fun.
You don't have to work so hard." They should have known their
daughter. Ellen would always get in. But then, he had two
younger girls.

Jeff went to Harvard. I went to Yale. I threw Leonard Mayer's
letter out and turned down Stanford. Cheating was behind me. We
were in now. We could afford higher standards. Ellen went to
Northwestern, and Kevin, in a last-minute reversal of everything,
stayed in California and went to Berkeley.

The French teacher asked Ellen and me to stay after class and
erase the blackboards. "I've known you two cheat," she said to
our backs, "and I want to tell you, you're going somewhere new,

you have a fresh start, and you both have everything going for you. There's just this streak—" Her own daughter had gotten a scholarship to Stanford.

At the end of the summer, the owners of the ice-cream store found it empty one day, a note left under a can by the manager. "No raise, no car, no flavors, no salt . . . Maybe Hawaii will be better." The three of them called me in and offered me the job. That day, I turned in my key and quit. My mother shook her head when I came home. "Don't you think you ought to take that?"

"Mom, I got into *Yale.*"

"Two hundred dollars a week is nothing to sniff at."

That is not the end of our story. Sharon transferred: to Duke, then to Princeton, finally to Brown, where she graduated when we did. She wrote me a letter to the Hanners' house, asking me to be maid of honor at her wedding.

Once, after that, Ellen and I saw her in New York. Ellen had left Jeff by then. We were in line for a movie. All of a sudden we saw Sharon. She looked thin, thinner than we'd ever seen her, and her hair seemed scarce on her head. She was wearing tight leather pants and high-heeled boots and an enormous fur coat, six inches out from her. Her face looked like a pale, curved bone. She stood with it tilted up to the tall buildings, as if she wanted to absorb their lights, while her husband stood buying the tickets. That minute, I felt I saw what it was nobody ever liked. It was nothing, really. Just the feeling that you wanted to turn around, go anywhere, be lost in a crowd before she saw you and called your name.

Ellen told me the hardest thing she ever did was leave Jeff. It took six years. Six years. But once she left, she kept going. She didn't just get an M.D., she got a Ph.D., too. Sometime before then, she turned reverent. You couldn't tell the difference between her and her East Coast friends, girls who had always done everything right, who had never had to cheat. When they put the tassels over her shoulder, she cried.

I'm still the same as I always was. I'm belligerent the way I seemed in high school. Things slip out. I'm a criminal lawyer, slated for judgeship. My life is bargaining. But I've kept going too. I'm married, with two little boys.

Ellen and I both have maids ourselves now. You're probably wondering, What do our mothers say? But they love it. Our mothers are the proudest of anyone. "Why should you spend the time, that's right, you hire her. And she's glad to have the work," my mother has said. My mother still lives with the Hanners, but she doesn't clean anymore. They hired a younger woman, a refugee. The Hanners built a house in the backyard where my mother has assembled all the MGM stills and records of Elaine Rogers.

The last time Ellen's mother visited her, the housekeeper walked out. Mrs. Teshima pointed to all the spots on the walls. "Excuse me, Miss, you forgot something here," she said, "it comes out, see you just have to rub a little."

Ellen doesn't think about her childhood much anymore. She sees her parents on scattered holidays, her father telephones, she listens. But once, she told me, in a foreign city, walking under sycamore-lined streets with a man she was in love with, she couldn't help thinking about her shoes. They were new shoes, bone calf, a nostalgic style worn in the American capital cities that season, and this was the first time she had worn them. The streets were dark, lit only with scattered lanterns, the air whirred with unlit bicycle wheels, the trees dripping. It had rained a few hours before. The streets were still dotted with puddles and trees and tin eaves were dripping. There was the sound of water and wheels everywhere. It was a night to be lost in, on the alien streets, with signs neither she nor the man she was with could read. But she carefully watched her shoes. And when she came to her hotel room, after he was asleep she crept up, stole into the bathroom and carefully cleaned the shoes with a hotel towel.

We don't live in the same city, but sometimes Ellen calls and we laugh helplessly into the phones. And all our talks end at Kevin, Kevin who's a million miles away back in California, a lawyer too, living with the farmworkers, married to a Berkeley woman, with his hair grown long, in a house full of dogs and children. He ended up handsome and sure, still wearing old clothes, and amazingly, no matter what we do, we eventually come back to him— he's the one we want and who always forgives us. We're the only rich girls he'll ever love.

Massé

LEIGH ALLISON WILSON

The truth is it's not much of a city. When I moved in two years ago, all I knew about it was from a Chamber of Commerce brochure I got free at the courthouse: WELCOME, it said, TO THE BIG CITY IN THE LITTLE VALLEY BY THE LAKE. I had six suitcases in the back of my car and $350 and a good reason for leaving the place I'd left. For a woman like me, that's all people need to know. You start explaining things too much, you start giving heartfelt reasons for this and for that, and then nothing becomes clear and people don't trust you and you start looking at your life from bad angles. I like things clear. But the truth is it's not much of a city, not much of a valley, and you have to drive five miles to get to the lake. These are simple facts.

In the brochure they said the population was twenty thousand, but it is really closer to sixteen or seventeen. One problem is that most of the Chamber of Commerce live outside town, in big houses on the lake, and so maybe they don't come into the city much, to get the accurate head count. One thing I'm good at is counting. On Sunday nights at the local P & C, the average customer head count is twenty-six; on weekdays it is fifty-four after five o'clock. I can tell you the price of leaded gas at ten different stations, the price of unleaded at seven of them. Anytime you get good at something, it's because of a habit; counting things is just a habit with me. Last week I counted twelve geese heading for Canada in two perfect lines, a perfect V, and twelve is enough to prove that spring is coming. You can sometimes live a good life figuring angles and counting things, if you're in the habit of it.

What I've done for the last two years is, I drive a UPS truck during the day and I play pool at night. I have had some trouble lately, but not because of the UPS or the pool. You might think that these are things that women don't do—drive trucks for a living, that is, and play pool—but I do them, and so you probably just don't know enough women. Take into account enough numbers, anything is possible. Phineas says that the opposite is true, that given enough numbers nothing is possible, but he is a bartender who doesn't like crowds. Very little he says makes any sense. I've been seeing him off and on for the past six months, mostly off.

I met him, as I said, about six months ago, when all the trouble started. It was November, but a clear day, and the wind was gusting to forty miles per hour. I know because I listen to the radio in my truck. Every street I drove down that day had hats in the air, like a parade, from all the wind. This is what you could call an economically depressed town, which means that everybody in it is depressed about money, so I remember that November day's weather in particular. It was the only time I have ever seen anything like a celebration on the streets, all those hats in the air and everybody running after them, their faces as red and distorted as any winning crowd on television. I do not own a television, but all the bars have them. There are thirty-three bars in this city, and only nine have regulation pool tables. This is just a fact of life.

That day I was behind in my deliveries, although mostly I am punctual to a fault. I have a map of the city inlaid like a tattoo in my mind—where the easy right-hand turns are, where the short lights are, where the children play in the streets and thus become obstacles. I had to memorize the map in the Chamber of Commerce brochure to get the job, but anyone can tell you that maps like that are useless to a good driver. Maps are flat, cities are not. Obstacles are everywhere, but the good driver knows where they are and how to avoid them. Picture the city as a big pool table, right after the break in eight ball. Your opponent's balls surround you, like seven stop signs all over the table. You must deliver the

goods in a timely fashion. Knowing the correct angles is everything. The simple truth is I know all the angles in this town. But
that day I was behind in my deliveries and Danny, the dispatcher,
kept coming over the radio, kidding around.

"You're late, you're late," he said. "Frankly, I'm appalled.
Frankly, your ass is in a slingshot." He was in his silly-serious
mood, jazzing around with the radio, bored to death with his job.
He used to be a big shot on some high school football team in the
city, but that was years ago, and although he is still a huge,
bruised-looking man, the only big shots in his life now come from
bars. He drinks too much is my meaning, but in a town like this
that goes without saying.

"It's the wind," I told him, clicking the mike. "It's the wind
and about fifty zillion hats. I'm not kidding, there's exactly a
hundred fifty hats out here today."

"Ignore 'em," he said. "Run 'em down," he said. His voice
came out high and crackly, as though any minute he might burst
into weird, witchlike laughter. Radios do this to everybody's
voice.

"What's the matter with you?" I asked, but I could tell that
he'd already signed off, was already kidding around with another
truck, his big body hunched over the radio back at the office,
surrounded by boxes and handcarts and no windows anywhere.
Danny's life is highly unclear. Once I tried to teach him pool, to
show him a few straightforward things about the game. He handled the cue stick the way lips handle a toothpick, all muscle and
no control, then he tried a crazy massé shot that was all wrong for
the situation and ended up tearing the felt of the table. Finesse
and control are the names of the game in pool, but he would have
none of it. They kicked him out of the bar. I ran the table twelve
straight games after he left and picked up about seventy dollars—
a very good night for me.

I made my last delivery at about four o'clock, the wind buffet-
ing the truck every yard of the way. Usually I am punctual, but
the fact is the elements are an important factor in any driving job.
That day the wind was a factor. For another thing, there is always
the customer factor. If your customer is in a hurry, he just grabs a

pen or pencil and lets it rip; you get an unclear address and end up wasting precious minutes. My advice is, always use a typewriter. That way there is nothing personal to get in the way of the timely execution of your business. Chaos is no man's friend, clarity is everything.

I parked the truck in the lot at four-thirty, tied up some loose ends inside the office, then went outside to my car. It is a '73 navy Impala with a lot of true grit. Most people picture a good car and they think of bright color or sleek line or some other spiffy feature. This is all wrong. The best part of a good car, what makes it a good car, is its guts: pistons that never miss a beat; a carburetor so finely tuned it is like a genius chemist, mixing air and gasoline as if from beakers; a transmission that works smoothly, the gears meshing like lovers. This Impala has guts; even Phineas says so. I drove home and on the way counted smokestacks, eight of them, all rising above town in the shape of cigars stuck on end. Then something strange happened.

I was driving past the pet shop where I buy fish, only six blocks from my apartment. Up ahead the street was empty as an old Western set except for a few newspapers, seized by the wind, that tented up in the air, then fell and lay flat on the pavement. Along the sidewalks on both sides telephone poles stretched way into a distance I couldn't quite see. Maybe being late that day had me all worked up. I don't know. But I began to imagine bank shots with my car. I began to figure out at exactly what angle I would have to hit a telephone pole in order to bank the car across the street and into the pole on the other side. Then I began to do it with buildings—double banks into doorways, caroms off two fireplugs and into a brick wall, a massé around a parked car and into the plate glass of the corner drugstore. By the time I parked at my apartment, the knuckles of my hands were pale on the wheel.

Overhead, slightly distorted by the windshield, I could see Mrs. McDaniels, my landlady, leaning over the second-floor railing of my apartment building, her eyes magnified by bifocals and staring straight down, it seemed, onto my knuckles. I put my hands in my lap and stared back at her. She is a businesslady, never misses a trick; she calls all of us tenants her "clientele," just as if she were the madam of a whorehouse. The apartment building looks like one of those ten-dollar-a-night motels—two stories with lines of doors opening onto a common walkway that has a wrought-iron railing down the length of it. But Mrs. McDaniels runs a tight ship, no monkey business.

"Have you tried goldfish?" she called down when I got out of the car. "My sister says she has goldfish you couldn't kill with a hammer."

"I think so, I don't know," I called back. My hands were shaking so much I had to put them in the trouser pockets of my uniform, fisting them up in there. When I got up to the second floor, I began it again, this time with Mrs. McDaniels—I figured I'd have to put a lot of left English on my body in order to graze Mrs. McDaniels and whisk her toward the right, into the doorway of my apartment. I brought out a fist with my keys in it.

"You're late," she said, her eyes large and shrewd as a bear's. "Are you drunk or what?"

I quit listing sideways, then jiggled the keys. "No," I told her. "Just a dizzy spell. It's from sitting down all day. All the blood goes to my butt or something."

"Goldfish," she said, sniffing the air around me until, apparently satisfied, she moved to the side so I could get to my door. "Well?" she asked, and she asked it again, "Well?" For a moment I thought Mrs. McDaniels wanted to shake my hand, then I noticed the Baggie of water between her fingers. In it two goldfish held themselves as rigid and motionless as dead things. And they might as well have been, because I knew right then that they were doomed.

"I don't know," I told her, opening the door with one arm so that she could go inside ahead of me. "I think I tried goldfish first thing."

Once inside the room Mrs. McDaniels began to war with herself. She prides herself on being someone who is easygoing and friendly with her tenants, but when she gets inside your apartment, she can't help herself. Those eyes behind the glasses glaze over with suspicion, search for holes in the plaster, gashes in the parquet. My apartment is one large room, with a kitchenette and a bathroom off it, a couch, a card table, three chairs, a bed, a dresser, and a fish tank. She went directly over to the couch, studying my new poster of Minnesota Fats.

"You're fixing the place up," she said suspiciously.

"I used the special glue, Mrs. McDaniels. It doesn't peel the paint."

"Oh!" she cried. "I don't mind at all, not at all. Not *me.*" I could see that good humor and business were tearing Mrs. McDaniels apart, but finally business won out and she pulled a top corner of the poster away from the wall. It came away cleanly, just as the advertisement for the glue had predicted, though after that the corner bent over and didn't stay stuck anymore. "Silly me," she cried gaily. She was in high spirits now. "I really like that poster."

For a year and a half I had lived in the apartment without anything on the walls. Every time Mrs. McDaniels came inside, she'd say, "You live like a transient, just like a transient." And I always said, "I like things neat." And I did. But this Minnesota Fats poster caught my eye. In it Fats is crouched over the cue ball, looking into the side pocket, which is where the camera is. You don't see the side pocket, you just see Fats looking squint-eyed at you, looking at you as if he knew a pretty good trick or two. And he does. The poster cost me two-fifty but was worth every penny.

"I think I tried goldfish about a year ago," I told her. "They didn't last."

"You never know," she said. "I think these guys are winners." She held up the Baggie and studied the fish for flaws. I did not bother to look at them; I knew. They were already as good as dead.

When I first moved in, the fish tank was the only piece of furniture in the room, if you can call a fish tank furniture. The tenant before me had skipped out on his rent but had left the tank as a kind of palliative gesture. Inside there was even a fish, still alive, roaming from one end of the tank to the other. It was rat-colored, about three inches long, with yellow freckles all over its sides—an ugly, sour-looking fish. I called it The Rockfish. After a month or so, I got to thinking maybe it was lonely, maybe loneliness had made it go ugly and sour, and so I went down to the pet store for some companions to put into the tank. The guy there gave me two angelfish—two pert, brightly colored fish that he said got along famously with each other and with just about anybody else. I put them in with The Rockfish and waited for something to happen. The next day I thought to look in the tank, but there was no sign of the angelfish, not a trace, just The Rockfish patrolling all the corners. After that I tried every kind of fish in the pet store —guppies, gobies, glassfish, neons, swordtails, even a catfish bigger than The Rockfish. They all just vanished, as if the tank had pockets. Mrs. McDaniels became obsessed when I told her about it. From then on nothing would do but that we find a fish good enough to go the distance in the tank. We didn't know whether The Rockfish was a male or a female or some sort of neuter, but we tried everything again: hes, shes, its, they all disappeared. Soon I wished I had never told Mrs. McDaniels anything about it, because I could tell she was beginning to associate me with the fish. She started dropping hints about what a man could do for a woman around the house, about how a woman like me could use a good man to straighten out her life. I just told her I already had all the angles figured, thank you, and that a good man wasn't hard to find if you were looking for one, which I wasn't.

"Listen," said Mrs. McDaniels, shaking the Baggie. "My sister says these guys don't know the meaning of death. They're right from her own tank. She should know."

"She should," I said, "but frankly, Mrs. McDaniels, I think they're dead meat."

"When are you settling down?" she asked absently. She was bent over the tank, flicking the glass in front of The Rockfish, her glasses pressed right up against it. I wondered then, because it seemed strange, whether Mrs. McDaniels's eyes, magnified by the glasses and the glass of the tank, whether her eyes might look huge as billiard balls to The Rockfish. No mistake, it had to be a strange sight from that angle. "Here's hoping," she said. Then she dumped the goldfish in. They floated for a few seconds, eye to eye with The Rockfish, but then they seemed to glance at each other and, before you could blink, the both of them shot down the length of the tank and huddled behind a piece of pink coral, sucking the glass in the corner for all they were worth.

"They know," I said. "One look and they knew."

"Look at the bright side," she said. "Nothing's happened yet."

"Not yet. But nothing ever happens when you're looking. It waits till you're at work or shopping or daydreaming or something—that's when it all happens."

"A big girl like you," she said, giving me the once-over. "Ought to be married is what you ought to be."

"Thanks for the fish, Mrs. McDaniels." I showed her to the door.

"Listen. Keep me posted. My sister says they're tough buggers, says they can eat nails."

"I'll keep you posted," I said, then I shut the door. For some reason, I began to snicker like crazy as soon as Mrs. McDaniels left. I went over to the tank, snickering, but The Rockfish only hung in the middle, sedate and ugly as sin. The two goldfish were still sucking away in the corner. I had to lie down on the bed to keep from snickering. For a few minutes I thought maybe I was having a heart attack. There were these pins and needles in my arms and legs, this pain in my chest, but then it all went away after a while. I lay like a stick on the bed, trying to get some sleep, counting my breaths to relax a little. Maybe being late had me worked up. Usually I got through work at two in the afternoon, home by two-thirty, but that day I was all off. I couldn't relax and I kept thinking about how I couldn't, which of course just made things worse and aggravated me and gave me the feeling I was in a fix for good. I got to thinking, then, that my life was going to take a turn for the bad, that somehow I would be off-balance and out of step for the rest of whatever was coming. Across the room I could see the unclear, rat-colored shape of The Rockfish swimming the length of the tank, banking off the far walls, then swimming back again at the same latitude, back and forth, patrolling. And I wondered, to keep from snickering, to ward off the heart attack, I wondered if it knew I was watching. Did it know I kept count of things going on in the tank? Did it know I had all its angles figured, its habits memorized? Did it think I'd almost masséd my car around a fireplug and into a telephone pole? Did it think I was a friend?

I slept like a dead man, because I didn't wake up until around ten-thirty that night, my neck twisted at an odd, painful angle. The only light in the room came from the phosphorescent green glow of the fish tank. Mrs. McDaniels must have switched the tank light on earlier, because I almost never did. It gave me the creeps, as if the tank were the window onto some obscene green world where the tiniest ripple had profound ramifications, the kind of world you always suspect might happen to you suddenly, like Kingdom Come, if you lost all your habits. You lose your habits, and then you can kiss everything you've gotten good at goodbye.

I got out of bed, but things were still off somehow; the feeling of things gone wrong was like a fur on my tongue. Usually I got home at two-thirty, ate something, then slept until about ten o'clock, when business at the pool tables got going good. But that day I'd overslept and was late to begin with, and I knew as if I'd been through it before—which I hadn't—that trouble was just beginning. All I did was grab my keys and I was out of the apartment, almost sprinting to my car. Outside the wind grabbed hold, but I tucked my chin against it until I was inside the car, gripping the wheel and breathing hard. I figured by hurrying I could get a jump on whatever might come next, though when trouble comes, mistake number one is hurrying. I knew that, but I hurried just the same.

On the way to the bar I kept my mind on driving, no funny business. There are nine bars in this town with regulation pool tables, and I always go to a different one each night, until I have to start over again. That night I was due for a bar called The Office, which is a nice enough place if you can stand seeing type-writers and other office equipment hanging on the walls. Oddly enough, it is a favorite hangout for secretaries during cocktail hours. They seem to like the idea of getting drunk surrounded by the paraphernalia of their daily lives. At night, though, the clientele switches over to factory workers and middle-level management types—supervisors, foremen—and you can pick up a nice piece of change. All the way to The Office I kept myself rigid as a fence post. Only one thing happened. I was passing the button factory, a big yellow building with two smokestacks that went at it all the time, burning bad buttons maybe. It struck me, as I passed, that those smokestacks looked a lot like pool cues aimed right for the sky—that's all I thought, which was strange, but nothing to knock you off-balance. Nothing like banking your car off buildings. I'd even begun to think I could relax a little by the time I got to the bar.

Because The Office is situated among gas stations and retail stores, it gave off the only light on the block except for occasional street lamps. The plate glass in front glowed yellow like a small sunset surrounded by nothing at all and out in the middle of nowhere, the kind of sunset people plan dream vacations around, and a sure recipe for disappointment. For a moment I thought better of the whole thing, almost turned around and went home, but the fact of the matter was, I knew that if I did all was lost, because once you gave in you kept on giving in. A habit is as easily lost and forgotten as hope for a better shake in things. So I went on into the bar.

As soon as I got inside I thought it would be all right. The two tables were busy, mostly guys in blue workshirts rolled up to the elbows, holding the cues like shotguns. It was promising because anyone in town recognized the blue workshirts. They came from the nuclear power plant up on the lake, the one that might or might not ever get built, which meant they had money and didn't much mind throwing it away on a fifty-fifty possibility. I had played a foreman from the power plant once, a year before, and during the course of the game he explained that even though the job was dangerous half the time, the money they got was the real health hazard. "More of our men die from drunk driving," he said, "than from touching the wrong wire," and he said it in a proud, feisty sort of way. He was an electrical engineer from east Tennessee, where he said anything that happened had to happen big or else nobody noticed it from one valley to the next. I took him for twenty dollars, then he got unfriendly. But that's the way with those guys: they see a woman playing pool and they automatically assume a fifty-fifty chance, usually more. Then they get unfriendly when they see you've got a good habit. They just don't know enough women. Numbers count.

In The Office, to get to the pool tables you have to finesse your way through about twenty tables full of people who have had too much to drink. Cigarettes, flitting through the air on the tail end of a good story, are obstacles, and so are wayward elbows and legs. One sure sign that you're drunk is if you're in somebody's way. But I got through that part. I made a beeline for Bernie, who was chalking his cue at the second table, the good table, the one with a roll you could figure.

"You are tardy," he said in his formal way, still chalking his cue. Sometime during his life, Bernie was a schoolteacher: astronomy. On certain nights he'd take you outside and point out the constellations, his old nicotine-stained fingers pointing toward the stars. He knew his stuff. And he knew pool, too, except for a tendency to grow passionate at the least provocation, a tendency that combined with old age and Jack Daniel's was ruining his game. Given a population of sixteen or seventeen thousand, Bernie was the only rival I had in town. But we never played together, sometimes never saw each other for weeks; we just appreciated the habits we'd both gotten into.

"You are tardy," he repeated, giving me a dark look. "And the stars are out tonight." He meant that people were spending money like nobody's business.

"I think it's the wind," I told him. "I think there's something funny in the wind."

"Ha!" Bernie cried. He put down the chalk and picked up his cigarette, puffing on it. Then, in a cloud of smoke, he wheeled around to the table, brought up his cue, and nailed the eight ball on a bank into the side pocket, easy as you please. It threw his opponent all off. His opponent had on a blue workshirt that was either too small for him on purpose or else was the biggest size they had: his muscles showed through the material as though he were wearing no shirt at all. On the table only one ball was left, sitting right in front of a corner pocket, and by the look on the guy's face you could tell he'd figured he had the old man on the run, the game sewn up. What he didn't know was that Bernie's opponents in eight ball always had only one ball left on the table. But the guy was a good sport and paid his ten dollars without muscling around or banging his cue on the floor. Sometimes with your big guys chaos is their only response to losing. It is just a fact of life.

"That is that," Bernie said, putting the ten in his wallet. "The table is all yours."

"Where you going?" Bernie always stayed at the tables until about midnight, and if he was around, I just watched and took pointers, waiting for him to get tired and go home before I got busy. Usually I took over where he left off. "It's only eleven," I said, "and you say the stars are out."

"I have a granddaughter coming in on the midnight train." He made a face that meant he was tickled pink, the corners of his mouth stretched and stained with a half million cigarettes. "All pink and yellow, like a little doll. She can point out Venus on the horizon with her eyes shut. A beautiful girl. You should meet her."

"Maybe I will."

"Seven years old and she knows the difference between Arcturus and Taurus. For Christmas last year, do you know what she told her mother she wanted? Guess what she wanted."

"A pool cue," I said, which was exactly what I would have asked for.

"No, you are insane. A telescope! She said she wanted to get close to the sky, close enough to touch it. She's no bigger than a flea and she asks for a telescope!" Bernie slapped his palms together, then sidled closer. "Between us, she is a genius, has to be. My granddaughter, a genius."

"You must be proud of her," I said. All of a sudden I wanted Bernie out of the bar. His very breath smelled like trouble. Then I noticed his shot glass of Jack Daniel's was missing from the stool he usually kept it on; he was sober as a judge. I wanted Bernie gone.

"Oh, she is going places, I can feel it. I can *feel* it!" He slapped his palms together again, bouncing on his feet a little, then he swung toward the men in the workshirts and opened his arms enough to include me in the sweep of them. "Gentlemen, I leave you with this young lady as my proxy. Do not be fooled by her gender." He looked at me appraisingly. "Do not be fooled by the uniform. She can handle herself."

"Thanks, Bernie," I said, but I didn't look at him then, and I didn't look at him when he left. Instead I looked at all the guys in blue workshirts. At first they each one had an expression of irritation and rebellion: they didn't like the idea of me usurping command of the table just because the winner knew me. And I didn't blame them, except that the next expression on each of their faces was a familiar one.

"All right, George, you're up," one of them said. "Take her and then let's us get serious," he said, which was exactly what I had expected from their expressions. I could read these guys like a brochure. Any other night I would have grinned and aw-shucked around, leading them on a little bit. I might have even offered to wait my turn, humbling myself to the point of idiocy, until they said, "No, you go on, honey," gallantry making idiots of them, too. That night, though, something was wrong with me. For one thing, the whole day had been all wrong. For another, seeing Bernie sober and giddy as a billy goat really threw me. I hadn't known he had a granddaughter or a daughter or even a wife. I'd never seen him sober. Something about it all set me going again. I imagined flinging myself headlong into the knot of blue workshirts, sending them all flying to the far corners of The Office, like a good break.

"O.K., little lady," said the one named George, winking and grinning to his friends. "Let's see how you deliver." He could not contain himself. "Did you hear that? Did you hear what I just said? I said, I asked her, 'Let's see how you deliver.'"

They all snorted, stamping their cues on the end of their boots, and I regretted not changing out of my uniform. It was a bad sign because I'd never worn it to the bars before, just one result of hurrying trouble. You never knew when somebody might take a wild hair and try to mess up your job, somebody with a poor attitude toward losing and a bad disposition and a need for spreading chaos. I felt dizzy for a minute, as though I'd been submerged in water and couldn't make the transition.

"Winners break," George said. Now he was all business, ready to get the game over with so he could play with his friends. He strutted around, flexing his workshirt. Most nights, when I had the break, I would try to sink a couple, then leave the cue ball in a safe position, ducking my chin and smirking shamefacedly, as though I'd miscalculated. The point is, never let the guys waiting in line see that your game in no way depends on luck; it scares them if you do, shrinks their pockets like a cold shower, so to speak. But that night I was crazy, must have been. George went into an elaborate explanation of how he had to go to the bathroom but would be back before his turn, how I'd never even know he was gone. I said, "Five bucks." He rolled his eyes comically, performing for his friends, then said it was all right by him. "You're the boss, Chuck," he said. I don't know what got into me. Before George was out of sight, I broke and sank two stripes. Then I hammered in the rest of them, taking maybe three seconds between each shot. By the time old George could zip up his pants, I'd cleared the table.

"Fucking-A," said one of George's friends.

"Whoa," another one said. "Holy whoa."

It was a dream, that whole game was a dream. I had read somewhere that a sure sign of madness was when life took on a dreamlike quality, when you started manipulating what you saw as easily as you manipulate dreams. Those pins and needles came back into my feet, prickly as icicles. George came back, too. I figured the night was over. They would all get pissed off and quit playing and begin to attend to their beers. But—surprise—they ate it up, practically started a brawl over who was up next. It wasn't anything you could have predicted. I guess it pumped them up with adrenaline, or else with a kind of competitive meanness, because for the rest of the night they banged the balls with a vengeance. They were none too polite, and that's a fact. Whatever happened during those games happened in a dream. A wad of five-dollar bills began to show through the back pocket of my uniform trousers. The guys in blue workshirts were like a buzzing of hornets around me, their faces getting drunker and redder every hour.

Near closing time, around two in the morning, George came back for a last game. I'd been watching him play on the other table, and even with the handicap of a dozen beers he could run five or six balls at a time, which is not embarrassing for bar pool. But there was real hatred on George's face, sitting there like a signpost. All those beers had loosened his features until his eyebrows met in a single, straight-edged line, the kind of eyebrows the Devil would have if he had eyebrows. Some men just can't get drunk without getting evil, too. I suggested we call it a day, but George would have none of it. He swaggered around, foulmouthed, until I said all right just to shut him up.

"Fucking dyke," he said, loud enough for me to hear. I kept racking the balls. He was the one who was supposed to rack them, but now I didn't trust him to rack them tightly.

"I said," he said, a little louder, "fucking *dyke* in a uniform." He was drunk—and I should have known better—though, as I've said, that day was the beginning of trouble. One rule of pool is never get emotional. You get emotional and first thing you know, your angles are off, your game is a highly unclear business.

"Asshole," I told him. "Fucking *asshole* in a uniform." My hands shook so much I gripped my cue as if it were George's neck. I am not a grisly or violent person, but there you go.

"Just play, for God's sake," said one of his friends. They were all grouped around the table, their faces as alike and featureless as the balls in front of them. I imagined that their eyes were the tips of cues, blue, sharp, nothing you wanted pointed in your direction.

"Radiation mutant," I said. "Rockfish." Then I broke. Sure enough, emotion had its effect. None of the balls fell.

"Fifty bucks, you pervert," George said, rippling those eyebrows at me. "No, make it a hundred." All that beer was working up some weird, purplish coloration into his cheeks.

They say that during important moments time goes by more slowly, elongates somehow just when you need it most. It is a falsehood. Time goes slowly when you're utterly miserable, or when you might be about to die, and both are situations any sane person would want to go by quickly. When you really need it, time isn't there for you. I wanted to study the table for a while, get myself under control and ready. I wanted to go outside and have somebody point out the constellations, show me the difference between Taurus and Arcturus. I wanted somebody to give me a fish that didn't die in the tank. I wanted somebody, anybody, to tell me that I was living a good life, that my habits were excellent, that I was going places.

"This is all she wrote, Chuck," George said, leaning over the table like a surgeon. It looked grim, not because the spread was all in George's favor—which was true—but because I had gotten emotional. Nothing was clear anymore, not the angles, not the spin, nothing. My cue stick might just as well have been a smokestack.

"Shit!" George cried, and he slammed a beefy hand against his beefy thigh.

He'd run the table except for the eight ball, leaving me with some tricky shots—stop signs all over the table. By now everyone in The Office stood around the table, watching, belching, not saying a word. I thought about what Minnesota Fats would do, how Fats would handle the situation, but all I saw was that corner of the poster, unstuck and curled ominously over Fats's head. I wondered what would happen if I picked up each of my balls and placed them gently in the pockets, like eggs into Easter baskets. Crazy, I must have been crazy.

The first couple of shots were easy, then it got harder. I banked one ball the length of the table, a miraculous shot, though it left the cue ball in an iffy position. I made the next one anyway. After each shot I had to heft the stick in my hand, get the feel of it all over again, as if I were in George's league, an amateur on a hot streak. Finally the game came down to one shot. I had one ball left, tucked about an inch and a half up the rail from the corner pocket, an easy kiss except that the eight ball rested directly in the line of the shot. There was no way I could bank the cue ball and make it.

"All she wrote," George said, "all she by God *wrote!*"

I hefted my cue stick for a massé, the only thing left to do.

"Oh no," cried George. "No you don't. You might get away with that shit in lesbo pool, but not here. You're not doing it here. No sir. No way."

"Who says?" I asked him, standing up from the table. I was sweating a lot, I could feel it on my ribs. "Anything goes is my feeling."

"Bar rules." George appealed to his friends. "Right? No massé in bar rules. Right? Am I right?"

"Phineas!" somebody called. "Phineas! No massé on the tables, right?"

Phineas came out around the bar, rubbing his hands on an apron that covered him from the neck to the knees. He had short, black, curly hair and wore round wire-rimmed glasses, the kind of glasses that make people look liberal and intelligent somehow. He looked clean and trim in his white apron, surrounded by all those sweaty blue workshirts. For a minute he just stood there, rubbing his hands, sizing up the table.

"What's the stake?" he asked philosophically.

"Hundred," George said. He was practically screaming.

Phineas puckered his mouth.

"Well," he said, drawing the sound out. Maybe he was buying time. Maybe he was leading them on. Or maybe he was a bartender who didn't like crowds and didn't like crowds asking for his opinion—which is exactly what he is. "Anything goes," he said. "Anything goes for a hundred bucks is my opinion."

"I'll remember this," George said, snarling, his purple face shaded to green. "You prick, I'll remember this."

"Fine," said Phineas, almost jovially. He folded his arms across that white apron and looked at me. He might have winked, but more likely he was just squinting, sizing me up.

"Massé on the ten into the corner," I said stiffly, formally, the way Bernie would have done. Anybody will tell you, a massé is ridiculous. You have no real cue ball control, no real control period. You have to bring your stick into an almost vertical position, then come down solidly on one side of the cue ball, which then—if you do it right—arcs around the obstacle ball and heads for the place you have in mind. It is an emotional shot, no control, mostly luck. And anytime you get yourself into the position of taking an emotional shot, all is pretty much lost. I hefted the cue stick again, hiked it up like an Apache spearing fish. Then I let it rip. The cue ball arced beautifully, went around the eight ball with a lot of backspin, then did just what it was supposed to do—kissed the ten on the rail. The trouble was, it didn't kiss the ten hard enough. The ball whimpered along the rail about an inch, then stopped short of the pocket. A breath would have knocked it in, but apparently nobody was breathing.

"That's all she wrote," I told Phineas. He just smiled, looking liberal and intelligent behind his glasses.

The upshot was, George won the game. I'd left the cue ball in a perfect position for making the eight in the side pocket. Any idiot could have made that shot, and George was no idiot, just a drunken jerk. He even got friendly when I paid him his money, wanted to take me home, his breath hot and sour as old beer. But then Phineas stepped in, cool as you please, and said that *he* was going home with me. Between the two there was no choice: I told Phineas to meet me out front at my car. "A '73 navy Impala," I told him. It was not that unusual, even though the day had me off-balance. I'd had a couple of guys over to my apartment before, after the bars closed, the kind of thing where in the morning you find yourself clenching the pillows, hoping they don't use your toothbrush or something. Even if I did see those guys again, their faces would mean no more to me than the faces of former opponents in a pool game.

The wind had died, nothing moved when I went out to the car. On the way to my apartment Phineas told me about how he hated crowds, how there was nothing possible with those kinds of numbers. I told him numbers counted, but he didn't argue the point. Then he told me how nice my car was. "True grit," I said. "Nothing spiffy, just good guts." He put his hand on my thigh. We rode like that for a long time. When we passed the button factory, I told him about the smokestacks looking like pool cues. Then, for some reason, I told him about driving my car into telephone poles, banking it off buildings.

"You shouldn't get all out of control over a game," he said. After that I didn't tell him anything else, pretended I was concentrating on his hand against my thigh.

Inside my apartment I didn't turn on the lights. The green glow of the fish tank let me see all I wanted to see, maybe more. Phineas, of course, went right for the tank, which was what everybody did when they came into my apartment.

"How come you only have two fish?" he wanted to know.

"That one there, with the yellow freckles. It kills everything I put in there. Wait see. In the morning that other one won't be there. It's a shark," I said.

"No kidding," he said, peering in at The Rockfish. "Really? A shark?"

"No. It's just an it. A killer it."

Phineas straightened up. "What's your name?"

"Janice," I said.

"At least in this town it's Janice," I said, revealing myself a little, although I wasn't about to go into heartfelt reasons for this and that. It didn't matter because then he kissed me, hard, standing there in front of the fish tank. In a minute or so, he broke away.

"You can play your ass off in pool, Janice," he said. He began to unbutton his shirt. It was flannel, which matched his glasses somehow; the apron he'd left back at the bar. I took off the trousers of my uniform, then he kissed me again, his hands down low.

"You look real nice," he said. "Out of uniform, as it were." He laughed, and I laughed, too, in a strange kind of way.

After that I was on the couch with him on top of me. He got busy. I put my hands on his back, but he did all the work. The whole time I was thinking, my head to one side, staring into the fish tank. I was thinking that maybe I would leave town. Maybe I would pack up my car and move and get around my trouble that way. I could leave the fish tank, skip out on the rent, just like the guy before me had done. Let The Rockfish chew its own gristle, I thought, let Mrs. McDaniels drop hints to somebody else. The Rockfish was patrolling the tank, whipping beside the lone goldfish like terror on the move, and the goldfish sucked madly on the glass in the corner, behind the pink coral, wriggling whenever The Rockfish swept by. It struck me as the saddest thing I'd ever seen. Then I began it again, with Phineas this time. I imagined he was performing a massé on me, several massés, coming down hard on one side and then the other, one emotional shot after another, only I wasn't going anywhere. I must have snorted, because Phineas worked harder all of a sudden.

"Feel it?" he said, or asked, whispering, and I could tell that he'd come to a crucial moment. "Can you feel it?" And I said, "Yes," I said, "Yes, yes, I can feel it," but I couldn't. I shifted slightly to make things easier, but I couldn't feel a thing, not a thing—nothing.

Flight
LINDA SVENDSEN

It was Queen Victoria's birthday; I remember because the schools were closed and I'd felt slightly guilty all day, as if I should have been someplace else. After beating Penny at Ping-Pong, I biked home. At the bottom of the crescent I could make out my mother and sister on our front porch. I pedaled hard and pretended I was going to crash into them. "No brakes," I shouted. "Save the children and run for your lives."

At the last second I swerved, crushing a clump of daffodils. They hadn't budged. Joyce still wore sunglasses, although there was nothing to shield her eyes against. "Hi, gang," I said. "Why are you sitting out here in the dark?" The lamp on my bike beamed across their laps and they seemed to be hypnotized by a growing family of moths meeting at the light. It was then I realized something wasn't right. I said, "What happened?"

"Joyce is leaving Eric," my mother said carefully, and I was struck by that word *leaving*. Joyce had not actually *left* yet, although her body was beside ours and not his. "She's going to stay with us until she's on her feet."

"Oh," I said.

"I'll let her tell you. I'm going to bring the mower in before somebody steals it." Mum stepped over the zigzag of half-cropped lawn and tugged the machine out from under the dogwood. She called over the rattle, "Doesn't the grass smell good?" and disappeared into the garage. She was crying.

I put my arm as far around my sister as I could. Joyce was twenty-four then, ten years older than me. She peaked at six feet, on a full breath, and was pretty—with dark hair, a very long neck, and skin white as rice. She stared over the yard. "Eric couldn't hold a job," she finally said. "There was nothing to eat except Quaker Oats."

This confirmed what I'd heard: Eric was a dreamer. Instead of buying bread or socks, he shopped for airplane parts, and the skeleton of a wing had been suspended in each shabby living room since the honeymoon. He had promised me a flight to Djakarta when he had propellers. He didn't pay bills and made long long-distance calls to an aviator pal in Gander Bay. He used Joyce's name to apply for a phone when the old one was disconnected. I had thought him shrewd and romantic, and Joyce blessed.

"And he hit me," she said, and slowly rolled up the sleeves to show me her right arm, left, and turned, and raised the glasses, to show the side of her face, and neck, all the rich blue marks.

The next day Mum urged me to skip school to help keep my sister company. I was also supposed to fetch my mother if Joyce stayed longer than ten minutes in the bathroom or glanced at her reflection in a sharp blade. I missed an oral report on French verbs and my friend Penny telephoned to see if I was sick or what. "Joyce's marriage failed," I said. "She has to talk to me about it. This is bigger than French."

"Very interesting," she said. "That means Eric's free now." Penny fancied herself a temptress. She patterned herself on Joyce.

Joyce had wound up with Eric when our family was between fathers. Mum had worked two jobs, dated a chef, and brought home doggy bags of sirloin that she cut up and fried with our eggs for breakfast. My brother Ray had longshored; my oldest sister, Irene, had instructed a gentle Belgian immigrant in English (she'd eventually wed him and proceeded to do boring Belgian things—bake sour pastries, fuss with tulips, and raise a prim daughter). Joyce had quit grade eleven and lolled around the airport with Eric. She could identify unseen objects by their purr in a cloudy sky. They'd married when Eric was wait-listed for ground school. She'd been twenty.

Late that afternoon, Mum rushed out to buy last-minute onions for supper. Joyce was listening to a Herb Alpert and the Tijuana Brass cut called "The Lonely Bull." She didn't want to snack or consult the Ouija board or talk. "You're haunting me, Adele," she said.

"Why don't we walk the dog? Groucho could use the exercise."

"I don't need a nanny." Joyce got up and replaced the needle at the beginning. The trumpets blared.

I convinced her to bask in the sun because exposure might hasten the healing of her bruises. She borrowed two of our mother's bandanas (Eric had used her bathing suit as a hazard flag on a U-Haul and lost it on the freeway), and wrapped them snugly around her breasts and hips.

It was hot and our Welsh corgi, who was old as me, panted under an evergreen. After a few minutes, Joyce asked me to bring out the Crisco. She slathered little pats of shortening on the tops of her legs, and smeared the insides of her elbows and thighs until she glistened in the rusty chaise longue, which I'd also set up.

"Cook me, sun," she said, closing her eyes. "Fry away."

I opened my French textbook and read about Jacqueline bumping into Paul at the Arch of Triumph. *Quelle coïncidence.* The theme of the new verb list was "getting acquainted." I looked up from the glossary, after I'd found the *nth* translation, and noticed tears running down my sister's face. "Hey," I said. I went over and rubbed her slippery shoulders.

"I will never love another man," she said. "Never."

"You will," I said, wishing my mother was home.

"You have a whole life ahead, Adele."

"Not really," I said. "Not like you."

When our stepfather, Robert, came home from the docks, she pulled herself together. Mum grilled cheese on raisin toast, Joyce's favorite, and mashed a potato salad. Joyce wasn't biting, and when Mum asked why, Joyce said she hadn't liked that kind of sandwich since she was a teen-ager. Robert discussed Eric.

"I'd like to go over there and torch the bastard's plane." He looked Joyce's and my way. "Pardon my Greek but I'd like to cut off his balls with a dull razor." He meant well, but Mum saw Joyce's solemn face and changed the subject. Robert and Mum eventually decided to phone the skip tracer, whom they'd stalled for months, and deliver their son-in-law's current address. They needed to do something.

I had been lonely in the house, and in the world, after Joyce married Eric. She'd baby-sat me when I was a tyke and played "Mother May I Cross the Golden River?" commanding ten dinosaur steps backward until I was out in the street in the traffic. She had threatened to phone the Nazis if I didn't brush my teeth. Then, in our baby dolls in the living room, we had pretended to be Peggy and little Janet of the Lennon Sisters singing on Lawrence Welk—

> Up in Lapland little Laps do it
> Let's do it
> Let's fall in love.

I had adored her.

One night when Mum and Robert drove to a nursery, Joyce brought out a tray of ice and gave me a pedicure so I would learn how to give her one. While she sucked the cubes, and clipped and buffed, she talked a bit about Eric. She felt guilty about leaving him; after all, everybody fights (she cited Princess Margaret and Lord Tony, and the bickering couple on "Bewitched"). And she was hurt: he'd told her no other fool would give her the four best years of his life, and she would die a shrew.

"But if you'd stayed with him, you would have died of malnutrition," I said. "Anyway, when I graduate in three years, we can live together and be bachelorettes."

"Right." She switched feet. "Can't wait."

On Sunday, Mum, Joyce, and I brunched at a pancake house. Mum had deliberated about including Irene, but Irene's zest usually depressed everybody else. We ordered crumpets, raspberry jam, and tea.

"Thank God there were no kids, Joyce," Mum said. "At least you're free to look for work."

"Not yet," I said.

"I think a job would do wonders for your self-respect." Mum cornered Joyce with her gaze. "You'd be paying your own way, you'd meet people. It's important to circulate during a separation."

Robert had ushered Joyce to the lawyer a few days before. She had now legally left Eric. She didn't charge him with assault, saying blame was fifty-fifty and he'd been provoked. Nobody asked how.

"I don't want to circulate, Mother," she said. "And I'm entitled to welfare."

"Not when you're living in Robert's house. Not when you're not sick."

"Then I'll move," Joyce said.

"I'll go with you," I said.

Mum banged her spoon against a cup and the young couple in the booth behind us turned attentively. "Listen," she said. "I've contacted somebody about you, Joyce." Our mother played piano. Her connection for Joyce was a store manager she knew from the music business, who handled fashion shows and similar illusions. He understood Joyce's beauty and charm recommended her as a demonstrator. Mum implied a future in modeling.

"I refuse to wear an apron and give away cheese," Joyce said.

"Look." Mum spoke earnestly and with love. "You never listened to anything I said while you were growing up. Maybe you could give my ideas a shot now."

Joyce slowly dunked a crumpet; our mother sensed a little victory. She picked up the bill.

By the start of June, Joyce had opened a savings account in her own name, gained seven pounds, and seemed shorter. Penny and I caught a bus downtown on a Saturday afternoon to watch her demonstrate.

We saw a ring of umbrellas in front of Woodward's window, and we elbowed our way through the men, muttering, "Press." Joyce, in black terry shorts and tank top, idly pedaled a stationary bicycle. She advertised the ultimate elasticity in panty hose. Her legs, the shade of steeped pekoe, clashed with her pale arms. On a break at the back of the store, Joyce rested against a wall of shoe boxes. "The chain catches," she said. "I've snagged every pair."

Penny and I sympathized with her until the manager tapped his wrist, and Joyce headed back to the window. We watched her a while longer, then waved good-bye and searched for a cheap palm reading. We couldn't find one in our price range. Penny broached the prospect of Eric again and I said he'd been despondent and volunteered for the Air Force, which was a lie. She asked where he was stationed.

When we reached home, soaked, Joyce was erasing an answer in her TV crossword. She'd been fired at three o'clock.

Mum couldn't bear to see any woman manless. She and Robert equated Joyce's lost marriage to falling off a horse; she must mount again, the sooner the better. And if Joyce wasn't employed, she'd better find a man who could support her. (Actually Joyce was working again; she'd signed up at Manpower and been temporarily hired by a paper mill taking inventory. She counted bundles of foolscap.) Of course, our parents didn't air their misgivings around Joyce, and I didn't repeat what nobody knew I'd gleaned.

I guessed something was afoot when Mum invited Joyce and me to dine at the Grouse Nest, where she was playing all week. The restaurant crowned a nearby mountain. "You should both dress," she said.

Joyce wore a cream Boussac suit of Mum's, and I sweated in kilt and Nordic sweater set. Mum spotted us in the lobby and struck two dramatic chords. I wanted to duck; Joyce flanked the maître d'. At our reserved table a waiter introduced himself. Dietmar was taller than Joyce and his eyes were the washed-out green of pears. Mum tinkled "Kismet."

"Joyce?" he said. "I hope you have an appetite." He trimmed the wick and lit it. He slipped the linen napkins across our knees. He wore a ring on his left pinky.

"He's what the doctor ordered," Mum said, driving us home in her Impala. She extolled Dietmar's manners and mused about what to barbecue when he came for dinner: sockeye or steak. Joyce twisted the radio dial until she heard something familiar. "Paul Anka," she said. "That's him, eh?"

Dietmar was our mother's choice; Robert's was Rex, an independent tugboat owner out of Portland who hauled barges of cedar. He popped in one afternoon, when we all coincidentally happened to be in the backyard, to borrow an adjustable winch. Joyce sunned in Mum's bandanas; Mum checked my conjugations in the shadow cast by a willow. *"Croire,"* she said to me. The test was the next day.

Rex also towered. He had blond hair, whiskers, and the grin of an otter. I liked him.

"Hi." Joyce tightened her top bandanna.

"Hello, Rex," said our mother. "Say hello, Adele."

"Hi there," I said, noting his name was only a consonant away from sex.

"Pull up a chair," said Robert. "What you drinking?"

The men griped about Soviet fishing vessels trespassing in North American waters. Groucho started lapping up Rex's beer, which was in a stein by his feet, and Robert cursed. He threatened to donate the dog to science and I gave him a dirty look. Joyce watched the rock garden as if it perceptibly grew.

Mum interrupted. "Rex, do you keep a girl in every port?"

"Hardly." He glanced at Joyce.

"Why not?"

"Mum," I said.

"Don't have time," Rex said.

"Good for you," Robert said. "I run a harem and they're trouble."

"He's teasing," Mum said.

Joyce stood and stretched and we stopped talking to admire her. Her ribs still stuck out, but she was slightly tanned, the bruises faded; she picked up Mum's poncho and shrugged it on. "What's the boat's name, Rex?"

"No name yet. I'm repainting it. That's why I need the extra winch."

"Oh."

"You should see it when I'm done," he said.

"Soon?" Mum said.

Three days later Joyce and I boarded Rex's bright boat in English Bay. It was the first of July, Dominion Day, and I was chipper about graduating from grade nine. Penny suffered at a camp with permafrost a foot below, and I looked forward to Joyce and summer holidays.

Rex let Joyce steer, and explained in a low steady voice about courtesies of the sea. He pitched me a coil of rope and showed me how to tie a simple knot. Then we ate tuna on kaiser rolls, sipped club, and puffed menthol cigarettes.

We droned toward our mooring in twilight. Joyce asked Rex about sound traveling more clearly over water, and he cut the inboard. The waves slapped cheeks. He asked what she was listening for.

Joyce straightened her head. "I don't know," she said.

Rex kissed us goodnight at our door, but kissed my sister last and longer.

"If you married Rex you'd be an American," I said to her, after he'd gone.

"I am married," she said.

A twelve-unit motel on Kingsway hired Joyce as a relief maid. She scrounged skinny bars of soap, which we tucked in our boots, and gossiped about people she met from different parts of the continent. But they were all motorists and therefore duller than people who flew places. Since Joyce was constantly exhausted, Mum hounded me to finish her chores around the house.

The supper for Dietmar fell on a Monday, when the restaurant was closed. Irene and her husband and daughter arrived, bearing perishables. They were leaving the next day to visit a hamlet outside of Luxembourg where all the Belgian in-laws aged. Irene talked to Joyce and me while squeezing extra heads of iceberg into the crisper.

"Let's face it," Irene said. "Eric was a rat. You need somebody more mature, Joyce."

"He wasn't a rat," Joyce said.

"Why do you still stick up for him?" Irene swiveled, and her eyes also searched me. "He beat you, for God's sake."

Joyce focused on the stack of green heads. "Adele, get my cigarettes from upstairs."

"Later."

Joyce pinched me, hard, on the arm. "Now."

"Don't talk while I'm gone." I dashed upstairs ("I thought you quit," Irene was saying) and grabbed the pack off Joyce's pillow. When I got back, Irene had her arm awkwardly folded around Joyce. She had to reach up.

"I love you," she said.

"I love you, too," Joyce said.

"I want to see you happy."

They both looked at me. They had nothing more to say; they didn't seem to be sisters.

"Here's the baby," Irene appraised me and let go of Joyce.

"I'm the baby." Joyce took her cigarettes. "Adele's the after-thought." It was the old family joke.

Irene bent over the remaining vegetables. "You'll take good care of the animals while we're gone, won't you, Adele?"

I nodded. Robert and Dietmar and Peter, Irene's husband, chuckled outside.

"Who's this Dietmar fellow?" Irene said.

During the meal, he snickered at Robert's Newfie jokes, buttered Mum up by saying she was better than Liberace, praised the Low Countries, and doted on Joyce. She enjoyed the attention, but flinched when he picked the slivers of bone from her fish. Irene helped with dishes, conferred with Robert about a lift to the airport, and whisked her family home. Mum and Robert tied Groucho to his doghouse and turned in strategically early. That left Joyce, Dietmar, and me in the living room. His head was behind hers and he was murmuring something about her nape.

"Do you like music, Dietmar?" I hunted for the polka album.

"No."

Mum called from upstairs. "Adele. Lights out."

"There's no school," I yelled.

"There's no nonsense," she said.

"Goodnight," Dietmar said to me.

"Going?" I said.

Joyce laughed, then stopped herself. "You better exit," she said to me.

In bed with a detective story, I read to the first murder, then skimmed the end. My guess was wrong. Then I heard their footsteps, Joyce's door shutting, and I thought about how modern our family's morals had become. I let my light burn.

Joyce showed up in Dietmar's shirt after midnight and seemed disoriented. "I want to come in," she said.

"You're in."

She stood rubbing the bridge of her nose, the lines of cheekbone, as if reassuring herself of a face.

"Do you want me to get Mum?" I said.

"No." Joyce lowered herself onto the floor, easing her spine against the boxspring. "What is that man's name?"

"What?" I didn't understand what I'd heard.

"What's his name?"

"Last?"

"First."

"Dietmar," I said. "Dietmar something."

"Oh." She pulled the comforter over her hair.

"What?" I said.

"Nothing," she said.

"Sure?"

"Nothing."

I had to check. "What's *your* name?"

"Joyce."

While Dietmar snored alone next door, we shared a pillow in the single bed. She fell asleep. Her closed eyes flickered in dream and I wondered what Joyce saw in that other world. I touched her cold ear with my finger.

I didn't wake up Joyce on time and she was dismissed from the motel. A nonsmoking guest had already complained about ashes in the sink and the owner claimed her lateness was the last straw. Mum was upset because she'd knocked on Joyce's door in the morning and, when there was no answer, trusted Dietmar had driven her to work. She was shocked to find my sister with me, and called a summit conference before she'd even flossed her teeth.

"What are you going to do now, Joyce?" Mum perched on the top stair and twisted a strand of the shag rug.

"I don't know," she said. "I don't feel so hot."

"She needs sleep," I said.

My mother didn't say anything. After breakfast she dropped us at Irene's fussy brick house on the southern slope. Irene was paying me ten dollars a week to feed the bird and Siamese fighting fish, and to perform humdrum tasks. Joyce tagged along; she didn't want to be alone with the questions, or suggestions, of our mother. While I defrosted the fridge, Joyce spilled our niece's pouch of jacks and impatiently flipped them. "Double bounce," she said.

"Bravo." My fingers stuck to the ice-cube tray.

"What's the matter, Adele? You got a chip on your shoulder too?"

I did. Mum blamed me for harboring Joyce, letting her oversleep and lose her job. And Joyce was unpredictable: she said she loved Eric yet slept with Dietmar; she forgot Dietmar's name ten minutes after making love; she pinched me hard. But I didn't say any of that. I gave her the ice. "You always get off scot-free, Joyce."

"What do you mean?"

"You never help. I've got to do the fridge, then vacuum, then clean the birdcage, then make your lunch."

"Where's the vacuum, Delly?"

"Hall closet."

She ducked her head going through the archway and I heard the cord unwinding, a flick, and the monotone whine. She bustled in, holding a long and headless hose, the vacuum floating behind.

"Thanks, Joyce."

"I'll charge you later."

"There's an attachment," I said. "It snaps on."

She quickly did the kitchen, saying "oops" when a stray jack clanked in the machine. She advanced to the dining room. After lifting the steaming pots, one by one, and placing them in the freezer, I found the proper brush buried at the back of the closet and took it to her.

Joyce was dangling the hose through the small door of the birdcage. Sesame seeds, gravel, and a plume vanished. Irene's pink finch clung by its beak and claws to the cuttlebone, near the top of the cage.

"Joyce." I yelled.

She raised the tube as slightly, and deliberately, as her chin, and the brilliant bird disappeared.

Our parents hustled Joyce to an Egyptian psychiatrist and he recommended a thorough rest. He comforted Mum and Robert. Their intention had been correct; they were right to try to keep Joyce distracted. But she had possibly been too busy. He admitted her to Hollywood Hospital, a ramshackle mansion in New Westminster. In the fifties, disturbed film stars had recuperated there without hoopla; the asylum was discreet, off the beaten American path.

Mum and Robert didn't let on that Joyce was institutionalized; they told my aunts and acquaintances that Joyce was camping in the interior. They wouldn't even let me visit until the end of July, when Joyce was calmed down.

She swung in a suspended bamboo chair in the crowded common room. Her braided hair hung like a bellpull, slick as if she'd combed it with margarine. I kissed her hello, hugged, and wouldn't let her go until she gave me a tentative shove. "I hope you don't think I'm mental." That was the first thing she said. "I'll have you know I've got both oars in the water."

She insisted Irene's bird had been an accident. She thanked me for the poems I'd sent every day. She'd overreacted because she hadn't been ready to leave Eric and didn't know if she ever would be. "Has Eric called?"

"I don't know," I said. Joyce's lawyer had told us that Eric was filing for divorce.

"Do you want to see my room?"

She shared it with three other women, whom she diagnosed nuts. Joyce waved me onto the unmade bed and dragged over a chair. When another guest poked her nose in, I felt self-conscious, as if I were the patient.

"What does your doctor say?" I said.

"The sphinx?" she said. "Time. More time."

"What's wrong with you?"

Joyce shook her head. "What's wrong with you?"

I didn't know what to say. There was probably lots wrong. "What do you do every day?"

"Rotate," she said. "The earth turns around. I turn with it." She blew on a short fingernail. "You do too, Delly."

I visited every afternoon after that. I pretended Joyce and I were tenants in a building with eccentric neighbors. We played Fish and tetherball. We lamented, with some other patients, the macaroni and the weather, but it didn't matter much. Joyce was right; we simply rode Earth.

One day Joyce and I were learning the bossa nova on the lawn, taking two steps away and shuffling towards each other when Rex beckoned from the veranda. He brought Joyce two books—one about a man sailing around the world by himself, and an atlas. She handed them to me.

"The P.N.E. opens Saturday," Rex said to Joyce. "If you're out soon, maybe we could go."

"I don't think so," she said. "But thanks."

I examined the atlas. I felt sorry for both of them.

"I'm not anxious to see anybody, Rex."

"I understand," he said. "But feel free to call me, Joyce. Even for a cup of coffee. Call collect."

Joyce shook his hand at the electronic gate, then came back and we lay on the lawn and watched the patients rhumba. "I wish everybody would leave me alone," she said.

At supper, Robert asked if Joyce had cheered up during Rex's visit.

"Not really," I said.

"Why not?" Mum said.

"She cheered up when he left."

"She changes her mind so much," Mum said. "One day she hopes Eric's killed in a plane crash, and the next day she's depressed because they didn't have children. She doesn't know what she wants."

"She wants to be left alone," I said coldly. Robert looked up, suspecting my tone of voice. "Why don't you both leave her alone?"

Robert mumbled something about the peanut gallery and walked out the back door and turned on the water; he was soaking the grass. Mum waited.

"She's all right when she's with me," I said.

"She was with you when she got sick," Mum said. "She's a woman, Adele. She needs *somebody.*"

"She just needs me," I said, trying not to cry.

Joyce was free to leave whenever she wanted and she chose to come home the day after Labor Day. Robert booked off ill with flu to celebrate the reunion. It was overcast, but we sat outside and broke open a bottle of domestic champagne. I'd memorized an original toast but Mum clinked "To life" before I'd filled my glass. Then they gave Joyce a new bathing suit, one-piece, turquoise.

She was upstairs, seeing if it fit, when the bell rang, Groucho roused a bark, and I ran to the front door. An older guy wearing a Nehru jacket trimmed in silver cuddled a trumpet under his arm. "Is your mother home?" he said.

"Who are you?"

"Rudy, from the Musicians' Union. She said to drop by today."

"Everybody's in the yard," I said.

He walked around the corner of the house and Mum hailed him. I hurried inside.

The suit fit beautifully. "Should I model it?" Joyce said.

"I wouldn't. There's a trumpet player on the loose."

"Oh," she said. "Did they hire a band to welcome me back?"

We joined them on the patio. Mum served a platter of cold cuts, sliced rye, and gherkins and they talked about live music in Canada. After Rudy built his second open-face sandwich, he told us he was counting calories and newly single. His ex-wife, the ambitious vocalist, had transferred to Toronto.

I pretended I couldn't find the horseradish and summoned Mum into the kitchen. "Did you invite that creep here today?"

"Yes," she said. "He is not a creep."

"Why today? For Joyce?"

"No, I'm thinking of forming a trio again."

"I bet."

Mum tugged my chin and I had to meet her eyes. "It's terrible to lose somebody close," she said. "I've been through it twice and I don't wish it on you, Adele. But when you're older you'll know." She let go of me. She turned and found the condiment exactly where she'd left it on the sink, then joined everyone outside.

I watched through the window screen. Robert trotted by on his way to find another bottle of champagne. Mum stood listening to Rudy loudly outline the requisites for a hit: how the melody should be catchy, the chorus easy to remember, and how the lyrics should always be about falling in, or out of, love. Joyce was listless. She watched our dog, under Rudy's chair, flatten into sleep. Then she made a visor of her left hand. I saw my sister look up at the sky at something going awfully fast.

Printed in the United States
by Baker & Taylor Publisher Services

Printed in the United States
by Baker & Taylor Publisher Services